ANGRY, WAS HE?
I DID NOT CARE

I had cared very much, once. Khys had been kind to me that first night. I had no recollection of other men before him, though surely there had been some. In my lost past lay all that had occurred before I came to the lake of Horns in Cetet of '695, two years, two passes back.

He told me he would do many things. He had done some. He had seen to it that I was reeducated. I had been looked after, but not by him. He had also said that some-day the band of restraint I wore would be removed from me, that I might explore my talents. That he had not done. After the pregnancy, he had promised, when I lay near miscarriage by my own hand. But no release had been given me after I birthed him his precious child.

and accomplish my

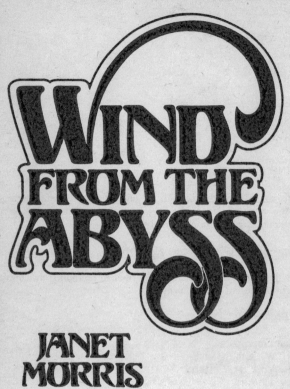

WIND FROM THE ABYSS

JANET MORRIS

A BAEN BOOK

WIND FROM THE ABYSS

Copyright © 1978 by Janet E. Morris

A Baen Book

Baen Enterprises
8-10 W. 36th Street
New York, N.Y. 10018

First Baen printing, January, 1985.

ISBN: 0-671-55932-X

Cover art by Victoria Poyser

Printed in the United States of America

Distributed by
SIMON & SCHUSTER
MASS MERCHANDISE SALES COMPANY
1230 Avenue of the Americas
New York, N.Y. 10020

to
my sister

Contents

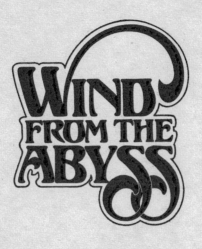

Author's Note

Since, at the beginning of this tale, I did not recollect myself nor retain even the slightest glimmer of such understanding as would have led me to an awareness of the significance of the various occurrences that transpired at the Lake of Horns then, I am adding this preface, though it was not part of my initial conception, that the meaningfulness of the events described by "Khys's Estri" (as I have come to think of the shadow-self I was while the dharen held my skills and memory in abeyance) not be withheld from you as they were from me.

I knew myself not: I was Estri because the girl Carth supposedly found wandering in the forest stripped of comprehension and identity chose that name. There, perhaps, lies the greatest irony of all, that I named myself anew after Estri Hadrath diet Estrazi, who in reality I had once been. And perhaps it is not irony at all, but an expression of Khys's humor, an implied dissertation by him who structured my experiences, my very thoughts, for nearly two years, until his audacity drove him to bring together once more Sereth crill Tyris, past-Slayer, then the outlawed Ebvrasea, then arrar to the dharen himself; Chayin rendi Inekte, cahndor of Nemar, co-cahndor of the Taken Lands, chosen son of Tar-Kesa, and at that time Khys's puppet-vassal; and myself, former Well-Keepress, tiask of Nemar, and lastly becoming the chaldless outlaw who had come to judgment and endured ongoing retribution at the dharen's hands. To test his hesting, his power over owkahen, the time-coming-to-be, did Khys put us together, all three, in his Day-Keepers' city—and from that moment onward, the Weathers of Life became fixed: siphoned into a singular future; sealed tight as a dead god in his mausoleum, whose every move but brought him closer to the summed total, death. So did the dharen Khys bespeak it, himself. . . .

I

In Mourning for
the Unrecollected

The hulion hovered, wings aflap, at the window, butting its black wedge of a head against the pane. Its yellow eyes glowed cruelly, slit-pupiled. Its white fangs, gleaming, were each as long as my forearm.

I screamed.

Its tufted ears, flat against its head, twitched. Again and again, toothed mouth open wide, it battered at the window, roaring.

Once more I screamed, and ran stumbling to the far wall of my prison. I pounded upon the locked doors with my fists, pressing myself against the wood. Sobbing, I turned to face it.

The beast's ears flickered at the sound. Those jaws, which could have snapped me in half, closed. It cocked its head.

I trembled, caught in its gaze. I could retreat no farther. I sank to my knees, moaning, against the door frame.

The beast gave one final snort. Those wings, with a spread thrice the length of a tall man, snapped decisively, and it was gone.

When it was no more than a speck in the greening sky, I rose clumsily, trembling, to collect the papers I had strewn across the mat in my terror. They were the arrar Carth's papers, those he had forgotten in his haste to attend his returning master's summons.

1

I knelt upon my hands and knees on the silvery pile, that I might gather them up and replace them in the tas-sueded folder before he returned.

Foolish, I thought to myself, that I had so feared the hulion. It could not have gotten in. I could not get out. It could not get in. Once I had thrown a chair at that impervious clarity. The chair had splintered. With one stout thala leg, as thick as my arm, had I battered upon that window. All that I had accomplished was the transformation of chair into kindling. The hulion, I chided myself, could have fared no better.

Hulions, upon occasion, have been known to eat man flesh. Hulions, furred and winged, fanged and clawed, are the servants of the dharen. I had had no need to fear. Yet, I thought as I gathered the arrar Carth's scattered papers, they are fearsome. Perhaps if I had been able, as others are, to hear its mind's intent, I would have felt differently. My fingers, numb and trembling, fumbled for the delicate sheets.

One in particular caught my eye. It was in Carth's precise hand and headed: "Preassessment monitoring of the arrar Sereth. Enar fourth second, 25,697."

I had met, once, the arrar Sereth. Upon my birthday, Macara fourth seventh, in the year '696 had I met him, that night upon which my child had been conceived. I had read of his exploits. He frightened me, killer of killers, enforcer for the dharen, he who wore the arrar—chald of the messenger. Sereth, scarred and lean and taut like some carnivore, who had loved the Keepress Estri, my namesake, and with her brought great change upon Silistra in the pass Amarsa, 25,695—yes, I had met him.

I sat myself down cross-legged upon the Galeshir carpet, papers still strewn about, forgotten, and began to read:

The time is approximately three enths after sun's rising, the weather clouded and cool, our position just south of the juncture of the Karir and Thoss rivers. I highly recommend that you look in upon the moment.

The arrar Sereth, on the brindle hulion Leir, touched his gol-knife. It was the first unnecessary movement he had made in over an enth. My presence, alongside upon a black hulion, disquieted him. The brindle, gliding at the apex of its bound, snorted. He touched its shoulder, and the beast, obedient, angled its wings and began its descent.

When its feet touched the grass, he set it as a grounded lope. I followed suit, bringing my black up to pace him.

Sereth regarded me obliquely. I, as he, served the dharen, he thought, and touched his hulion to a stop.

We had been riding all the night, up from Galesh, where I had met him with the two beasts. He had served dharen, most lately, in Dritira. And before that, in the hide diet, and before that upon the star world M'ksakka had he dealt death and retribution at Khys's whim. And dealt them successfully, though those tasks had been fraught with deadlier risk than a man might be expected to survive. His thought was wry, recollecting.

"How did you find M'ksakka?" I asked, to key him, to bring something else above the impenetrable shield he has constructed. My hulion growled at the brindle he rode, and that one answered.

"I will make a full report to Khys," he said, slipping off the hulion's back. "Let us rest them."

I joined him where he lay upon the grass, staring at the sky.

"I missed this land," he said. "The sky there is dark and ominous, always clouded. M'ksakkan air stings eyes and lungs. Everything is covered with a fine black dust. I would not go again off the planet."

"Perhaps he will not send you," I conjectured.

He saw M'ksakka, and that seeing was colored by his distaste, both for the world and the work he had done there. The methods he had employed displeased his sense of fitness. The value of the M'ksakkan's death was to him obscure. I saw the moment: the adjuster's surprised eyes, wide and staring as Sereth's fingers closed on his throat, around his windpipe; the M'ksakkan's clawing hand upon his wrist as he ripped out the man's larynx, vocal cords dangling; then the blood, spurting, and the sound of the adjuster's choking death.

And I saw others he had killed, those who were anxious to try their skills against a real live Silistran. He had been hesitant to do so, but more hesitant to face an endless line of their ilk, so he had killed the first three. Again, his thoughts sank below readable level. The hulions lay quiet, lashing their tails. The clouds scudded heavy over the sun. A soft, drizzling rain commenced.

"The dharen is pleased with you," I said.

He sat up, his mind absolutely inviolate. "What do you want, Carth?" He stared down at me. I lay perfectly still. He made no attempt to read me for his answer. He merely waited.

"A first impression. You are coming up for assessment," I answered, rising up. "We want to get some sense of you. Your mental health is now our concern."

He tossed his head, ripping grass from the sward.

"You brought child upon that wellwoman in Dritira," I prodded.

He saw her. In many ways she had reminded him of the Keepress. It had been passes since he had taken a woman. On M'ksakka there were females, but nothing he understood to be a woman. He had not couched many of them. And in hide diet, there were only forereaders. In Dritira, with that woman who reminded him of the Keepress, he had spent his long-pent sperm. Four times he had used her, before *she was more than a receptacle in his sight. And he had abused her, more than was his custom.*

"Get me the forms. I will collect my birth-price," he answered. He did not want the woman.

"You should take her. We have been considering her. She might yet make a forereader."

"Then it is a pity she caught. From inferior sperm can come only inferior stock."

"Khys has asked me," I said, "to bid you welcome to any of the forereaders we hold in common at the lake. Spawn from such a union would be doubtless possessed of talent. The bitterness you hold is out of proportion to the reality. We all, at one time or another, find there is something we want that we may not have."

He did not answer me, but rose and went to his hulion. He thought of her as one thinks of the dead; with acceptance, and then of his life, and what compromises he had made to keep it. What he let me know, I have no doubt, will please you. What he did not—that is what concerns me. He allowed me nothing else for the duration of our return.

His shield, as you will see, is set lower and much farther into his deeper conscious than any I have encountered. Most of his processing must take place behind it. Deep-reading him is out of the question. He visualizes barely enough to verbalize his will. That he is functioning superbly is attested to by his works. That he feels it to his advantage to serve us at present is a certainty. I worry over what might occur, should he choose, eventually, not to serve us.

My formal recommendation is for a complete and detailed assessment. Also, I feel some attempt might be made to pacify him, in light of what he is fast becoming. Or perhaps even to eliminate him, lest he become, like Se'keroth, the weapon turned upon the wielder.

And it was signed *Carth*.

"Carth!" I gasped, as a dark hand snapped the

sheet from my grasp. Still upon my knees, I twisted to see him. His dark eyes gleamed. He ran his hand through his black curls.

"Did you find this informative, Estri?" he asked, towering over me, the paper crumpled in his fist. Carth was furious. I dared not answer.

I started to my feet.

"Pick them up!" he commanded, pointing.

I scurried to obey him, scrambling for the sheets strewn upon the web-work, my stomach an icy knot. Once before, I had seen Carth this agitated, when I had written for him a certain paper. And he had called it audacious, and destroyed it. I finished, and rose to my full height, handing the tas envelope to him. My head came to his shoulder. He looked down at me, sternfaced.

"You were ill-advised to do this," he said. "He is not pleased with you. This"—and he threw the crumpled sheet across the room—"will only aggravate matters. You had best make some effort to placate him."

"What do you mean?" I demanded. "Has he taken some sudden interest in me?" I had seen the dharen precisely three times since I had come to reside at the Lake of Horns: the night he had gotten me with child, the day following, and once while I lay near death when the child had driven me to seek it. He had not been at the Lake of Horns when I bore his he-beast into the world. I had cried out for him during that premature and extended labor. He had not been available. Now, nearly eight passes later, he had returned.

"Do not be insolent!" Carth's voice snapped as his palm slapped my face to one side. Tears in my eyes, I put my hand to my cheek. It was what I had thought, not what I had said, that had brought me punishment. Shaking my head, I backed away from him. Though I had known Carth a telepath, a surface-reader, rarest of Silistran talents, never had he shown his skills before me, one who neither spoke nor heard the tongues of mind.

"Estri, come here."

I went to him, my hand trailing from my cheek to the warm, pulsing band locked about my throat.

When I stood before him, he lifted my face, his hand under my chin, that I might look into his eyes.

"He is very angry, child. You must realize that what you think is as audible to him as what you say. I know it was not intentional, that you read what you did. Forget it, if you can. Concentrate upon what lies before you." He patted my shoulder, all the anger gone out of him.

"I do not want to see him," I said, toying with the ends of my copper hair, grown now well below mid-thigh.

Carth pursed his lips. "You have no choice. He will see you in a third-enth. Make ready." And he turned and strode through the double doors that adjoined my prison to Khys's quarters. Khys, my couch-mate, was again in residence. The dharen of all Silistra, back from none knew where, would again rule at the Lake of Horns.

Make ready, indeed, I thought, combing my hair. I had only the white, sleeveless s'kim I wore; thigh-length, of simple web-cloth. My jewelry was the band of restraint at my throat. I retied the garment upon my hips. Throwing my hair back, I regarded myself in my prison's mirrored wall. My body, copper-skinned, lithe, only shades lighter than my thick mane, postured at me, arrogant. I had thought, for a time, that the he-beast had destroyed it, but such had not been the case. Exercise had given its grace and firmness back to me. My legs are very long, my waist tiny, hips slim. Pregnancy had altered me little. My breasts were still high and firm, my belly flat and tight. Good enough for him, surely. I widened my eyes suggestively, then stuck my tongue out at her. She made a face back. I grinned and wondered why I had done so, turning from that wall that ever showed me the boundaries of my world.

At the window, I waited, looking out upon the eastern horn of the lake. The fall flames of Brinar, harvest pass, fired the forest. The grass was losing its battle, browning. Hulions and forereaders and Day-Keepers strolled between the tusk-white buildings that circle the Lake of Horns like some wellwoman's necklace. The green lake was calm and still, wearing the sky's clouds for masquerade.

Angry, was he? I did not care. I cared no more for him than that he-beast he had put upon me. I would not care.

I had cared very much, once. He had been kind to me that first night. I had no recollection of other men before him, though surely there had been some. In my lost past lay all that had occurred before I came to the Lake of Horns in Cetet of '695, two years, two passes back. And I had cared for him, he who first touched me, Khys.

He had told me he would do many things. He had done some. He had put on me a son. He had seen to it that I was reeducated. I had been looked after, but not by him. He had also said that someday the band of restraint I wore would be removed from me, that I might explore my talents. That he had not done. After the pregnancy, he had promised, when I lay near miscarriage by my own hand. But no release had been given me after I birthed him his precious child.

I touched the warm, vibrating band at my throat. I hardly minded its tightness. I could often forget that it was there. But its true significance I could not forget. Khys had explained to me that I wore the band for my own protection, lest the mindlessness reach up again and take me. I had learned otherwise.

Early in my pregnancy, when they still humored me, I had begged to be allowed to stay with the forereaders in the common holding, that I might have the company of womankind. Reluctantly, Carth had agreed.

I had sent for him to take me back, weeping, upon the third day. Among the forereaders, I was an outcast. Those born at the Lake of Horns feel themselves better than all others. My skin tone resembles theirs. Those who come from the outside, or "Barbaria," as the Lake-born call it, are an even tighter group. I fit neither. And I was the dharen's alone. They were jealous, commonheld. Or so I thought, until I saw an angry dharener stride into the women's keep and collar a moaning, pleading forereader. So do they punish wrongdoers at the Lake of Horns. As long as she wore the band of restraint, the forereader could not practice her craft. She was isolate. She was blind, deaf, and dumb to mind skills. She could not sort. Neither could she hest. She was helpless. She was shamed. She was marked, disgraced. As was I.

When Carth had retrieved me, I had demanded to know, sobbing uncontrollably, what it was I had done.

He had for me no answer, but that I wore the band for my own protection.

But after that, I began to wonder. I wondered until the child began to make itself known within me, until I could think of nothing else. Ravening, it tried to destroy me. In time, I tried to destroy myself, first, that perhaps I would not spawn such evil upon the world. But it would not let me die. It enjoyed too much the torture to which it could subject me from within.

When it was born, finally, after thirteen enths of labor, I refused to look upon it. I would not feed it. They forced me twice, but the he-beast was so agitated, red-faced, and howling, and its teeth so

savage upon me, that they desisted. I had never
heard of a child born with teeth, but I had known
it would have them. I felt their bite a full pass
before the thing demanded exit. I was glad to be
rid of it, a pass before it was due.

He could not blame me, surely, if he had seen it.
If his mind had touched it, he would not be angry.
I leaned back against the window, waiting.

It was more than twice the third-enth Carth had
given me before those doors opened and he motioned me to him, his concerned eyes admonishing
as I passed by him into Khys's personal quarters.

The dharen stood by the gol table, stripping off
trail gear as blue-black as the thala walls. His
copper hair glinted golden from the tiny suns, Day-
Keeper-made, that hovered near the hammered
bronze ceiling.

Carth crossed the thick rust rug, soundless, to
speak with him. Then only did Khys look at me. I
pressed back against the doors, trembling. His face,
in that moment, had been terrible with his wrath.

Carth made obeisance to him, and left the outer
doors.

The dharen paid me no mind, but stripped himself of his leathers and weapons. I watched him,
the only man that had ever touched me. I had
forgotten him, his long-legged grace, his considerable mass so lightly carried, his ruddy, glowing
skin.

In his breech, he went and poured himself some
drink and took it to his rust-silked couch. Upon it
he sat cross-legged, sipping slowly, his eyes regarding me over the bowl's golden rim. The crease
between his arched brows deepened. He threw the
emptied bowl to the mat, where it rolled silently
upon the thick pile.

My throat ached, looking at him.

Then I recalled to myself that which he had
done to me, and that which he had not done. I

tossed back my hair and pushed away from the door.

"I was told you wished to see me," I said quietly, my fists clenched at my sides.

He stared at me a time in silence through those molten, disquieting eyes. I felt my palms slick under his indolent, possessive scrutiny.

"Take that off," he ordered. "I would see how childbearing left you."

I flushed, but I untied the s'kim and dropped it.

"Turn," he said. Shaking with rage, I did so, kicking my abandoned garment from my path. When I came again to face him, I put my hands on my hips.

"Well?" I demanded, shaking my hair over one breast.

"Do not stand like that!" he snapped. My hands went to my sides. "Come here."

"Khys!" I objected. My head exploded with pain. I sank to my knees, my hands clapped over my ears. But they could not keep out that roaring. Then another pain, and my head was twisted back by the hair. By it, he pulled me up against him.

"How dare you withhold sustenance from my son?" he demanded. I thought my neck would snap. His other hand held my wrists against the small of my back. "How dare you come to me in such arrogance?" He shook my head savagely, his words hissing a fine spray upon my cheek. "You have disobeyed my expressed wishes. You will not do so again. When I am finished with you, you will not be so presumptuous." Lifting me into the air, he threw me against the wall above the couch. I struck it with my back and shoulder with such force that the breath was driven from my lungs.

He stood, spread-legged, looming over me. I did not move. I lay very still, as I had fallen, that I might not further enrage him. My mouth was foul with fear. My mind cried and whimpered. I raised my face to him, pleading. His thick-lashed eyes, half-closed, were unreadable.

"Khys, please," I begged him, hoarse. "I could do no different. It is a monster, a beast. Please, I tried. It drove me mad. It tried to kill me. Punish it, not me."

His nostrils flared. He shook his head, his mouth twisted in disgust. "Sit on your heels," he commanded.

I did so, my whole body sheened with sweat, my knees pressing into the couch silks. My arms clasped about me, I shivered in spasms. I hardly knew him, the dharen. Never before had he raised a hand to me.

"You had not given me cause," he said. Still did he breathe heavily, still was his body taut with rage.

I ran my hands through my hair, tearing it from my eyes, trying desperately to stop thinking. But I could not. I was hypnotized by him, poised menacing above me. I felt as I had with the hulion—trapped, defenseless, vulnerable.

"I am frightened," I whispered, my eyes downcast.

"That shows you are not totally mad," he said. Hearing the amusement in his voice, I raised my head. I recalled his face as it had been when I had lain near death with his child in my belly, his concern, his compassion. I saw, now, no trace of such emotions.

He stripped off his breech. I saw very still, watching the play of muscles across his back.

"Once," he said softly, straightening up, "you asked me to teach you your femaleness. I thought you too weak, then. I did what needed done, and nothing more. Doubtless your failure to function as a woman lies partly upon me. I am going to attempt to remedy the situation before it kills you."

But when he came toward me, I could not do it.

I could not sit and let him vent his anger upon me.
I fled, as far as he allowed. When he chose, I found
myself imprisoned within my own body, and it, of
its own accord, returning to him. He stood calmly
by the couch and took my flesh from my control. I
could not speak. I found myself at his feet, my
head pressed to the mat.

He let me try those bonds, for a while, let me
dance upon the brink of madness. When he took
his will from my limbs, I did not move.

He flipped me casually onto my back, crouching
down, menacing. His large head came close to
mine.

"Lie still, and do as you are told. Only that, no
more." And I did so, until I forgot, in my need, his
instruction. The taste of blood in my mouth, the
flat of his hand against my searching lips, reminded
me. I laid my head back against his thigh as my
body leaped to him, pleading. I heard my voice
repeating things he had bade me say, without
understanding. And later, when his teeth and tongue
were upon me, did I beg for his use. And I did for
him what I had not known a man would ask of a
woman, whimpering. And he, raised on stiff arms
above me, laughed. As he thrust into me, I sobbed
his name, my love for him, my need. And then his
weight came down and I could but cling to him as
he rocked me. When I thought my bones would
shatter, he grunted, shivered, and lay still.

He stayed with me, holding his weight upon one
arm, stroking my hair back from my forehead.

"I needed you so much when I had the child
within," I whispered.

"I know," he said. "I have a world to run." His
eyes narrowed. I felt him, I thought, in my mind.

"Do you know how lonely it is for me, locked
up?"

"I can do nothing else with you." He rolled away,

onto his side. "But I will be here. My works are progressing nicely. I need not be elsewhere.

"I want you to understand something," he continued, taking me into his arms. "I have what I wanted from you." His voice was gentle. His hands wandered my hips. "I must see a radical change in your behavior to justify the trouble of you. Carth tells me it is doubtful that you would survive another pregnancy."

"I do not take your meaning," I said numbly.

"There are more than two thousand forereaders at the Lake of Horns, many extremely attractive, all skilled and cooperative. I cannot, for reasons I will not explain, put you in common holding."

I rolled away from him.

"Did the child please you?" I asked.

"Yes."

"But I do not." My voice shook. I had been breeding stock to him. I was no longer useful as such.

"No," he said. "You do not."

"I did the best I could," I flared. "I am ignorant of couch skills."

He laughed, touching my lips with his finger.

"It was a start," he admitted. "If you live, you might learn to serve a man properly. You misunderstand me, or I give you more understanding of life here than you have." He sat up, and pulled me by the hair into his lap.

"I had not intended to breed you again. If I do decide to do so, you may not survive it. I am not in need of a contentious, undisciplined female. Either you will become otherwise, or I will have to breed you to justify your existence."

"Have to?" I asked. My terror of pregnancy and that of death balanced even.

"You are coming up for assessment. I must follow my own rules, if I expect others to obey them."

I shivered, buried my head in his lap. I thought

of what I had read; I could not help it. I waited for
the pain of his displeasure. It did not come. His
hand went around my throat, lifted my head. He
bent and pressed his lips to mine. I felt him move
against my thigh. My hand sought him, and he
allowed it. He bent his bite to my nipples, erect
and waiting.

Something, within me, turned and rustled in
that couching, and halfway through it, when
I choked and gagged on him, it woke itself to my
aid. I shifted position, arched my neck slightly,
and my discomfort disappeared. Easily, sure, I
worked upon him, my lips against the very root of
him, my nose in his golden hairs. And he shuddered and his hands came upon the back of my
neck, and I let him slide forward, that I might get
the taste of him. As he pulsed in my mouth, I ran
my tongue, fast, hard, up and down the underside
of him. And the dharen moaned and twisted, his
hands convulsive upon me.

When he cursed, softly, laughing, I sat up to see
him. My strangeness still upon me, I noted his fine-
chiseled lips, swollen with his heat. Then I bent
again, licking, nipping, and took from him that
last aftertaste.

By criteria I had not known before, I read his
body's response, my cheek against his hard belly,
that I might feel his excitement, judge it by the
wane.

"Tell me again, dharen, what you might do to
me, if I cannot sufficiently please you." And I heard
my voice, deeper and more upon breath, and it
seemed to me that it was a stranger's voice, with
an accent I could not place.

He grunted, sat slowly. He cuffed me lightly,
pushed my head from his lap, crossing his legs
under him. I regarded him, discerningly, and found
him not wanting.

"Insolent saiisa," he growled, grinning.

And I knew the word's meaning, though it is man-slang, and Carth never spoke crudely. The word means coin girl, of the cheapest variety and questionable skill.

"I wish I were even that, rather than living my life in that chamber," I said, the mood gone, and with it that odd confidence and comfort.

"You may have the both of them, yours and mine, for a while." His eyes probed mine. "Is that one of those things a woman instinctively knows?" he asked, and I knew what he meant, but I had no answer. I smoothed the rumpled couch silks.

"Perhaps I read it," I said. I wanted to crawl into his lap, curl into a ball, and sleep. More than I had wanted the child out of me, even, I wanted his approval. I recalled those nights, alone, I had cried myself to sleep over him.

He stared at me, his head slightly cocked.

I remembered my humiliation, that he would not even deign to use me, that he cared not even enough to check on the growth of his child in my belly.

I laid my hand upon his forearm, upon the copper, silky hairs there. His skin, a reddish gold, was shades lighter than mine, and the glow upon it was more pronounced.

"Khys," I whispered, "keep me with you, please. I will be whatever you want. Just give me time." I did not look at him. Tears I had thought long spent came and drowned me. "I love you," I blurted, miserable, not understanding.

And he pulled me up beside him, and in those arms I poured out my pain to him, my confusion, my doubts. I begged him to explain why I wore the band upon my neck. I pleaded for my past, or some way he might know to make me whole without it. And I asked him of the child, and why it had been such a curse while residing in my womb.

He said nothing, until I had finished, dry of words and tears both.

"I will discuss it with you," he allowed, still holding me. "I am not prone to patience. I will speak of these things once, only. You will never ask me again."

I nodded, my head pressed against his chest, where his copper hair grew thick.

"First the band. When and if you show signs of emotional stability, we will consider removing it. When you were progressing so well, those first passes, I had thought we might have done so by now."

"It was the child, and the pain from its growth," I whispered.

"And it was you who chose to experience your pregnancy as you did. Another woman would have, perhaps, enjoyed it, loved the child, and cried when it was taken from her. Still another might have filled her time with study, or some creative work. Females have been bearing young for thousands upon thousands of years."

I pulled away from him. He looked at me narrow-eyed.

"I am not insulting you. I am going to explain something to you. You were, so to speak, born anew two years ago. You still gather the experiential perspectives most acquire when they are babies. You could not get them from lying, hungry, denied mother's milk. You could not get them, learning to walk. You still gather the experiential perspectives; those upon which adult behavior must be based. Wait!" he snapped, as I sought to interrupt him. I sat back upon my heels.

"You wear the band. It is my will that you continue to wear it. If it pleases you to feel that you are unjustly marked by it, then feel so. The fore-readers in common holding did not ostracize you because of the band. Where there are women, there

are great stores of information. I am sure they
know all about you. You are not common-held.
You come from the outside, but are complexioned
as a blood princess among them. And those women
from outside, perhaps rightly, hate the superior
lake-breds. When I allowed it, I was sure you would
not stay. I wanted you to realize the value of your
isolation. You did not.

"No one has barred you from any studies you
might have wished to pursue. Tutors of all sorts
might attend you. One makes what one wants of
the opportunities life presents."

"But I may not walk the lakeside. I may not
even walk the dharen's tower."

"You attempted suicide. We found it necessary
to restrain you."

"Before that?" I tossed my hair forward. It fell
shining, past my knees, copper ends on the rust
silks.

"It was too early. You were not ready. You are
still not ready. If your memory does come back to
you, and you have not become ready, it will destroy you. There is nothing I can do to hasten its
return, nor would I choose to do so." His voice had
a tinge of impatience. He closed his eyes for a
moment.

"And my child?" I asked him.

"Your child is no monster, only the first of its
kind."

"How can that be?" I shifted, knees aching.

He rose and filled two bowls from that golden
pitcher and brought me one. I tasted it, found it
fine kifra, dry and live. I sipped, laid the cool
metal upon my thighs.

"Look at yourself," he commanded. A muscle
ticked upon his jaw.

I did, and back at him, my hand upon the bowl
to balance it.

"Once the fathers spread their seed widely upon

the land. We have long been about gathering up those offspring. You are one we missed. Surely you knew it when you saw your resemblance to the lake-born."

I had considered it, but felt it some pretentious fantasy.

"But there are other children."

"Other attempts. This is the first that has matched my vision."

"I still do not understand."

"I did not expect you would. But I have told you that you at least have some truths to work with, building your particular reality. Build it well, for you must live within that construction." His voice had an edge, and he drained the bowl he held and set it down. My stomach lurched, tightened, as he approached.

"What is assessment?" I asked.

"You will find out, soon enough," he said, taking the bowl from my lap. His long fingers fondled my breast. I twisted, that I might free myself.

"Do not flinch from me," he ordered, but softly. "I would give you a few more truths for your reality. You are mine. I will do with you what pleases me. Lie back."

I lay back, stretching my aching legs out straight.

"I do not wish to be touched, not now," I objected, but I did not move away from his hand.

"Then do not wish it. Your wish has very little bearing upon what will occur, at this moment, or any other. But you will wish it shortly. I promise you."

I was his. And he did what he pleased with me, and within an enth, all I wished was his couching.

I found myself alone, in his chambers. The doors were not locked. He had looked back at me, almost smiling, and left one door ajar.

And I had risen to my feet and gone to stand before them, my arms clutched around me, shivering. Freedom lay, doubtless not, out those doors. He would see me disobey him. Or perhaps he would see that I could not.

For I could not. I stared at the open door, sank to my knees. If I ran, he would find me and bring me back. I remembered his wrath. I recollected his strength. And I found that not only did I dare not run, but that I dared not displease him. I wondered how I could sit calmly with the open door beckoning, and not try.

I sat cross-legged, a luxury he would not have allowed me. Above my head, the tiny suns had dimmed, as ever when no Day-Keeper is within their range. To the miniature stars, each within its prison, I did not exist. I wondered if they were sad, and restless, as was I in my constraint. And if there were any of them, for the bronze ceiling hosted twelve, that felt love.

I lay upon my stomach, on the rusty Galeshir carpet, humming softly, under my breath. My acknowledged couch-mate, the dharen, whom I had so fully served, was possessed totally of me. A responsive female, he had made me. I smiled to myself. I was other than I had been, a few enths ago. And doubtless he would teach me to become still a different creature. I shivered. I wondered if the fear of him would pass.

Sighing, I rose and wandered the dharen's lair, that I might know what such a man would choose to keep about him. Without a word, he had left me. I found myself at the gol table, a featureless translucent slab, upon which he had piled his trail gear. A straight-blade lay there, half the length of my arm, in a chased scabbard of green stra metal. Its hilt was inlaid with titrium wire, the butt of it a single fire gem.

I slid it from the scabbard, my hand upon the hilt. A strange thrill went through me, holding the weapon, as if I had held such before. Upon the stra blade was engraved a legend, in some unfamiliar script. And a symbol, one I had seen repeated upon the scabbard and hilt, a bursting spiral. And then I recollected the tune I hummed: Se'keroth.

Chilled cold, I replaced the sword in its housing, and stepped back. I did not touch the gol-knife there, or the strange sharp-edged circles of steel piled beside it. "Se'keroth, Sword of Severance," rang in my head.

Wordless, he had left me, in an unlocked room filled with weapons. I ran my palms along the inner thighs, still damp without moisture. I paced the chamber's confines, trailing my hand along the smooth northern thala that paneled the walls, my bare feet soundless upon the Galeshir mat. I could kill myself, if I chose. I could arm myself and run. I did neither.

My hand found a panel, forward of the others. I slid it back. Bound books and scrolls lay there, orderly, behind a second wall of glass. Among them I saw his own works, numerous volumes, including *Ors Yris-Tera*, "Book of the Weathers of Life." And what must have been the game itself, yris-tera, the three-level board and leather shaker. Inside that shaker, I knew, were sixty bone pieces. Another creation of Khys's, *Ors Chaldra*, lay near it. Divination and morality had been Khys's concerns, in hide-days, when he and some few others attempted to put Silistra back together again, after the fall. Disquieted, I slid the panel back in place. How could I aspire to him?

Upon the gol table, among his other gear, had been Khys's own chald. He did not, as do most Silistrans, wear his chald soldered about him. The great chald of Silistra, in which every strand given upon the planet was woven, lay like some sleeping slitsa among his leathers.

If I had had a chald, a testament to my skills and accomplishments, a prideful statement of my chan-tera, the will of the life, I would not have left it casually upon some table. But I bore no chaldra. If I had ever, it was lost, along with my past. It is a shameful thing, to be chaldless. I had been told that someday I might bear the arrar's chald, the highest attainable. But that was before my madness, before the child.

I found I had come again to the beckoning doors. I turned and surveyed Khys's keep once more; the rust-silked couch, the gol table, the windowed alcove floored with cushions. Above my head, the tiny suns flickered, dimmed again. I went and collected the three bowls near the couch and placed them on the stand that held their brothers, and the golden kifra pitcher. I smoothed the silks over the dharen's sumptuous couch.

Once more the door drew me. Doubtless, he would tire of me. I, barely literate, unskilled, was no fit companion for such a man. He had gone, leaving me unrestrained. I might not see him for another two years. I remembered what he had said, that there were better than two thousand women at the Lake of Horns. And what he only implied, that any of them would be honored to stand in my place. He had gotten already that which he had desired from me.

I put my hand upon the door's bronze handle, pushed it back. Standing in the doorway, I regarded the tapestried hallway, the vaulted ceiling with its myriad tiny stars for illumination. The floor was of stones, squares of blue ornithalum and green-veined archite. I put one bare foot upon that smooth coldness.

And then I heard him, his voice edged with anger. From the left, around a sharp turning by a tapestry depicting battling hulions, he strode into my sight, another beside him.

I stood frozen, caught with one foot upon the hall stones. Not even did I move to shake my hair over my nakedness before a stranger. Khys's companion looked enough like him that they might have been brothers, except for his hair, shades darker than mine. He wore a full loose robe of blue-black, with a glittering spiral at his left shoulder. About his waist was a chald nearly as grand as the dharen's, wide and thick, imposing in its magnitude.

". . . as I please!" said Khys to his companion. They had not yet noticed me. I stood witless, unmoving.

"It seems to me," said the other, not intimidated, "that your passion clouds your judgment in this matter." I clutched the door's edge, leaned upon it.

"You will come to think differently," said Khys, his mouth an angry white line. "I can . . . Estri! Come here." They both stopped there before the hulion tapestry.

Trembling, I hastened to obey him. His companion's eyes assessed me coldly. I knelt to him, as he had taught me, my hair falling over his feet, my knees upon the cold floor. It was not easy, before another. I felt my skin flush.

"Doubtless you can make her obedient. That is not a factor," said the other.

"On the contrary, it is the factor. But one must define obedience. I feel," said Khys, "that even though you have prejudged matters, what I have done may still enlighten you. This is no time to discuss it."

And he bent and touched me. I rose, my hair over my breasts, shining in the soft light. Khys's eyes seemed concerned. The other's glance was openly hostile.

"Walk with us," he said, and they moved apart, that I might be between them.

"This is Vedrast, Estri."

"*Presti m'it*, Keepress," intoned Vedrast, his full mouth feigning a smile.

"You mistake me, arrar." He took my arm, as if to guide me back into Khys's keep. I felt a slight shock, at his pressure, then a sense of presence. I grabbed Khys's wrist, fearful. He shook his head imperceptibly. I dropped my hands to my sides.

"My apologies, lady," said Vedrast, enigmatic. His eyes were decidedly amber.

Khys turned to close the double doors, and the light in the keep brightened.

The arrar Vedrast crossed the room and poured himself a bowl of kifra, taking it to the alcove, where he lounged back upon the cushions there. The spiral glittered upon his robe. I turned from him, to Khys, behind me.

My couch-mate stood with his hands upon his hips, his face abstracted. He seemed elsewhere. I waited, wanting to run to him, seek shelter from this other, who glowered, intimidating, from amid the cushions.

He motioned me to him, took me in under his arm. He was scowling, but not at me.

"You had best lighten your touch, Vedrast," he said to his guest. "It is the entire monitoring system that stands to judgment here."

"I do not take your meaning," said Vedrast slowly, his jaw a grim line. Whorls of sparks danced in the air between them. Khys stiffened.

"This that you do here is at best, a formality. I will do, as I have always done, my own will. Properly handled, the monitoring you want as its own authority will uphold me. If it does not, then it has been improperly done."

The arrar blanched visibly, put down his bowl, and got purposefully to his feet. Khys pushed me gently to one side. They considered one another.

"Will you gainsay rules of your own creation?"

"I made guidelines that, properly adhered to,

would serve as safety factors in complicated hests of long duration. If the sorting of the monitor is not free from preconceptions, the work is valueless."

"I would take these points up with all us present," rasped Vedrast, flicking those intrusive eyes my way. I was shocked that he would speak so to the dharen.

"Do your business here, now!" Khys commanded. "And I warn you, see to your skills while you are about it."

The arrar Vedrast closed his eyes for a moment, searching composure. He found it, and walked purposefully toward me. I retreated from him.

"Stand still, Estri," Khys commanded.

"Come sit with me," said the other, extending his hand. I looked at it. He did not withdraw. Timidly I extended my hand to his. This time there was no shock, but I felt again, unmistakably, a cold touch within. I twisted my head to the dharen.

"Please, Khys," I petitioned him, as Vedrast led me firmly toward the alcove. He only looked away, his face gone cold.

"Sit there. Good. Khys, if you will . . ." And he motioned to a place on his left.

"Thank you," Vedrast said when the dharen had seated himself, his back against the draped windows.

"Now, Estri, I am going to sedate you. It will not be painful, and the effects will last only a short time." And he reached over and put both his hands around my neck, fingers meeting where spine joins skull. I felt only a drowsiness, an urge to sleep, and a receding of sensation. I concentrated upon staying upright. My body was weighty, recalcitrant.

Vaguely, I knew the man's hands had left me, and that Khys's had replaced them with his own. And I saw, blurred, that when his hands came away, they bore with them my band of restraint.

But I had only enough strength to keep myself erect.

The arrar's hands were again upon me, and he peered at my throat for a time. I wanted desperately to lie down and sleep.

Then they asked me of hulions. And I heard myself answer, speak of what had, this very morning, occurred. I was asked to remember in detail, and I did.

Then did Vedrast ask what the paper I had read had brought to mind. And of the arrar Sereth, did he question me. I answered him as best I could, that I had only once met him, and that I had, upon occasion, dreamed of him, as I had much of my namesake's life.

"Why do you think," said Vedrast, "you have those dreams? Do they trouble you?"

I shook my head to clear it. Something within screamed that my answers were important, even crucial, but all I wanted was to lay my head in the dharen's lap.

"No, they do not trouble me." I struggled the words out upon an unwieldy tongue. "I have no past of my own. Hers was of great interest to me. I chose her name, also. I would be as she, but I know what was in that book was hers, and not mine."

"I see," said Vedrast. I squinted, that I might see Khys's face, but I could make nothing of it.

"Tell me, now, about the child you bore."

I did so, seeing the hateful beast, remembering my swollen belly.

"And about Khys," he pressed me.

I tried to rise. I could not. I could feel him, strolling through my memories, kicking what did not interest him from his path. My mind was filled with tangled thoughts, impressions, a patterning I could see extending out into the unborn time.

"Tell me," said Vedrast, his amber eyes, close to mine, prying.

"I serve him," I whispered. "I want what time he will give me, nothing else," I said. Then I felt Vedrast at our couching. Enraged, I met him there boldly, with a skill I had not known I had. And I drove him back. The arrar, shaken, retreated.

Khys replaced the band upon my neck gently. I felt his second touch, tightening it. And his third, upon my forehead, and my lethargy was gone, lifting like some oppressive gravity just repealed.

Vedrast, shaking his head back and forth, rose and pulled back the draperies, staring out into the waning day.

"Perhaps you can hold her," he said grudgingly.

"Doubtless I can hold her," Khys said, stroking my hair. I had been without the band, and I had felt the difference. I turned to him.

"I would do anything to have that freedom, to see, and hear, and feel as you do," I breathed, fighting tears.

"And I would love to have you whole," Khys said. "When the time comes, rest assured, it will be done."

"Did I pass?" I asked him fearfully. "Will I be eliminated?"

Khys laughed. Vedrast turned from the window, solemn-faced.

"Answer her, then, O dour one," directed the dharen.

"One does not usually give the subject the results," he temporized.

"Make an exception." And the dharen's tone had lost its humor.

"It is not up to us, in truth. You have heard that. If it were, I might be tempted to precipitate some crisis and see how you handled it." Vedrast turned to Khys. "There is no use in this, I will send you a written report."

"You will make one before you leave here. And bring it before me, that I may see what it contains, and I may sign it. I may not. At any rate, I would hear what will be in it." His hand, upon my back, stopped moving.

"This is a farce!" the arrar exploded.

"Indeed, as is all of civilization. But it is workable. As one farcical primate with delusions of spirituality to another, let me adjure you to walk with greater care in my presence. I might be tempted to break you in half and feed the remains to the hulions. Now, in ten words or less, how do you find her?" the dharen said, rising.

"Neutralized. Reasonably adjusted. Potentially dangerous. May I go?" His words hissed from fat, full lips upon a fine spray.

"Go, then, and make your report. I will expect you to attend me at moon's meal."

"I have business elsewhere," said Vedrast, stepping carefully over my outstretched legs.

"Cancel it. We have more pressing business here."

The arrar wheeled and made exaggerated obeisance, strode angrily from the keep, slamming the thala doors behind him.

Khys went and secured the locks, and when he turned, he was grinning widely.

He came and stood over me, fists upon his hips.

"Still dreaming of Sereth, are you? Perhaps I will give you to him for a night. Would you like that?"

I shuddered and crept through the cushions, back against the window. I shook my head repeatedly. I wondered what was going to happen to me. Had I been assessed? Would the recommendation upon my papers be the same as the arrar Sereth's? I had no hope but Khys's protection. I thought of Vedrast, trembling.

"Speak to me," he ordered, squatting down, his bulk closing the alcove into a cube.

"No, dharen," I whispered, cowering amid the rust and evening cushions.

"What?"

"No. I would not like it. Yes, I will serve you however you wish." I would not cry or scream. I dug my nails into my palms and took deep breaths. I thought what it had been like without the band, then I tried not to think.

"Your life," he said, stretching out among the cushions, "rests in my hands alone. Such decisions have always rested with me. They might recommend. But they, in their turn, are also assessed. The council had no power but what I have given it. Over you, I have given it none."

And I looked at him, turned sideways, and knew that he was a man who gave away nothing. He had ruled Silistra so long, so well, so silked was the hand of steel, that few upon the outside conceived him to be a living being. They quoted him, venerated chaldra, threw yris-tera to guide them in their lives. They thought him more a force than a man, some long-dead priest of justice and truth.

And that priest of justice and truth cornered me against the window, that I might testify to his manhood and be blessed by his use.

When it was over, he slept, and I lay beside him, rubbing my hipbones. I thought long of fear and love, and wondered how I would have felt about him had things been otherwise. But they were as they were, and I found no solace in such speculation. I turned and laid my head against his shoulder. He growled in his sleep, and my heart scrabbled for escape. Partly wakened, he put an arm across my chest, pulled me to him. Half-thrilled, half-terrified, I lay hardly breathing. Alone so long, I had dreamed of just this. Yet, he had structured my experiences to suit him. Doubtless, how I felt now was more his choice than mine. I fell asleep finally, upon the uneasy conclusion that love, no matter what its roots, feels real when it is upon one. There seemed to be, then, no way to test it, for I loved my life the most. If Khys had taught me not all of love, he had taught me what he desired, and that would keep me alive. If he kept me alive, he could have my body, my mind, my love. I would deal, somehow, with my fear. Perhaps, I thought, drowsing, I might even wake up free of it. And I dreamed I saw with the Keepress, she all I had ever envisioned her— magnificent, haughty, her skin and eyes aglow with the father's fire. Upon a barren crag, she sat with me. Khys, she said, deserved better. I, she judges, shortchanged us both, with my conception. I argued that it was not my conception, but that put upon me by others, those around me. And she stood and stalked about that peak, vital, uninhibited. She demanded to know the identity of her who inhabited my body. I was a woman, born to flesh, she stormed. Female by birthright, she called me, and deaf to the law within. I am no animal, I raged. Then you are not of the living, she said, and knelt down, her wide-set molten eyes glowing, her tiny winged brows knit with concern. The wind whipped around her, keening. It reminded me of my place, and before whom I sat.

So did the Keepress come to me, and adjure me not gainsay myself. Live your heritage, she demanded fiercely. Do not make judgment, only listen, and live. Make no less of yourself than you are, and she turned me within, to see the fullness there.

And when Khys woke me, entering me from behind, I found a different way to move against him. As the Keepress, I leaned into his cupping hands, clutched him, let my body couch him, unconstrained. I was not disappointing, to him or my brazen self.

"Perhaps one should not query such a gift," he said, wiping sweat from his upper lip, "but one may surely remark upon its quality." His eyes narrowed to slits.

"Did I not please you?"

He laughed. "Is that what you call it?"

"I love you," I reminded him, running my hands over my taut belly.

"You assured me of that before we slept." His finger touched my lips. I nipped it.

"I had a dream," I said, remembering.

He cocked his head. "May you have them more often," he said, after a pause. But he stared at me, disquieted. He reached out a hand, caressing, and my body leaped, joyous to his touch. He took his hand away and rose up on his knees.

"Sit up," he said.

I curled my legs around me, leaned upon one straight arm. It was not my way of sitting, nor a way Khys had taught me. My breasts and belly, and the curves of my hips and waist, were well displayed. I threw my hair over my right breast, and it fell between my slightly parted thighs.

He surveyed me minutely. I found it exciting, that he looked at me so.

"I have meetings," he said finally. "They will take the rest of the day and most of the evening." His voice was level, only.

"Take me with you, please," I begged, wide-eyed, leaning forward. "I would not be here alone. I will do nothing to displease you."

He rose up without answer. I waited, following him with my eyes, my breath held. Near the hidden bookshelf, he pushed back a thala panel. From within it, he took a night-blue robe, and dark breech, and sandals. I wondered how many of the common-held forereaders he had couched. Doubtless, many. I found a joy in his movements, that of a woman's eyes upon a fine male.

Belting on his chald, he came around to face me, his arched brows slightly raised.

"I think, upon another thought, that I will allow you to accompany me. What rises within you has taken my interest. Clothe yourself."

I bowed my head, smiling, and went searching my one garment. When I had tied it at the neck and hips, he beckoned me close.

Amusement flickered in his eyes. He looked me up and down and bade me turn.

Then he untied the s'kim's strap, knotted behind my neck, and retied it loosely. He pulled the second tie tighter across my hips.

"It will have to do," he said. "I must get you some other garment if you are going to sit to council." His manner drove me deep into my meager store of Stothric teachings, where I searched the ice of distance to soothe my indignation. He did not fail to mark it.

"Be silent," he admonished. "Be obedient. If you do not perform creditably, I assure you, you will regret it." His hand went around my throat. By it, he pulled me roughly against him, into those arms that could have crushed me lifeless.

"Yes, dharen," I breathed when he released me. I shivered.

Beside him, I walked with attention, proudly. Unaccountably, I laughed at my fears. Doubtless, he might kill me. Rightfully, I feared him. All women fear such men, who know them. Such men, who do not fear themselves, must always be feared. But that, also, is the attraction of them, the fearsome ones, who take from us what is only such men's to take, and not a woman's to give. A woman may give her body, but a man must demand the rest, that which is his alone. A woman, Khys once said, is like owkahen—the time coming to be—which is either what a strong man may make of it or what a weak one will be made by it.

"Heed yourself, Estri," he advised, cryptic, as he stopped before a door and reached across me to push it open. His robed arm brushed my breasts, and they responded. I had been considering myself— walking the most priveleged keep at the Lake of Horns, beside the dharen of all Silistra. At the will of such a man, my best would never be too much. Even Estri the Keepress, my namesake, who had found herself often overqualified in her dealings with men, had, before this man, fallen. She would, I was sure, have approved of me, in my new perspective. My freshly wakened body preened itself, much aroused.

The room behind those thala doors was seven-cornered. One great window, dark-hung, looked out upon the Lake of Horns. The ceiling, high above our heads, was of hammered gold, ruddy and gleaming, lit by clusters of entrapped stars.

I found myself trembling, chilled, as if the cool gol under my feet was instead colored ice. Upon that strange symbol, of a bursting spiral, I turned, slowly, full around. Khys, by the window, watched me intently. Again I surveyed it, that empty hall of gold and thala. At either side of the double doors stood high-chalded arrars, lake-born by their fire-licked skin, still as statues, in the blue-black of Khys's service.

The dharen called me to him. My limbs, as I obeyed him, seemed numb.

"I have been here before," I murmured to him, and the room took my voice and returned it to me, louder, echo-edged.

"In your dreams, doubtless," the dharen said, indicating that I should kneel before the window.

As he taught me, I sat there, upon my heels, my head bent, my mind whirling. After a time, I was conscious of his eyes no longer upon me, that he went and spoke with his attendants.

And then began the audiences. As each man was announced and presented to him, the supplicant knelt before the dharen and put his lips to the master's instep, as I had been taught to do.

The first of them, a Day-Keeper, was named Ristran, dharener of hide diet. Attired as a Darsti builder, with his red-haired head shaved in the lateral stripes of the period of history in which he specialized, he made obeisance to Khys, who did not see fit to allow him to rise, but kept him upon his knees the whole time.

Of Astria, the high Day-Keeper spoke to the lord of his kind, and of those problems he faced with some who had taken helsars there.

And Khys was displeased. He adjured the dharener to send him no more excuses, no matter how inventive, as to why he could not deal with the helsar situation himself. And of his misdeeds, was Khys aware. Cruelly, as Ristran attempted to explain himself, did Khys restrain him. Remembering the horrors of the dharen's flesh trap, I felt compassion rise up in me for the Astrian dharener. Helsars, Khys instructed him, were not to be apportioned. Those that lay still upon the plain of Astria awaited certain individuals, for whom they had been intended.

And the dharener Ristran, head bowed, only listened as Khys instructed him to open his school to those who had taken helsar teachings, or were about to take them. The dharener objected. He wanted no servers, no coin girls, no weapons masters of threxmen, in his care.

"What am I supposed to do with them?" he inquired, his voice atremble with fear and rage, still upon his knees.

"Train them, form them into a group, use them. At least that," Khys ordered, observing that though some who had taken helsars could barely read or write, they would soon be possessed of much greater skills. Further, he demanded an accounting of all those involved in helsar studies. He would have it, he instructed Ristran, within a pass. And then, in his most formidable voice, he informed the dharener that he was aware of attempts by those of hide diet to claim certain helsars, without regard to their rightful partners. If, said Khys, he heard again of such misdeads, he personally would put Ristran in a band of restraint.

And the dharener looked up at him in disbelief. And at me, with an expression I could not name. I saw his limbs suddenly tremble, as Khys released his flesh again to his control. Stiffly he rose to his feet and backed the long way to the thala doors, his eyes lowered, deferential.

The second petitioner that day, Brinar first fourth, was admitted even as Ristran made his exit. To him, a man called Brenath, adviser to Well Astria and Port Astrin, the Well's dependent city, Khys allowed, as he begged, certain aid in the rebuilding with which he was concerned. I learned, shifting there upon my aching knees, much of the state of Well Astria. I learned that in the holocaust of Amarsa, '695, the coastline of Astria had been markedly altered. The Liaison's Port, where off-world ships are accommodated, was only now ready to be reopened, in its new location. Also I heard tell of the new Well-Keepress, a forereader, hide-born, who had been installed there. And my discomfort, unexplainable, was such that Khys turned from the supplicant, his eyes, half-lidded, eloquent warning. I twisted my fingers together and sought to calm myself. The woman, named Yrisia Ateje diet Vedrast, was surely no concern of mine. Yet, mention of her, and her installation as high couch, discomfited me. Once more Khys turned. I saw him through tears, blurred, come upon me unbidden. That he might not chastise me, I put my face to the gol. He turned away once more. I found, when my resentments had cooled, that I had drawn blood with my nails upon my palms.

The next to seek him was a man high among Slayers, Rin diet Tron, of the Slayers' Seven of Astria. He was a much-scarred, grizzled veteran, in the end of his prime, and his distaste for the bending of knee and kissing of foot Khys required of him was ill-concealed. The Slayer's eyes kept returning to me, and they were blue and troubled when I met them.

He spoke, also, of helsars, at Khys's prompting, abstractedly, as if he had forgotten why it was he had come here, and wished he had not done so. He explained, with the aid of a man unused to problems beyond his power to solve, the perplexity of his men.

"Helsar talents," said Rin diet Tron, in a voice raspy and solemn, "seem more a hindrance than help to those Slayers who have acquired them. And when one needs them, in dealing with renegades also possessed of such skills, the carnage accompanying their use waxes out of proportion to all sense of fitness. I have seen men hurl chunks of mountain at each other. I have seen altercations between two take thirty to their deaths. The sort around Astria is so complexly muddled from all who wander about owkahen, none can get any use of it. My men whet their blades and long for the days when they could use them. Only a few find their new weapons welcome, and study their use. Most, myself among them, feel this whole situation unseemly. I would be rid of these gifts, but if I were somehow freed of them, I would be at the mercy of those who wield them with no conscience!" He stopped, spread his hands wide, dropped them. It was obvious he felt that even Khys had, for him, no solution.

Khys instructed him to send, in groups of twenty, his troubled Slayers to the Lake of Horns, to stay a pass, each group, and take instruction.

Dismissed, the Slayer got stiffly to his feet, backed wordlessly from Khys's sight.

The fourth supplicant was an off-worlder. I looked at him with interest, having never seen a M'ksakkan. He had no horns or tendrils, no tufted ears. His skin, except for an olive cast, was much like Silistran skin. He was not small, as I had conceived M'ksakkans, and his hair was harth-black. Ponderous he was, and overly muscled for my taste, with eyes like dirty ice. He wore a tight-fitting, strangely cut breech, black trimmed with gold, and a white tunic under his Silistran cloak. As he walked toward Khys, I saw that he limped pronouncedly, favoring his left side.

When he raised his eyes from Khys's feet, he stared at me openly from under bushy brows. I straightened my back, meeting his gaze. My legs ached so from sitting upon them, I could think of little else.

His name was Khaf-Re Dellin, and he was Liaison First to Silistra. I had heard of him. He was before Khys with a formal request for inquiry into the complicity of a certain Slayer who had been upon his home planet, M'ksakka, at the time of the M'ksakkan adjusters' death. His fear of Khys, I decided, must be second only to my own.

The dharen strode around him, where he knelt upon the spiral set into the gol floor. He suggested to Dellin that he look among his own for his culprit. He had, he said, been informed of the manner of the M'ksakkan's death, and found it not Silistran.

Dellin, diffident in the extreme, pleaded for a statement to send to his superiors.

That statement Khys gave him, an observation upon the harmonic workings of the Weathers of Life, caused him to cringe upon his knees. Thrice I caught his eyes upon me, and it seemed that he found me offensive in his sight.

Khys also noticed, and bade him explain his

fascination, at which time the Liaison begged to be excused. The dharen allowed it.

"Hold the rest," he instructed those who attended his doors, and strode across the chamber to where I knelt battling the strangeness that threatened to engulf my sanity. I first knew it when he put the flat of his hand on my head.

I quailed beneath his touch, fearing flesh-lock, discipline . . . I knew not what. My mind, despite my best efforts, was filled to overflowing with resentment and hatred.

Instead, he bade me rise. And I felt calmed, my hostility fading as circulation returned to my numbed legs. I rubbed my knees.

"What think you of our Liaison?" queried Khys.

And I felt invaded, and did not bother to answer him aloud. He had his answer, I knew, from my mind.

His aristocratic face expressionless, Khys toyed with his chald.

"You asked to come here," he pointed out. "Shall I return you?"

"To my confinement?" I spat. "No. I would rather even this."

And he indicated that I take up again my place before the window, which now showed the sun's set. Again sitting on my heels, under his scrutiny, I flushed hot with shame. A decoration for his audience room, I had become. And I felt much-fallen, though from what, I did not know.

He strode, his dark robe swirling around him, to the arrars at the doors. One, nodding, left the audience chamber. The other crossed his arms over his chest.

Six more men kissed the dharen's feet that evening, seeking his favor, his council. The night stars glittered in the moonless sky before he was through with them. My stomach growled and rolled upon itself. It occurred to me that the dharen might not feel hunger, that such a man perhaps did not need food. But I knew different, from a night I had supped with him. And then I was not sure at all that that night had ever occurred. Looking at his back, I seemed to see the bursting spiral there, scintillant. And he was another, so great that Khys was only a poor copy. Around me, I saw not thala but thick-leaved greenery, and above me was not gold, but the glory of the universe, not paltry as time lets us see it, but brilliant and much multiplied, its beginning and ending and all motion between chronicled there.

And I found that my hands squeezed my head, spread-fingered, and that I rocked back and forth, moaning softly, with Khys's concerned face close to mine. The tenth supplicant was no longer in the chamber, and the two arrars stood just behind their master, eyes distant.

I could not look at him, though he demanded it. When I did, his features danced and changed in the mist. I heard my own voice, begging aid. I am not here, I thought desperately. The dharen's flat palm cracked my head to one side, then the other. I barely felt it; rather was I conscious of the different sights before me.

Then I saw that golden ceiling, and the entrapped stars upon it, and knew that he carried me, for they were where the floor should be. Then I was not there, but elsewhere, and I bore that beast again, saw the cord between us cut, heard it scream.

It screamed and screamed. I felt something upon my mouth, and the screaming, mercifully, stopped. I heard my name, and forced my lids apart. And closed them tight against what I saw. But he would not let me be. I could feel him, within me, working. I fought him. Better to drift, forever. He would not allow it. He was stronger than I. He pulled me back. I felt the couch silks under me, and knew my chance was lost.

"Estri," said Khys, "look at me."

I did so. His face did not dance. The mist did not obscure him, nor the expanse of his keep, nor Carth, whose worried face peered over his shoulder.

"No." I denied it all—the madness, the hatred, the other I had seen. "Help. Please help me," I pleaded, in the face of what I feared most of all.

"Estri," said Khys. I met his eyes, unresisting, that he might heal my accursed madness. And it was as if one stood over a clear, bottomless well in which the sense of one's life floated, waiting to be dipped and drunk. I felt my heart rate slow, my blood chemistries come into balance. His fingers came together at the base of my spine; I partook of his strength. His face, as he worked, was transfigured, compassionate.

He sat back, again dharen of Silistra.

"Rise," he directed. I did, and dizziness assailed me. But the keep did not dissolve, and Khys's grasp on my arm was very real.

"Thank you, Carth," said Khys, not turning. "Send Vedrast my apologies. I will not be long here." And Carth, his brow still furrowed, left by the outer doors.

"Now," he said gravely, "let us discuss what has just occurred."

"I could not help it," I whimpered. "I am trying. Surely you know that. I cannot help it."

"There is no way out. There is no way but mine. There has never been." He spoke to that within me which still defied him. "I will not allow another of these fits. You will, should you repeat this performance, find yourself once more stripped, and I will start anew." And though I did not know then what he meant, the fine hairs on my body raised themselves. I clenched my teeth to stop their chatter.

He smiled grimly. "Your sensing is truly superb.

The worst is yet to come." He patted me delicately upon the head.

At the door, he looked back at me. "Have a pleasant evening," he said. "Tasa." And I heard the tumblers click as he locked the doors behind him. The stars dimmed.

I sat there, stunned, for a time. Then I went and tried the doors, both those to the hall and those to my chamber. All were secure. The trail gear and weapons were no longer upon the milky gol table. That panel I had seen him push inward did not respond to my touch.

I poured myself a bowl of kifra, to stay my shaking limbs and drive the chill from me. Sorely I had displeased him. I wondered what the night enths held in store.

"It is not fair," I said aloud, tossing the empty bowl to the rust-toned mat. It was not right for him to punish me. Surely the madness was punishment enough. I went to the windowed alcove, stared out at the night. The city was reflected in the lake. Another time, I would have been taken by the view's beauty. There was a wind, bobbling and rippling the lake's surface and the lights upon it. How long I sat with my leg thrown up on the sill, I do not know. At one point I stripped off my s'kim and threw it, petulant, among the cushions. At another, I thought I heard footsteps, and hurriedly reclaimed it, tying it as Khys preferred, tight over the hips, loose at the breasts. The knots of queasiness in my stomach I attributed to so long without food. I was dozing, my shoulder pressed against the cool pane, when the doors opened. I did not turn. The ceiling stars acknowledged him. I continued to stare into the night.

He came up behind me, in the alcove amid the cushions. Taking a deep breath, my sweaty palms clenched, I turned to face his anger.

And pressed back against the window; Khys had made good his word.

Before me stood the arrar Sereth. He wore a night-dark robe, loosely belted. Shadows hovered in his hollow cheeks, danced in the scar that traced its way from temple to jaw. Khys's height, but spare was the dharen's most deadly weapon.

I went down on the cushions to him, my lips to his instep, as Khys required. Abruptly, he jerked his foot away. Confused, my knees resting on my own hair, I stared up at him. He squatted down by my side.

"Do not fear me," he said, tossing his head. His hand found my shoulder. It seemed that his fingers trembled. "He asked me to come here, to use you." His voice, through unmoving lips, was very soft. "I will not, if you do not wish it." So gently spoke this man who ripped out throats with his bare hands, who got well-women with child and refused them. A deep V formed above his high-bridged nose.

I studied him, his clenched jaws, his tight-drawn face, all line and bone and scar. And I peered close, at those eyes searching mine. He was an arrar, I reminded myself. No doubt my thoughts were open to him. "You are my punishment," I offered timidly. "I will get worse, should I refuse to serve you." My words came out barely louder than his. This man, whose touch I had craved in dreams, scared me witless. He retrieved his hand, examined it as if it held the answer he sought.

"Estri," he said hoarsely, "do you not at all recall me?" He touched his fingers to my chin, ran them up my bruised cheek. His eyes narrowed as I flinched.

"I recall you," I whispered. "You once took me to my chamber. You would not stay with me. You asked that I leave you be."

He stood, crossed to the kifra pitcher, scooping

up my discarded bowl along the way in an easy, fluid motion. He moved like a wild thing, not like Khys, whose dignity ever weighted his flesh. He returned with two filled bowls and offered one out, hesitantly, as if afraid I would refuse him. I reached up and accepted it, trying to smile.

Those eyes took stock of me as if I were some carnivore's long-trailed dinner. Hungry was that gaze, with a hunger I had never seen in a man.

He sat beside me, cross-legged, and sipped his bowl, holding it in both hands. His eyes never left mine.

"How is it with him?" he asked finally.

"As he wishes it," I said, looking into my kifra, swirling it around.

"Does he often beat you?"

"He seldom does anything to me. This is the first I have seen him since before I birthed his son."

He was silent, then. When he emptied his bowl, he took it and refilled it. I pondered, watching, what he would do if I refused him.

"I wonder"—he sighed as he sat once more—"if he wants me to move against him. You would not know, would you?" His eyes were very bright. When he had drained the bowl, he threw it against the far wall so hard it rebounded to the middle of the room.

"Arrar," I murmured, "it would be a kindness if you would do what you came here to do. I would not face his wrath."

"I doubt if I can," he said dryly, and laughed, a sighing laugh like the winter wind rattling my tower window.

"I am sorry," I said. "I am afraid it is my fault." And I got up on my knees and stripped off my single garment. Before my nudity, he sat hardeyed. It occurred to me that this man, who had once refused me, doubtless had had better.

"Sereth," I whispered, "I will try very hard to please you."

He ran his hand across his brow. Then he unbelted his robe, shrugged it off his shoulders. Seeing him in his maleness, I shrank back.

"Come here, little one," he said, and took me into his arms. "So long," he groaned, his head buried in my breasts. He called me by name, repeatedly. After he had spent himself within me, he raised his head, and his eyes were red and swollen. I had never seen a man cry in orgasm. Khys certainly did not. And he had groaned strange sounds while about his stroke.

He lay half upon me a long time, his face buried in my hair, unspeaking. My fingers traced his chald, soldered around his hips, touched the carapace of muscle there. Wandering, they found themselves upon a wide scar running along his right side. He took my wrist, pulling my hand away.

"You got that upon the plain of Astria, did you not?" I asked softly.

"Estri?" he queried, suddenly leaning over me, his knees at either side of my hips.

"You are very famous, you know. And very different from Khys."

He sighed and kissed my forehead lightly. "It is good to be with you," he said, rising. "I only wish I understood his intent." And he went to the window, sat with one leg thrown up on the sill.

Upon impulse, I joined him there, my fingers finding work upon the knotted muscles of his shoulders. Leaning into it, he laughed softly. "We have come to a strange pass, you and I," he remarked.

"Arrar, do you not read thoughts?"

"Not when I can help it. And not those of a woman."

"I read Carth's report to Khys concerning you," I offered.

"Did you?" He slid out from under my hands. "What did it say?"

"That Khys should either eliminate you or seek to pacify you in some way."

"This situation could be part of either," he said after a time, in a voice like steel scraping ice. "You have risked his anger for me. Why?"

I regarded my ankles, sunk amid the cushions. My fingers attacked each other. I had doubtless done so.

"I do not know," I murmured. I sat beside him upon the sill, our thighs touching. "They say I am mad. Sometimes I am. I often do and think things that make no sense." Though I tried to hide my disquiet, my voice was husked and shaking. He put an arm around me, and I laid my head upon his shoulder.

"You are not mad," he whispered, almost angrily. "It is only what has befallen you, and the way he uses you, that makes you think so."

"In his way, he cares for me," I excused him.

He spat a word I did not know.

"What does that mean?" I asked him.

"It means that Khys cares for nothing but his hests. Nothing."

"Do you think," I ventured, suddenly near tears, "that he will let you come to me again?" The room flickered. I fought it and the aching sadness that came upon me. For a moment I saw him differently in my mind—at another time, another place.

"I do not know," he said, distant. "I will if I can."

But I cared no more for the answer. I slid from the sill and curled myself among the cushions, sobbing. I heard my voice, begging his aid. And he gathered me up in his arms and rocked me like a child, speaking to me in a language I did not know. When I was drained of tears, he again couched me, savagely.

"Clothe yourself," he said, slapping me upon the rump. "I have done all I can do for you." He fished up his breech, his robe, his sandals.

"Where are you going?" I asked, tying my s'kim about me.

"I am going to take you, as I have been instructed, to the dharen," he said, his brown eyes intent upon my face.

And though I tried to hide my fear, I know he saw it. I pulled my fingers from where they clawed at the band upon my neck, smoothing the s'kim over my hips with them.

His brows knit, he pushed me lightly toward the door.

"I should not," he said, locking it again behind us, "speak to you of these things, but I will. Do not let him terrorize you so. All masters pass. And you have, as a woman, certain constraints you might use upon him. If I were you, I would do so."

I looked up at him, uncomprehending.

"I have loved you," he added, low, "since I first saw you. We both live. For now, that must be enough. If ever I can aid you, know that I will surely do so."

And I walked upon awkward legs beside him, each footfall a surprise as my weight thudded down. I wondered what to do. Khys, who had fathered my child, had given me to this man, who would destroy him.

"Khys is my couch-mate," I reminded him, this stranger, before whom I had exposed my madness, weeping and begging for aid. His hand kneaded the back of my neck as we passed through the hall by the hulion tapestry. And the touch reminded me of his way with my body, so different, so much more, than the dharen's.

I thought again of Khys, and by the time Sereth pushed open the doors to the dharen's study, I was trembling. Within that room, mural-ceilinged, of

thala and silver, he sat at table with Vedrast. I
knew the room. My child had been conceived here—
not open one of the six narrow couches, but upon
the silvery mat, beneath the dark-draperied windows. Tapers were lit upon the round table, as
they had been that night, though clusters of entrapped stars hovered high in the keep's four
corners.

Khys and Vedrast rose, bringing their bowls with
them, and seated themselves upon the thala-toned
couches. Sereth propelled me gently forward.

I went to the dharen, brushed my lips against
his sandal, sat back upon my heels facing him.

"Sit down, Sereth," ordered Khys, indicating a
place at his right. Sereth slid down upon his spine,
crossing his arms over his chest, his head low.

Khys's glance met Vedrast's, who now lounged
supine on the couch to the dharen's left.

I shifted, and he took note, scowling, as he turned
to Sereth.

"How did you find her, arrar?" asked Khys
solicitously.

"Much diminished," he said, almost inaudibly,
meeting Khys's gaze, unflinching.

"But not so much so that you would not again
couch her," Khys predicted, over steepled fingers.

"No, not that much," Sereth agreed. His face
was pale with concentration.

"You did well for me, in Dritira. And in hide
diet, that which you did outshone my brightest
hopes. From what you did upon M'ksakka, there
have been repercussions, but through no fault of
yours. We were hoping that this"—and he indicated me—"might please you. We are not ungra-
cious." His eyes barely open, Khys dug at Sereth.
And that one's scar grew livid, and his body
stiffened. Sweat glistened upon his face. But he
did not take his eyes from Khys's. Between them,
the air grew wavery, sparking sporadically.

Vedrast stood abruptly, his shoulders hunched, his face distraught.

And then, amazingly, Khys laughed out loud, and extended his hand to Sereth.

The arrar wiped his sweat-slicked face before he grasped it.

"When would you like this thing done?" he asked.

"Now!"

And even as Sereth sprang from his place, Vedrast seemed to shake off his paralysis, whirling. They grappled briefly, Sereth's arm at the man's throat from behind. His other hand, I saw as he kicked Vedrast's legs out from under him and dropped him to his knees, held an open metal circlet.

Khys leaned forward with a sigh as Sereth stepped back from Vedrast, whom he had put in a band of restraint. That one, upon his knees, clawed at his throat, groaning his negation. I sympathized with him.

"And what you just did for me," approved the dharen quietly. "I have been trying to get done for a number of years."

Sereth grinned at him, his fists upon his hips. But his eyes, upon the piteously moaning arrar, were bleak.

"Take him, now, and dispose of him," Khys ordered.

Sereth, no longer smiling, bent to the restrained arrar, speaking softly. He tossed his head and raised the man up by force. Those eyes in that slack-jawed face were vacant. Vedrast, upon Sereth's arm, stumbled from the room, mewling.

I retrieved my fingers from my own throat, from my own tight band. Khys secured the doors Sereth had left ajar. Upon his way back to me he reclaimed a bowl, its contents spilled upon the mat, upset by the arrar's struggle. His movements were very different from Sereth's.

The whole time, I had not moved. I am well-trained, I thought to myself wryly as Khys again seated himself. I felt very small and helpless before him.

"And what do you think of all that has occurred, my little saiisa?"

"The man went mad when the band was put upon him." I quivered, upon my knees.

"Shock, only. If he were allowed to live, he would accustom to the silence. He had a great talent, and the use of it for more than a thousand years."

"And you needed Sereth to do it?"

Khys laughed. "I am still attempting to test that man's limitations. Only such as Sereth, with his oddly developed skills, could have restrained Vedrast. He has had that band, keyed to his touch, ready, since he returned from M'ksakka. But he did not know for whom it was intended." He chuckled, stretching. "I have long desired to see him work his craft."

"You value him highly," I commented.

"I have appraised him fairly. One must see what is, no matter how markedly it differs from one's expectations."

And then it was that he turned his attention upon me, blatantly invading my mind. Cruelly he visited himself upon my memories, upon my couching of the arrar. His probe I could not stop, as I had Vedrast's. When I tried to run, I found myself flesh-locked. Then I stood aside, within my own mind, and docilely watched him take what he wanted from my experiences. And of all Sereth had said to me, Khys apprised himself. And of how it was for me at the arrar's hands, did he take note.

When he released me, I let myself fall forward, lying passive until the tremors attendant upon flesh lock had passed. An informer upon the arrar Sereth, he had made me, and even upon myself. How, I demanded of myself desperately, can one live this way? And my thought reverberated in the hollow, ringing emptiness within me, coming back unchanged, unanswered.

He called me. I rolled upon my side and looked up at him, miserably. I had not the strength to do more. Or the inclination. I waited, passive, for him to make known his will. There was no more rage or horror or hatred or fear in me. I was only tired. One can fight just so long a battle that cannot be won.

"Good," mused Khys, as if to himself. "Soon you will be ready."

II

The Wages of Forgetfulness

I knelt upon the bursting spiral, in that seven-cornered room, before Khys's council. Or upon seven spirals, in seven such rooms, spaced the length and breadth of Silistra. One corner was empty. In one stood Khys—his flesh-and-blood presence. In the remaining five, the flame-licked figures flickered, behind each a window looking out upon the part of Silistra in his care. They were each in their places, and here also: the seven alcoves, identical; the seven spirals, overlayed; the five of Khys's council, bicorporate. And I—was I seven also, where I crouched upon the symbol that focused these widespread keeps into one?

There was a feeling to inhabiting that highly charged space, one of being enrapped, encased, embalmed in crackling force. I wore no band of restraint. I had been sedated, but such was no longer necessary. I seemed, to myself in my own vision, neck-deep in the congruent spirals, the arms twisted around me like some great slitsa. I could see my breasts, my knees, the true spiral upon the true floor, only through the others, semi-present, atop it. I averted my eyes. The sensation brought upheaval to my stomach and water to my mouth.

The keep wrenched sideways, churned, and it was no longer Khys that was flesh, but another. My knees were invisible, imprisoned, swallowed by the gol floor. Cold shriveled the edges of every cell of my body. The golden one smiled at me. Make heat, or die. Simple. I made it, using the pain I felt to kindle the conflagration. The crown of my head was that fire's fuel, and around the flames my interrogator paced, appraising. Damage he found there, and damage he did. Cringing, I received it, for I knew not how to resist.

"Speak to me of the sevenfold spirit!" my tormentor demanded of me.

I could not. There was, within me, only a yawning chasm where he sought. But he brought to be in that place a blue-glowing spark, and by the light of it, to him certain things were revealed. And I watched, without understanding, as he took what pleased him of those truths, for they were in a language I did not know. Written upon the walls of soul, sequencers for the electrochemical devices of power lay open to him. Within me, they had long lain. Great shocks of force ripped at those walls—blinding heat; and what remained was melted, charred. The wreckage dripped, steaming, as I was passed to another hand.

The second's touch was as smooth as gol, and he bade me fear him not, but make for him certain statements of mind that he called shaping. At his bidding I saw a scarred place with those skills encysted beneath, but I could not do more than gape. Once, I might have shaped. My ears heard a wailing, and knew it mine. Kindly, gently, he passed me to the third.

And I was more deeply imprisoned within the spiral at that one's hands, my substance again screaming as it was dragged into another realm, where the physical third held court. It was his pleasure to dismantle, within me, a certain projection of my being, like tenuous water-cast gold extending out into the unborn time. As he was about it, a wind came up, roaring. Extrusions of gale whipped around him, bound him there. The fourth hastened to aid him, weighted down by the others, whose hands were all joined across the abyss wherein the wind held one of their number captive. Straining, they extricated him, a molecule at a time, from chaos.

Then did Khys reclaim my flesh into his realm. I heard the fifth, who had gainsaid any further exploration of me, tirading unintelligibly. Though I had no understanding of their words, I knew with a certainty more chilling than the void-touch between their keeps that they debated my right to live. And Khys stood for me, against them, while I knelt, dizzied, weakened, within the spirals' whirl.

One by one, he reviled them. Layer by layer, the spirals thinned, vanished, each with the window alcove and its occupant, until there was only one window in the seven-cornered keep, only one man regarding me, and only one spiral, that upon which I knelt.

I took deep gulps of air, fighting nausea, as the room rotated slowly left to right. It did not cease until Khys stood before me. As he approached, he seemed to float leftward, disappear, be again, closer. I laid my head upon my knees and moaned, for I knew that he would put the band of restraint again upon me. I did not move to stop him as he brushed hair from my exposed neck and slipped it around my throat. Almost, I craved the silence, the isolation, the peace of the band. I pressed my forehead against my knees, my pulse thunderous in my ears.

They had shown me what I had been. And what remained of those strengths I had once been pleased to employ, they had checked. I had let them, in fear of his displeasure, in weakness, born of what I had become. No dreams did I harbor now about what I might be, should Khys take the band of restraint from me. Whoever I had been, that one had had great talent. But I had been made safe during my assessment.

Khys, who had taken a clean slate and written upon it what he chose, who had rescued a wounded animal, maimed and broken, and domesticated what was left of it, had saved his creation from extinction. So thoroughly had he conditioned me to him, so completely was I his, I had not been able to conceive resistance to his will. Not even in the face of extinction had I done so. I wondered why I did not bleed. Surely, blood should flow from my nose and ears, well up in mouth, and spill out onto the spiral from my ruins. Why could not the charred remains of my skills be smelled upon the air?

"Estri, cease this," he said, raising me, unresisting, to my feet. I laid my head against his shoulder, taking comfort in his touch, his support. He had saved me, after all, from death. What worse would have befallen me, at their hands, if he had not stopped them?

"It was the only way," he said gently, and I knew somehow that he was regretful. "What was destroyed was partly of our making. You have been made safe, it is true, but for your benefit."

I said nothing, only leaned against him. He stood a time, holding me thus, silent.

"You understand so little," he murmured to me. "If you had no defense against us, from whence came that wind? Truly, I tell you, none can take from another that which has been by the father given. Alterations may be made. Restraints may be applied. That, and no more may be done." His voice was thick with some emotion I could not name.

He took me, that same day, Brinar second fourth, to the high chalder of the Lake of Horns. It was late day, near to sun's set, when we set about it. Long had he lain with me upon his couch, only holding

me, as I had asked him. Even did he cancel his
meetings and audiences, all but two, whom he
received at couchside. And with them he was
subdued, preoccupied. We took a meal there, served
us by a deferential, scantily clothed forereader,
with the bronzed look of a lake-born. Upon her
skin, a finger's length below her collarbone, was a
bursting spiral, glittering—myriad tiny points of
light upon her skin. Khys bade her come near to
me, had me run my hand over it, upon her high
breast. The place was smooth. The feel of it under
my fingers was as silken, oiled flesh. And yet, to
the eye a microcosmic universe rested there.

"She is one upon whom I have brought child,
one I favored," he said to me, when he had dismissed her. "It is my custom to so adorn my
women. It is my wish that you, also, bear my
device."

"It will be my honor to do so," I said to him, my
eyes downcast. I felt rage, that he had other women;
jealousy that she bore the mark of his favor; horror that I might bear it; fear that I, too, might
someday be relegated to such a menial position. I
pushed away my plate and rose. I had no appetite.
His eyes followed me.

I wondered if such a mark might be removed,
and how many at the lake bore it.

"No," he said. "Not, at least, by a forereader's
skills." His mouth quirked with amusement, he
rose also.

"Does it matter to you, so much, how many
others there are? I have put much spawn onto
Silistra in my lifetime. I expect to put a good deal
more."

I did not answer him, but went and lay upon the
couch until he bade me make ready, that he might
take me outside. Thrice, during the seven days
since my couching of the arrar Sereth, had fitters
attended me, at Khys's behest. Among those gar-

ments he had provided were soft tas sandals, a
dusk-dark cloak lined with shorn brist fur, and a
number of lengths of silk and web-weave with
appropriate clips and cords. He chose for me from
that selection a brown iridescent web-weave, and I
fastened it behind my neck and at my hip with
two bronze clips.

"I will also," he said, his glance approving as I
secured the cloak at my throat, "have put upon
you the chald of birthing fulfilled, and that of
couchbond."

Gratefully I thanked him, pressing myself against
him, my cheek upon his blue-black tunic. He
laughed, and held me at arm's length for a moment,
bemused.

At long last I would bear chaldra. One woman,
and one alone, can be in couchbond to a man, even
such a man as the dharen. I hardly saw the imposing halls, the precious sculptures and tapestries
that decorated Khys's tower as we passed by them
and through the huge bronze doors, inlaid with
golden beasts, and out onto the broad archite steps,
green as summer grass. The attendants closed them
from within, soundless.

"Wait," I begged him, as he started down those
stairs two at a time, his grip firm upon my arm.
He allowed it, and I turned upon the steps and
regarded the tower of the dharen, white, seamless,
unadorned, rising a quarter-nera into the fading
day. The brisk breezes of harvest caressed me, the
moist air off the lake lifted my hair, whispered me
secrets. Its footprints waved the lake's surface, gray-
green as the sky, cloudless above the forested
horizon. From ground level, those tiny decorations
at the lakeshore proved to be great soaring con-
structions, casting huge dark patches over the skittering water. And the spaces between them, so
small-seeming from the tower, were each a half-

enth's walk along archite ways set into browning grass.

We passed three parties upon our walk to the high chalder, and each one stopped and bent to give the dharen his due. Along the promenade, at lakeside, strollers were numerous, awaiting the spectacle of sun's setting over the Lake of Horns.

The high chalder, who worked his craft upon the bottom floor of the Hall of Chaldra, was expecting us. In a small and luxurious chamber, thick-hung with blues and gold, did the master of chalders greet us. Behind his thala desk were displayed all manner of chald-work, single strands, belts great and small. There were chalds there knotted in every manner and worked in every style to be found upon Silistra—chalds I had studied from books, but never before seen.

"Khys, be welcome in your house," intoned the high chalder, coming around the desk to bend his knee of his dharen. Khys raised him immediately.

The chalder, a heavyset, fleshy man, wiped his hands upon his leather apron. His eyes gleamed as he searched his pockets, his mouth twitching like that of a man with a fine humor awaiting his chance to speak.

"It is, you will see, quite unique," he muttered, both hands now searching beneath the apron. "Let me just lay my hand upon it." And his smile broke free of restraint as he brought his hands back into the open.

"This"—he held out his closed fist to Khys, who extended his own hand, palm up—"is your birthing chald. It is only superior." He opened his fist. A sensuous length of gold, solid as a slitsa, and as supple, curled itself in Khys's palm. The dharen sternly inspected it, rolling it in his fingers. It was the width of a hundred hairs. He held it out for my inspection.

I took it from him, pretending to examine it. I

knew nothing of its quality. It seemed to me satisfactory. I nodded and handed it to the chalder, whose eyes scrutinized me minutely, unabashed.

"It is very lovely," I offered.

"This is Estri," Khys explained.

"Oh," said the high chalder, suddenly knowing, his glance now more than curious. And he turned from me to Khys, and again held out his closed fist.

"It is too bad she cannot appreciate it," he remarked, letting a strand fall again into Khys's palm. But the sight of it took my breath away. It was a couchbond strand, technically, being structured upon a frame of pinkish titrium. Four times the width of the birthing strand it was, a complex geometry of chain, set in places with matched bloodred gol drops, each the size of an eye's pupil. Khys held it a time, turning it in his copper fingers.

When he raised his face to the high chalder, his pleasure was evident.

"Next to my own, Miccah, it is the finest I have yet seen from your hand."

The high chalder preened himself, puffing out his chest and tucking his chins down against his thick neck.

"Then," he said at last, "I have only to enchald her." Forthwith he set about it, employing tiny pincers and a thing like a knife that was instead a tool that joined the chald links permanently, seamless.

The chalder bade me strip. I obeyed him, standing straight before his disinterest.

Low about my waist did he fit it, first threading the golden strand through tiny links in the wider titrium chald, making them one. His hair was very white, against a blushed scalp, as he fussed upon his knees before me with his tools. Khys watched him, abstracted, his fingers toying absently at his own great chald.

"And mark her, upon the left breast," he instructed the chalder, as the man got awkwardly to his feet. Miccah raised a pale, cowlicky eyebrow, and went behind his desk. When he returned, he had a cylinder in his hand. He rotated a wheel upon it.

"Khys . . ." I started, and stopped. His eyes warned me, heavy-lidded, imperious. I would bear this man's sign, upon my very flesh, for the rest of my life. I regarded him, prepossessing, lordly, the dark-garbed master of Silistra.

"It is not painful," said the chalder, testing the cylinder's end upon his own forearm. He held it a time, then again touched it to his own flesh. He nodded.

I found myself several steps retreated.

"Stand very still," the chalder entreated, low, "or you will have a blurred and imperfect mark." And before Khys's arch stare I did so.

The high chalder put one hand gently upon my left shoulder, and with the other pressed the cylinder against my left breast. I felt the bite of the myriad tiny needles the wheel had exposed in the cylinder's tip, hot and sharp, smelled a pungent odor. I bit my lip, that I might not whimper.

He removed the cylinder, took his hand from my shoulder.

"Do not touch it," the chalder warned me, peering close to examine the raised affronted flesh beneath my collarbone, "not until the morrow. Sleep upon your back. Good," he pronounced, stepping back from me. The mere breeze of his breath upon the mark had set my breast aquiver, burning. I blinked back my tears, that I might see Khys, determine if my comportment had pleased him.

He regarded me, his possession, with his device burned into my skin for all to see. He called me to him, his expression noncommittal, that he might examine the mark.

"My thanks, Miccah," he said after he had scrutinized my breast. His satisfaction, though I had sought it, chilled. His smile was replete, triumphant, as he bade me clothe myself. I clipped the web-cloth over my right shoulder, mindful of the chalder's warnings, through half-closed eyes, that I might not see the mark, raised stinging upon my breast. I draped the cloak over me, clear of that place.

"When it has settled, your beauty will be much enhanced," Khys remarked to me, his arm about my waist as we took leave of the high chalder and descended the broad steps of the Hall of Chaldra, into the early-evening dark.

Under the crescent moon we walked, silent. I could feel him within me, questing amid my mixed emotions. He stiffened, his cold probe aloof, as he searched me. I had deemed it an honor, beforehand, to bear his device. I tried to retrieve, or at least simulate those feelings before his mind's touch. But a part of me sobbed, disconsolate, regardless of the dharen's displeasure.

It came out of the night sky upon snapping wings, growling, hissing, a black shadow that placed itself between us and Khys's tower. Its great wings extended out straight, it snarled repeatedly, glowing eyes unblinking.

I screamed. Khys silenced me, roughly thrusting me behind him. The beast arched its neck, growling, its hindquarters twitching, its tufted tail lashing back and forth. The dharen stood calmly before it, his hands at his sides, unmoving. The beast, head low, paced left. The dharen matched him, keeping between us. The hulion skulked to the right, hissing. Khys was ever before him.

"Estri," said Khys softly, his voice urgent, "come stand beside me." I did so. The hulion sat upon its haunches, its ears atwitch.

"We are going to walk by him. Be as calm as

you can. Think as contented thoughts as you can manage." And he took me against him, as the hulion snorted and rose once more, and my legs threatened to gainsay me their support.

We assayed the passage, slowly. The beast reached out his huge head, snuffling as I came abreast of him. So close did that moist muzzle come to me that its long whiskers brushed my arm. It paced us all the way to the stairs that led up into the dharen's tower, its golden eyes glowing, its growling breath loud in my ears.

"Just walk," Khys snapped. "Do not look back." But I did, as Khys slapped the knocker ringing, and the hulion roared and roared, plaintive. It paced the length of the bottommost step, its gaze upon us, speaking in its alien tongue.

When the ponderous bronze doors were opened from within, the beast had its two front paws upon the lowest stair, its wings half-furled. The attendants' faces drained pale as its growls reached them. Khys pushed me ungently within.

"Wait!" he ordered. "Watch her!" he commanded them, and turned and ran down the steps three at a time.

"No!" I objected, as the attendants pulled the doors shut. They turned, wary, one leaving the doors to stand between me and the empty corridor at our rear.

"You need not fear for him, lady," said he who was still at the doors, amused. "One might rather fear for the hulion." He chuckled at his own humor, his thumbs stuck in his weapons belt, white teeth flashing in his black face.

I stood between them, breasts heaving, breath tremulous, waiting. What if he was wrong? My nails savaged my palms. What would happen to me, without him? At the mercy of those five others, I would be. And without him ... I stopped my fingers just before they touched the spiral new upon my breast, curled them into a fist, forced that fist to my side. The black attendant stood very still, his head cocked, as if listening. He no longer smiled. I licked my lips, sticky with concern for the dharen. As I did so, the knocker's summons reverberated in the vaulted hall, and they opened doors to admit their lord.

Unscathed he was, composed, his aristocratic nostrils, flaring, the only sign of his agitation. I wanted to run to him, but I did not; I only stood there with relief running over my skin like sheeting rain. He eyed me once, sharply, speaking low with his men. He touched one upon the shoulder, the black man, who nodded and cracked the doors, slipping out into the night.

He spoke no word to me, nor did he touch me as he strode down the corridor and I half-ran to pace him. The tendons stood sharply corded in his neck, and his heavy lashes seemed to meet. Not until we were within the baths, upon the underfloor of the tower, did the dharen's mood lighten.

He lay long upon his belly on one of the archite slabs, staring pensive at the hissing mound in the circular depression at the chamber's center, at the steam rising from rocks piled there. The baths were deserted, at this enth, when most would be about their moon's meal. We were alone but for those who tended the steam and the bathers, and they, sensing the dharen's preoccupation, had made themselves all but invisible.

The steam, he had said, had healing properties, and would be good for me. It made that place upon my breast throb, and fuzzed my hair, and the long strands, curling, stuck to my body and tangled and got sopped with my sweat and the moisture in the air. Perched on the edge of the slab, I worked upon him, as he had previously instructed me, with the heel of one hand and gathered fingers of the other, kneading oils into his skin. Rivers of perspiration meandered down my rib cage, across my belly, sluiced by the chald there.

"Enough," Khys decreed, when I thought I could not move my leaded arms again. I rubbed my eyes, which itched and stung from the perspiration in them.

"I am inordinately pleased with you," he grunted, sitting up and swinging his legs off the slab. He reached out to the mark upon my breast, and I drew back.

"Trust me," he said, and extended his palm toward me, just over the mark. The hand took up a rotating rhythm. That place tingled as if cool air blew upon it, around and around. When he took his hand away, the skin there was no longer angry or risen. It seemed, for the first time, to glitter softly.

"Still, you should not touch it," cautioned the dharen, slipping off the slab.

"You were very calm before the hulion," he remarked, his glance sidelong. He extended his hand, smiling. As I took it, those thoughts which I had earlier quieted came again to my mind, of the hulion's fate, and my own. The steam and the heat had calmed me. But I bore Khys's sign upon me, and within me also, as I had seen when he had gone out to meet the hulion.

"Did you kill it?" I asked, as he guided us through the wooden door and into the warmly lit resting keep, where our gear lay, neatly folded.

"No." He chuckled. "I did not even speak harshly to it." Over and over in my mind a thought chased itself. I did not speak it to him, but his eyes hardened upon me. Taking a wet sponge from its bucket, he threw it to me, that I might rinse.

He toweled himself dry, took my arm, and led me wordlessly to his keep. And through it, to that mirrored prison keep that had been mine so long,

stopping only long enough to get from his gear a
length of thick parr thong.

I looked at it, in his hand, at his face, so forbid-
ding, at our reflections upon the mirrored wall.
My keep held, as always, only a low plain couch,
one chair and a writing ledge below the window.
The walls and floor were silver gray. Too long had
I spent here.

"Strip," he snapped. I did so, dropping my new
finery about my ankles.

"Khys," I implored him, "do not hold against
me my thoughts."

"Cross your wrists at your belly!"

I did, and he bound them there, first to each
other, then looping the supple parr thong around
my waist and tying the ends behind my back
tightly.

"This way," he grunted, "you will not tear at
your mark in your sleep. And you might consider
your ambivalence, and make some attempt to control it. Or meditate upon your place. It would
please me if you could learn to keep it."

"Must you leave me here?"

"I will not spend this night in the tower." He
spun me roughly sideways, so that my full figure
was reflected in the mirrored wall. Standing behind me, he put his arms around me, cupping my
breasts in his hands. I closed my eyes.

"Look at yourself," he said.

I did not.

His touch insisted. I leaned back against him,
watching my heat igniting, steam. My wrists, bound
at my waist, fought their bonds. My master's sign,
just above his fingers upon my left breast, shone
softly. The chald at my navel rustled as my hips
began to move against him. When I moaned and
tried to turn to face him, he pushed me to my
knees, bade me stay still. As he left, he darkened
the keep to a bare dimness.

"Khys," I whispered to him after he had gone, "what do you want from me?" I knelt there, my need raging, a long time, lest he return and find that I had disobeyed him. The chald and his mark and my body slick with rut regarded me. In the semi-dark, barely limned, I might have been any woman who bore them. And I knew why, then, he had left me, hungry. Bound, upon my knees, alone, I regarded her whom I had come to be, and I was further aroused. The mark, I found suddenly, awareness rising in me with my lust, excited me. And I shook my head, that I might shake the thought away. I wondered where he went, if it was to the common-held forereaders he had gone. I resolved then that there would not be another night that I knelt thus, while he used some other because I had been less than pleasing in his sight. Alone with my need, I chastised myself. If I could, I would have given my body relief. His name went ringing in my head. The fantasy of him, after a long, aching time, gave me what my bound hands could not.

Gasping, little sated, I lay down there, upon the mat, and cried myself into a sleep that was no respite. That which cannot be given, he had taken. I saw him, in my dream, and he was indeed with forereaders. Can you be even half of what they are? he demanded. Of what you once were? And I spoke of love. Upon the word there came to be in that place another, who resembled me, and with her a great hulion. She bade the hulion devour him. I found myself between him and those gaping fangs. I saw even the spittle and the yellow fungus that bubbled and grew thick upon the beast's tongue. She would have pushed me aside, destroyed him. Upon slim bronze fingers she ticked off importunities for which she would hold him to account. Khys's laughter rang in my ears. And I, after each point she made, repeated the same answer. I could not allow it. The time, I told her, must be served, the will of the father done. He has gone too far, she thundered at me. And he then tired of the game. With a wave of his hand she was bound and collared and marked by my side.

And I woke from the dream as her answering tirade was muffled by the gag that came to be in her mouth, to find Khys's fingers loosening my bonds and the rays of first light shining upon my face. My body was cold, damp, my breasts heaving, as if I had run a long way.

He crouched, naked, above me. I rubbed my white-striped wrists. Surely it had been part of the dream. My fingers explored that place upon my breast. The skin felt unmarred. Heartened, I looked there. It glittered against my copper flesh, Khys's device, the bursting spiral. He nodded. I would have risen from my back. His hand stilled me.

"I stood for you in my dreams," I murmured, half-placating, half-accusing.

"It took well," he adjudged my brand, the quality of it upon my skin, brushing my hair back. He put his knees upon the mat, bent, and kissed my breast there. "And the night's meditation did you good." I saw him rising, and knew that the mark pleased him, that he would use me. And I was grateful that I bore it.

"Speak to me of what you have learned," he suggested, his hand testing, then making more eloquent suggestions. I did, withholding nothing of what I had come to feel.

"Consider it your heritage." He chuckled when I fell silent. "Long have you been destined for this end." And I would not have had it otherwise. His final taking of me was once again upon my knees, from the rear. I watched her couch him, wild-eyed, sweating, dancing unconstrained upon his manhood. She moaned and begged and cried for him, her rhythms punctuated by breathless whimpers. Then he pushed me forward from the waist, my head to the mat, and I could not see, but only receive his fierce thrust. For the first time, I heard Khys's lust escape his lips. It thrilled me, setting me once again aquiver, that he had cried out.

He did not let me rest replete, but stayed in me, rearousing my flesh. When he removed himself, too soon, I was again beginning to tremble. He touched my risen nipples. I looked at him, and had no doubt that he could have finished what it had pleased him to start. I rolled over, pressing my belly against the mat. I caught his eyes, imploring him.

He rose and stretched, looking down upon me. "Stop that!" he snapped. I stilled my hips, with effort.

"Yes," I breathed, anguished. "Anything. Khys—"

"No. Sit. Do not touch yourself. I want you that way awhile."

I sat, as he preferred, my shoulders well back. The air swirled cool against my blood-mottled skin. I pushed my hair back from my face.

"Why?" He turned from the door and came back to stand over me.

"Is it not enough that I wish it?" he said quietly.

"It is enough," I murmured. Would he lock me in here again? Had I not well served him?

"You have the run of both keeps. Stay within them. I have much to do. This evening I will take you with me, to a gathering of some small import." His eyes narrowed, sparking. I felt his intrustion, his deft, casual appraisal. I sat very still. And he was gone, out from both keeps, stopping only long enough to gather up his formal robes.

When I was alone, I rose and went and lay upon his rust-silked couch, slamming shut the doors to my prison as I left it. Do not touch yourself, he had said. The morning sun sliced the keep into sections, spilled over my turned hip. I rolled upon my belly and pressed myself against the couch. If I disobeyed him, he would know. I did not do so, only raged at him for what he had done.

I still lay thus when Carth, carrying a tas-wrapped bundle, entered the keep.

I sat up, clutching the rust silks around my body's nakedness. But I could not cloak my mind's lusting.

Tossing the bundle upon the couch, he sat beside me. Gently he pulled the couch cover from my hands, that he might examine my mark. His mouth pulled inward at the corners. His brows met above his eyes. He ran his hands over me familiarly. He had never before touched me in such a fashion.

"No." He smiled without humor. "I will not use you, now or ever."

I wished he would go away. I turned my face from his dark-robed form.

"Soon enough, child, your wish will be granted," he said dryly, tugging at the straps upon the tas binder.

"I did not mean that, Carth," I wailed, and threw my arms around his neck. All that one might feel for a father, I felt for the arrar Carth.

"And I did not mention it as threat or punishment. It is only a fact. Long he has had me at your care, assigning much vital work to others in my stead. He evidently feels"—and he smiled sourly—"that you are no longer in need of such stringent supervision. And I must say that, seeing you, I believe he is right." His fingers desultorily stirred the tas cover back, disappeared within the bundle.

"May I dress?" I asked dully. My stomach pitched and rolled with loss. Carth, answerer of quandary, soother of fear, Carth, the man whose approbation had sustained me, would be taken from me. I would be alone with the dharen. Oftentimes, this past set, his counsel had been invaluable in my dealings with Khys. How, I wondered, fearful, searching in Khys's wardrobe for a wrap, would I manage without him?

I knelt down there a time, my palms pressed against my eyes, out of his sight. I calmed my pulse with difficulty. Purposefully, as he had taught me, I sensed the pile under my feet, thick and soft. I tasted the air upon my skin, counted its waves. Thus was Carth's teaching for mental distress. Upon this day, I would show him I had learned it.

When I emerged from Khys's wardrobe, a white robe of Galeshir sheer belted around me, he had spread the contents of the bundle out on the rust silk. There were three volumes, ors, bound in patterned slitaskin. There was a gossamer-thin something, sunlight upon marsh mist, jeweled with dew. I touched it with my fingertips. It was as stroking a wirraget's wing.

"Oh, Carth, it is beautiful." I picked it up, and it spilled the length of my body. Such a wrap, though it could conceal nothing, would much enhance any who wore it.

"Thank the dharen, when you see him." The arrar was more than brusque.

"Where is he? What is this gathering?" I asked, slipping my arm between two layers of the webwork. It hugged my limb, overgleaming it with shadow-soft sparkle.

"He is meeting with his dhareners, and with those others who hold power upon Silistra. This"— he picked up one ors—"is what he gives them, why he had called them together." Abruptly he threw one book to me. I caught it, barely, opening it to the title page. Then I turned to the contents, scanned them. I closed it, holding it against my waist.

"Why did you give me this?" I asked.

Carth leaned back upon Khys's couch. His dark face was unreadable. He ran a hand through his black curls.

"Not me. He. It is some part of his hest concerning you. He has ceased to confide in me so far as you are concerned. I do not know why he wanted you to have it. With a lesser man, one might say that it is his newest creation, a work upon which he has spent more than a year, and he but desired you to read it."

"But you do not think it that simple." I sat beside him, regarding my toes peeking from under the Galeshir silk.

"The dharen is anything but simple. Let it rest. All who bestow chaldra have today received from him this volume upon the chaldra of helsars, and how it may be adjudged. Perhaps he would simply like you to be able to make polite conversation. None will have had the manual longer than you. The dhareners will be more confounded than you could ever be; not in twenty thousand years has there been a new chaldric strand for which to strive."

I put the ors down, trading it for the next.

"Do you think," I asked, touching Carth's arm, "that he might let me test for one?"

Carth took a deep breath, regarded the midday upon the Lake of Horns through the windows. He found the sight so intriguing that he left me, drew the rust draperies fully apart, and spent a long time in contemplation of the lakeside.

The second volume was entitled *Hesting, the Primal Prerogative* and was twice the thickness of the first. It was filled with odd diagrams and charts. I laid it by. The third was the *Wellwoman's Ors*, written by the foundress of Well Astria. To hold that in my hands sent thrills and tremors up my nerves.

"This," I whispered, half to myself, "I will read straightaway. I am in need of nothing more."

"You had best work first upon the others, and save that for your leisure," decreed Carth, coming to stand over me, shadowing the open book upon my lap.

"Why are you so somber. Carth?" I wondered, looking up at him, wide-eyed.

He, back-lit, silhouetted, laughed harshly. Then he squatted down before me.

"My little one is grown up. I suppose I regret it." He ran his finger down my nose, withdrew his hand. "That woman's trick proves it. Tonight you had better be as ready as he has deemed you."

My own fingers rubbed my left breast. I swallowed hard. I had not missed Carth's eyes upon it, then my face, lastly upon the band at my throat. Before all Khys's high ones, I would be shown, banded, marked. My skin turned hot as a bather's in midsummer sun.

"And with his couchbond strand at your waist," Carth reminded me sternly.

I touched it, grateful for another thing to do with my problematical hands.

"You will not be the only restrained one present, nor the only woman bearing such a sign. That everwelling pride of yours may yet be your ruination." He rose up, one hand upon his hip. Something in his stance before me had changed. I was conscious of him as male, as I had never been before. I shifted, knowing my own moisture, my eagerness, my body's response to his.

"It is you that have changed, have grown aware. Get up. In this one instance, such enlightenment will do little for you."

"Where are you taking me?" I said. Putting the *Wellwoman's Ors* carefully upon the couch, I rose obediently to follow him.

"Down into the common holding, that they may prepare you. Then to a meal, if you would like."

"Carth?" I asked him, pressing against his arm in the hall.

"Speak," he allowed, looking at me askance. He did not disengage my fingers.

"Will you be at this gathering?"

"Yes, along with a number of other arrars."

I took my hands from him, falling silent. In my mind I saw another arrar, and those eyes, so disturbing, seemed to hover before me along the corridors.

Out we went into the bright clear day, and along the ways by the lakeside. Carth, as if in reparation for his bad humor, allowed me to take up some rounded pebbles and dance them across the water. One, I found, as I was about to fling it, had been woman-formed by the lake's constant lapping. I dried it upon my robe and handed it to him solemnly, that he might have something by which to recall me. He clasped me to him, crushed the breath from my lungs. After a time he kissed me upon the crown of my head and pushed me away. Though I asked him, he would not speak of what concerned him, nor of where he expected to travel upon his pursuit of the dharen's will.

In the forereader's tower lies the common holding, plush, elegant, all in soft neutral shades, as if fall had come indoors, and installed itself in that great hall. Across the clear floor we walked, within which, set deep, were designs of colored earth that teased the mind and gave lightness to the spirit. I did not pay the floor attention, nor the great striped ragony table that encircled it, nor the furred and sueded and tapestried cushions piled along its circumference. At four places one might pass through the circle, across the floor, and out again among a number of grouped couches. Only, I wanted out of that place. I hated the feel of the gol under my feet, the dark cloying scent that seemed to sweeten my tongue. Here I had been ill-treated by those forereaders whose keep this was. Here I had seen the forereader restrained. I blinked away the phantom of that sight, the room suddenly filled with bodies. Even could I hear the musicians playing softly from their alcove, smell the roasted denter upon the air.

Carth's hand upon my shoulder, his sidelong glance, warning, rebuked me. I chased the past from my mind. We passed out of that hall into a cerulean passage of gold-flecked ornithalum, and through it to the right, down two flights of stairs. At the stairs' foot was an open door, into a large chamber, where six women lounged upon a great pool, divided into three sections.

There, Carth, with an admonition relating to obedience, handed me into the care of a forereader whose name I do not recall. I begged him wait, but he would not. The woman laughed, remarking upon the discomfort of men before a woman's beautifying arts. If she had used them upon herself, I thought, she must, aforehand, have been a horror to look upon. Her eyes, resentful upon me, bespoke how I had fared in her assessment.

Graciously I smiled at her, and allowed that she might, with alacrity, attend me to the best of her ability. Upon the last word I made it clear with a lifted eyebrow that I doubted her skill. She flushed, and stared pointedly at my band. I stripped off my robe, that she might see my chald and be made aware of how I stood in the dharen's eyes. As naked as she, I stood before her, taller, finer, and with his chald of couchbond, upon which was strung a fortune in gol drops, at my waist.

Her small and overly squat body stiffened. She was forced to crane her short neck to meet my eyes. In them she found nothing but contempt.

No other word was spoken between us during the two enths it took her, with her two assistants, to make me ready. Finally, my body soothed with oils and my hair confined by ten tiny braids through which were worked strings of fire gems, I was prepared.

I regarded myself in the mirror, my pubic hair

and nipples aglitter with a scintillant powder, my eyes gilded, the nails of my fingers and toes shaped and lacquered gold. Their avaricious looks, reflected in the mirror behind me, brought a warm feeling to my heart. Any of them would gladly have borne my restraint, my mark, any indignity, to be possessed of such a reflection. I smiled at myself, regarding my tongue as it flicked out to moisten my lips. I turned slowly full about. Khys's device upon my left breast took the light, pulverized it prismatic. Then I saw Carth there, and his expression was eloquent tribute.

The squat forereader brought my creamy robe and held it for me. Belting it about me, I approached him.

"What think you?" I whispered, teasing.

"I think I had better feed you," he mumbled. I found his consternation delectable fare, but I only nodded and brushed by him, into the corridor, that he might observe from the rear my begemmed mane.

"I have been thinking," I informed him as he came up beside me, his arm encircling my waist.

"About what you would like to eat, I hope?" he said, turning into a side passage of brown taernite.

"About the hulion that attacked us yesterday, and about what was done to me by the dharen's council, and about the literature you gave me."

"You must be fatigued," the arrar remarked.

"When they assessed me, one of his council undertook to dismantle a web that extended out from me. What was it?"

"Ask the dharen," he evaded.

"I will not have your invaluable counsel much longer. Please, Carth, do not withhold your aid from me. Was it a hest? It seemed to me to bear a resemblance to a diagram I saw in Khys's text." I turned my face to his, my eyes imploring. He watched the floor before him, intently.

"Only can I say to you, it might have been. If it was, no matter; it exists no longer. As for those other questions you have, I am not empowered to answer them."

"Will you not, this once, bend his rule upon you?"

"Not even this once." And the arrar's face was as dark as I had ever seen it.

"Return me, then, to his keep," I said, toneless. "I would study the texts before I am called to him."

"As you wish," Carth said, reversing our direction in the passage.

All the way to the dharen's keep we made in silence. When he had gone, I stood by the window until I saw him pass along the ways, in the direction of the arrar's tower. He stopped and spoke awhile with another, by the lakeside. Before them, on the lake's surface, a disturbance arose, as if unseen stones skittered there. Far out upon the water, almost to the opposite shore, the lake skipped and danced. Both men watched, it seemed, but neither had taken up stone or raised arm to throw. After a long time, they separated, each headed the opposite way. And the water of the lake was becalmed, meditative.

I turned from the view, went and got Khys's texts from the couch, and settled with them among the cushions. Long did I struggle with his discourses upon hesting, though I could make no attempt to put his instruction to work. Khys defined hesting as the introduction into experiential time of probability not inherent in the sort. But I had little understanding of sorting, the forereader's skill. Stochastic restructuring, or hesting, demanded apprehension of what was natural to the time. I could not sort. One must see the sort, the spread of probability, before one can alter it. I touched the band upon my throat, ran my hand beneath the creamy Galeshir robe, over my left breast.

With the subject of helsars, I was at an even greater disadvantage. I had never seen one. I knew they were material things, small crystals that were a kind of teaching aid to the skills of mind. I knew how they had come to be upon this plane, having read the Keepress' papers. But I scanned the material stubbornly—the many adjurations and warnings and fail-safes Khys recommended—should one be about that questing. For so it appeared to be—a journey, an exploration of a different reality. When I sighed and rubbed my eyes, stretching, I realized the ache in them was caused by the fading light and the failure of the entrapped stars to recognize my presence and increase their glow.

I put down the treatise upon helsars and glared up at them, hovering, dim.

"Be bright, curse you," I muttered at them, arrogant reminders of my mental insufficiency. I was sorry that I had pressed Carth, and thus lost his company.

I lay back upon the cushions, staring up at the bronze scales upon the ceiling. I had no interest, I told myself, in such a dangerous trek as Khys's guidelines revealed helsar teachings to be. I thought of Khys, and wished he would come use me, release me from my frustrations. Upon the arrar Sereth my mind dwelt also, he who rode hulions. Possibly he would be among the arrars at Khys's gathering. The thought cheered me. I stretched again, arranged my hair upon the cushions, closed my eyes. It might, I thought, be a lenghty evening.

Sleep was not tardy attending me. But it was a sleep restless and draining, during which it seemed that I was called into a presence which named itself my father. I replied I did not know him. You may be he, I allowed, looking calmly upon a man form, bare outline, from which star-stuff spurted

and flared. I was not afraid; rather was I filled
with longing, and an overwhelming sense of be-
longing. Let me stay, I petitioned that darkness,
which of a sudden had great glowing eyes. In each
could be seen a universe, spawning. Have I not
done enough, been enough, suffered enough, to suit
you? No. Bring me my fruits; he spoke without
words, the sound of it great bell peals in my brain.
Take it, and the father also, I spat. I would be free.
And he laughed, and the gale of it picked me up
like paper and whirled me back into the bondage
of flesh. I had one last glimpse of that place, over
which a great winged slitsa with fire-clawed appendages hovered, its tail wound in the ascending
lines of force that skewered the world in its care. I
heard its thrumming, sensed the harmonic it provided as it pulsed the gravitic song that binds the
substructure of space to the weathers of time. And
then the song was gone, and the pulse also, and I
sat up in the dimmed keep to see the stars and the
new moon rising, and the dharen, silent, leaning
over the gol table in the near-dark. I rose up. He
noted it and lit the keep, rubbing his eyes. He had
sat straining, rather than wake me.

"Khys, you should not have let me sleep," I said,
conscious of his hunched preoccupation as I crossed
the mat to stand beside the table, where he had
spread what seemed to be a list of names, with a
number of columns after each, in some of which
were noted numbers and cryptic symbols. He
shrugged, straightened up.

"They did artful work upon you," he said. "Turn."
I did so.

"Carth tells me you had a number of questions
which he could not answer."

"I would not bother you with them," I excused
myself, stepping back from his molten, half-lidded
gaze. "It was only . . ."

"I know." He smiled warmly, as he seldom did,

showing those white and perfect teeth. "If, by the pass's end, you still have them, I will speak with you. For now, set your thoughts upon the moments upcoming. Do your best for me this night."

"My best at what?" I queried him, noting his humor, still lingering as he gathered up the papers, sheafing them on the gol. Khys did not deign to answer, but busied himself secreting the lists in his bookwall.

"The cahndor of Nemar," he said, donning his plainest and most elegant formal robe, "has brought his couch-mate here, and his heir also." His face swathed itself in shadow as he made fast the chald at his hips. "Both the woman and the child will reside at the lake for a time. She will be, understandably, nervous and ill-at-ease. If you can do anything to comfort her, I would appreciate it." All the while he talked, I could feel his cold probe, intruding. "Mind-seek," so the Strothric teachings label it; invasion, it seems, to one who has no comparable skills, and hence no choice.

"I will do what I can," I said quietly, fleeing to couchside on pretext of retrieving that miasmic wrap which I would wear, and also of his choosing, and not my own. "But that is not what you want."

"No," he agreed, reclining, his humor evaporating like water in full sun. "You are right. The pretense must serve us both, for the moment. Know you how to peg the time?"

I nodded. Carth had seen to it that I was not wholly ignorant of the Stoth traditions that Khys so highly prized. I slipped the wrap over my head. It closed about the right shoulder, falling open down the whole right side. The seamed side lay low against my left breast. My mark, in this fashion, was well displayed. I smoothed that fabric, as light to the skin as an evening breeze, over my hips. Khys reached out and put his large hand flat on my belly, his stroke following the cloth down.

I stepped back from him. He made no move, but stood silent, brooding. A muscle twitched repeatedly at his jaw. Disconcerted, I knelt before him, my palms flat upon my thighs.

"Dharen," I whispered, "you make me uneasy. Surely, if you would speak in more detail, I could better serve you." I wanted to touch him, to taste him, to bridge the gulf between us with my body. I bent my head to his feet, and my braids, heavy with the gems wound through them, flogged my shoulders as they fell to the mat.

"I will, this night, lend you to the cahndor of Nemar," said Khys quietly. I sat up. Accusingly I stared at him, bit my trembling lips.

"It is not discipline. I am not displeased with you." He pushed himself upright and touched his palm to my cheek. I took his hand in both of mine, held it there, kissing his open palm. I saw tiny beads of perspiration in the creases. I ran my tongue in the folds, tasted his salt.

"What, then, is it?" I dared, in my softest voice, staring up at him, his palm pressed against my cheek once more.

"An old obligation, a part of some larger hest of mine." His brows arched, but he did not rebuke me. "It is necessary that you perform creditably. If you can do only as well as you did with the arrar Sereth, I will be satisfied." His tone had turned dry and pointed. I dropped his hand, sat back upon my heels, raising my head high.

"I will try," I said, barely audible. I knew now why he had been preparing me. My heart seemed frost-burned. I blinked away my tears fiercely, lest they mar the gilding upon which the forereaders had spent so long. I reminded myself that if I were a wellwoman, I would have served a different man nightly, without such qualms. But I was not a wellwoman. I watched him, moving about the keep, his dark-robed figure stiff and tense, his movements belying his calm. Perhaps it was an obligation, but surely it was not his pleasure, this that he proposed. I wondered what would constrain such a man, what would make him act against his own will.

He whirled about, eyes blazing, leaning back against the gol slab. I could see his hands whiten as he gripped the table's edge.

"Be still, or I will have him put a child upon you, and be freed from your self-conscious mental babble permanently." I lowered my head miserably, that I might somehow silence my thoughts.

"Get up." I did so, pulling the open side of my wrap together as best I could.

"Pull it through your chald." And as I hesitated, he bore down on me. Reaching out, he raised the wrap and slipped it under the chald I wore, jerking the material tight. The soft, glimmering wrap was now chaldbelted, turning the slitted right side from blatant openness into restrained invitation. I smiled up at him, uncertain. Simple things, I did not know, such as how to wear a chald to advantage. Khys's intrusive gaze turned gentle as my mind bewailed my inadequacies.

"I do not want to couch another," I said needlessly. "It is only your touch my body seeks."

"But you will do as I instruct you," he said. I could only nod.

He spoke then, as we descended the back stairs and crossed the walkway to the common holding, of what had been achieved in his meetings. He had never before done so. Most of it was beyond my understanding. I learned that some helsar chaldric strands had already been bestowed, and that the strand given was of luricrium, a rare and costly metal which has to it a tinge like storm clouds forming. I learned that the odds against completing helsar work unscathed were twenty to one, that prerequisite to such an attempt was the successful obviation of space. I did not learn what happened if one failed. Nor did he make clear what might be gained, that such a risk was worth the taking.

I endeavored to think as little as possible, and not at all about the exchange Khys proposed. But I could not silence my heart's wailing. Generously, the dharen said nothing, but instead encircled my shoulders with his arm, against the evening's bite. The wind, gusting, seemed to snigger at me, that I so venerated this man, who doubtless only used me, as the arrar Sereth had said, to serve his hests. Whatever they were.

Between ornately trapped sentries we passed, through the brass-inlaid doors that proclaimed this tower the residence of women. In the entrance hall we passed small knots of robed and wrapped lake-born, and the smells of flesh and flower mingled with the acrid tang of narcotic danne and set my head spinning. Clutching Khys's robed arm, I pressed close against him as we passed into the common holding, and I saw just how many attended this gathering. Crowds, their buzz and roar, their close-packed smell, their threatening diversity, were something with which I had no experience. My eyes searched the strangers, seeking a familiar face. I saw neither Carth nor any other I knew at the drink stand, nor before the musicians who rolled out a pulse-matching Dydian chromatic piece in seven-four time. Near the easterly bank of sheer-draperied windows, yellow smoke hung heavy in the air, dancing phantasmic as it rose toward the star-glowed ceiling of greened brass. The round, hollow table was set with all manner of gracious utensils. Whole carcasses, fruited skins gleaming, lay upon huge serving trays encircled with pastried tuns, their crisped outer crusts dusted with salt. The enclosed floor was so thick with celebrants that it could not be seen. A plethora of forereaders

circulated among the guests, all bare-breasted, their
hips diversely wrapped, their soft flesh shining.
Here were representatives of every bloodline, surely,
that thrived upon Silistra. From palest white to
starless evening sky did their coloring range, and
those forms were dressed all differently, from bare
nakedness to one dark-skinned, tiny women of
whom all that could be seen were her eyes and a
tiny patch of forehead. She was elsewhere swathed
in layer upon layer of green translucence, the edges
of which were fringed with little golden beads that
tinkled as she moved. Toward her Khys headed
me, to where she stood with a formidable-appearing
man who wore upon him a magnificent cape of
black feathers, like ebvrasea's wings, sprouting from
his broad shoulders. To another he was speaking
animatedly, a man near his own build, whose back,
dark-robed, was turned to us, and about whose
waist snuggled the arrar's chald.

The woman saw us first. Her velvet eyes widened.
She touched her companion's arm, and that rana-
skinned man turned his own black eyes upon us.
His dark lips drew back, those white teeth, startling,
augmenting his fearsome aspect. I thought he might
roar, rather than speak, as he slid gracefully toward us, the crowd parting for him as if in long-
rehearsed formation.

Down upon us he swept, that carnivore's smile
flashing, and when he reached us, his great arms
went about me. A hand cupping each of my buttocks, my body pressed to his leathers with their
metal fittings, he lifted me off the ground and
whirled me around. I shook with fear, my head
against the tight-curled hairs of his leather-strapped
chest, biting my lips.

"Estri," he said in my ear, his lips nibbling down
into the hollow of my neck.

"Please, put me down," I begged timorously.
Laughing the roar I had expected from this hulion

of a man, he did so, his fingers uncupping my hips regrefully. I stepped back and found myself against Khys, who put his own hand to the nape of my neck. The dark man's eyes seemed to cloud, as if a curtain blew over them. His mouth tightened; his hand found the point of his shoulder, rubbed there.

"I thought," he said to Khys after a long time examining me, "Sereth spoke allegory, part-truths, born of his distress. I see now that such was not the case." He kneaded that place upon his shoulder, looked about his feet, eyes darting. Then he raised them.

"I am appalled," he said, not softly, to the dharen, his censure snapping like a whip, making a circle of silence and attention around us. I shivered, my skin crawling under the many-eyed stare of the curious crowd. I sighted the tiny woman, her breasts and hands pressed against the arm of the arrar whose back was toward us, her body straining. She was shaking her veiled head to and fro. I tossed my confined hair forward, over my left shoulder, that it might obscure from the dark man's eyes my mark. Khys's fingers tightened upon my neck, reminding me of the band that pulsed there.

I quivered under the dark one's stare, from those oddly filmed eyes.

"Appalled, are you?" said Khys softly to him. "Or perhaps it is another emotion you feel, birthed out of your own inadequacies? Could you, Cahndor, have done such a thing? Is it not your fear that appalls you, your own vulnerability that causes you such unease?"

The cahndor of Nemar shifted upon his feet, his fists wrapped in his many-stranded chald. "Doubtless," he growled, "that is the case. At least, partly."

Khys brushed my hair off my shoulder. His device twinkled at the cahndor, who could not take his gaze from it.

"I would not have Liuma so degraded," the

cahndor said in a lowered tone, running his dark talons through tight-curled hair. Upon his arm, so displayed, was a winged slitsa, wound around a recurved blade, drawn upon the skin in umbers and ochers. It slithered and writhed with the movements of his bicep.

"She is yours. We will do with her only what you wish. If you want her not at all improved, do not leave her with us. It matters not to me. It is the child who should concern both of us." And he let go of my neck, pushing me gently from him. "As with her, it was the child that gave her value." I stood frozen between them, like a hapless moon eclipsed, wishing I might at that moment cease to live within flesh.

The cahndor of Nemar extended his hand. Hesitantly I surrendered my own, watched as his grasp engulfed it. By that grip, inexorable as gravity, he drew me nearer. I saw, briefly, the woman, still held by the arrar. Her huge eyes were luminous, fearful. My own, I was sure, showed no more composure. The darkling prince enfolded my trembling frame, and I understood the filming of his eyes: nictitating membranes, snapping forth and retreating, cloud-glitter on an obsidian void.

"Speak my name," growled this savage to whom Khys was obligated.

"I will, Cahndor, if you would but inform me of it," I breathed, compliant as any obligation about to be discharged, beseeching his patience. His grip tightened. He spoke a number of sentences in some unfamiliar tongue. Then he turned his head and barked an order in that same guttural speech. He intoned his full name gently. I repeated it, fascinated by that gaze that immobilized me as surely as Khys's flesh lock.

"She knows nothing?" he demanded of Khys, loosing his grasp.

"She knows a great deal. She remembers nothing of her life before she came to the lake. We have deemed it safer not to remind her of what she herself will not recall."

"As you predicted," said Chayin rendi Inekte harshly.

"As I contrived it," amended Khys, his well-modulated voice silky, in contrast to the desert monarch's imperious growls. My knees grew infirm. Both of them, then, knew my history. Khys had never before admitted it. And the other thing he had said ... I faced him, not wanting to believe what his veiled threat to the cahndor implied.

His lucent gaze stayed me, my questions, my hurt. My tears dried in my eyes unshed before the cold breath of his hauteur. I turned once more to the cahndor.

The diminutive dark woman, upon the arm of the arrar Sereth, had come up beside her couch-mate. She eyed me with terror unrestrained. Her lips were dried with it; her tiny limbs trembled like a sapling in the path of a northern gale. She leaned heavily upon Sereth's robed arm, her finger clawlike. I had no doubt that she was in need of his support. And that one regarded me impassively from under his thick brown mane, as if we had never couched.

"Sereth," I whispered. He did not answer, but only regarded me, his attention upon my left breast. Stung that he would not even acknowledge me, I turned my head away, staring at the floor, for I knew not where else to look. My fingers found Khys's strand of couchbond at my waist and tangled themselves in it. I could feel my palms weeping, the moistness they imparted to the web-cloth upon my belly.

Khys introduced me to the cahndor's couch-mate by her first name only, an insult that was not lost upon her, she who was Nemarchan, forereader and highest among the tiasks of that desert land, Nemar.

He took her resentment from her mind, surely, for he told her courteously that while at the Lake of Horns she might not use titles, for here no such accounting of rank was kept; even her hide name, and her mother's and father's, mattered not at this place, only what she was and what she might come to be. I watched Khys weave his spell upon that tiny woman in a matter of moments.

"Let me see her," Khys ordered of Chayin. She made no objection when her couch-mate stripped off her veils, and, spinning her, unwrapped her miniature beauty that Khys might assess it. In the puddle of her diaphanous, gold-beaded greenery she poised, her proud carriage not diminished. Around us, the crowd had cleared back, many pointedly turning away. We were alone amidst the well over two hundred that feted in Khys's common room. He studied her a time, indolent, and I knew from his face that his intrusive thoroughness had laid bare her mind as easily as the cahndor's hand had stripped her body. I closed my eyes to her distress, feeling it my own. When I opened them, I saw the arrar Sereth's face, unguarded for a moment, and the pity upon it was mine, not the Nemarchan's. Unthinking, I moved toward him, those few steps.

He regarded me, silent, his dark eyes indrawn.

"How are you?" he asked in his most inaudible voice, a mere rustle of breath.

"Frightened," I whispered back, leaning toward him. He reached out his hand, stopped it, between us.

"Touch it, if you would," I invited him. He ran his rough palm over my left breast, over the softly glowing spiral there. He tossed his head. I could hear his teeth, grinding upon each other. He shot his gaze across Chayin and Khys, speaking together intently, and over Liuma, who at Khys's bidding was redressing.

"Estri," said Sereth, leaning close, "you have no need to fear Chayin. He would never do you harm. There might yet be something salvaged, with his help." And he took his hand from my breast. "Did it hurt?" he inquired, about the mark.

"Not unduly," I replied, holding my head high. Helpless as I was he before Khys's will. I resented what he had said to me, about the cahndor. "It is easy for you to tell me not to fear," I snapped. "If you find the cahndor so lovable, you couch him." At my rebuke, he half-smiled. I wondered what comfort I had found in him previously. "I suppose," I hissed archly, "that one could expect no different from you. You are, after all, no more than his servant." And I turned my back upon him, my fists clenched before me. His hand came down hard upon my shoulder, whirling me once more to face him. He held me a moment, his grip crushing my shoulder. Then he let me go, turned, and strode through the crowd, bumping several innocents from his path.

Khys, breaking off his conversation, stared after him, then at me, questioningly. A moment, he closed his eyes. Comprehension lit his face. He laughed softly, and drew me near. Somehow, I had pleased him. I did not even bother to wonder why, only congratulated myself, basking in his oft-withheld approval. In the shelter of his arm I stood, with the Parset lord of Nemar's alien eyes upon me.

They discussed, then, the disposition of Liuma's child, while she listened, distraught. I did not understand her agitation. The heir of Nemar would be raised and educated at the Lake of Horns, privy to the Greater Truths that are not taught elsewhere upon Silistra. No woman at the lake retains a child after its second year. The child, born Brinar second fourth, 25,695, was two years, one day this sun's rising, that of second fifth. Perhaps, I postulated, children are not put into common care in the Parset Desert. I shrugged, causing Khys to pull me closer. It was no concern of mine, her distress. And if she would couch the dharen this night, it was to my advantage that she be out of sorts, preoccupied, as she so obviously was. I felt deeply the sharp pain of my jealousy. I wondered how he would ever fit in her, she being so small. And then I regarded Chayin, her couchmate, and knew that she could not be a problem, if she had been used by the cahndor, had borne him a son. I felt Khys's silent chuckle, and knew he had eavesdropped upon my thought.

"Assuredly," he whispered in my ear, "none of her ilk will ever replace you." I pressed, in answer, my buttocks against him, and was rewarded by his stirring beneath his robe. "Hold them both for a time, Chayin, while I go and soothe the Ebvrasea's ruffled feathers." And Khys departed, threading his way through the crowd to Sereth, whose dark head was just visible to me, wound around with danne smoke, near the banked windows.

When Khys had reached his arrar, and not before, did Chayin speak.

"What," the cahndor demanded, "did you say to Sereth?" And, not knowing whether or not he read thoughts, I answered him truthfully. Chayin blew his breath hissing through his teeth.

"Of all men, he should be free from your censure!" he snapped. I only stared at him. Liuma, his couch-mate, tittered, a tinkling sound.

He whirled upon her like an enraged hulion, snarling. "Think you I would not wipe this floor with your carcass, should it come to me to do so?" And though she fell silent, her eyes still danced with humor. Assuredly, Liuma had no love for the arrar Sereth.

"Of all men," I said softly to Chayin when he turned his dark glare back upon me, "only Khys has that freedom with me. It is he to whom I am couch-bound." And I met his fury without comment, as he cursed in that barbaric tongue of his. When he ran dry of words, he spat at my feet. I looked from that small wetness, up at him, his taut form, and knew I had said too much. I found, myself retreating into the crowd. Two steps, he took, and retrieved me.

"By the wing of uritheria, Estri, this cannot go on! Do you not have any understanding of your situation, or of the shadows it throws over us all?" I saw Liuma's hostile gaze, watching, her ears fairly pricked.

"No, I do not. Perhaps you will enlighten me," I petitioned him, as he led me back to her.

"It is my fervent hope," he said wryly, "that I will be able to do so." Roughly he placed me upon the right of his Nemarchan, Liuma. Then he looked about him, hailed an arrar with Khys's spiral upon the left breast of his robe. That one, blond and golden-eyed, was quick to attend him.

"Do not allow them conversation," he instructed the arrar. "Let neither one out of your sight. I will return for them presently."

The arrar nodded, standing opposite us, legs spread, arms crossed over his chest, as Chayin made his own way through the crowd to join the dharen.

Liuma caught my gaze, eyed the arrar significantly. I nodded to her. We had, neither one of us, been ordered to stay with him, directly. I set myself leftward, toward the banked windows, as Liuma hurriedly put bodies between her and the startled arrar, heading toward the right. He hesitated, undecided as to which one of us to pursue. I increased my pace, looking backward, sliding between a marked wellwoman and one who was not her couch-mate. The arrar closed upon me, frowning.

I stumbled right into him. Hands, fiery gold, took my upper arms as I staggered. Murmuring an apology, I raised my eyes to him whom I had jostled. And stared, witless, at the first of Khys's council, he who had so harmed me during my assessment. He was plain-robed in black. His hair and eyes were black also, and yet the fathers' fire shone hot from him. I made to kneel. He held my arms, shaking his head, saying that the time had not yet come for such obeisance. And: "Where do you go in this unseemly haste?" Strong fingers dug troughs in my arms. But his eyes looked elsewhere. I twisted in his grasp. The blond arrar had stopped.

The man who held me had the blond's attention. He jabbed a finger in the direction Liuma had taken. The blond nodded, set off that way.

"I will deliver you myself to Khys," he mused, smiling coldly. "How goeth the dissolution of the dharen?" he asked at length, his piercing eyes exploring the depths of mine.

"Please let me go," I begged. He did not, but ran his long-nailed hand over the dharen's device on my breast. He laughed softly.

"There is an irony," he remarked as we negotiated a trail through the crowd, "in his marking you thus. I would be there to see his face the day he realizes it."

"I do not take your meaning, arrar," I said.

"I am Gherein," he replied. "And you will, soon enough. Remember me to your father, when next you see him, and convey to him my awe, that he could put into the time such a force."

I wondered if he were mad. Again he laughed, a sound starting low but ending in a high, squeaking yip. As he hustled me down the path ever opening before us, I recalled him; and those unmeet actions, that destruction he had wrought within my helpless mind, he who had first explored me during my assessment.

Before Khys, he ungently clapped the dharen on

the shoulder. That one turned from his conversation, and the shadow of his annoyance grew darker.

"I have something of yours," said Gherein.

"Indeed," answered Khys. "And how did you come by it?"

"What is loosely held is often misplaced." The arrar Gherein, first of Khys's council, shrugged. "She escaped, you might say. I returned her to you." He stepped backward.

"You have my thanks," said Khys dryly.

"As ever"—Gherein smiled, bowing low—"I am but the instrument of thy will."

Khys, his glare upon me, snapped his fingers. I knelt at his side. He turned from his council member, and that one melted into the crowd like some malevolent spirit.

"Escaped, did you?" said Khys, staring down at me, his tone severe. I shifted upon my knees, touched his thigh, pressed my cheek to it. I said nothing. Those with whom he had been speaking, Carth and some dharener I did not know, passed a pipe between them. To my left, against the window ledge, leaned Sereth, with Chayin's arm thrown companionably about him. They, also, smoked danne, the yellow psychotropic herb.

Khys called Sereth to him. The arrar was languorously obedient, his eyes off in the crowd. Chayin received Liuma from the blond arrar and set her upon the window ledge.

"I think," said Khys to Sereth, who studiously avoided looking at me, "that I have a new commission for you."

The arrar Sereth grinned. "You will lose me yet, with these easy dispatchings." He tossed his head. "He is not Vedrast."

"Do you not feel up to it?" Khys inquired of him, matching his soft tone.

Sereth raised his head, stared long into Khys's eyes. After a time, he raked his hand through his hair, pushing it impatiently off his forehead. "It might work," he allowed. "Doubtless"—and his voice was very soft—"you will be well rid of one of us."

Carth, long silent, reached out and touched Khys's arm. The dharen stepped close to him, away from me, motioning me up, almost as afterthought.

Sereth's hand closed about my wrist. His eyes caught mine. I bent my head, that I might avoid them. My fingers, trapped in his, could find no escape.

"Come with me," he whispered. I shook my head. But he pulled me along after him to the window. My eyes, entreating Khys's intervention, did not obtain it.

He took from Chayin the pipe upon which the cahndor puffed, and held it out to me, his straight brows knit. I hesitated. I had never smoked it.

"Try it," he insisted, with some dark humor that crinkled his eyes and colored the scar upon his cheek. Liuma, I could see, had partaken. She leaned back against the draped windows, her shoulders slumped, her posture far from that of a woman before men. The cahndor touched Sereth's arm, began a circular rubbing upon the arrar's back. Sereth grinned at him obliquely.

He retracted the pipe, puffed upon it until smoke billowed from the bow. Then again he offered it to me. I received it from him.

My lips on the narrow stem, I pulled in deeply and was rewarded by a paroxysm of coughing. Through blurred eyes, shaking my head, I handed it back.

"Not so much," he instructed me, demonstrating. But I would taste no more of it. Loosening was danne. It made tenuous the bond between body and mind. I had fought that sensation often. I needed no drug to bring it upon me. I said so,

tossing back my hair, forgetful of the dharen's
mark it obscured.

"Does he never feed you?" criticized Chayin, of
my thinness, reaching out to touch my left hipbone
where it flared below my waist. His fingers, upward-
moving, counted my ribs. I shrugged.

"Answer me when I speak to you!" growled the
cahndor of Nemar. Liuma tittered upon the window ledge. Sereth hoisted himself up beside her,
his eyes never leaving me, that voracious gaze
raising the small hairs of my skin.

"He feeds me. I often do not eat. If I had choice,
it has occurred to me I might never eat."

"You could use more flesh than you carry. You
will eat this evening, while I have you."

"As you wish it, Cahndor. But one meal will
make little difference in my figure. I know for
certain that Khys has a number of voluptuous and
highly skilled forereaders. I am sure he will allow
you the use of any other you choose in my stead."
And I excused myself, intending to inform Khys of
Chayin's disgruntlement and perhaps save myself
from his hands.

He snarled my name. I turned back to him, quailing before this more-than-appropriate anger. I ran
my palms over my cheeks. My eyes itched from
the particles of gilding that had made their way
into them. I rubbed them gently.

At that moment the chimes called our seating.

Khys himself came to collect us, and with him
Carth, leading a bronzed girl who had about her
the look of one not lake-born. Sereth slid off his
sill seat, his thumbs hooked through his chald, his
whole bearing one of marked displeasure. Chayin
looked at the woman, at Sereth, then went to the
arrar's side. There they had what seemed a heated
discussion, in the cahndor's tongue, very low.

The woman leaned upon Carth's arm, her eyes

on the arrar Sereth. Carth spoke to her, patting her reassuringly.

Khys summoned me, drew me to table with him. Liuma and Chayin followed, the cahndor's expression ominous. Beside Khys, upon his left, was Liuma seated, while Chayin took the place upon my right. Carth, when he came finally to table, had with him the long-limbed female, whose tanned skin had not the fiery touch of the fathers' blood. Sereth, when I turned to seek him, was nowhere to be seen. After seating the woman, Carth came to Khys and leaned between us, whispering in the dharen's ear.

Khys listened, nodded, waved a hand impatiently.

"You have done," he told Carth, "enough, more than might have been expected of you. Let it rest. Take her yourself, if you like." Carth grinned at him, straightened up, and returned to his seat between Liuma and the unidentified woman.

"Who is she?" I whispered to Khys, my hand upon his arm, as the dhrouma drums began a polyrhythmic thrumming, and the dancers filed through the four openings in the table, to take their place in the enclosure.

"A wellwoman, new to the Lkae of Horns. Carth thought she might be of interest to Sereth. Evidently he was wrong." He grimaced. The dancers waited. Khys raised his hands, smacked them resoundingly together. The entire orchestra took up the tune. The women, in slitsa skins and feathers, began their undulations. I took no notice.

"Really?" I breathed, leaning forward to peer around Khys, past Liuma and Carth, at the wellwoman. I had not, to my knowledge, ever seen one. Beside her was an empty place. She seemed subdued, her long-lashed eyes lowered, her chin almost resting on her chest. I had thought such a woman might sit differently, carry herself some other way, have about her some air to set her apart from all lesser creatures. I saw it not. She was indistinguishable, to my eyes, from any forereader. I sat back, disappointed, to see that my plate had been filled to overflowing.

Khys eyed it, amused. I turned to Chayin, who evidently thought I could eat as much as three grown men. He pointed firmly to my plate with his knife, tapped the stra blade resoundingly against the plate's silver edge.

I ate as much as I could—some of the tiny meat pastries, filled with ground denter, herbs, and cheese, the crust off a mountain of creamed tuns, the fruited skin of a harth breast. I contrived to hide the kelt eggs under a tas chop from which I had carved one bite. Khys served that night a bloodred kifra, of eloquent vintage, bursting with life, and I drained my silver goblet. The attentive forereader who served us hastened to refill it. I placed my hand over the goblet's mouth. The lakeborn stepped again to our rear, to join her sisters, of whom Khys had provided one for every four feasters. In the enclosure, the dancers whirled and spun, now together, now separate, their skins shining with sweat. The slitsa-women, slithering, gave stylized chase to those leaping feathered ones, caught them, struggled, and even seemed, with the magic of their art, to consume the bird-plumed, whole. Litir players screeled their cries for them, dhroumaists conjured whining desert wind.

Three goblets of kifra did the cahndor consume, and two full plates of food, before he pushed back his chair and sighed, his attention upon the dancing. When those girls fell to the floor, panting, when the muscians took the moment between dance troupes to retune, Chayin rose up, stretched, and harshly commanded me attend him. Khys, who had been with consummate politeness hearkening to Liuma, touched by thighs beneath the table, slid his hands between them.

"I would hear a good report of you," he said softly, withdrawing his hand and his attention, turning back to the Nemarchan.

I sighed, rising, and went to the cahndor, who firmly guided me out the rear of the common room. Along the taernite passage he led me surely. The cahndor had been in these halls before, where the forereaders couch those who choose them. My mouth grew dry, my heart double-paced, as I followed him. The darkness made him loom larger in those soft-lit halls. The whites of his eyes glittered cruelly. He spoke no word to his evening's entertainment.

My breathing grew so loud in the silence that I could stand it no longer. I swallowed hard, and the sound was as a tree kepher propositioning her mate in a Galeshin swamp. I ran my palm over my forehead, felt the moisture there.

"Who was that woman?" I asked him, to crack the unease between us.

He laughed, flashing his large strong teeth. "An appeasement they had meant for Sereth, who, perhaps unwisely, will have no such." He licked his full lips, eased us down a side turning, stopped before a door there. "There was a time," he said accusingly, his black eyes boring deep, "when he would have had more sense than to refuse her. She bears his child." He pushed open the simple ragony door and shoved me gently within. Until he entered, the keep stayed dark. Evidently the entrapped stars recognized the cahndor of Nemar as worthy of their light. They brightened, then became dimmer, as he adjusted them to his liking.

"You seem familiar with our ways, Cahndor. Have you been before at the Lake of Horns?" I asked, to camouflage my nervousness. I sought the cream-silked couch, sat upon its edge.

Chayin rendi Inekte growled his laugh, a rumble deep in his throat. Standing in the middle of the brown-hung couching keep, he dropped the cloak of harth-black feathers from his shoulders onto the creamy mat. His breech and leathers followed them, and his thigh-high boots. I found my breath caught in my throat at the sight of him revealed. It is said that what is dark appears smaller than what is light. That revelation made Chayin seem to me, in that dimness which gave him its substance, immensely powerful, gargantuan in his mass. About him was little of civilization, nothing at all of the refinement that marked Khys.

"You and I," growled the cahndor, stalking about the keep, pulling back the hangings, checking the windows so revealed, "are going to have a little talk."

I pulled my legs up on the couch, crossed my arms upon my drawn-up knees.

"Disrobe," he snapped abruptly, throwing himself upon the couch, rolling to one hip. I scrambled to my feet to obey him, my fingers fumbling as I pulled the web-work up through my chald and over my head. I held it between us, folding and refolding it.

"Come, Estri," he said impatiently. I dropped it where I stood, and walked toward him, keeping my hands at my side with difficulty. I wished he had even more darkened the keep. "Sit," he said, patting the creamy silk. I sat there, my back straight, separating my hair, that I might clothe myself in it.

"No," he snapped, lounging upon his side, his chald glittering wide and full upon his dark skin. "Tell me about yourself."

There was little to tell. I told it as succinctly as possible. He chuckled, a bitter sound, when I told him of my naming, and why I had chosen as I had.

"The dharen," he interjected, "is as close to omniscient a man as I have ever seen."

Of the arrar Sereth he asked me, and since I had
felt him in my mind, I answered truly.

When I was finished, he sighed and sat up, crossing his legs under him, his large hand kneading
the place where his right shoulder met his neck. "I
cannot directly inform you of your past. Khys has
forbidden me. But there is a chance that I might
be able to bring it back to you, if you want it.
When once such was discussed, it was postulated
that my hand on you might achieve it." He stared
at me, the membranes snapping back and forth
across his eyes. I saw then, upon his other arm,
uritheria, the mythical desert beast, winged and
clawed, whose fiery breath had manifested upon
the plain of Astria in Amarsa, '695. "What say
you?" he demanded.

"Khys says if it comes upon me, and I am not
ready, it will destroy me," I whispered, trembling.

He shrugged. "Khys says what serves him.
Part-truths, and twistings, thereof, are tools he is
not averse to using. I doubt if your past will destroy you, though when you realize yourself, you
may have some difficulty with what you have become since you lost cognizance. But the risk is
there." He rose. "I, for one, am in favor of taking
that chance. It is not easy to look upon you thusly."
He searched among his piled gear and returned to
me, a tiny pouch clasped in his hand.

"Here." He held it out to me, unstoppered. "Take
a small taste only. Put your tongue to the opening,
then tilt the pouch back." Under his scrutiny, I did
so. It was bitter, a nerve-curling burning saltiness
that left my tongue and throat numb.

"Sereth had two of these, once," he said, fingering the gol drops mounted on my chald. "He saved
them long for the Keepress, and when they came
together after a lengthy separation, he gave her a
blade, the match of his own, with such a gol drop
embedded in the hilt." He turned the chald at my

waist, counting the drops. "One is a fortune, for an ordinary man. Khys holds you high."

"Not high enough to keep me for himself," I murmured, shaking. The drug was strong.

"He promised me more than a cursory use of you, once. He cares, I suppose, or he would not have amended his word." His eyes searched mine for some corroboration they did not find there. His large hand ran up and down my back, his nails scratching lightly. I fought the urge to turn and bite it. The room air whined around me, geometrics dancing like motes of dust wet with dew. I rubbed my eyes.

Chayin suddenly pulled me down beside him, his hand holding both my wrists, with ease, above my head. His other hand, exploring, demanding, was unbearably arrogant. I fought him. I bit and kicked and writhed and turned, forgetting all my promises to Khys. I sank my teeth into the fanged creature that lurked upon his bicep. He laughed, struck my head away. I saw, suddenly, another place, another time I had struggled thus with the cahndor of Nemar. Above me were no longer the brass scales of the forereader's common keep, but a desert apprei, whipping in the hissing wind.

"No," I wailed, and he, just entered in me, grunted and strove harder to split ne asunder. "Chayin," I gasped, when I could, "let me go, please." My wrists would surely crack, imprisoned in that grip. As I thought it, he tightened his grasp upon them.

"Estri," he rasped, kneeling over me, his knees upon my hair. "Recall me, or what Khys gets back will be greatly different from that which he lent out!" He did not give me time to answer, silencing me with his need. I had been helpless under him, another time. Still, I would not see it. I saw the Keepress' life, her couching of the cahndor, as she had described it. Swallowing, convulsive, it burst upon me with his sperm, with the taste of him in my mouth. I found my hands free, clutched at him, my whole universe shifting like a bondrex in sucksand.

He held me while I wept, my head pressed against the curling black hairs of his chest. I thought I might never raise my head, that I could not live with such shame. And another thing, I thought, over and over: Khys, what have you done to us? Sereth, my love, my couch-mate—how could he ever forgive me? Santh, my own, whom I had raised from a whelp, how might I explain my absent love to him? Chayin, who still loved me, whom again I would gainsay for another, who had better served me than any—what might I do to repay him?

But out loud I only wailed, again and again, my spread fingers clutched over my ears: "Khys, what have you done to us?"

III

Seeking Stance in the Time

Chayin slapped me hard with the flat of his hand. Thrice, before my hysteria subsided. His rage had his great arms quivering.

"Estri! Cease this now! Speak to me! Later you will have time for tears."

And I put my arms around his neck and brought him down upon me. "Chayin," I wailed. "What am I going to do? Help me. I am so sorry. I could do no different."

"I know, little one. You seem destined to be ever some man's crell." His tone much softened, he kissed my closed eyelids, out of which tears squeezed anew. I sobbed against him. "I do not know, truly, what you can do. As always, you have my support, anything I have, whatever I can do. And more, if you come to want it." His hands, with their own wisdom, brought calm upon me.

"What I said to Sereth—how could such a thing come to be? If there is any sanity in this universe my father made for us, I fail to see it." I pushed at him, that I might see his face. Chayin's eyes were red, his upper lip beaded with sweat, his brow furrowed. I knew that what I had to ask would hurt him.

"Do not think," I said softly, taking deep breaths, trying to clear my thoughts, "that I am not aware that no other could have brought me to myself." I ran my fingertip over his lips. Crouched above me, he nipped it. "Always, it will be you to whom I am indebted." I raised my head, kissed him, a long time. "I will find, should I extricate myself from this, some way to repay you that will cause you to look back upon this day with joy. Will you do for me, right now, what must be done?"

"If I can, little crell." He grinned at me, bit my neck.

"Find Sereth. Bring him here to me. I beg you. I must explain myself, salve the wound I dealt him."

His body stiffened against mine. He brushed stray hairs from my forehead with his lips.

"That I cannot do. When he left the meal, he left the lake. He was much offended that Khys would put such a mark upon you." I felt his probe, turned my face away.

"It is my father's sign," I whispered.

"Not upon Silistra," he said, taking his weight from me.

"What is the time, Cahndor?" I demanded, dizzy with confusion. Once, it was I to whom Chayin had come for such counsel. A great reversal had come to be in our positions. "What reason had Khys for allowing this to come to be?"

"I know not, little crell, what he has in his mind. The time, so muddled with all who now set hests within it, yields me little." He sat up, crossed his legs under him. "I thought he might let me have you now, since he got the child. He will not. He told me once I might breed you. He will not allow it. Yet he allowed me this couching, doubtless knowing what I intended."

I saw upon him his northern chald, and the new strand woven there, that of helsars. With both minds, I knew him. He who had so afrighted me without my memory was a comfort in my sight. And yet his altered chald showed him also Khys's crell.

He shook his head. "Little can I do for you, Estri, or for Sereth, or even myself, before him. I asked for you. He refused me. I petitioned him for Sereth, that I might have an arrar's aid in calming the chaos that is now upon the Parset Lands." He laughed harshly. "He allowed me an arrar—Carth. Such is the dharen's humor. He wants you both here to serve his hests, whatever they are." He fell silent, brooding. I could get no sense of him, of what emotions raged within him. Nor could I keep him out from my own mind.

"What are you thinking?" I queried him helplessly.

"About you and Sereth. He was angry that I would try this, even that I sought to free you. He believed Khys, that it was uris which in truth destroyed you, and that you were better off unknowing if you remained in Khys's hands. What was left of you mattered so to him that he would not have risked it."

I said nothing. My fingers found Chayin's, entwined them as of old.

"You did," I assured him, "the right thing. I will be better off, after I have correlated what information I have. It is only the shock. I will be fine." I did not believe it. "If you would restrain your attention from my thoughts until I have them ordered, it perhaps would be easier upon the both of us."

"It hurts me," he growled, "to see you so helpless. Before, when you did not know, it lay easier upon you." He rose and paced the keep, ever the desert stalker. "I know now what has set Sereth upon the edge of madness." He kicked his piled gear, scattering it.

"Could you not seek him with your mind, tell him what has come to pass, that I am restored to myself, that you did me no harm, but invaluable service?"

"I cannot. He likes not such conversation, and has spent much time upon a shield to keep him isolate. I doubt if even Khys can crack it," he said proudly.

"Let it be. I will see him presently." I sat up, tearing the braids and the fire gems from my hair. My skin pebbled as my mind began to function.

"Chayin," I asked softly, turning my head to follow him around the keep, "what will Khys say? What will he do to you for helping me? They destroyed the last hest I set before I was banded, while about my assessment."

"Little crell," Chayin snarled, striding across the keep to stand over me, fists upon his hips, "I care not. He cannot destroy me. He needs me to hold the south. Far-reaching changes he intends in the Parset Lands. Without the trust my people have in me, none of his seeds could bear fruit. Jaheil has made very clear to Khys the connection between my life and his goals." His white teeth flashed in that fearful grin I so loved. He sat beside me, encircled me with his arm, pulled me onto his lap.

"But do not underestimate him. He is an awesome talent. Doubtless he knew of this probability. Perhaps it is, in some obscure way, his intention. I set my hest interlocking with a larger conception that encompassed yours. If I had set it upon yours, I would have lost it. It is a trick I learned from a certain Keepress when I restudied her works with a helsar-trained eye." He squeezed my breasts. I nestled my head against him.

"You hooked into Khys's hest?" I echoed. It made no sense.

"I know not whose it was; it was of such enormity I could only attempt to employ a tiny section, placing my own coeval with what I could apprehend."

A knock, twice repeated upon the door, precluded my answer. I pulled the couch cover around me. Chayin grinned, striding to open it. I thought it not funny. Within me were the emotions of Khys's

Estri, as well as my own. I lowered the cover from me deliberately as Chayin pulled open the door. He who stood there was an arrar, that blond who had held Liuma and me so clumsily in the common room. He bid the cahndor come with him and attend at once the dharen. The woman, he instructed, inspecting me coldly, was to be left here. Another would come and collect her. Chayin could make no objection, even when the arrar shackled my hands behind my back. He only stood by, helpless, as the blond arrar lifted me bodily from the couch and put me on the mat beside it. I was struck dumb in my fear. He took from his robe a chain. Then he lifted my hair, held me by it while he snapped one end around the band of restraint I wore. The other end he attached to a ring set low in the couch's side. I could not rise upon that short tether.

The arrar strode out into the hall, looking back impatiently when Chayin did not immediately follow. The cahndor knelt down and kissed me, holding me so tightly that all breath was forced from my lungs.

"Tasa, little crell," he growled in my ear. "If I can, I will see you again before I depart for Nemar." He rose. I watched him, unspeaking, my hands in chains behind my back, kneeling as Khys's Estri had been so well trained to do. The door shut behind him with a muffled thump. I slid my legs from under me and slumped back against the couch frame, waiting. Estri Hadrath diet Estrazi, you have come to occupy a most untenable position, I thought bitterly. Khys—unconscionably had he treated me. Yet, not knowing him culpable without my memory, I had loved him. I sought within me for some vestige of my skills; found, as I had expected, only scars and reminders of what had once been. I waited, fearful and defiant, for the dharen to come collect me.

My mind skittered and whirled and paced in the silence provided by his band of restraint. Desperately I sifted the memories of him I had acquired, for some hint or sign, some clue, overlooked in my ignorance, that I might now put to use. I found it not. I came upon only my weakness. If they had not so thoroughly dealt with me in my assessment, I thought, I might have fared better. I recollected him, with both minds, and shivered at the ambivalence that was mine. It had been such ambivalance that had destroyed Raet, Khys had once confided. I struggled in my chains, to no avail. What would he do with me? I lunged against my tether. The couch, set into the floor, remained unmoving. The chain hummed, held. The band of restraint at my throat did not so much as bend. Half-choked, my neck badly wrenched, I leaned back against it once more. I sought the sort, saw nothing. My skin sheened with sweat. It dried, lay there like a dusting of salt.

When the door opened, I scrambled to my knees automatically.

He pushed it wide, paused there, regarding me critically. I awaited him, sitting upon my heels, my wrists chained behind, my head bowed, my chin touching the tether that bound me to the couch. I fastened my gaze upon my copper thighs.

I heard the door close, the sound of him moving. I saw his sandaled feet before me, and I knew for what he waited. Stiffly, I bent my head as far as my tether would allow. My unbound hair fell over his feet. A thousand pulsebeats he kept me so before he bade me rise, long enough for my shame to set my body afire, long enough for my terrorized mind to babble to him all he might choose to hear.

He squatted down and touched my shoulder. I flinched, sat back upon my heels.

"Keepress," he greeted me, even-toned, shadow or humor dancing at the corners of his mouth in the dim light. A terrible wrenching took me as I tried to make some accord between my two views of him. Those molten eyes sought mine. I avoided them, until his hand under my chin forced my head up.

"Dharen," I managed. I could hardly hear my own voice.

He raised one arched brow, ran his familiar, alien hand down me. I quivered, fighting the old hate, the new love within my heart. "No repudiation?" he queried, low, in that silken voice. "No threats, no imprecations, no judgments upon my use of you?"

"No," I whimpered. She who had not known him had not known her danger. I appraised it, saw my defeat in every molecule of that father-bred body. He whom my father had chosen for me was more than my match. "You do not have to reteach me, dharen." I tried to keep my voice steady. "I have no doubt of your power, your skill." I stared into those eyes, so like Estrazi's, drowned there. In them was no hint of what he intended.

"Do you know now what I have done?" he said gently.

"No," I whispered, my wrists by their own will fighting the bracelets that bound them. I searched his face, desperate for some hint of his intent. There was none. I wished, agonized, that he would hold me. My skin crawled at the thought. I moaned, closed my eyes, tossing my head as if I could shake away my pain.

Khys laughed softly. "Talk to me, Keepress!" he commanded.

"What are you going to do with me?" I asked, shuddering at his presence in my mind. He took from me all that I had felt with the cahndor. I did not attempt to defend myself. I sat straight, my head raised before him.

"What I choose," he said, freeing the tether where

it had been snapped to the couch ring. I thought
wryly how great an honor it was considered, upon
the outside, to be allowed to come to the Lake of
Horns. He wrapped the end of the chain around
his fist. Again he wrapped it, and again, drawing
me toward him.

"Khys"—the wail burst from me—"please, tell
me how I may serve you."

He let loose the tether, a wrap at a time. I sat
back from him.

"Tell me," he suggested, "about Sereth."

"What do you want me to say? I wear your
band, your brand, your couchbond. He, as I, live at
your whim." My eyes beseeched him, prayed his
mercy upon us. "I beg you, do not hold us to task
for our feelings, for what has gone in the past. Do
not take vengeance upon him for what failings you
find in me." I blinked, his form gone blurry before
me. "Estrazi meant me for you," I whispered, my
mouth stumbling over the words. "Your will, and
his, brought me here. I have loved you, freed of
my past. If you allow me life, I doubtless can
repay you in service. Perhaps, in time, I can come
to terms with my ambivalence. I am more than
she whom you have known in my stead." I stopped.
He only regarded me coldly. "I have borne the
child you desired, Khys. Within the limitations
you have put upon me, I could still be more to you
than any other you might come to use." My nails
bit my slippery palms behind my back. My breath
came hard to me. He cocked his head ever so
slightly.

"Now," he said at last, "you are beginning to
see." And his quietly triumphant tone brought a
moan to my throat. I swallowed it, and the taste
was bitter.

"Is there need for you to gloat over your success
with me?" I flared.

"It pleases me, to see you finally aware. What

think you your arrar might say, could he see you petition me so wholeheartedly for my favor?"

I said nothing, shifting upon my aching knees before him.

He slapped me across the mouth. I tasted my own blood.

"I know not," I whispered. "Khys . . ." I hesitated, stopped. I remembered the shield Esyia had taught me upon Mi'ysten, tried to build it. I could not hold the image. I had not the power.

He sighed, reached beyond me, hooked the tether to its ring. He turned me roughly, so that my buttocks faced him. I did not scream as he entered me abruptly, not even stripping off his robe. Tears ran down my face and stung upon my cut lips as he tore his way into my rear passage. One arm around my waist, so that I could not ease myself, he serviced himself with me.

When he released me, I fell forward and lay there sobbing softly. My wrists jerked convulsively in their bonds.

I heard him at the door.

I rolled to my knees. "Khys, do not leave me here!"

"After you have had some practice upon your old skills," he said, "I may collect you, if you have come to wish it."

"Please, dharen, do not punish me. Take me with you." He paused in the doorway. I felt his probe. He stood there longer than was his custom. Then he came and unsnapped the tether from the band of restraint at my throat. I leaned against him, sick with relief, as he unshackled my wrists. He did not let the bracelets fall, but safed them in his robe. I dressed before him, clumsy, and retrieved, as he ordered, the strings of fire gems I had strewn petulantly upon the mat.

My fingers toyed with the chald he had put upon me. Its testimony was no longer obscure.

He took me, through untraveled corridors, out of the forereader's keep.

The night lay soft upon the Lake of Horns. We walked it, he intent upon my thoughts, silent. I, buffeted by the wind from the abyss that brought with it dawning comprehension, hardly noticed his presence. Along the lakeside we walked, the sharp Brinar breeze whistling around us.

"Khys, may I speak?" I petitioned him, knowing he would allow it.

"Surely," he affirmed, he who had so long awaited this moment.

"It is of Estrazi I would speak to you," I cautioned him.

"I know," he said, hesting a stone up into the air, out across the lake. The spume it made, skipping, glittered in the moonlight.

"If you had come to me in Arlet, before Sereth, before Raet, and gotten me with child then, you would have had from me all that you desired. You would have needed to put no band of restraint upon me. You would have had, then, more than I can offer you now." My fingertips ran over the band pulsing warm against my throat. If he had not wanted more from me than my unknowingness could provide, he would have kept me free of remembrance. I sought his face, but the moon's light sat like a mask upon it. How I craved my skills, with this man, before whom I was so little without them.

"And you would have borne my son upon Mi'ysten. That way, in all its variations, provided a lesser yield. Only as regards what might have been between us was it a superior path. As you found, yourself, such selfish choosing must often be sacrificed for the greater good." And I heard the loneliness, the bitterness in him that I had often felt when concerned with choosing between possible futures. Khys, much older than I, bearing upon him a world's weight for so long, must have often made such decisions. I felt an empathy for him, a tightness in my throat, over burdens I presumed to think only the two of us had ever borne.

He put his hand upon my neck, propelled me forward toward the keep where I had been so long a prisoner.

"Many will walk that path, lit as it has come to be by the light of so many helsars. That, also, could not have been, had we blazed a different trail."

"There are things about my father you do not know, Khys."

"And will you give me that knowledge?" he asked softly, for he and his council had tried, and failed to obtain it.

I opened to him a certain portion of my memory, stepped aside. Without comment, he absorbed what was there, what had been denied him, even with all his power. What his council, in their assessment, had tried to take from me, I gave him. Not by my skills had that information been withheld from him, but by Estrazi's. The fathers' shaping sequences I gave up to him, my own child's father, lest the boy be denied his heritage, should I not be enfleshed when he came of age; and that Khys would know I harbored no resistance to him. If the man would stand against the fathers, he would need them, and more. And I had nothing else to give. I could provide him with little else—I might have, once, been a formidable ally, but no longer. I had not the power to put those skills to use.

"Do you want to see the child?" he asked me after a long time.

"No," I said. He squatted down, drew in the soft sand.

"I will not take the band from you."

"I did not expect it," I said. He looked up at me, and I knew his mind weighed the change he saw in my carriage, my voice, my heart. I saw his hesitant smile, not meant for my eyes, that his hest had come in. All this time, though he had my form, he had not possessed what had driven him to seek me. I knelt down before him, throwing my hair off my shoulders. His mark sparkled upon my breast.

"This way," I said softly, "surely as you intended, none but yourself may be so tempted." Shaping skills had been no blessing to me. I knew, even then, the importance of that moment, when Khys received from me what Estrazi had meant for him, and him alone.

"Estri," said Khys, very low, "you should see our son."

"No, Khys." I shook my head, got to my feet. Avoiding his hand, I stared out across the lake. "Not until we take him before his grandsire."

Then he rose also. Had I kept the thought within, he would have marked it as complicity against him.

"Do you not see it, dharen?" The wind caught my words and carried them back to him. His arms encircled my waist. "Estrazi will have his fruits."

"I have gone to a great deal of trouble to avoid such a confrontation," he said in my ear. "It has been long since you have sorted. Much has changed since you set your last hest. Let me worry about owkahen. I have managed alone a very long time." His words were sharp, but his tone was pleased, prideful.

My fingers went to my chald, caressed the gol drops there. I shivered, and he propelled me toward the keep, solicitous. I almost laughed. Deep within me, my rage growled, rose, and circled, seeking a smoother spot to sleep. I heard it, muttering, settle once more.

Though I tried not to think of him, my thoughts turned again to Sereth. As we mounted the steps to his tower, Khys asked me what I would have him do.

"Let us settle it between us. Only a woman can ease a man about such things. Or allow him my use periodically. You might, in time, tire of me. It would be not unfitting to cede me to him, if such came to be the case."

"It is not in the sort," he said shortly, as the guardians of the doors held them open for us. He stopped just within to speak with them, as was his custom.

"If harm comes to him," I said when he again paced beside me, "I will bear the weight of it. You would not use him so recklessly, but for his feelings for me."

"It would be worse upon him if I gave him nothing with which to occupy that mind." I heard the warning there, knew I trod near the edge of his patience.

"He is no match for Gherein." I sighed, fretful.

Khys smiled bleakly, said nothing. Up the back-passage stairs of brown taernite he guided me. And into his keep, where the rumpled couch silks answered for me a question I had felt it importunate to ask. I moved away from him, to the couch, and stripped it.

He stared at me as I did so. When all the coverings lay upon the rust mat, I turned to him and asked where I might find fresh couch clothes. He told me. I redressed the couch. It is not my practice to sleep on another woman's sweat.

"How did you find her?" I asked, smoothing back the outer cover.

"Sufficient," he allowed from the kifra stand. He turned from it, offering me a bowl. "I was, I am afraid, somewhat preoccupied with you and Chayin. She is a talented forereader, if a trifle melodramatic by nature."

"Why are they here?" I queried him over the edge of my bowl.

"Things in the Parset Lands change too fast for some of its inhabitants. Also, he being Raet's son, his spawn deserved better than the schools of Nemar."

"It is a little young, is it not, for school?" I asked innocently.

Khys drained his bowl, put it down. "There is no temporizing with you, is there? If you please me, I may update your information. I have told you that I abhor questions. I have spent long teaching you your place. I adjure you: do not forget what you have learned."

I took my bowl and set it, half-done, upon the stand. I stripped off the lucent web-cloth he had given me, walked past him, and put it in its place, a small space he had allowed me in his wardrobe. It had taken longer than I had expected to come to the end of his tolerance. Khys had bestowed upon me a great latitude, along with my memory. I was not displeased.

When I emerged, he was in the alcove, stripped down to breech, leaning with one arm against the window frame, his eyes upon the waning moon as it bid farewell to its twin on the wind-ruffled water.

"Tomorrow evening," he said, not turning, "we shall sup privately with the cahndor and his mate. At sun's rising I have an appointment with the high chalder. Then some rather dreary business in which I will not involve you. I will collect you at mid-meal, and we will discuss the situation in the south. Your observations might be valuable, you having more extensive experience with tiasks than most."

"Your will is my life," I acquiesced, waiting, reading the tension in his muscles as easily as my skills would have given it to me from his mind.

"It is what I said to you about Estrazi that troubles you, is it not?" I asked.

He made no move nor answer.

"I had a dream in which he identified himself to me, expressed his intent, though I could make nothing of it at the time."

"Do not give it credence. You know better, do you not?" he snapped. "Go to sleep!"

And yet, for a probability he would shun, he himself posited too much attention upon it. I shrugged and turned to slip between the fresh couch silks. He darkened the keep, all but for two stars in the alcove. From his library he got the charts he had lately been studying and took them there, settling back among the cushions in the dim light.

"I do not need dark to sleep," I offered.

"It will be light soon enough. I know them by heart. I use them as a focus. Do not concern yourself."

So I turned upon my side, my back toward him, and sought the restorative waters of the sea of spirit.

But though I walked with determination along that shore, as I chased each wave, it receded before me. I could not sleep. From my memory of the gathering in the common keep, I conjured a tune, that I might have what little privacy such a simple ploy would afford. Beneath the melody, I took note of his regular breathing, its deep slow rhythm, and knew Khys worked upon his projects from a vantage point not afforded by his keep's window.

I pushed myself deeper, slowing my respiration, my life processes. But I could not slip my flesh's hold.

Khys, in the alcove, muttered to himself. He was all that once I had adjudged him, in my hate, and more. Yet he was also what Khys's Estri had seen—a man who had slipped entropy's hold and lived twenty lifetimes, a man of obscure but un-

questionable morality, who had made the adjust-
ment I had sought and not found between life
enfleshed and life overwhelming. Khys was an extremely successful organism. His fruits lay ripe
and bountiful upon Silistra, and near a million
were nourished thereby. When I had refused him,
he had afforded me a lesson in perspective the
magnitude of which was only beginning to come
clear to my sleep-befuddled sensing.

I wished desperately that I could seek my father's
help. I could not slip Khys's band of restraint. The
dark beyond my closed lids was dark only; the
silence, but for my rustling mind and the tune I
proffered as flimsy shield—the silence was deafen-
ing. He had gotten his child from me. I had invited
him, in my ignorance. He had used my life more
efficaciously than any band of restraint upon my
former couch-mate, Sereth. And Chayin, also, did
Khys's will. All three of us he had bent to his
purpose as easily as if he were a chalder melding
strands of soft gold. What purpose? Even the
cahndor knew not, and Chayin had been, even
before we rode to battle upon the plain of Astria,
formidable in his forereading skills.

I felt the chald, the gol drops pressing into my
back as my agitation tighter-fleshed my mind.
Miccah, the high chalder, had remarked it a pity
that I knew not the chald's significance. He could
have meant by that only one thing. A man receives
a couchbond strand to bestow as he pleases upon
reaching puberty. Low chaldra is such a strand;
and no invocation, no Day-Keeper's hand, is needed
to add a couchbond chain to a woman's chald. But
Khys had not had such a strand to give. He had
had Miccah make one. That he might once have
had one, and lost it somehow, occurred to me. But
I did not think so. I shifted, adjusting the chald so
that no drop lay against my backbone. I recollected how he had treated one woman upon whom

he had brought child—she who bore the mark of his favor, she who had served us a meal. She, surely, had never worn such a strand at her belly. The dharen had amended his custom to enchald me thus. I wondered if I were enough of my old self to be able to turn his interest to my advantage.

I heard him again, the rustle of his movement about the keep. I wriggled upon the couch, rolled onto my side, facing the sound of him.

"Khys," I whispered, breath-soft, opening my eyes to the coloring dawn. "Tell me a thing, lest sleep never come to me."

"Ask it," he said, sliding back the book wall, safing his charts within. His back was to me. He had dressed as if he might work his body, in a practice breech and light weapons belt. He turned finally. I had waited, that I might see his face.

"What is the significance of this chald, that upon which the high chalder remarked? I still do not see."

"If you did not see, you would not have asked," he remarked. "But I will give you the acknowledgment you seek. I would not want you to lose sleep over it. As you surmised, I had not such a strand to give." He pushed away from the book wall and came to the couchside. "Silistra has never before had a dhareness."

I stretched under the couch silks.

"Do not make more of the fact than it is," he advised sternly. "It is your bloodright, procured for you by your father's grace, by your genetic strengths and the potential inherent in the son you produced for me. It is him I honor, not you." The sun invaded the keep, fanning the fathers' fire upon his skin.

I laughed softly at him. Honor his son, would he? I saw no honor in the band of restraint I wore, but I saw a look upon his face I had seen often before upon other men's. Fleeing, it hovered there, before he chased it from his countenance.

He stared a moment longer at me, in the rising light, then turned and strode from the keep.

When I judged him gone down the stairs, I threw off the couch silks and went into my old prison. In the mirror there, I regarded myself. I spent a time coming to terms with that image, with his works upon me. I saw the painful thinness of my frame. I saw a tone to my muscles that did not please me. I would, I vowed, get Khys's permission to work my body into some kind of fitness. My inner thighs did not suit me. My skin did not have the healthy tone it normally carried. But those things I could remedy. His device upon my flesh, I could not. I tried one final time to loose Khys's band of restraint. An enth, I sought the power to interrupt the flow of energy that held it there. I failed totally.

I wondered what I might wrest from this situation, what might be gained. One must know where one stands, and what one wants, to even peg the time. So I was, nominally, dhareness. The title did not assuage my exacerbation. Estrazi, how could you allow this? My father did not answer me. Was Khys, truly, enough to stand against the fathers? "Have you joined with those who oppose me?" my father once asked me. And I had threatened that I would do so. He had told me then, truly, of all that would occur—even of my subjugation, my loss of memory, at Khys's hand. And he had come to me, in a dream, even before I had recalled myself. I turned from the mirror and hastened out from the prison that had so long contained me.

I had, at least, the run of the dharen's keep. I took up his book upon helsars, and that of hesting, and sat with them in the alcove. I could not read. Sereth, and the cruelty Khys had shown him, obsessed me. I could see no reason in Khys's actions. If, as Carth had said, Sereth was resigned to my

loss, why had Khys given me to him, and brought
more pain upon him? You are, after all, only his
servant, I had said to Sereth, and Khys had laughed
and hugged me close. I sighed, rolled upon the
cushions. Was this how M'ksakkans felt among
Silistrans? Short so many senses, I found myself
unable to use my reason effectively. It will come, I
told myself, in time. One can adjust to anything.
But my spirit shriveled at the things I had done
and said in my ignorance, and my reason had no
salve for the pain in my heart. Somewhere in that
sea of tears, I drowned, and slept.

I would, I knew upon awakening, contrive to
speak again with Chayin. He, I was sure, knew
more than he would say. Before, he had withheld
from me that which he had adjudged me too weak
to know. I rose, rubbed my eyes. Squinting out the
window, my hand crushing the thick-napped drap-
ery, I guessed it an enth before mid-meal. In the
sky, full greened, I saw tiny specks rise and fall,
chasing each other upon the wind. Hulions romped
above the Lake of Horns. What part did they see
for themselves in Khys's hest? Why would they aid
the dharen? One cannot constrain a hulion. They
are the freest of creatures, primal proponents of
the law within. If they lent their strength and their
wisdom to Khys, his works must be potent indeed,
in their sight. I longed for the sort, the spread of
probability, to make itself known to me. I quivered,
standing there, remembering the strength of the
hesting skills I had once had. I, Estri Hadrath diet
Estrazi, who had once made a world, who had
once claimed the heritage of the sevenfold spirit,
had by my own will come to this moment; undone.
I had set my will against my father's, and he had
sent me to another who did likewise. But I had not
known. The failing, as Estrazi had once warned
me, was not in the power, but in the conception.
My incredible foolishness had come to tithe its

due. I had spent my power unwisely. You will not interfere with Sereth's destiny, Estrazi had decreed. No, I would not. I could not interfere with a wirragaet's destiny, now.

I threw myself upon the cushions, curling into a ball. Khys's books jabbed at my hip. I could not, in any conscience, blame the dharen for what he had done to me, lest I shortchange my father. But my rage was deaf to reason, blind to the pattern I was only just apprehending, as it had been when it came to me, aforetime, and precipitated all that Khys had done to erase it.

I rolled onto my back, my fists clenched around the chald I bore. If I had not blared my hate at him when first we laid eyes upon each other, how might it have gone? But the hate had come unbidden, out of owkahen, out of what he would do to me, and thereby made it impossible for him to do differently. My head ached. I rubbed my fingers over my temples, unable even to rid myself of simple physical pain. I did not like what I had seen, these past enths, and I felt no better for the seeing.

Blame him? Myself harangued me. Of course you can blame him. He demanded that he be ceded casual responsibility when Sereth, Chayin, and I had been brought before him, battle-torn, bleeding, and bound. I am the sort and the hest, he had said. All that you have done is my will, he had boasted. And my father's hest—he had claimed it his tool, and called it paltry. The hest of a Shaper, a world creator, he had downgraded.

I rose, pressed my head against the cool pane, watching my breath mist its surface. There was no use searching relevance in Khys's actions, no more than in my father's. I had learned that lesson upon Mi'ysten. The only relevance is that of consummated will, upon the plane where Khys and Estrazi did battle.

But the question remained in me—whose hest had Chayin locked into with his own? Was it a father's, or Khys's own machinations upon the time? And whose will, between them, would be done? Often hests run congruent for a space, gaining power from such synchronistic periods, causing great chunks of crux when they part. I sighed, backed from the window. My foot came down upon one of the dharen's volumes, twisted. I stumbled amid the cushions, knelt down to rub my wrenched ankle. I recalled Carth's anger when he had read that paper I had long researched for him, in which I postulated certain conclusions drawn from the genealogical records kept at the Lake of Horns. His anger, that I could have suggested Khys's longstanding breeding program faulty, was vehement, of greater violence than I had deemed him capable, so great that he had refused to pass the work to the dharen, so great that he had, before my eyes, torn it into tiny scraps. And he had made me do another, upon a specified subject in which I had no interest. I wondered, sitting there, rubbing my aching ankle, why I had recalled it.

You may be mad, still, I chided myself, my mind bucking and twitching like some unbroken threx at first saddling. This situation might bring madness upon a more stable mind than my own. I thought, momentarily, of the child, then chased the image from my mind. I cared not what they did with it, nor into whose hands its care devolved. I had wanted, desperately, to bear a child to Sereth. Circumstance, or owkahen, had prompted Sereth to refuse me. Surely it would have been a child of which both of us could have been proud. But he had refused, and I had not the will to go against his wishes. I saw him, a cascade of memories we had built together, upon the trail to Santha, at Tyith's death, under the falls, with Estrazi's cloak upon his shoulders as he had been that day we did

battle upon the plain of Astria. He had lost, and
lost again, and yet he lived. There was that. He
lived. I took comfort in it. I would, I avowed, do
nothing to endanger his life. If I served Khys well
enough, I might even come into some small influence over the dharen. If so, I would be able to
discharge some part of that obligation I felt. But
to do so, I must quiet the love I had for Sereth.
There was no trickery I could play upon Khys, no
deceiving such sensing as the dharen possessed. So
I came to it, the decision I made upon my recollection of self, with so little cognizance of my true
situation. But any choice is better, I told myself,
than making none. That rule, first of mind skills,
always holds true. I would serve Khys, who in my
best evaluation was an unknown. I had been placed
here by a convocation of will that I might do so. I
would let the past go. If I could, I would ease
Sereth, free him of his love for me. Unencumbered,
he could seek another; one the Weathers would
allow him. I would do my best not to further
enrage the dharen. I would come to some terms
with my crippled state without seeking to place
blame, for in truth, there is ever only will, and the
responsibility for one's actions.

I guessed it near to mid-meal, bare iths from the
time the dharen had bade me be ready. I looked,
unhappily, at his books, regretful that I had not
even started them. Khys had, I was sure, specific
reason for presenting me his works. I gathered
them up, slid back the wardrobe's thala panel,
placed them with my things there. I promised myself I would attack them with my full attention at
the earliest opportunity.

There was a white length of off-world silk, laced
with threads of silver, among the wraps Khys had
provided. I chose it. I would wear my old colors,
those of Well Astria. I wondered, as I draped the
short length around me, fastening it with a spiral

clip of silver at my throat, at the gift my father
had left within me for the dharen. I ascertained,
reviewing my assessment, that he had not himself
tried to extract any knowledge from me at that
time. He had only watched, while his council tried
their skills upon me. Rethinking it, I saw that
they, in those moments, had also been assessed by
their master. I giggled, a bit hysterically. He had
either known I would give the sequences up to
him, or made me do so. He had been in no hurry. I
wished him better luck with those skills than I had
had. They were not meant to be wielded in the
domain of space and time. I had learned them
upon Mi'ysten. I had paid dearly for them. Even
upon the dharen, I would not wish such as had
come to me, when I used them against Raet. I
sighed, taking up the comb of carved bone he had
allowed me. I needed it. There was a time I might
simply have hested my hair smooth and shining. I
stepped from the wardrobe, intending to avail myself of the alcove's midday sun.

He was standing there, his hair water-sparkled.
He must have just come from the baths.

"Have you been here long?" I asked, nonplussed.

"I do not need to be near you, to hear you if I
choose," he said quietly, brushing past me into his
storeroom. He took a circlet tunic of dark, soft tas,
and buckled it about him. Then he clipped a cloak,
upon which the Shaper's seal blazed brightly, to
his shoulders. It might have been the one Estrazi
had given me, or its double. I did not ask. He did
not volunteer the information.

I tucked the white and silver silk beneath my
chald, set the hip clip tighter, conscientiously driving each question from my mind as it appeared.
He slid shut the panel which enclosed the wardrobe,
leaned against the night-dark wood. I stood still
and straight under his scrutiny, aware that he
might take exception to the colors I had chosen, or

the way I had fastened the silk at my throat, obscuring my band of restraint.

"You look lovely. I question the ease with which you have taken to your new perspective."

"I look reasonably well. I could do with a circle partner; daily work upon my body must soon commence. Also, with your permission, I would be allowed an enth, say at sun's set, for dhara-san. As for perspective, I have not enough information to have one currently." I heard my own voice, soft and sure, poised. I smiled to myself. I had me—much more than Khys's Estri had ever had.

"I will find someone," he granted. "A man, most likely. We do not have a woman in training for the Slayer's chain, here at the lake."

"You do not wholly approve?" I licked my lips, widened my eyes at him.

"On the contrary, I think it wise of you to find some way to vent your frustrations. Just do not kill any of my arrars," he said, mocking, fiercely.

"I promise." I grinned genuinely. "I will not. It would much ease me if you allow me a less sedentary life."

"As trustworthy as you prove yourself, that much more freedom will I allow you. Are you hungry?"

"Desperately."

He inclined his head, ran his fingers through his still-damp hair. "That is the first time you have ever, since I have known you, expressed any interest in food." One of his brows drew down. He extended his hand to me.

"You have not known me, Khys," I murmured, taking it, "only in battle shock, and then that shadow child you made me."

The claok he wore, with the Shaper's seal upon it, brushed my arm. My hip, as he walked beside me, rubbed against his thigh. He did not bother to lock his keep, but left the doors ajar.

I examined the passage, the tapestries and artwork displayed upon its walls, with an eye that could appreciate them. He allowed me stop before the hulion tapestry. Long I gazed upon it. Only in Nemar had I seen its equal. Tenager, First Weaver of the Nemarsi, had attained near the skill of the artist who had worked those hulions upon the grid. So real were they that their eyes, as one shifted, took deep glow and seemed to follow, so real that it could not be said for certain that those tufted tails, one black, one red, had not just twitched as one looked above their bloody heads at the krits that jabbered soundlessly, ever-leaping from branch to branch above their pointed ears.

He touched me lightly, his palm at the small of my back, led me toward the stairs.

"I would see Santh," I whispered, unsteady, leaning against his arm.

His glance, sidelong, was ruminative. The tendons in his neck corded. I was about to withdraw my request, my foot descending the second stair.

"After the meal, we will see to it," he said. I almost stumbled. Still were the effects of uris on me, I thought as I caught myself. And that brought another thought to mind.

"It was not uris, was it?" I ventured. It had not been uris that had stripped me of skill and self-knowledge.

"It was uris that so weakened you that I could take you. It was uris that caused the scarring you yourself have seen. But it was not any one thing, unless one might call the Weathers to account. Or Shapers. It was my will, but if I could have done it some kinder way, I would have." He glanced at me again, his jaw slightly forward, his fine nostrils flaring.

I said nothing. Khys was many things, kind not being one of them. And yet, I knew nothing of the constraints put upon him by his hests. And if he would shape, he would be even further bound. Or did he think that upon that plane he could, as he had done upon Silistra, make his own rules? I paced him down the stairs, silent.

"Estri," he said to me when we gained the landing of the ground-floor hall with its ceiling of golden scales, "are you actually concerned?" His tone held some little incredulity.

"I am empathic by nature," I mumbled. He snorted softly. "I once went against Shapers. I set my will against Estrazi's. I lost." I straightened my shoulders, remembering that my first manuscript had never appeared upon Silistra. "I thought, in my audacity, that I might free us from the manipulation of Raet's ilk." I laughed, then wished I could call back the ugly sound of it.

He pushed open the door to his study, held it for me. The round table was set. The entrapped stars that lit the muraled ceiling came alight with their master's entrance. I swallowed, and then again, as water came anticipating into my mouth.

"What your father left for me will be of great aid in achieving that goal," he said, motioning me to table.

"I hope so. But I wonder. I think you have not been with him. He left you a gift. It had some purpose. That information was never accessible to me. I knew not of its presence until you bespoke it." I settled into the thick-padded chair. Khys served me charred denter, red-running with blood, a heap of zesser greens. The drink in its silver pitcher was a light-milled brin. It frothed in the silver goblets, whispering.

"Your concern is duly noted," he mused. At least he did not discount my impressions. I was heartened. Half an enth later, he leaned back in the chair, regarding me over steepled fingers.

"Little saiisa," he called me. I looked up from the fat edge of my meat, where I had been searching another edible bite. "You may have more."

"No," I demurred, pushing my plate away and my hair back from my face. "I must increase my intake with moderation." He himself had only half-cleared his plate. Khys's Estri interpreted his narrow-eyed gaze, quailed before it. I steadied my breathing, pushed back my shoulders.

Khys leaned forward, his elbows upon the table. The robe fell back from his hair-gilded forearms. He laced his fingers. "Tell me of Mi'ysten," he commanded.

As I did so, I recollected the time he had spoken to me of fathers, of Shapers. All that he had said had been concerned with their work in space-time. When I spoke of Estrazi, he leaned forward, almost imperceptibly. Twice he nodded. Once he asked me to repeat information—that which Estrazi had said to me concerning him. Having done so, I fell silent. Innumerable questions threatened to overflow the dam I had constructed in my mind to hold them, wash me away with their tide. Sweat formed beneath my breasts, rolled down my rib cage, past my waist, before the silk absorbed it.

He rose abruptly, and the whirl of his cloak as he turned away sent his silver goblet clattering, spraying brin to the floor. He paid no attention. I retrieved it, placing it carefully upon the table. It stood askew upon its base, dented. I took a meal cloth and set to sopping up the brin puddling the silvery mat, glad for something upon which to turn my attention.

"No," he said softly. I stopped what I was doing, sitting back from the stains over which I knelt.

"Dharen?" I said. Did he wish me to leave the brin to soak into his priceless mat?

"No, I said," he repeated, whirling, the cloak lashing around him. "It cannot be that simple. You are the courier of his propaganda."

And I remembered that, even to Estrazi, Mi'ysten hests are invisible when set within time. How much more, then, to Khys, would Shapers' design be obscured?

"Estri," he said, exasperated, "be silent." I had said nothing. I crouched small upon the mat. He sought and regarded his domain through the cloud-draped windows.

And the bearer of his gift was I, also: I had come to the dharen complete with couch-gift, available only to the mate for whom I had been intended. I cursed them both. A deadly gift it might come to be. The thought cheered me, as my ambivalence hissed and slithered in its cave deep within my heart. I pressed my palms against my temples, that I might quiet myself somehow. I held my breath, fearful. But Khys either heard not, or cared not.

"Let's us go and find your hulion," he said, abandoning the window.

I scrambled in a most ungraceful fashion to my feet. A grin, fleeting, lit his features. He swept by me, out of his study. I trotted after him.

"If you were in charge of the standardizing of the Parset Lands," he asked when I had gained his side, "what would you do with rebellious tiasks?"

"Against what are they rebelling?" I found it hard to pace him. We took a left into the main hall. Tiny, down that interminable corridor of archite, were the great doors and those who attended them.

"We have outlawed the wordship of Tar-Kesa, torn down his temples. We have now in the south real dhareners, and uniform chaldra, and Slayers. There is no place for a force of such women. A number of them, disdaining Well work, have gainsaid their chalds and roam the land in bands."

"I can imagine." I thought of Nineth as a well-woman. I laughed aloud. "Are there still crells in the Parset Lands?" I asked.

"Yes. What they do with their chaldless is their own affair."

"Catch them. Make crells of them. Even better, for each tiask put in crell chains free a female crell and install her in your new Wells. The gene pool will be served, both ways. As crells or well-women, the tiasks will get men's use, according to their desirability. And there are some worthy women, crells in Nemar." I recollected Khemi, and those dark girls Chayin had kept in Nemar North. "It is harder to envision a tiask as well-woman than crell," I added. "They are not fond of men, as a principle."

Khys laughed as we came up to the doors. "I will suggest it to the cahndor. It is much less complicated than his plan, or mine, and a good bit more realistic." He touched me, left me to converse with the black guard. When he returned, his straight nose was bracketed at the brow by two deep lines.

"Come," he said very gently, "let us seek the hulion." He put his arm, protective, about my shoulder. His long-fingered hand, closing on my shoulder, squeezed reassuringly. He led me, thus, out the doors into the midday.

"What is it?" I blurted, my throat aching, the hairs standing away from my skin.

"Nothing I can discuss with you," he said, still in that compassionate tone. I shivered, though the day was mild and fair. Down by the lake he guided me, along the promenade, settling finally upon one of the white gol benches.

He sat, pensive, staring out over the lake's green-gray raggedness. That same breeze had me holding my mane at the base of my neck, that it not blind me. Khys's copper hair whipped around his face. The wind, up out of nowhere, died abruptly.

"I cannot call him," I reminded Khys's sullenly.

"I had thought you might like to try." His eyes

closed momentarily, as a bitter laugh escaped my lips.

Santh was quick to answer Khys's summons. From the southeast he came, from behind us. His snapping wings sounded warning only moments before he landed. Khys, of course, had known from whence the hulion came. He had only stared off across the glassy becalmed water. Gone where I could not follow, was Khys.

"Santh," I cried, delighted at the sight of him. I was on my feet, running, as his clawed forepaws touched the ground. Wings furling, he roared his greeting, loud as the falls for which I had named him. His great mouth open wide, tongue darting amid blade-sharp fangs, he trumpeted again. And I stopped. The hulion flattened his pointed ears to his head, his tufted tail lashing. His pupils distended, muzzle jerking, he twisted his head about. His growl was distinctly angered. I put out my hand, the right, very slowly. The hulion sank to the grass.

"Santh," I whispered. One ear twitched. Muzzle shivered up, exposing his weapons, white and gleaming. "I know, Santh, I know. But it is me." The hulion was upset. I could not hear him. His mind-touch could not reach me. He snarled, rose sinuous to all fours, sank down again, belly first, upon the grass. His great claws clacked, repeatedly retracted. "Santh." I got down upon my knees, that our eyes be level, still holding out my right hand. He stretched his neck, his hindquarters wriggling. His wet, hot-breathed nose nudged my fingers. I scratched there, watching his luminous pupils dilate. He extended his neck still more. A rolling rumble began in his throat. Those great eyes closed. His tail curled in against his side and lay still. Swallowing the catch in my throat, I stuck my hand deep in his ear, rolled it around, fed him the wax I scooped out. He opened one eye. His right paw reached out. He laid it upon my closed thigh. Its spread covered them.

I heard Khys moving about. Santh's ears flicked forward, stayed pointed behind me, upon my left. He ceased his satisfied growling, muttered to himself. The hulion retrieved its paw from my lap, sat up, front paws tucked between rear. Santh had much grown since I had last truly seen him. I found my fingertips at my band of restraint, with an effort disengaged them.

Santh regarded me, speaking plaintively in hulion. His tail again flogged the grass. He rose up, took a step forward, butting his huge head against my chest. I threw my arms around his furred neck, buried my head there, smelling the pungent airiness of him. Oh, Santh, I love you, I thought, wondering if he could hear me.

He pulled his great head away suddenly. A thrill of fear constricted my belly. He hissed. I had never heard such a sound from him. He backed away, his head snaking low, from side to side, growling. Then he whirled, and in one bound had the air, the crack of his wings blocking my ears, the wind of it slapping me back. I watched until he was a dot in the deep green sky, until the dot disappeared.

I turned to Khys. I had seen the hulion. He had allowed it. His one hand toyed with the great chald of Silistra, the other hid within the cloak licking around him. He watched me intently.

I would not cry. I had upset my tenuous equanimity. I had disturbed Santh. I rubbed my naked arms with cold, moist palms.

"I will take you back," he offered. I nodded, fell in beside him. He put arm and cloak around me, for warmth. I smiled up at him, thankful for the small kindness. You are not what you were, I told myself fiercely. You will never be. Be at least strong. Behave with grace.

"As befits a Shaper's daughter," remarked Khys, softly mocking, or commiserating, I knew not which.

"Have you any message for me, from Santh?" I asked, as he headed us toward his tower. The sound of it was more bitter than I had intended.

Khys turned his head toward me, the parentheses that enclosed his mouth suddenly graved deep and sharp. "He considers you unfortunately afflicted," he said.

"What price are you exacting from me, to treat me thus? What debt have I incurred?" I would not scratch at my band. I clasped my hands behind my back, my eyes upon the white walkway ahead of us.

"Any other would have destroyed you out of hand," he said wearily. "I may do it yet, to save my own sanity. I am constantly urged to do so, by those who know just how great a power you unleashed upon the plain of Astria. One might say you incurred a debt there great enough to wipe out your life-right. Some, Gherein included, have demanded that payment. More vehemently will such demands be made of me, now that you know your identity. You are not free. It is that simple. Should I imprison you in some undertunnel, feed you upon stale crusts, until you enter that fact into your conception?" he demanded. His hand grasped my arm hard above the elbow.

"But as you yourself pointed out once, we did only your will! You did not imprison Sereth, nor feed stale crusts to the cahndor of Nemar!"

"Would that owkahen allowed it," he muttered, squinting ahead, toward his tower. His grip upon me loosened. I felt my blood rush to heat the squeezed flesh. "I have to fill my council's empty seat. Then I will see about your circle partner," he added, almost companionably, as if regretting his harshness.

"My thanks," I managed.

His gaze flickered over me, though he did not turn his head. I pushed my hair, wind-tickling, off my forehead. Up the wide steps he propelled me.

"I must go do my work," said Khys as the attendants answered his ringing summons and the doors opened before us. "The keep is unlocked. Stay there until I send for you. Baern!" It was to the dark attendant he spoke. "See her safely to my couch."

The guard reached out. Khys pushed me toward him. Then he was gone down the steps.

"Lady," the guard invited, his eyes lowered. I preceded him, taking the front passages, those of ornithalum and archite, that I might pass the hulion tapestry upon the way. Before it I stood a long time gazing, until the man made small noises in his throat, his body rustling its impatience as he shifted. He was darkly hirsute, rather like some brist that had learned to walk upright, if ponderously. When I adjudged him distressed unto the verge of speech, I moved off toward the dharen's keep.

The doors were still ajar. Without a backward glance I slipped within. By the time I had turned to face them, they were closed and locked.

I smiled to myself, as I went and pulled back the alcove's curtains. I sat upon the ledge a time, watching the water, attempting once more to cut my mind adrift.

It was a sound like wind's wailing. Like standing atop the Keening Rock of Fai-Teraer Moyhe on the eve of winter solstice, with the Embrodming Sea rumbling below. That wretched, that lonely was the sound that emanated from my prison keep. I have been there, where the heart of the world beats the dirge of the spirit upon Silistra's bones, and I know. I crept toward the doors to my prison, stealthy. They were not locked.

With infinite care I parted them, drew them back. Upon my couch in that gray holding keep lay Liuma, curled into a ball, my own white robe wrapped around her velvet darkness. I hovered there an ith, undecided. She had not seen me.

"Presti m'it, Nemarchan," I said quietly. She stiffened, sniffled, uncovered her head, using her arms instead to push herself upright. I saw the horror in her swollen eyes, the trembling of her puffy lips. She drew her knees up to her chin, crossing her wrists about her ankles.

"Chayin said you recalled yourself," she said shakily, not wanting to believe otherwise.

"I do," I admitted, leaning against the door frame. "Whatever it is that troubles you, it might ease you to bring it out here." I motioned behind me, to Khys's keep. "We could drink some kifra and consider it."

She looked at me warily, at Khys's device, at my throat, where beneath the silver and white silk nestled his band of restraint, warm pulsing against my skin. If I had been she, I would have been much affrighted at what I was—what the Keepress Estri had become.

"There would be no harm in it," she decided muzzily. When she rose, her movements were slow, uncoordinated.

I turned from her, went to fill two bowls. "Sit in the alcove," I suggested. I poured the kifra, brought the drinks to her where she sat beneath the window. When she reached up to take one, her light-nailed hands shook.

"Would you speak of it?" I asked, sitting cross-legged upon the cushions, my elbows upon my knees. I thought of Khys, and how displeased he would be to see my limbs so arranged.

"How can you stand it?" she demanded, her black eyes gigantic over the golden bowl. She did not sip, but gulped her kifra down. Her lids closed, pulse showing on their gilded backs, she found more tears to shed.

"What?" I asked, discomfited.

"Him," she sniffed, discarding her empty bowl, smearing her tears across her cheeks.

"Khys?" I wondered what he had done to her. Very probably, he had done little. I had seen her tears before. "What did he do to you?"

"He ... I ... He is ..." She looked at me, imploring, as if I should know.

"He is dharen of Silistra," I supplied. She nodded, her lips twitching. I waited.

"Did you catch with Chayin?" she asked, her membranes fluttering like crier's wings.

"Did you catch with Khys?" I queried her back.

She started, rose to her knees, clasping her belly. "Uritheria protect me!" she moaned. "I pray not. Please, did you?"

"No," I said. I understood part of her tears. If I had spawn by Chayin, he would have choice between them. She did not want her son's position endangered. Her fear, that I might bear Chayin a more worthy heir than she, was not unfounded.

"I saw your son," she said, sitting up, relief taking the weight from her shoulders.

"Indeed," I said. "And how did you find him?"

She shook her head, spread her hands wide. They still trembled, pink-palmed. She licked her lips, red tongue darting. "Awesome," she said.

"Have you taken a helsar?" I asked, to cover my confusion. My child was eight passes old, surely too young for such an appellation.

"No," she murmured. "Nor do I wish to." Those slanted eyes shot black fire at me. "Chayin, under its influence and that of the dharen, has become a stranger to me. He is worse than ever. There is no controlling him."

I only smiled. That would bother the Nemarchan. When he had been afflicted, she had worked her will through him.

"He was not even interested enough in the affairs of this world to be present at the birth of his son," she said, upon a hiss wet with poisonous spray.

"I bore mine, also, alone," I said, in what I hoped was a commiserating tone. "Where is the cahndor?"

"With Sereth." And that hiss was sibilant in the extreme. "They couch!" she spat, leaning so close that her breath rained upon my shoulder.

"They have long made such assignations their practice," I admonished her, startled. "I would not attempt to get between them. You might lose your place altogether." She straightened. I recollected something she had said, long ago at Frullo jer. "You still live. You did not fulfill your prophecy and die the death Chayin had in mind for you."

"Not yet, I have not," she said. Then: "I would have died, had I been fool enough to linger near the coast of Menetph. I was inland, in Menetph North, when the sea rose up and smote the city."

I had not known Menetph smitten. But if the coastline of Astria had been changed in the holocaust, then why not elsewhere?

There was a silence between us. I rose to refill her bowl. She grabbed it up and stood. I could look down upon the part in her black hair.

"Is Sereth well?" I asked her, as she followed me to the kifra stand.

"I doubt that I have ever seen him well. He is recovered from his temper of last evening, if that is what you mean." I wondered what Chayin had told him of me.

"It would be a great favor if you would tell Chayin I must speak with him," I said, pouring her golden kifra from the moisture-beaded pitcher.

"About what?" she said softly.

I almost slapped her, then recalled that I sought her aid.

"About the arrar," I said, even softer.

She inclined her head. Understanding crossed her face like a hulion's shadow.

"Are you not afraid of Khys's wrath?" she murmured, making the jump. I reminded myself that Liuma was an accomplished forereader.

"One would be a fool not to fear him," I said coldly, seeing her recollect her own fear in whatever had passed between her and the dharen. Her eyes found my chald. "I might be able to keep him away from you," I offered.

"Could you?" Gratitude afore the fact has always confounded me. Her fingers found my arm, squeezed. I resisted the impulse to shake her hand away. I lifted my full bowl with my free hand to my lips. The keep grew dim, as if a cloud obscured the sun.

"Perhaps," I said, as if I was sure. "But I must know your purpose here."

She took a step backward, her eyes opened so wide they seemed dark stones amid fresh-fallen snow. Her mouth fell open. Wheeling, spilling kifra down my leg, I saw what she had seen, and my bowl dropped from nerveless fingers, splashing its contents upon the rusty mat.

It had been no cloud before the sun. There was a blinding flash, a crackling as of burning parchment. An acrid wind, upon which rode stinging grains of window, rattled the keep's locked doors. Tiny Liuma grabbed me around the waist, buried her head against me. I stood, unmoving, stroking her hair, her whimpers rattling my flesh. Through the pulverized window, beyond which hovered a creamy egg-shape, came a metal ramp that secured itself around the sill with hooked claws. The metal screeched upon the stone. Over that bridge, into Khys's keep, scrambled two men, clothed but for heads and hands in black form-fitting garb. Around their waists were wide, blinking belts. I saw the red eyes of M'ksakkan death cubes. Their booted feet, first one pair, then the other, hit Khys's glass-sharded mat.

"Which one?" said one intruder, halting, arms akimbo. I moved toward the prison keep, away from Liuma. She moaned, huddling.

"That one!" said the second, whose belt blinked more than his fellow's.

I kept moving, wishing I had retained the bowl, toward the prison keep.

"Stop!" said the first, approaching. I stopped. I was far enough. The second M'ksakkan, his attention upon Liuma, had his back to us. I moved hesitantly toward the blond, my hands at my throat. Well away from the wall I stopped again.

He came slowly toward me, head jutting forward, eyes alert.

"Please," I moaned, my voice atremble. "Do not hurt me." I begged in clumsy M'ksakkan, omitting the contraction.

"Just come along," he said, in his own language, relieved. "No one will hurt you." I walked slowly toward him. Temple, windpipe, throat?

"What'll we do with the other one?" he called to his fellow, turning his head. I leaped for it, hand drawn back, arm scissored. My three stiffened fingers deepened the hollow in his throat, as my feet touched the ground. He gurgled, fell unconscious. My arm hurt, burning pain to the shoulder. I stepped back, clutching my fingers. The other M'ksakkan just stared. I doubted that his friend was dead, but from the feel of my hand, he should have been. I cursed my sluggish body.

"M'kinlin!" bawled the remaining M'ksakkan. I heard a scrabble upon the bridge.

"Come take me," I invited the second, in proper grammar. The man I had scored, I decided, was dead. He had yet to breathe. I felt uplifted, turned my full attention upon the first, and the man who now jumped from the swaying bridge into the keep.

"Come on, M'as ... What?" He froze, eyes widened. I heard noises, perhaps upon the stairs. "This one ... let that one go! Help me." He started toward me, not deterred by the corpse. I backed toward the prison keep. He had a decidedly un-M'ksakkan frame, graceful for all its bulk. The belt at his waist was a veritable galaxy, blinking. He sidled. I retreated from him. He grinned, gray eyes slitted.

"M'kin hadn't the authority to use one of these on you," he said to me, closing. Deftly he herded me, toward the corner. "I do. And I wouldn't mind a bit," he added, his eyes touching his dead companion. In his hand was the incinerating device, its twin red eyes alight with baleful promise. "If you aren't on the ship at the count of three, you're dead." He spoke M'kaskkan, without any interest in whether or not I understood him.

"One," he said. I nodded, walking toward him.

"Two," he said, turning on his heels, the death cube trained upon me. I realized then that he would do it. I ran, gained the ledge, my skin aprickle, waiting for the hot tongue. I crouched there, in the wind. The bridge, rivet-rough, swayed. Below, tiny, was the walk-wayed grass, behind me, the black-haired man.

"Two and a half," he said, grinning, touching my shoulder with the cube. I looked across it, at the opening into the hover. I saw two more men crouched there, squinting across the gap.

He pushed me lightly. I fastened my eyes upon the opening, crawled onto the ramp. It lurched. My fingers clutched its edges, curling around them. One leaned forward from inside the ship, extended his hand. The wind took up my hair and blinded me with it. A hand slapped my buttocks. I crawled, unseeing, my breath as loud as the high-tower wind. Crawled more, my hands never leaving the edges, my hair fouling my arms, pulled by my

knees. A hand touched mine, grabbed my wrist.
Another, at my shoulder, pulled me in, out of the
numbing gale. I stumbled; the hands held me
upright. My feet touched a resilient, fleshy surface.
I shook my vision clear. The M'ksakkan loosed his
hold upon me. The gray-eyed man, the casualty
upon his shoulders, jumped down into the hover.
Then I saw, through the hatch, what the last man,
the blond, found to do with Liuma. He lifted her
up to the window ledge. It seemed to me that she
slept. Her arms swung loose, her body untenanted
as he dropped her out the window. Running
crouched, he crossed the gap. Humming obediently,
the bridge let go the tower's sill, retracted itself. I
saw the claws come over the sill as the hatch sides
met. I swallowed hard, wondering if her body had
yet splashed upon the grass.

I turned from the featureless star-steel doors.
About one of the hover's six couches the men
clustered, all but the gray-eyed one, who sat with
a leg thrown up on the hatch-side console, arms
crossed watching me.

"So you're what all the fuss is about," he drawled,
insolent.

"And who are you?" I asked him. The muttering
from the couch tinged angry. I could have taken
two M'ksakkans. "You seem no M'ksakkan." It came
out ill-phrased in Silistran syntax.

"No M'ksakkan I am," he mimicked me. "As for
my planet of origin, you have never heard of it."

"I doubt that," I said, thinking that I was going
to be sick. I pressed my palms against my stomach.
The vibration coming up through my feet increased.
The ceiling, lighted squares, flickered, steadied.
The gray-eyed one turned and slapped three toggles,
punched up a visual display.

"No input! Maref, let's see your stuff! Manual
till they cut in from their side." A red light was
blinking angrily. The hover bucked, shuddered. I

sank down upon the springy floor, my stomach distraught. Twisting my head, I saw more red lights glowering. At a console beneath a grid viewer, Liuma's killer lifted a panel, clucked, held up a reel, bent-flanged, from which a chewed tape edge dangled.

"Splice, my ass," I heard him mutter. "I knew this would happen. You can't mix systems." Another, blond, with two boxes in hand, came to aid him. The brown-haired one hurried toward us, turned a couch to face the console upon which the gray-eyed lounged, set to work there.

"I'll have lock for you in a minute," said the man at our console, fingers flying over the input keys, replugging buses, cursing softly. Near the gray-eyed's shoulder, a reel began to whirl, jerkily. The brown-haired, slight man leaned back in the couch. It wriggled under him. "Got it," he sighed, a green light igniting to uphold him. All across the console, green replaced red. The brown-haired man laced his hands behind his head. "Shouldn't you tie her up or something, M'tras?"

The gray-eyed one took his eyes from the display grid across the hover. "Why? She won't be any trouble. Will you?"

"No," I said, curling my legs under me, leaning upon one arm. I wished my stomach would cease its rolling.

"Stand up," M'tras said. I complied shakily. He grinned, let his eyes rove me. He snapped his tongue loudly. I could imagine what it meant. The brown-haired one chuckled, leering, and made some comment in a slang unfamiliar to me.

"Now, Maref, you can't do that," he admonished. "At least, not yet. Me first." He slid off the console's edge. "Would you like to take a couch—a seat, that is?" I thought of the numerous ways I could have killed him if I had been free of Khys's band of restraint.

"No, thank you," I said, feeling the hatch's star steel cold against my back. I wished I had worn, this day, more than the short length of white and silver silk. Green blinking shot sick shadows over my skin, colored the neutrals of the hover, turned the white silk upon me sky green. Then it ceased.

"What'll we do with M'kinlin?" asked Liuma's killer, raising his head from the guts of the console.

"Let him decide, M'as! You can stand it until we dock," snapped the brown-haired man, in the tone of a superior. The black-haired one who seemed to have my charge had called him Maref, no contraction, which put him either very high or very low by birth in the M'ksakkan hierarchy.

"Where are you taking me?" I directed my question to him.

He held up both hands, palms toward me, as if to ward me off. "Ask M'tras," he suggested. "I can't even talk to you. I never saw you. I'm not really here. I'm vacationing on the moons of Dyriyiil. Wish it were true!" He chuckled, leaning back.

I turned once more to M'tras, whose belt had come to many-eyed life. He quieted it with a touch. Then he reached over the console to slip a head-rest from its housing. Holding the spidery wires to his ear, he spoke into the distended mouthpiece, his other hand raised to me, that I keep silent. I turned away, my eyes circling around the hover. My fingers ached, those of my right hand. The nails throbbed. I might, I thought, have cracked a carpal, from the way my arm felt. I rubbed it with my left palm. The two blonds, archetypically M'ksakkan in their pale slightness and their skin-fitting black uniforms, had swung the black contour seats toward the display grids. They lay upon them, talking low together. Upon the seat to our right was the dead one. The next seat of the circle lay empty; the one upon its left held the brown-haired Maref; the next, closing the circle, was also empty.

None of their uniforms had any familiar insignia; nothing but the belts, whose meaning I could not read. By omission, then, this was not a Bipedal Federation Liaison Unit.

They had killed Liuma.

"You had best get away from the hatch," said M'tras, pointing firmly to the unoccupied seat before me. I sidled past him and sat upon its edge. It sought to clasp my buttocks. I sought a solid surface. I wiggled, it writhed. I sighed and made my hips still. It quieted. M'tras laughed, seated himself beside me. The lounge quivered, reformed under me as it added his comfort to its task.

"Now, if you'd lain down, you would have been better off," he commented, resting his elbows upon his knees, regarding me sidelong. He reminded me of Dellin, though he was lighter-muscled. His hair, unruly, harth black, was cut to the nape of his neck. His skin carried a gray-green tinge beneath it darkness.

"This is a large hover," I observed.

"This," he corrected me, "is a special hover. Show her." Maref grunted, but raised a hand to his belt. The grid before him disappeared, to be replaced by the coldest black I had ever seen, in which few stars attempted a desultory sparkle.

"I am going to be sick," I warned them, doubling over. From somewhere into my swimming vision came a white receptacle. A hand held it against my mouth while I heaved. Very little did my stomach give up, but it was long before it ceased trying. I was no longer upon my planet. I was in a tiny craft adrift in space. I conceived every catastrophe I knew possible in such a situation. My skin slicked with fearful sweat. The bag was gone from my sight, replaced by a lined palm upon which two tiny spheroids rested.

"Take these." I managed to swallow them, holding the proffered sack of water in both hands, squeezing it up through the nipple.

"That's enough, or you'll lose it," advised M'tras. I handed the water sack back, first squeezing some into my palms, that I might cool my burning cheeks with it.

"You might have said you get star-sick," he admonished me.

"I did not know," I said shakily, shifting upon the undulous couch. I must have blanched.

"Look at me," he snapped. I did so. He had a webbing of tiny lines around his eyes. "Good. Ask me questions or something. Keep your mind busy till the pills work."

"Who are you?"

"I am"—and his lips curled— "Trasyi Quennisaleslor Stryl Yri Yrlvahl. Most call me M'tras, in the B.F. worlds. You might say I am an adopted M'ksakkan."

"And in what function do you serve the Bipedal Federate worlds?" I asked. He had been right: I was not familiar with any world that named its male children in such a fashion.

Nor did I know a speech that rolled off the tongue so musically; I had never heard such a language. I would have remembered. The reels upon the datagraph of the hatch-side console twitched, rolled, stopped. The board chattered. Hot, dry machine breath filled the air. Insulation, carbonized, tickled my nostrils. I hoped this ailing beast in which we rode would make it whither-bound. "What are you?" I asked again, risking a turn upon the blessedly quiescent couch to face him.

"A mechanic" He shrugged. "When the machine that runs the B.F. malfunctions, I fix it. However I choose." His eyes flicked up, caught mine. I arched my back, rubbing my arm.

"How did that bring us both here, now? What do you want with me?"

"Now, that is very complicated," he said, sitting up. He raised one arm over his head, bent at the elbow. The other he twisted behind his back, grasping hands between his shoulderblades. He flexed, pulling hard. He repeated the actions, exchanging the positions of right and left arms. Such muscular easings are universal among those who use their bodies. He took a deep breath, judging the effect. "You know anything about politics? Most Silistrans, I've been told, don't."

"What kind of politics?" I said suspiciously.

"Interworld. Silistra and M'ksakka, for example?"

"No," I said. He made that clicking sound; two click, two notes.

"Then I can't explain it to you. I'm not going to kill you. I don't think. I'll probably make some kind of deal with your people that'll get you back home." He frowned, running his thumb over his lower lip. "But you can't tell, with Silistrans. Yours is not the most rational of races." And I caught the change in speech pattern, the musical inflection of his last sentence.

"How did you hide your hest?" I asked him, using the Silistran word, for M'ksakkan has none.

"What?" he said, one brow, the left, diving downward.

How did you implement your plan, without Khys, who sees and controls a great amount of owkahen, the time-coming-to-be, finding out and obstructing you?"

"I don't know." He grinned, a flashing of teeth. The commander, Maref, rolled upon his side, facing M'tras' back.

"Come on, tell her. I'd like to hear it. Craziest thing I've ever done in my life—and in broad daylight!"

M'tras shot the other a warning look. His gray eyes were chilled when they returned to me.

"I got a little help. And that"—he turned his

head, speaking over his shoulder—"is all I'm willing to say. Do not continue to question me!" Music, once more.

"Khys will surely reduce you to component atoms for this," I said.

"Your playmate?"

"Couch-mate," I corrected him.

"That's why I went after you, not him. All our calculations say that he will deal, with you among the stakes. The probability of me getting in there, killing him, and out with my life, was minus—less than nil." His eyes were black-ringed, like frozen clouds. I thought I needed nothing less than one more assignation, but his whole bearing screamed that determination.

"Probability." I laughed coldly. "What know you of such things?"

He laughed also. I marked it strange, as he shifted, slid closer. "I'm a stochastic improviser. My planet is provisionally entered in the Federate, the provisions upon our side being that some aspect of the B.F. prove itself to be more than tonally boring. I'm part of the test group." He leaned forward, toward me. "I'm doing what might be akin to discharging chaldra, if I understand the concept."

"Are you telling me you sort?" I asked, my fingers at my throat, at the band beneath the silk.

"I guess," he said. "Musically, mathematically; I have a talent for asking the right questions of a very specialized computer. I interpret that output. Then I hear it, and I guess. I'm an aural symbolist. But sort? If what Dellin and M'lennin have reported is accurate, we don't do anything like it."

"Had Dellin a hand in this?" I demanded.

"No." He clicked once, sharply. "He didn't know. He is due for a lengthy rest. Those last reports we got from him had a great deal of misinformation in them. Men don't last long upon Silistra." His wandering fingers found my thigh, climbed it. I wondered why he did not simply use me and have done with it.

"What kind of misinformation?" I asked dully.

"That you were amnesiac, helpless, little more than a vegetable, an easy score. That you would be there alone." The light flickered. I flinched, staring around anxiously. The M'ksakkans lay quiet, undisturbed.

"It's nothing, just their remote commencing docking procedure," he assured me.

"It was not nothing the last time," I said, still with an effort as his arm went around my shoulders. Maref, from the adjacent couch, made derisive noises.

"I brought that reel with me from home. The tolerances, capstan tensions, weren't close enough. It happened in the trial run. We spliced it and made a copy. But you lose clarity in a copy, so we went with the spliced tape. It held pretty well. You saw the difference, felt it, running on the second-generation mix. You'll realize it now that the Oniar-M has us remote." And indeed, I could feel the lessening of vibration. The lights were steadier.

"What is the Oniar-M?" I adjudged him agitated. The pulse beat under his jaw, hasty.

"Our transportation to M'ksakka. That'd be a big trek for this sailless boat." His finger, thick-nailed, touched Khys's device. "That's permanent?" he asked.

"It is the dharen's mark," I said, throwing my shoulders back. "Shouldn't we lie down, strap in?" I had, I noted with satisfaction, properly contracted.

"You didn't answer me," M'tras observed, his lips drawing tight, removing his arm.

"The device," I said, "is permanent." I met his eyes, which I had been long avoiding.

"Somebody did that to me, I'd kill him," he said.

"I do not think the dharen would even consider you," I said archly.

He put his elbows on his knees, regarded the floor between his feet. "You'd think someone in your position would be grateful to be gotten out of it. I thought you would. Logic pointed to it. Instead, you kill one of my people. I play a sus-chord, and you respond with a dissonance." He chewed upon the inside of his cheek.

"If you want me grateful, remove the band at my throat with your formidable technology," I suggested.

"And what would your playmate say, if we did that?" he asked innocently.

He knew, then, exactly what he was about. Either he was intending to return me to the dharen, or for his own reasons wanted me tractable. I sighed, letting my fingers play in my chald. His body, relaxed, gave me no clue to his temper. I had no sense of him, talentless degenerate though he doubtless was. All his disarming banter had been just that—and of no consequence. Yet he had taken me, out from under the care of Khys, with Chayin and Sereth close at hand. They had had no inkling. Liuma, in her weeping, had known something. She would never know anything again.

Maref, with a grunt, sat up in answer to the blinking console's summons. He put his ear, then his mouth, to the headset. Then he ripped it off his head, eyes slitted, and brought it to M'tras, playing the cord out behind him. "For you." He grimaced.

Rising, M'tras received it. The two blonds sat up, diving for their own receivers.

"Let him," M'tras said into the mouthpiece, chin tucked in, his body an S-curve of defiance. His fingers drummed upon his belt, sharp taps in the silence. I stood. M'tras motioned Maref toward me. He came, fingers to his lips.

"Lick it, for all I care. We can't afford to further

implicate ourselves." Pause. "No. Let me talk to him." He clicked an intricate pattern, three times. I decided, watching him, that when Khys destroyed him, I would like to be present.

"Look, man, this is no time for nerves." He snarled into the headset, his eyes closed. "I don't care what he said. Don't worry. He couldn't." Pausing, he tapped his belt in a definite sequence. The hatch-side console came alight. A geometric graph showed there in green. Across it grew two root systems, one red, one white. Where they intersected, numbers flashed, changing as fast as heartbeats. "Some kind of illusion. People don't just appear out of thin air. All right, sparkling air. No, no such thing. Wait . . ."

He lifted the phone away from his ear. The two blond M'ksakkans were crouched at the foot of the far console, sputtering with suppressed laughter.

"Look," M'tras continued. "I will, if you do not calm down, disconnect." A short pause. "I'll push the papers through, if that is what you want. But if you're right, you'll be safer there." His tone had lost its sureness. His gaze, rapt upon the ever-changing numbers, grew shadowed. His frame straightened up. The M'ksakkans were no longer amused.

"The situation has altered markedly," he said. "I'll send someone for you. No, nothing urgent. Just that since you know, now, you're useless. We might as well save what we can. Two hours, at the port." Smile. "How long is that in real time? It's close. Try." He took off the headset, extended it to the empty air, his attention on the graph, whose white lines had taken on a tinge of blue.

Maref took it from him, waving his hand before the larger man's abstracted face. "We don't read minds, M'tras."

Clicking, M'tras lowered his head, quieted the

console from his belt. "Call Oniar-M. Have them pick up Dellin at Port Astrin."

"I could go back and . . ." Maref offered, broke off, shrugged, and hastened to the board. M'tras, who had turned his back to him, glared at me, crossing the distance between us in three strides. He grasped my arm urgently, turned me toward the seat I had so gladly vacated. Meekly I let him push me toward the half-sentient black couch.

"What occurred?" I asked, coming to terms with the soft, ever-moving plush of the seat. His left leg pressed mine. Again he balanced his elbows upon his spread knees.

"I'm not about to tell you," he said angrily, his head in his hands.

"Let me tell you," I said, joy making me careless, smug.

"Don't! Don't make me covet what information you have. You wouldn't enjoy our methods of extraction." His reproof was sharp.

"Dock in three minutes," Maref announced. M'tras did not seem to hear.

"Tell me!" he said, straightening up, his brows drawn down over his eyes. "Go ahead. What has occurred?"

"You spoke with Dellin. Khys or one of his council appeared to take him to task for what you have done. Seeing that he knew nothing, that one gave him a demand for my return and a threat of retaliation. Dellin was never very brave. He wants out. I cannot see how Dellin came to know of you, but I would call it some machine-aided determination."

"I thought you were talentless while wearing that collar," he said softly his eyes crinkled.

"I guessed," I said. "I know Khys."

He bit his cheek a moment. "I wish I did," he said. "Sparkling air, yet. He can do that?" He surveyed the hover, as if looking for Khys behind him.

"Two minutes," said Maref dryly.

"And so much more I doubt that you could conceive his limits."

He awakened his belt, I thought I saw something spinning among the lights.

"Could he," he said very clearly, "destroy something—say, this ship—from his present position upon Silistra, without mechanical aid?"

"And therefore, indefensibly, to a machine culture. . . . Yes, surely, though he might hesitate to do so with me aboard."

"Might?" His belt suddenly quieted, as if sharing the concern that froze him.

"He has what he desired from me—a male child. He would spend me, doubtless, if the prize was dear enough." I did not believe a word of it, but I wanted M'tras to take the falsehood, camouflaged so lavishly with truth.

"One minute," said Maref.

IV

The Gulf of
Alternate Conceptions

Ijiyr was the name of the instrument M'tras played. The sound of it, coaxed by dextrous fingers, tomed sonorous around the cabin. Crystalline, piercing, thick as running water came that quarter-tone composition, for a time that was not long, but so meaningfully filled it stretched eternity.

As he put it by upon the table, a sad yearning filled me, to be again where those sounds had winged us. He had taken me with him, where the music spirits go, out of cabin, of confinement, to a place where I bore no band of restraint, nor the heavier weight of my Shapers' heritage. Brought almost to tears by the melody's beauty. I could only sit a time, breathing. M'tras himself was quiet, loose-muscled, leaning back in the cabin's marsh-gray chair.

I sat in the other, which was green-toned and mercifully inanimate. Between us was a burnished table of some metallic-seeming substance. The cabin was sectioned, diffusely lit, windowless. Between the two sleeping slabs was a partition, subdivided, that served food, information, entertainment.

One wall offered a panoramic view of the Western Forest. I had asked M'tras, had been told that the Western forest was the greatest natural wonder upon M'ksakka. It looked like any other forest, save that the colors, beneath a gray-brown sky, seemed dull. The tree shapes, if you looked at them closely, were not quite right by Silistran standards. The opposite wall held some rather soothing Torth wall sculpture, four pieces that meshed the space between them, light green, into an integral part of the artists' conception. The cloud-toned wall held the door, with its red-glowing, oblong palm-lock. Across from it was the entry into the cabin's washroom, flanked by storage units, doored and drawered with the warm, dully burnished metal. That same metal floored and ceilinged the cabin, pedestaled the table and sleeping slabs securely in place. The covers and hanging that might be drawn for privacy around the slabs were a rich brown velvet.

I had gone and sat upon one of those slabs, despairing of ever learning to sleep so high off the ground, upon such a squishy, uncertain surface. The pills that had calmed my stomach were wearing off, as was the drug's attendant easing of my nerves. When, I wondered, would Khys reclaim me? I hugged myself, cold, frightened.

M'tras had not troubled me, but gone to his slab and gotten the ijiyr from its case. Trilling some tentative scales, he had been unsatisfied, clicking, his dark fingers running agilely upon the lucent keys. He placed it upon the table, gone to rummage in the storage drawers. When he returned with a tiny cube and a brace of tools, my curiosity had drawn me to the thing, lying silent, as long as my forearm, upon the metal. It was a keyboard and stringed instrument both, with a tiny and complex square of exposed wiring, under which were dials and switches.

He ministered to it, concentrated, intent. Thrice he touched a string, twice reset a red-switch.

"What is it?" I asked when at last he sank into the gray chair and pulled the instrument into his lap.

"An ijiyr. I think with it," he had said, sinking his chin to his chest, his right hand striking the first chord. I do not remember sitting down. Only the sound that took life and inhabited the air, do I recall. The scale he employed pivoted, metamorphosed, engaged. He joined modes in ways I had never before imagined. That level of sophistication in music is oft inaccessible. M'tras was eloquently, spiritually direct. Upon Silistra, a musician of such stature would have been high-chalded, a dharener among his kind, But he was not of Silistra. He was some kind of mechanized Slayer, about the business of Bipedal Federation. I felt momentary disgust, that they would waste such a talent, as I looked at him, his spirit slow returning from its outward fight, his jaw and neck aglitter with moisture.

"You should not do else but that," I said to him honestly.

He clicked, eyed me without turning. "I am no planner," he said cryptically. "I haven't the stamina to play that much." Then he did turn, put his elbows upon the table, resting his face in his palms. "I have this feeling you and I keep talking just to the left of each other—we think we're communicating, but we're misapprehending, and it's getting worse."

"The gulf of alternate conceptions." I nodded. "We have no contexually agreed upon symbols for what might be expressed—there are none in M'ksakkan, certainly." I recollected twice, since the hover had discharged us into the great gleaming tube leading inship, that such had occurred. Once he had asked me what type of restraint Khys's band put upon me. As my ears cracked clear, in the enclosure that had come to be around us, I had tried to answer. When the metal doors slid back, exposing a yellow, bright-lit corridor, he held up his hands in defeat, conceding that since we could not determine a common concept of either time or space, we could not sanely try to discuss events pertaining to them. Then, as the M'ksaddans who had manned the small craft left us, in that central hub, many-legended, which gave access to every level of the huge craft, he had asked me if I would watch the ship take sail. And I had refused, venting my distaste and discomfort at being inside a machine, my life dependent upon the perfect function of a number of tiny nonsentient devices.

"And how would you get across the void?" he had demanded, somehow hurt by what I said.

"By my will, if I so choose," I had snapped defensively.

And he had laughed derisively, saying that he would like to see it. I assured him he most probably would, stung by his disbelief. We kept, in common accord, a long silence that ended only with his music.

"What does your alternate conception dictate that I call you?" he said, poking his ijiyr. It whispered a tritone. He straight-fingered the strings, sliding down an octave. "Well-Keepress?" He tasted it, surely his preference, his tone rich with connotation.

"Dhareness, if you will. Or Keepress, though long past is that. Or crell, or saiisa, I care not. My given name, when I have borne it, has most times seemed sufficient." I thought of that time as crell when even my name had been stripped from me, at Chayin's hand. Near to five years it had been since I lay back upon the high couch of Astria to service whomsoever the moment dictated. "You may," I said in a much-softened tone, "if you choose, call me Estri."

"I would like that," he said, his voice a stream coursing gravel, his eyes upon his hand upon his instrument. "I would make this as pleasant as possible for you," he began hesitantly. "I haven't yet bound you, or hurt you, though you proved yourself deserving of both when you killed M'kinlin." He looked up from under his brows, head still bent. "I don't know if I believe all this supernormal stuff, but seeing you, I believe a lot more of what I've heard about Silistra."

This, I knew, was the moment. "I would be indebted to you if you would keep me from Dellin's hands," I said upon my softest breath, letting my fingers twist in my lap, biting my lip. "He has reason, perhaps, to abuse me." I trembled.

"Don't worry," he assured me gruffly, "this is my project. I have to be *able* to return you to your couch-mate." He grinned, that he had used the proper term. If one would seem less a danger, seek aid against some small threat.

"You must be sure of your safety, to wait upon him," I observed.

"If I left him there, knowing of us, I'd be a fool." He sighed, sat back in his chair. "Your friend Khys gave us a time limit within which to return you. My guess is, he's pretty busy right now, and that he'll wait. If he's got all that power, he'll take you when it's convenient. If not, I don't have to worry."

"What happens at the end of the time limit?"

"If we don't return you?" Softly, plucking tiny high notes. "He'll relieve us of our most distant moon, Niania." His eyes searched my face, his own expression uncommitted. "That moon is populous," he added. "The destruction that such an unprecedented occurrence would wreak is incalculable. There are the other two moons to consider. And upon M'ksakka, earthquake, flooding, possible volcanic eruption, axial realignment, violent turbulence—too much to conceive." I only sat and looked at him. I was not shocked, as he seemed to be. "Could he, realistically, do such a thing?"

"Before the battle of Amarsa, '695, even I could have done it." I raised my arms above my head, stretched, wriggling. "Of course he can. It is easy to just unmake something, especially something large. Harder it is to take a thing and change it, leaving all else around it unchanged. Did he choose to take such drastic measures, he would, I am sure, contain all side effects. Khys has a great reverence for life. He would not kill so many as you project."

M'tras shielded his eyes with a spread hand. "You think he'll do it, then," he said from under it. "You think he *can* do it."

"I have never known him to break his expressed word," I said solemnly. "Give me back to him now, and you might avoid all that will otherwise follow."

"I can't do that. I have great deal at stake. I need time."

"Khys has given you time," I whispered, wishing he had not done so.

"I don't *believe* any of this," he spat. "I can't believe it. I'm sitting here actually considering aborting a project because some back-space monarch threatened a not-much-saner local officer who is long overdue for a rest: 'Divest you of your smallest moon' was the quote I got! It's unreasonable to demand that we stretch our credibility that far." He rose and paced, stopped before me.

"What did your computer say?" I asked

"Can't get a sane answer out of it, either. The basic information we fed it has shown up faulty. I'm going to have to tear down the program and start again. All I want the bastard to do is negotiate! Behave like a civilized being, that's not too much to ask, is it?" He glowered down upon me, his hips jutting forward. "Is it?" he snarled.

"Losing," I said, craning my neck to meet his eyes, "is not in Khys's conception."

He looked at me with evident disgust. "I don't know who you people think you are," he said through curled lips, as the partition between the sleeping slabs began chiming. His boots slapping the steel floor, he hurried to it, palmed its face, and flopped down upon the velveted slab before it.

"What!" he snapped at the partition. "It better be good."

"Uh . . . we have collection on Dellin, dock fifty-seven minutes." The partition spoke in Maref's voice. "Systems check out fine. Your favorite toy thinks it needs alternate instructions, having aborted when the probability low you specified was reached. The boss wants to talk to you. We're rigged right to jump, and holding." I found myself halfway to the slab, stopped, crossed the distance.

"#67-a4-32. It's a Systems A reel I brought with me," said M'tras, his belt as jitter-lit as the partition, where a small replica of Maref's face chewed its lips.

"Wait. Got it," said Maref, pleased at whatever he saw offscreen. A blurred figure passed behind his head, was gone. M'tras patted the slab beside him. I perched there. "And where"—Maref grinned— "will that take us, if you don't mind me asking?"

"My place. Wide elipse. Orbit only," said M'tras, in the tone of one who will hear no argument, sprawling more widely upon the slab.

Maref raised one tiny eyebrow. "You'll clear it?"

"My presence clears it. But I'll call the lady and confirm, gladly."

"Fine with me," he said, miniature eyes roving. "Having any success?" They stopped upon me, well-replicated M'ksakkan blue.

"Some," M'tras said. "I'll let you know later."

"You ought to spend some of that charm on you-know-who. She's feeling resentful, usurped. This side trip won't help."

"It might save her unfortunately extended life," he said. "I'll call you back." And the face was gone, the screen panel retracted, replaced by what

I had first seen there: an attractive arrangement of geometric light forms.

M'tras stretched hugely, muscles sliding under the black, clinging uniform. I wished I had retained my seat at the table. What might lurk there, beneath the cloth? His appraising glance was unmistakable. I hoped he was not barbed, as are the men of Katrir, or overly acid-bearing, as are the Oguasti. He was from a world with which I was not familiar. What microorganisms might he bear within him?

"Does your race have a compatibility index number?" I said, as he continued to stare meaningfully at me.

".8888, if it eases your mind." He chuckled. "Come here."

It did ease me. Physiologically he was no danger, I presumed to think. "Hadn't you better finish your business?" I temporized, rising from the slab edge. Blurfast, his hand reached out, imprisoning my leg just above the knee. Cruelly he pressed the nerves there. I moaned, sank down upon the slab, my fingers unable to loose his grip. He took his hand away, tapped his belt, silent. I wriggled upon the plush, feeling the slide of silk against it. Rising, he slapped casually at the partition, just below the geometric display. A woman's face cleared upon the screen even as it moved forward. Behind her tawny head was deep blackness, and the stars. I shivered.

"It took you long enough," she said without preamble. Pale eyes avoided me with determination. Around her mouth were shadowy brackets of flesh. She twitched one. "I wish you'd tell me first, in the future, before you countermand my orders!"

"If I did that, you'd likely not have one. I'm concerned with timing. That means exactly the right move at precisely the right time. Not three seconds' error can I allow. You can't even talk that fast, let alone think. Do what I say, and don't bother me, and we'll be rid of each other soon enough. I don't like this any better than you."

"I ought to countermand, and you can walk home from M'ksakka!" she raged.

"If this project blows, there might not *be* a M'ksakka," said M'tras, squinting.

She snorted, twitched her mouth again. Into the screen came a many-ringed hand bearing a gemmed stylus. She pursed her lips upon it, gnawing contemplatively. I saw her seek her dignity, pull it around her like a palpable cloak. The stylus and the blunt-fingered, bejeweled hand bearing it, were withdrawn. Then it reappeared.

"You there!" she blared, pointing the tooth-marked instrument at me.

I flinched. M'tras covered his lower jaw with his hand.

"Yes?" I acknowledged, throwing my hair over my breasts.

"You killed one of my people. When they finish with you, you're mine. And I assure you, you're going to wish you were dead!" And the screen depicting her suddenly livid face went blank. I pushed my hair out of my eyes. My fingers rubbed my temples, and they were clammy. Behind the woman had been the stars. I had taken some comfort in this larger ship. It seemed solid, like a building upon stolid earth. But it was just a slightly bigger craft, floating precariously in the ever-dark.

"Now, don't get sick again," he growled, as I slumped forward, my arms pressed around me. "She can't touch you. It's nothing, don't cry." M'tras rubbed my back.

"Why don't you just imprison me? Do whatever you're going to do and get it done?" I gulped for air, shaking spasmodically. His hand upon me stilled.

"Sure, leave you alone. That's all I need. I'm

responsible for you. I acquired you. I have to hold onto you long enough to use you."

"How long can this go on?" I wailed it aloud, though softly, of a sudden anguished, so far from home, in a band of restraint. I pulled my legs up against me, my arms around my knees, soles on the slab.

He found some obscure humor in my discomfort, shaking his dark head, chuckling. Rising from the slab, he carefully divested himself of his blinking belt, wedging it securely between cushion and wall at the slab's head.

"It will be," he said as his clothing swelled a puddle of black upon the burnished floor, "about three days until we orbit my home world. 'This' can go on, doubtless, that long. Khys's ultimatum gives us twice that." He turned to face me: .8888 normal; wide-sprung ribs, short-coupled torso, ridged belly. His arms and legs were long, his neck and middle fully sheathed in muscle upon large thick bones. His sex seemed to the eye unremarkable, adequate, awake in its lair of black curling hair. I was not in the least interested. I have, I thought, been away from the couch too long. My tastes have become overly rarefied. There was nothing wrong with this man who stood before me. He at present held my life, he would at any moment have my use. And I was mind-locked. My body felt only numb and cold, though it could not, surely, have been the wind from the abyss. Not here, not under these circumstances; it could not have followed me here. I fought to find the present, my flesh, to stand upon the moment, peg the time, as befitted a Shaper's daughter.

The ache in my throat came first to me, and with it I bought delay. "Might I have water?" I petitioned him. He brought it from the partition dispenser. Sipping, I regarded him from under my hair.

"I've let you sample my skills," he said when I put the drink by. "Now I'd try yours." I could hear it in him, the fascination for my calling, for *what* I was, rather than who. I sighed, and rose, brushing by him, letting my trailing hand make the first touch. Only did I greet it, soft as a wirragaet's wing, as I put sufficient distance between us. Revealing the body before a man did I then review, in its most extended version, that I might in that time fan the fire low within me. M'tras, with instinctive etiquette, stood silent participant with me; he also rising, fists upon hips thrown aggressively forward. Deep below my navel, my heat hissed and grew. I turned full around, slowly.

⸳ He lifted me clear off the ground in mid-turn, and it was his face then that warned me. But truly, it was late. Customs differ. Morality is only a selective overlay. I saw the outline of his fist against my belly. I clamped my teeth upon my wrist, tasting my own blood. No M'ksakkan was M'tras.

"You're small in the hips," he said coldly, in the way of such a man after couching. I noted the beaded sweat upon his upper lip, the deep intake of his breath.

"Still, think you?" I said in Silistran. I lay upon my back, my hips turned, assessing my damages. He laughed, with clicks.

"Have you been long without?" I asked, still in my language.

"Long enough," he grunted, rolling onto his side. He leaned upon a crooked arm. His pulse beat hard in the veins that rode, webber-like, near the surface of his skin. His Silistran was hesitant, unaccented. "Something new, perhaps?" he postulated, over what he had done.

"My body knew it not," I admitted, not adding that I had seen Sereth do such a thing, to another man, upon a time.

He ran his free hand over my hip, under the dharen's chald. His fingers counted the goldrops. If he had wanted to shock me, to make me wary, respectful, he had succeeded. "How did you find it?" He smiled over the Silistran phrase.

"I would not add it to my practice, given the choice. But I am willing to admit I will never forget it." Lest he again strive to make himself singular in my sight, I spoke, praised his skill. Tentatively I moved my body, moaned, lay still.

"Please do not give me up to those others, M'tras." I reached out my hand, let my fingers trail his chest. I thought of the woman, and shivered. My kidneys ached. Slowly I drew up my knees. He seemed to be considering me. My skin cooled as his eyes ran along it. He clicked twice, stretched back for his belt, still wedged at the slab's head beneath rumpled plush. My fists clenched, I studied him, searching a clue to his temper in his alien ways.

He spread the belt on the velvet. Whistling softly, he slid a metal cover, exposing a narrow visual display, quiescent. I twisted toward it, so close my nose caught the machine breath's tang. Numbers flashed replies to his deft finger-questionings. Grunting his satisfaction, he stopped it, covered the twelve-digit face.

"M'tras," I whispered, daring a light touch upon his hirsute forearm, "please. I am long removed from wellwork. Such demands as yours tax me to my limit." Those black-ringed eyes met mine, calculating. A tiny tic flashed over his left lid.

"If it means something to you," he said, flat voiced, "I could arrange it. But we'll trade favor for favor. Deal?" Once more, it was M'ksakkan he spoke.

"Your will . . ." I acquiesced, releasing the breath I had held. Even the touch had been chancy, upon a man who fancied no aggression from a female. I waited for him to make his move. Stochastic improviser, he had named himself, and aural symbolist. What those words meant, I could only conjecture. He rolled onto his stomach. One of his hands remained upon his belt. His eyes did not leave me. I could get no sense of what lurked behind them. What was he? Surely more than he seemed, to have acquired me. He had gotten help, he had told Maref. I let my gaze catch his, across the belt.

"Why did you kill Liuma?" I asked him softly.

"The other woman? She was a witness. She shouldn't have been there."

"It did no good. Many might have witnessed what occurred, from the lakeside."

"I'm supposed to ask you the questions," he growled, propping himself up on an elbow. "How do you think he figured it out so fast?"

"Khys? Most probably, someone saw you. He might have had it from my mind. Often he has monitored me. Or he might have looked in upon the moment, having easily accessible perameters like the breaking of the window and Liuma'a death. Or he might simply have gotten his information from the sort. I doubt that there was more than one path leading here. Or—"

"Stop! That's all garbage," he snapped, scowling. He jabbed his belt alight. "Let's say nobody saw us. I was assured that no one would. I'm going to give myself that much credit. It didn't have to be us. Anyone with that much power has enemies." Pulling at his lip, he fell silent. Cautiously I gathered my legs under me. My thighs trembled with tetanus. Who, I wondered, had assured him? Who could give such assurance?

"That leaves," he said dourly, "him eavesdropping upon the whole escapade by means of your mind. I'm not willing to believe that. Or you think he might have reconstructed what happened. I can believe that, more easily, but not the way you put it. That last—that he would have known it was us because it *was* us—I can't find any way to state that in terms I can work with." He squinted at me, though the light had not brightened. Reaching out, he traced the band of restraint at my neck. "If the first is true, what assurance have I that he isn't 'monitoring' us now?"

"None," I said. "He might be."

He grinned. I met his humor solemn-eyed. A shiver ran perceptibly over his flesh. "I'm going to start over. Do you know anything about Silistran politics?"

"You asked me that before," I reminded him. His flat palm stopped in mid-strike, the wind of it buffeting my cheek. "No." I cowered, startled. "Not much, anyway."

"That's better," he said. "Now tell me how a bunch of anachronistic savages managed to destroy two brand-new, unmentionably expensive M-class Aggressives. I know you were involved." His scowl, brought ominously close, was terrifying.

"At the battle of Amarsa, you mean? It was only a peripheral effect. The energy I was using to fight Raet as Uritheria threw a whole section of Silistra out of sequential time—" And he did slap me resoundingly. I put my hand to my stinging cheek.

"Try again," he spat, thrusting his face close once more. The veins at his temple pulsed his outrage. "What caused the destruction of those ships?"

"Please, I have told you the truth," I whimpered. "Would you make me lie?"

A long time he questioned me, over and over again the same words. And I answered him as best I could, trying to keep my answers consistent. But he wanted other knowledge than the truths I had for him. Unaccepting of my replies, he sought for those he had preconceived. My throat was dry and sore and my mind spinning when he finally desisted, truimphant at having extracted from me an admission that the old weapons of prehistoric Silistran wars still existed.

"Somewhere"—I had stumbled over my tongue my eagerness to please him—"they are, in the hides. But they are old, so old, and long untended. It is not our custom to cherish such things. Thousands of years they have lain there. I would doubt that any are still functional." Huddled opposite him, I fell silent. I could retreat no farther, my back already pressed against the wall that spawned the slab. I thought of Chayin's threat to exhume those weapons, when the M'ksakkans tried to treat with the Parset Lands.

"That," he said, crouched menacingly above me, "makes more sense." His bearing blared his triumph, that he had found truth that suited his preconception. "That's the whole key to it, isn't it! Old weapons, from a more sophisticated culture." He grinned widely. "I'd be willing to bet that some of them are still functional," he mimicked nastily. "Functional enough to blow a hole in the B.F. budget, that's sure."

I lowered my gaze to the brown velvet of the slab. My fingers made light strips running against the nap. Let him, by his own will, be misinformed. When Khys blasted his M'ksakkan moon from time and space, M'tras would learn.

"Whatever the source," I offered, hesitant, "would it not serve you to avoid a confrontation with weapons against which you have no defense? Return me to the dharen. I have some little influence." I lied then, but he could not know it. "I will see to it that there are no reprisals."

"No chance," he grunted. "As close as I can, I'm going to stick to my first conception. I'm going to hold you. He'll deal. If he could have just snatched you, he would have done so by now. If he were sure, he would've arrested Dellin." he added, crossing his legs under him. He watched me attentively, waiting. I only stared.

"What are you thinking?" he demanded.

"That you had better ask these questions of your friend the belt. Its answers suit you better than mine. But you are a fool to so shortchange the dharen. He will, when it suits him, do exactly as he wishes with all of us." I wondered why I bothered, rubbing my bruised cheek. Shifting off one aching thigh, I was reminded of the coarseness with which he had set about demoralizing me. "I was"—I raised my eyes to him, chin high—"once, very powerful. Suspend for a moment your disbelief. Grant me my blood right. It was I, not Khys, whose power destroyed your ships, offhandly, while about a much greater undertaking. With gods did I contend. My father is greatest among the Shapers, those who created this apparent time and space in which we live. And I fell to Khys. Totally and completely did he denude me of my strengths, until I could be taken by even the likes of you. That fact alone should warn you." I broke off, for he no longer listened. His belt, upon his lap, spoke in its strange language. He sat very still, attentive. After a time he straightened up, pulled spread fingers through his black hair. His discontent lay upon him like a sneer.

"Get dressed," he snapped, rising to take his own orders.

Obediently I wrapped my silk short-length about me. It seemed skimpy, insufficient covering for this place. It was quickly done, and I stood, uncertain, awaiting him as he layer by layer donned his fitted gear. When all that could be seen of his flesh was above the neck and below the wrist, I ventured to ask it.

"Is it a point of economics that concerns you? Is

it recompense for what you lost at our hands that brought you to this foolhardy action?"

"Partly," he grunted, fastening his belt over his hips.

"Then you and I could resolve between us all differences, peacefully," I blurted, excited with the simplicity of the idea.

"How?" He disbelieved, fists resting on his black-clothed hips. A surreptitious finger set his belt whirling. It hummed softly, content to be in service to its master.

"I will leave with you my chald. One could buy a yra of such ships with its worth." I grinned at him, expecting approbation.

He came and ran his hands over it, nestled against the white and silver silk at my waist. "I didn't think it was real," he muttered. Then he clicked, raising his eyes to mine. "A man could, with that much gol, buy an A-systems computer, even." His fingers twisted in the strands, relaxed. But his body was stiff, his breath moving shallowly in his chest. I knew he considered it. "I can't do that," he said, pushing me away. "Lives were spent. Even that much wealth can't replace them."

"And spending more lives will? A moon full of lives, perhaps? If I were you, I would warn those who dwell upon that sphere that they may flee the dharen's wrath." I turned my back to him, tense, waiting for a blow that did not fall.

"I've done that," he said, still subdued, as I made my way to the slab upon limbs that shook despite my best efforts. There I crawled to the corner, faced him from its comforting security. He only watched me, a bemused expression upon him. I knew that he would click his tongue a second before I heard the sharp tone.

"What do you want, then, from Khys?" I asked, the distance between us emboldening me.

"I want," he said in a flat, cold voice, "the man

who killed Mossenen. I want recomprense in se-
rum for every man lost along with those ships; I
want their weight in drugs. The only replacement
fitting for their lives is the gift of life." I hardly
heard the last. Sereth's life, he would demand. Khys
would never cede it. And if it came to a trade, I
would give mine gladly rather than see such an
occurrence.

"Khys will never agree," I hissed, and the
vehemence of my tone drove his dark brows down
over his eyes. With measured steps he approached
me.

"He will. Or you'll bear the whole weight of our
displeasure. Mossenen was the most-loved adjuster
ever to rule M'ksakka. We can't have your killers
picking us off at their leisure. It's principle. We let
him get away with this, we might as well hand him
the Bipedal Federate Group."

"If you—" Chiming interrupted me. I bit my lip,
swallowing what I would have said. It occurred to
me, as he slapped the partition to life, that he
might not know whom he sought, who had killed
the M'ksakkan official. And I had almost enlight-
ened him.

Revealed upon the screen was Maref, an infin-
itesimal muscle jumping in his miniature jaw.
"Dellin's on his way down there. There was no
stopping him." His tone was apologetic, his palms
raised to the screen.

"That's nice," said M'tras dryly. "What are you
doing up there, playing with each other? Get three
men down here. I want them waiting outside the
door!" He slapped the screen away, growling deep
in his throat. As he crossed to his strange instrument and sank with it in his lap into the green
chair, I could not help but remember a thing Khys
had said, when first we stood before him, Chayin,
Sereth, and I, and he derided us. Of Sereth he had
spoken his disquiet, that such a seemingly talentless

one had come to stand before him, and in the
company of such "blood" as was possessed by the
cahndor of Nemar and me. Later, Khys had said
that when a man comes forcibly into your circle
by means of outstanding accomplishment, one cannot gainsay his right to be there, however much
his very presence might alter some cherished
preconception. Thus, I reasoned, it must be with
this alien, M'tras. His music rolled and thundered,
the anger in it prodding my adrenals. Cold it was,
a summoning from the abyss. Bass clef only, of
that score that holds the worlds aligned, did M'tras
call forth from his stringed machine. His head was
down. His lips upon occasion moved, mouthing
the sounds his fingers made. His work-set face
glittered like Khys's seal upon by breast.

He palmed his strings to jarring quiet as the
door panel blinked. The partition upheld the palm-
lock, chiming. I found myself pressed back into the
corner, thinking of what the three of us had done
to Dellin that time we sought Celendra. I pulled
the velvet up around me, dragging it loose from
the slab foot.

M'tras was looking at me. The door chimed
again. He turned away and touched his waist. The
door slid aside. Dellin, leaning there in northern
leathers and cloak, short-sworded, chalded, straightened up slowly. His eyes were bleak. He had still, I
noted as he crossed the keep, ignoring M'tras, the
limp I had seen upon him in Khys's audience
chamber. He had, I thought, cringing back, velvet
cover crushed in my fists, lost the weight he had
carried excessive in '695. M'tras merely turned his
chair upon its pedestal, that he might observe. He
ran a thumb over his lower lip. Then I could not
see him; Dellin's bulk obscured all else.

"Estri!" His knees were upon the slab, those
hand reaching out toward me. "Are you hurt? By
the gods of my mother, I assure you, I had no hand

in this." He grabbed me up in his arms, held me.
Shocked, I was limp against his sweet-smelling
circlet armor. He lifted me from the slab, placing
my feet upon the floor.

At arm's length he held me. In Silistran he had
spoken. I answered him the same.

"Presti, m'it tennit, Liaison," I replied. "I am
well enough." His fingers dug my shoulders. "Among
these artifacts of your culture, Khaf-Re, think you
the both of us seem out of place?" His fingers
loosened, dropped away to his chald. I had marked
it augmented. Besides the Slayer's chain, he bore
that of threxman and one gold strand, that of birthing fulfilled. I caught his troubled glance, made a
sign that I knew he knew. M'tras watched, per-
plexed, as Dellin pulled me against him.

"Estri, there is no use in it," he whispered, gain-
saying the Slayer's sign I had given. "Do not ask
me to go against my own people. I have seen the
dharen. You need no more help. Let me salvage
what I may," he continued, in thick dialectic
Arletian. "I had thought you deprived of self. I saw
you once, and you knew me not. I had sniffed such
seemings upon the breeze, but the Weathers called
it Khys's hand." I pushed back, grinning, to meet
his grim smile. Let M'tras decipher that with his
tape-learned Silistran.

"Aforetime," I agreed solemnly, "such was the
case. Yet I recall the moment, and even that I
knew you not. We ride the crux wind again, you
and I."

"And you with the dharen's seal upon your skin,"
slurred Dellin.

"That's enough," snapped M'tras. "Dellin, sit here.
Now! You"—he pointed at me—"over here on the
floor where I can watch you." The M'ksakkan
mechanic's eyes roved Dellin as the larger man
obeyed him. "Only one out of fifty go native," he

said, sardonic. I knelt before him, realizing, only after the fact, that I sat as Khys had trained me.

Dellin, in his trail gear, shifted uncomfortably. "I had to get to Port Astrin," he said in M'ksakkan. "I had to get through the streets, into the port."

"You could have stayed," said M'tras, voice edged like honed stra.

Dellin cursed in M'ksakkan. M'tras leaned back in his sky-green chair. "It's me he'd abuse, not you," M'tras said, eyes narrowed, "She seemed to think," he remarked to Dellin, "you'd show me a little Silistran woman-beating if I let him in here. I'm disappointed." Together they looked little alike. Only their coloring was similar.

"If anything happens to her, none of us are safe!" said Dellin loudly, leaning forward upon the burnished table. His short sword clanked.

"That Khys really put a scare into you, didn't he?" said M'tras, stretching out his legs. One hand played, below Dellin's line of sight, upon his wakened belt.

"Look at me, M'tras," said Dellin. M'tras did so, as if bestowing great favor.

"I am telling you, it's all real! They do affect probability. According to their skills, they do control the future. I'm not crazy. You are. Send her back to him. He is inestimably dangerous. Look at her, if you don't believe me!"

M'tras looked at me raised an eyebrow. Then he shrugged and turned back to Dellin. "I see her. I've got her. He doesn't. Now, if you'd stayed down there, you might have been able to help. You wanted, you said, out. Well, you're out. When the ride is over, you're going to have to face your uncle. You're confined to three deck until that time."

"You can't . . ." Dellin scowled, straight brows drawn.

"I could confine your uncle on this ship. I have

a personal override. I just wanted to see some Silistran discipline. I'm not going to see it, and I'm not interested in anything you've got to say. File a report, if you must. You have an A-systems input in your cabin. Make it to my attention. Maybe I'll read it. Now, get out!"

Dellin, his face as pale as the hand strangling his hilt, rose wordless and limped to the door. His slap upon the palm lock was loud in the silence. M'tras sat with lowered head until the door slid again across the entrance. Then he touched his belt, and the palm-lock turned from red to amber. We would not, while it glowed that color, be disturbed. I moved to rise off the metal floor. M'tras, with a sharp signal, stilled me. I sank back upon my heels, my face raised to him, as he removed his belt, stretched it upon his lap.

Thinking he had forgotten me, I again made to rise. "No!" he snapped. I shrugged, sitting back. The burnished metal was warm. It seemed to vibrate.

Something in his face as he played with his machine gave warning. I wondered what his world might be like, what place would spawn such a man.

"On my world," he said, as if he had read me, "we don't put that much store by females. I still don't see what's so special about you, except that fancy brand."

"I had gathered that much," I said to him, making a hollow for my silked rump between my heels. I could feel the rough callus snag the silk.

"You'll gather more," he promised, eyes heavy-lidded. "But its time for me to gather what I can. Dellin believes everything he said." He tapped the readout of his belt, as if the machine upheld him. "I'm going to try to be open-minded about this. Do something uncanny. Show me you're more than King What's-his-name's favorite slave."

"I cannot. You know it. I wear Khys's band of restraint."

"How do I know it's not just another fancy collar?"

"Try and remove it," I suggested.

He shrugged. "It's bad manners to take a collar off a woman if you aren't going to keep her." His gaze, openly hostile, stripped me. I found I clutched my arms about my waist. "He's trained you well," he remarked, supercilious, warning. I straightened up, my plams on my thigh. "What did Dellin say to you?" So abruptly did he snap his question, I flinched, my throat gone dry.

I told him, all but the meaning of the sign, lest I embroil Dellin in my troubles. As was his custom, he asked the same things of me repeatedly, comparing the results. I considered what he had said of women, and etiquette as regards to collars, and the fact that he still held me kneeling before him.

"Please," I petitioned him, "let me rise." My knees ached, my calves were run through with hot needles.

He snorted softly through his nose. "You stay there. I'm not that raw that I don't know the difference between free women and whatever they call it on your planet." His belt let out a audible beep. He attended it, his mood lightening perceptibly. "And confirmed," he grunted, grinning. "We now have"—he smiled unkindly—"a tentative fix on every underground depository on Silistra. Look at me!"

Uncomprehending, I raised my head. My back ached intolerably. "Why tell me?"

M'tras leaned forward, buckling the belt again around him. "Because," he said, upon a cadence, "if your master is monitoring you, I want him to know. If we don't get some response from him fast, we're going to blast a few holes in your planet's precious crust. And some of those underground installations seem to be right below heavily populated areas." His threat was potent. I though of Well Arlet, beneath which lay hide bast. And the Well Astria, which lay less than seventy neras from hide diet. Intently did M'tras' pale eyes study me. "You seem a little taken aback. Perchance you don't believe all you aver. Doubtful, are you, that the dharen will get my message?"

"I cannot know it." I reverted, in my perplexity, to Silistran. His hand darted out to encircle my throat. By that grip he pulled me to him, until I knelt between his spread legs, my shoulders pinned by his thighs.

"But you believe it," he accused. He reached under the table. When his hand returned, it cupped the red-eyed death cube. The whole time Dellin had been present, M'tras had not moved from the table. I had thought him brave, indolent. He had been, actually, cautious. "I have your readout. Something is affecting the electrolytic balance of your body fluids. Possibly that band, which even A system can't analyze. " His knees pressed my shoulders. In his hand, lightly juggled, was the death cube.

"I do not take your meaning," I said.

"Anything"—he sighed—"that affects such electrolytic balances affects the stimulus response times of sensory receptors. Within you is a complex set of electrochemical rectifiction and negative resistance devices, the carriers of which are ions— sodium and potassium. The band seems to be interfering with the permeability of certain membranes, membranes that are the junctions of these devices, those that separate fluid-bearing tissues. Your sensory receptors, unable to function normally, cannot sufficiently stress these membranes—change their permeability. Thus the positive ion flow from one fluid to another, which should result in a specifically ranging change of charge in fluid, has been drastically and specifically impaired."

"I am lost. What means this?"

"I'm not sure yet. Receptor cells in sensory neurals and their associated membranes—differential membranes, through which ions flow more readily in one direction than another—are remarkably similar for all senses, and should, when functioning normally, produce similarity in the characteristic stimulus times. The intensity of stimulus is a function of the number of pulses in the pulse train carried along nerve fibers to the brain. The imput pulse to the circuit is the result of some change in a sensor. In the case of, say, hearing, it's a change in stress upon the hairs along the basilar membrane in the cochlea. If this selective masking of imput were affecting your hearing you'd be tone deaf, as well as intensity-impaired. But the effect, obtusely selective, is not impairing your hearing. What it is affecting, I don't know, unless it's the transduction of energy.... Wait a minute." He barked a laugh, and consulted his belt.

When he looked up, his eyes were very bright.

"Do you know anything about the kinetics of a photoreaction cycle?"

"No."

"Well, A systems says the band is acting as an uncoupler, selectively deprotonating. An uncoupler allows electron transport to proceed, but in effect disconnects it from phosphorylation. In a sense, you're photosynthesizing, or were before they put the band on you. More specifically, that melaninlike pigment that causes your skin to glow is photoreactive under the aegis of a chromoprotein that absorbs at much longer wavelengths than those of the visual spectrum. It's not phototaxic, but powers a metabolic function that we call proton-plumping. Your skin can convert light energy into an electrochemical gradient—or could if that uncoupler weren't around your neck. We've long known that an organism lacking chlorophyll can capture and convert light energy and use it to drive metabolic processes; the Coryf-dennen do it exclusively, using a chromoprotein closely related to visual pigment in animals."

I nodded; I had met one Coryf-denne. They do not eat, neither do they sleep, and their rough skin glows so bright that one cannot look upon them without discomfort.

"We have also long been aware that light can power the uptake of energy by envelopes of sodium and potassium ions and of amino acids independent of the high-energy bonds of adenosine triphosphate, by some thought to be the primary energy carrier of living cells."

I shook my head, but it did not help. The dizziness that oft assails me when faced with making sense out of such concepts danced all around me.

"So," he said, triumphant, "you are being physiologically constrained by this all-sense blanketing. But from what?"

"My hearing is fine," I said.

"That's the point. Where is this energy you aren't receiving supposed to go? What I know is that the band is impairing the conversion into free energy of an electrochemical protein gradient of the chemical free energy of light or of some oxidizable substrate; that the band disconnects you, so to speak, from photoreaction and energy-bond conversion, deprotonates this light-driven proton pump in a sort of attenuation of the energy-transducing mechanism itself. And it's not directed at any one system I'm set up to scan. It impinges upon all senses, in a consonance that is most distressing, without any effect on your five senses. They are functioning exquisitely, acutely, despite the field effect, or whatever it is, of the band." He stopped, clicking, exasperated by what he did not see upon my face.

"I think I understand," I said. And I did. "It is as I have told you. Those skills with which you will not credit me are those you have found impaired. Sensing is no separate organ, but an all-pervasive network, the primal receptors." I spoke it softly that he might not strike me for speaking of what he would not hear.

He shifted. His left knee ceased its pressure upon me. One eyebrow descended to meet the frost of his gaze. I would have scrambled from him. I dared not.

"What," he demanded cautiously, "exactly, could you do, without such constraint?"

"Move my flesh from this place to anywhere I chose. Hear and see within my mind. Marshal what forces I chose from the energies about me. Often are such bands used upon wayward forereaders and dhareners; they keep the wearer reduced to five senses, incapable of escape in time or space. The worst of it is the silence." I heard the thickness in my voice. Fearful, from between his thighs I peered up at him. He had asked, but he had struck me before at such answers.

"But you could exit this ship, in the same manner as Khys entered Dellin's complex, if you didn't wear it?"

"Long since, I would have done so," I affirmed.

M'tras, nodding, made entry into his belt once again. So close, I could see the whirling layers of prenumbers at their deciding. I watched it think, blink, glow with its chosen wisdom. He leaned down, neck craned, and considered it. Shaking his head, he laughed low. As he sat back, his body was fight-tense.

Mine, shoulders entrapped by his thighs, went tight also. For in the telling, I had seen a thing— that Khys could not just drag me flesh to him, as he might have, through the plane worlds, had I not borne the obdurante, warm band at my throat. My fingers twitched, found their way between his clamping thighs to run its vibrating curve. Alone I was, in space, hurtling upon sails of gold. Where?

"Estri," he said, slurring his tone a half-step, his hand under my chin. I liked not those storm-morn eyes, cold as Opirian nights. I tried to turn my head. His thumb pressed down upon my chin, three fingers up into the soft tenderness behind and beneath. "You just might be right." His hand toyed again with the incinerating cube.

I shivered before him. "How long," I asked faintly, "have we been off Silistra?"

"Six hours, fifteen minutes," he said, of his own knowledge. An hour is about twenty-one twenty-seconds of an enth, the Silistran twenty-eight-enth day being only fory minutes shy the B.F. Standard day of thirty hours. It was near moon's meal upon Silistra. The moon would be up, over the Lake of Horns. I wondered what had come to pass this day, Brinar second sixth. Of Chayin I thought, tasting his pain, and Sereth, with whom he had lain whilst this strange creature abducted me. And Khys? Had they come and told him, in his meeting while he was yet filling the vacancy of the southeast corner? Whom had he chosen for these lands, to oversee Dritira, Stra, and Galesh?

"Why?" he asked me, shaking my shoulder.

I only regarded him. Could he not see what loss I mourned, what loss my world was to me? His fingers fell to the dharen's mark, swirled upon it.

"Why did you ask the time?" he demanded in a voice that scraped bone. How, I wondered, would he have treated me, were he not planning to return me to Khys? His hand slid about my throat, longing. I saw him restrain himself, whatever violence crossed his mind. He shook my head about savagely.

"I am only hungry," I choked.

"I have no intention of feeding you until we've finished our little talk. How and why was the band put upon you in the first place?" I marked him disquieted. He believed the artifactual evidence upon me. His machine had spoken for my truth. M'tras clicked, shifted. I took comfort in his unease.

"Did not he from whom you obtained aid explain that to you?" I dared.

"Don't push me." His fingertips played a syncopated pattern upon my throat.

"It is rather complex, what you ask." I sighed. "As to how it is done—it is simply done. When Khys had me brought before him, I was much wounded. He merely put me in flesh lock and slipped it about my neck. He made me hold up my hair while he did it."

"What's flesh lock?" he rejoined, eyes narrowed.

"You would surely be angered if I tried to explain it. The band is fastened about the neck of the victim by he to whom it is keyed. It must be removed by that same hand. Not even the high chadler, who has charge of the bands until they are keyed, can remove them." My eyes begged his, that I might be silent.

"Where do they come from?"

"Normally they are produced by the dharen's council. One puts a band of restraint upon a highly skilled person only, one who may not be bound otherwise. They are little used. I had never heard of them upon Silistra until I was taken to the Lake of Horns."

"You have not told me why you wear it," he prodded, implacable. I shifted upon icy limbs between his legs. I did not want to speak to him of my diminishment, my shame. I did not want to think of what I had been—so highly skilled, so arrogant, so foolish. His hand twisted in my hair. By it he pulled me closer.

"I abrogated, in hauteur, my chaldra. I became couch-mate of a chaldless outlaw. We caused a great deal of bloodshed, hearkening to the law within. Khys did not deal harshly with us. He left us our lives. He wanted a child from me. I would not give it. He stripped me of my memories, that I might not object. When it was done, I did not object, but asked for his seed." Blinking back tears, I regarded him. His face was emotionless. His grip upon my hair relaxed. I sank back, resting on my heels.

"How did he get you to put the band on you, if you were, as you put it, so highly skilled?" I thought him further disquieted. His brows had both descended. I had been reminded, relating what had occurred, of the damage done to me. Could I ever, I wailed silently, be again what I had been before Amarsa, '695, what I had been with Sereth, upon Mount Opir? Even might I regain such skills as I had been pleased to employ when I found myself in the Parset Desert? I doubted it. I dropped my eyes to M'tras' belt. Doubtless I, too, would need such a machine to think for me, to direct me as to what owkahen had in store, and how to meet it. He cuffed my head to one side, against his thigh. I let it lie there, slumping against him.

"How did he acquire me?. He hested it. He brought his will into the time. He waited, and when the moment matched his sensing, he sent men to fetch us. I had fallen unconscious. I awoke in the hands of his minions." Without my power, and without most of my sensing, I recalled. "We were brought before him. He tried and sentenced us as suited him. He, as I just told you, put the band upon me. The rest also I have told you." From my slanted viewpoint, his face seemed gray, alien, forbidding. I raised my head, held it straight. His hand freed my hair, touched his eyes, rubbed there.

"Sit as you wish," he said, releasing me totally. I did not try to rise. I would not have been able.

By my arms I pushed myself backward and slid my legs out and around. I could not feel them. In a few moments, I knew, I would long for this state. They were clumsy, as if another owned them.

"What are you thinking?" he demanded, rising. He stretched, his hands at the small of his black-clothed back. His boot heels thudded on the metal as he went and stood before the real-seeming Western Forest, truly upon far M'ksakka. We were not going, I knew, to M'ksakka. "If you want to eat, you had better be responsive," he warned, turning to face me, arms crossed above his wakened belt.

"That we are not going to M'ksakka. I wondered where we were bound. Then how long that might take. They I took thought of you, and your machine-symbiote. Does it speak to the ship's computer?" I rubbed my calves, slapped them. The pain was begining.

"This ship has an A-systems unit, yes. I couldn't wait for relay. M'ksakkan devices are nowhere as sophisticated. The brain that runs this ship is M'ksakkan. The A-systems unit we carry is as advanced in comparison as I am to my cave-dwelling ancestors." Looking at him, I wondered if he knew how close he was to those of whom he spoke. The burn-tingle had reached my ankles. Water-rush presaged it in my calves. My knees were still frozen. I recollected what Khys's Estri, without, comprehension, had read of the dharen's new writings. He had brought forth a volume containing odd references and analogies to computers, accompanied by charts. In it he had put forward the belief that hesting is a survival characteristic in all races, that to some degree, oft under the control of the deeper conscious, all men hest. How these hests are experienced, Khys postulated, is greatly affected by conditioning and conception. Furthermore, he affirmed, and I do believe him, that in a mechanistic culture where survival is removed

from the individual's control, the hesting skills may
turn and prey upon the experiential reality of the
conscious mind—may become a tool of the powerful and divided selves, the inimical, fragmented, constrained remnants of the law within so doggedly
supressed by such as M'ksakkans. He had called it
Hesting: The Primal Perogative, and in it he had
adjured the reader to study will and responsibility,
and take thought as to the get of one's actions. The
gift of owkahen did Khys offer in such language as
might appeal to a man like M'tras. I lowered my
head, fastening my gaze upon my quivering thigh.
Perhaps Khys would spend me, if the gain were high
enough.

M'tras came to me with a tray: yellow, birthed
of the automated partition. Such food as was upon
it was not unfamiliar to me. I had been a year in
couchbond to the Liaison First when that one was
named M'lennin. Often had I myself punched up
similar meals in the Liaison's automated keep.
Jaundiced plate and cup and bowl held jeri, a fruited
intoxicant drink; a synthetic meat-textured loaf,
steaming; some round green vegetable the name of
which escapes me; and a sweet dessert, siw-es-ar,
which I abhorred. Next to me on the steel plating
he set it, and took his own to the table. I looked at
it, resting on that metal the color of Khys's hair.
The enormity of my difficulties rushed in upon
me. Tears filled my eyes. I turned my body. The
cost in pain was high, but worth it. I did not want
M'tras to see my distress. With blurred vision I
reached the tray close. I ate off it, bites often salted
with the crying that would not stop. I thought of
proton pumps and sodium ions and bit my lips,
that my mouth not speak out upon his overvaluing
of these minusculities, and his failure to see through
them and comprehend the whole. And the weight
of those thoughts dragged me deeper into tears,

like some clandestine undertow. My shoulders, despite my best efforts, betrayed me to him with their shaking.

I did not hear his approach, but only felt his hand rubbing my back. He bade me cease, but softly. It took a time for me to regain control. Dragging my hair from under his hand, I pulled it veillike about my face. Sniffling. I took the absorbent fax he proffered and wiped my cheeks dry.

"What brought that on?" he asked, still crouched by my side.

"You," I said miserably. "You and your machine. What need have you for it? Does it think for you? Surely no machine is more than the mind that conceived it. Are such beasts of metal and plastic the ruling species upon your planet, as they are on M'ksakka? It is said that the ruling species upon a planet proliferates a suitable environment to its needs. Upon M'ksakka, the Western Forest is vestigal, the last trace of a time when another race ruled there, one that breathed air and depended upon nature for its survival. No longer, I have heard, can M'ksakkans breathe their own air without aid from that planet's ruling species: the machine. Is it so upon your world? Are you, also, in bondage to the artifact, crell to your creations? If so, I beg you, do not take me there. Of all things, I fear such constraint the most. I will surely die, without the sun and the grass and the wind and the company of those creatures that thrive upon nature." My hand, when I had finished, went to my mouth, as if, after the fact, it could prevent those words' escape.

M'tras' storm was no longer contained by his eyes. His whole face scudded dark, ominous. The rage that issued forth from his mouth snapped and roared like shifting earth, each indecipherable curse shaking me as gusts pummel yearling trees immured on a hill crest thunderstruck. But that thunder, still riding his alien tongue, brought no lightning trailing behind, but rather took up a plagel cadence; became righteous, spirit-speaking. M'tras, sure in his truths, found need to express them in Standard, most exact and somber of tongues. And I, knowing that there is no one truth, did not then mark (nor do I now recollect) the moment at which his speech became intelligible by virtue of words; for through my band of restraint and across the gulf of context his meaning had already leaped, that we two take up that ongoing battle between form and substance, between man artifactual and woman ineffable, between innovation and replication.

Thus do I recall them, those words spoken in moments transformed, by some alchemy agreeable to us both, from the interrogation by captor of captive into that interchange (which never began and shows no sign of ending) between the proponents of physical and metaphysical:

"My little primitivist, how is it that you set youself up to adjudge a culture of which you know nothing, a context about which you may be sure of only one thing: that it is other than your own? It is said of your people that they seek the law within. Where is it written, upon those books, that one idea is good and another evil, that an idea in seed, when nurtured by these five fingers and given spatial reality that it be numbered among the items of creation, becomes tainted, while another, swathed in numinosity and wraithlike for lack of palpable existence, does not?"

"The ideas of our mechanists sent the remnants of a world scurrying into burrows, there to wait interminably for the fruits of their methodical poisoning of air and sea to disperse," I pointed out.

"And so you say to a man: this is too dangerous, this you must not do. But you allow the sword, and pharmacology, and all that suits you, though the dangers of each are as great as that of a hand communicator or a death cube. Is a man less dead when killed by a blade of stra?'' His visage, jutting forward aggressively, drew from my mouth the admission that a man, killed, was as dead by aegis of knife or limb as by incineration; but I felt compelled to add that one man so armed could not destroy a city, nor a forest, nor a mountain.

M'tras took a moment before he replied: "Then ban fire, for with it city and forest might fall by way of a single well-placed torch, and even a mountain be scoured bare of all life she hosts. It is held by you an ineluctable truth that technology destroys, and yet it is ideology, morality, and all the cogitations which you hold so dear and elevated that bent the metal of inventor's alchemy to the desecration of nature you so loudly decry. It is not truth of which it is said: 'Herein lies destruction,' but man's use of it. The world which spawned me, like all others, took the trial of fire: that of subjugation, by *means* mechanistic, of greed overwhelming and lust blind to tomorrow. It is said by us that the true test of spirit lies therein, that only when man waxes godlike, when he consigns into his brothers' hands the means for elevation or destruction of his own civilization, does he learn the validity of the conglomerate of survival decisions called morality that his world has constructed.'' His dark hands, whose fingers might within their own sum of days smite my beloved Astria from afar, twisted together, whitened, then released. Staring at those digits, it came to me that he was in a sense right, that it is not the product of their labor that destroys, but the intent of the mind that directs them.

"Khys,'' I offered, taken aback with sudden enlightenment, "must have considered these things, else why did he allow commerce with the star worlds to commence, and bring to us once again the temptations of such power?''

M'tras smiled. "Temptations, are they? I think,

instead, a road to growth upon which man either becomes wise or perishes by his own folly. Unlike M'ksakka, we chose not to befoul the nest of our descendants that the progenitors' coffers overflow with wealth. Nor did we, as upon Silistra, raze to the ground those who believed differently than we, deeming even the obliteration of plant and beast meet price, that an idea offensive to our minds be no longer promulgated by men who, more by their samenesses than their differences, loomed iniquitous in our judges' sight. Upon my world it is said that we have three billion religions, and of philosophies an equal number; that of the total sum of men living thereupon. And to those of us most insightful it remains an eternal source of wonder that two may speak together from out of each one's singular reality, and that from out of these cross-indexed similitudes of meaning, understanding is birthed and communion upon ideas achieved. Against all odds of logic and reason, man speaks with his brother, and that brother hears." Those hands that might at their whim reduce every hide upon Silistra to poisoned ash stroked his jaw, awaiting my rejoinder.

But I was struck cold and cautious, asudden aware of the dangerous ground upon which I trod. How wholeheartedly might anyone, in my place, have debated with his jailer? I shook my head, my eyes lowered. I would not chance speaking to him of relevance, nor of the low esteem in which I held logic and what preferences one man will label "reason," and another "irrationality."

And so, he chose to continue: "My home is magnificent. You will not see it. You have no more place there than one of your mutated carnivores in the void, nor would you survive even as long. But know you: there is no sphere I have seen among the M'ksakkan worlds as green, no range of climate as exulting to flesh and spirit, no world anywhere among the civilized stars that boasts the fecundity of Yhrillia. Is is said of her that He practiced upon the firmament, and perfected upon her bosom. But notwithstanding, none of yours will ever discern that truth; we open not our doors to this universal rabble of which you are a part. With you and these M'ksakkans in my company, even I would not be allowed to land." And this last was finally spoken in M'ksakkan: the converse was ended, that temporary immunity he had bestowed upon me perceptibly revoked. And as he pulled about him yet another alien tongue, he seemed to cast away his righteousness, or to secrete it again in that pocket we all construct to keep our selves sacrosanct, lest they be tarnished by the diverse oils come from a mulitude of fingering strangers.

But I had seen; even banded, I did not fail to mark him.

"Then why," I injected into that demanding silence, "approach Yhrillia at all?"

"I want to let the A consult with cohort," he informed me brusquely. "I want also to make sure that I live through this. The ship can negotiate for M'ksakka from wherever I choose. I can make this journey and be back orbiting Silistra in quicker time than you might suppose, with the ship on an A-systems slave basis."

"I did not know machines took slaves," I said, moving my left leg, which now only ached. Experimentally I stretched it out in front of me, straight, pointing my toes. "Could you not just call this other machine?"

"I can't use their communications systems for A to A. It's too complex to explain. And it would be too dangerous to prematurely update their system so that I could use it."

I nodded. Once we had sent a message to M'ksakka, Sereth, Chayin and I, or rather we had caused such a message to be sent. The delay time from planet to planet was three Silistran days, dependably. It had been important to us at that time. We had needed the lengthy delay. Silistra is far from the nearest congruence, so far that it was a B.S. light-day and a half that signal traveled, upon a lasered beam, before entering the congruence. Exiting immediately at the M'ksakkan equivalent, it had then traveled a light-day and a quarter to M'ksakka.

"So we're just going," added M'tras. "We'll have our orbit before morning."

"How can you have morning in a place like this?" I stretched out my other leg slowly.

"We observe M'ksakkan days and nights." He shrugged. "I've gotten used to it." His smile was grim, like dawn burst upon the northern sea. "You're making it hard for me to be pleasant to you," he observed, bouncing in his squat to loosen his own calves. His belt, quiet, seemed only ornamented black leather.

"Such was not my intention," I said. He was stretching a point, I reflected, to call his treatment of me pleasant. I looked at my hardly touched food, took the jeri, for something to hold in my hands. I thought, any moment, he would sit. He sat himself down, cross-legged. Upon my tray still lay most of my meal. I remembered my resolve to gain back some weight. I shrugged. M'tras, misunderstanding, grinned, a curling back of lips. I decided I cared not if I was too thin, sipping the jeri, which was, blessedly, not synthetic, but clear and tangy. And it would, I knew, relax me, and blur the ache in my body from enths of kneeling.

"What do you think of Dellin?" he asked.

I sighed to myself behind the cup. It was beginning again, if on a lower key.

"What would you like to know?"

"I'm curious." He raised his arms away from his body, showing his sleeping symbiote, curled around him like some somnolent slitsa. "Why did you think he would hurt you?"

"Sometimes," I said quietly, "with Dellin, one forgets he is not Silistran. I did, I suppose, nothing for which he would hold me to account." I ran my tongue along the cup's yellow rim, catching an escaped amber drop. I could see him only above the shoulders, over the rim. He waited. I could not imagine that M'tras did not know what the Ebvrasea, the cahndor of Nemar, and I had done to Dellin, in his own keep, before we went to take Celendra out of Astria. "It has been years since he and I had converse," I added. "When last I saw him, he bore no birthing strand, nor the strand of threxman at his waist."

"Birthing strand?" prompted M'tras.

"He has gotten, I would venture, a Silistran woman with child. The gold strand is not easily acquired. Dellin has built a good start for a chald."

M'tras rose fluidly from his cross-legged seat. As he approached the slab before the partition, he touched his belt. By the time he stood there, the screen glared bluely, out from hiding.

"I thought you had nothing to say to me." It was Dellin's voice, truculent.

"Did you get some local woman pregant?" M'tras demanded, lounging sprawled across the velveted slab.

"No." Dellin's surprise was evident. I imagined him: touching his chald somewhere upon three deck. I stayed where I was beside my tray. "It was a political move I made." Condescending, was Dellin. "I took up the chald of another, with respect to one child only. It is a complicated chaldric matter, nothing you could understand. The fitness was debated for four passes by Silistran authorities before any decision was made. It's very delicate, this whole thing. Or was."

I thought his words oddly tinged with pride for

one who fled his chaldric commitments. And with regret. M'tras, also, marked it strange.

"Whose child is in your care?" he snapped viciously. "Or was?"

"That of Tyith bast Sereth, out of a coin girl," Dellin said with gravity. One never names such a woman in giving parentage. It is bad taste. Sereth, I thought, would not have been pleased if such knowledge had come to him. No, he would not have been pleased to know that his grandson had been in the hands of Celendra; and passed by her to Dellin, doubtless as part of their extended couchbond. The decision, I realized, must have been pending while Dellin was in our hands. Pending and ratified when Celendra was accounted dead or crell. Yet might she live, in the Parset Lands. Perhaps Jaheil had found her pleasing. But I could not know it. I did not know if she even survived the wounds she had sustained when Jaheil used her as shield before him in the battle upon the plain of Astria. "It is a son," Dellin added, doubtless for my ears, "and healthy, favoring his grandsire."

"Can't you speak your own language?" M'tras growled at the miniature Dellin I could not see.

"Surely," came the answer. "I hear you're going to counterthreaten Khys. You're a fool. There's nothing in the hides but old books and older philosophers. One-quarter of that planet's population lives within a hundred B.F. miles of one hide or another. You're talking about direct hitting a quarter of the human life on the planet. They don't have any buried secret weapons."

"And what's he doing? There are plenty of lives involved in his threat to the moon Niania."

"This is like a nightmare," said Dellin, and an absence of light play upon M'tras' body let me know that Khaf-Re Dellin had broken the connection.

M'tras grunted, lying back upon the slab, one hand rubbing his eyes. "Come here," he advised, fingers at his belt. Regretfully I did so.

"Lie there." He indicated the slab near the wall. I obeyed him. "Take this, I want to sleep." A small round tablet, white, nestled in his palm. I looked at him in horror. "It won't hurt you. Take it." His palm was closer. I took it, lest he force it down my throat. It melted, sweet and soft upon my tongue, taking the world of the senses with it. The last thing that concerned me was urgent, and I fought for time to deal with it. But even for the hides, the drug would give me no time.

From that heavy sleep I gained no insight. Awakening was a gradual rising through less-dark clouds. There was the press of no-sound upon the ears, then a rhyming of thuds, which became blood and pulse, red as the clouds that were then eyelids. Lastly, I felt the vibration beneath me, and named it. Remembrance of my whereabouts caused my direction sense to tilt crazily. I was not at the Lake of Horns. I opened my eyes, saw the mechanic M'tras awake. He was propped against the wall, brooding, his face abstracted, fully dressed, with the remains of his first meal about him—crushed clear containers, yellow tray, yellow eggs of machine-bird.

I knuckled my eyes, stretching. He had, at least, thrown a cover over me, I thought. "Has your machine spoken to its brother?" I said, turning over to face him, on my belly. The velvet slid soft and slick along my skin. And he had undressed me. Considerate, was M'tras.

"Yes," he said, not raising his head. "It has. We have broken orbit. We make our way back to Silistra. If he wants to talk, he'll go to his local liaison, who'll call us."

"Do you not fear to get too close to our ancient weapons?" I asked, yawning.

His eyes narrowed shrewdly. "That's a small chance, but a good excuse. If he can hit something as far away as Niania, where could we hide? We're small. We're moving, fast and random. I told you, I don't believe most of this, really." His actions, I thought, belied his confidence. I shrugged.

"Can you not feel the ship yaw, tacking?" I said, as the slab dived under me like a hulion descending. I envisioned those great diaphanous sails, golden, astretch far into the star-pored blackness. Drug-calm, I found no terror in the vision, nor the moan of the solar wind in my ears. Again the slab dropped, rose. M'tras, crouched on his hands and knees, sank down beside me. He rolled onto his side, eyes closed, his fingers awork. A screel shot my ears to fragments, was gone by the time my sheltering palms reached them. Lights flickered, died. Only M'tras' belt gleamed redly. I heard a moaning, steady, far off. I clutched myself. M'tras offed his belt, brought it up to our heads. It lit him from below, redly, and my hand upon his shoulder, digging there. He cursed unintelligibly. I liked not the sound of it, so soft.

"What?" I moaned, pressing my head against his arm. I ground my teeth to keep them from clacking together, breathing deep, as if I could store the air away for future need. The sound was raspy in the dark.

"We hit something," he said quietly, disbelieving. "You don't hit things . . . I mean, it just doesn't happen when you . . . But we didn't. We're on gravitic. What's left of the sails are in. But one, which is frozen. And it's dragging against the edge of whatever we hit that isn't there. We can't go any farther in the direction we were headed." Out of the red-dark hissed his voice. He seemed some hoary spirit, underlit. "It happened within seconds of the moment we dropped out and extended them."

"How far are we from Silistra?" I asked.

"Not far," he said, as the lights came on, and we were both bleached pallid, blinking. My heart acquiesced; it would remain resident in my chest. I rolled on my back. "We don't use the normal congruences. We punch a tight hole, so to speak. It's self-sealing."

"You could take a helsar, then," I remarked, dream-high with relief.

"What?"

"Breaking through a plane where there is no natural entry. It is a plane, through which you obviate space, is it not?"

"I suppose," he said, "in the broadest sense."

"What are you going to do?" I asked.

"Sniff along the edges of this thing, if it has any. Best guess now is that it's a circle the diameter of which is twice that of Silistra's solar system, and centered around same."

"Oh," I said.

He rose upon his knees and called out once more the viewing screen. It showed only whirling color. The slab beneath me shivered. M'tras, arisen, slid back a panel beneath the viewer, consulted his belt. Still, no face or form came upon the screen. It occurred to me then that none had sought his advice or consulted him for orders, he who held singular control over this metal world in which we rode. It would not have been so among the Slayers, nor the jiasks, nor the dhareners at the Lake of Horns. With a steady stream of discordant adjurations he demanded performance of the screen. He did not receive it. He grunted, a mix of pain and surprise, and jerked his hand out of the thing's innards, shaking it as if burned. Furiously he slammed shut the panel, dimissed the screen, and sought his ijiyr.

I thought it strange that he would seek it. He took it to the table, sat. But he made with it no music, holding it in his lap. I saw that the palm-lock, which he had turned amber, had returned to its red color. Only did he hold the ijiyr a time, caressing the strings. Then, carefully, wiping the strings beforehand, he closed its case around it, placed it upon the table.

It must be, I reasoned, that men do not attend the ship's flight, but machines. Men would surely have called to discuss this disaster with him who led them. Men are not, like machines, inured to crisis.

M'tras took council with his belt. Beyond him, at the door, the palm-lock died, its red eye going dead and gray. Wondering where he had hidden my clothing, I rose, went to stand before the real-seeming Western Forest. His eyes followed me, but he made no objection.

"What will you do without the sails?" I queried him, low. I wished I had water, recollecting the Stoth position in the debate we had so recently held (and which I had not put forth), that a skill making use of machines other than that of flesh is too conditioned by artifice; that it is flesh that must learn to fly, or fall like a stone from the back of mechanical perversity it rides.

"I'm not sure yet. Don't worry about it. Things will just take a little longer. Whatever it was we hit is gone now. We can ride ..." He stopped, his mouth hanging open. I recalled the death cube, resting beneath the table.

I need not have considered it. M'tras, aural symbolist, stochastic improviser, M'kaskkan mechanic, could not even close his mouth. His eyes, terrified, followed me as I crossed the metal floor and knelt before him who stood there, pressing my lips long to his sandaled instep.

Khys did not raise me, but leaned down, brushing my hair off my neck. I felt his fingers move there, upon the band I had so long worn. When he took his hand away, releasing me with a touch, the band went with it. I did not move, but knelt still, my lips against my couch-mate's foot, within the curtain of my hair. Joy raced my blood like uris. My neck tingled. Tears flooded me, wet the dharen's sandal.

"Crying, little saiisa?" he said to me in that sonorous voice. "Let me see you."

I straightened my back, brushing my hair over my shoulders. My mind cowered. So long it had been entrapped, I had truly forgotten the life-songs. I raised my tearstained face to the dharen. Freed, I still feared him. Inscrutable, indomitable was Khys. What had he in his heart, in his mind? Weakly I sought the sort.

He scrutinized me, those flame-licked eyes warming my flesh, adjudging my condition, the extent which M'tras had abused me. "Stand," he allowed, a half-smile on his face. I stood before him, naked, he in his blue-black leathers and cloak, his waist weapons-belted. I threw a glance over my shoulder, at the M'ksakkan, still in flesh lock. Khys's copper-lashed eyes closed a moment. I felt his presence, considering my emotions, my reactions. He nodded. I trembled, fearful, though there was nothing within me that would displease the dharen, only gratitude, relief. And the knowledge that the leavings of my skills were as nothing before his. He had left me little.

He raised a hand to my cheek, took a tear rolling there, tasted it. I stood still, my gaze resting easy in his, waiting for him to speak. In this alien keep, surrounded by the artifacts of our enemies, he had removed my band of restraint. Doubtless he felt I could better serve him without it. I hoped I would live to do so.

"I do not doubt it," he said, brushing a stray hair from his mark upon my breast. "I have long sought this moment. I regret only that it was birthed in such an unseemly womb."

"Was there another way?" I asked, for it would be long before I had steady stance in the time.

"Evidently not," he said slowly. I sensed the self-reproach in him. It edged his voice, tightened his belly, made him still before me. "No one," he added, "is omniscient."

"Estrazi himself has said that to me," I told him gently. I wished he would hold me. He did so, taking me abruptly against him, his touch smoothing the quailing of confusion from my muscles. I did not deem it unfitting that he had used me in his hesting. I whispered it to him, my lips against his leathers. His grip upon me tightened. Even in the strength of it, I sensed the tremors. "I am unhurt," I murmured. I pushed back slightly, that I might raise my gaze to his. "I killed one of them," I said.

"I know it. I am proud of you." He tucked in his chin, his eyes heavy-lidded. His lips brushed my forehead, my eyelids, then pressed savagely upon mine, his teeth bringing blood to my mouth.

"Liuma?" I asked, hesitant, when I could.

"Dead." He spat the word as he released me. "That part, I had not foreseen. And from it, other unforeseens came to be. I am late here. I would not have left you so long, helpless before them. I had a different thing in mind." He shrugged, as if it were nothing, but his rage roared over me like the Embrodming breaking on the eastern cliffs, and I knew his hest had been altered by another hand. "I would not see you again at the mercy of such as he." He said it even-voiced, deathly low, inclining his head, to the flesh-locked M'tras, motionless in the gray chair. Within Khys, I sensed his reticence, his unwillingness to believe what he saw within me, in the face of what was, to him, his own glaring error. I reached out tentatively to soothe his self-condemnation. His lashes met momentarily. His shield, impregnable, snapped tight. I stepped back.

"Can there be any doubts of my feelings?" I wondered aloud, amazed, hurt. "You have, how often, taken the truth from my mind? Take it now, Khys."

I saw him, with an effort, compose himself. "I have released you, have I not, from your restraint? I have done so not to commune with your mind, which in any case is open to me, nor to see you as equal, which you will never be, but that your welfare be less a burden upon me. I can use your strengths in what lies before us. I do not need them, but I can use them."

"You have them. As always have you had that which you desired from me."

His nostrils flared. He inclined his head, his majesty a wrap pulled close. "Keep in mind," he advised, "that this freedom I give you is highly conditional. If you prove unready, I will return you to your former state." He brushed by me toward M'tras, unmoving at the table. Upon the dharen's cloak, emblazoned on its back, glittered the Shaper's seal. His copper hands found the ijiyr. M'tras, unable to do more, closed his eyes. Khys turned the case, opened it. His countenance was severe as he lifted the instrument from its bed. And he played upon it, calling forth from the strings such sounds of wrath and magnificence that my blood halted, ice-bound, in my veins. I heard the scrabble of M'tras's mind, near madness, as Khys replaced the ijiyr in its case. I had not realized that the instrument meant so much to him. Slowly I made my way to join the dharen, feet slippery on the metal plating, struggling with my own emotions. Did he, I wondered, know of the threat to the hides? And I answered myself that he must.

Nor was I wrong to keep silent, lest I belittle myself with the inadequacy of my conception.

Khys spoke a musical sounding. I guessed it some greeting in M'tras tongue. The tone of his skin near-matched the burnished metal. Easy, relaxed, was Khys in his dark leathers before the M'ksakkan, as if we hurtled not in some wounded thing's stomach through the void. And while I thought it, the dharen leaned upon the table, both hands clenching its edge. Not understanding, I went to him, touched his arm, my mind sending support to the best of my weakened ability. But it was no indisposition upon Khys then, no sudden-revealed infirmity. Seeking, I saw a shore, cold and forbidding, and a strangely formed rock, through which the wind keened. And then a sun spewing gold-red tongues blinded me. Singed and blinking, I retreated, retrieving my hand from Khys's arm. That one looked at me. His eyes had carried away the solar flame. It burned in him for a moment, undamped. Then he pushed himself back from the table's edge.

"I am going to free your tongue, Trasyi Quennisaleslor Stryl Yri Yrlvahl. You will speak only at my bidding." I saw his lids' barely perceptible flicker, as he altered his flesh-lock upon the mechanic. M'tras kept silent. His skin was very gray as he sat there, unmoving, his hands in his lap, his mouth at last his to close.

"I have cause to do what I will with you. Your intentions, and those of your superiors, distress me. I will not, of course, allow any such to manifest in the time. I granted you an opportunity to reconsider. You did not choose to seize it. Did you think that by drugging the girl you could shut my eyes to your machinations?" He smiled grimly. "There is the sort, and the hest. And there is the assessing of minds, in the now. All are particulars of sensing. One does not consider depth perception apart from seeing. You know, you are thinking, nothing of sorting and hesting. I shall begin to teach you. Silence," Khys snapped as M'tras twitched his lips. He could not, I was sure, even turn his head. I threw my leg upon the table. The metal was cool to my bare flesh. As best I could, I hardened my heart to M'tras plight. I had craved this moment, that of the dharen's retribution. Upon me, I found it less than savory, as grating upon my spirit as Khys's M'ksakkan to the ears.

"Let me divine for you the sort," offered the dharen, his eyes flashing. I quaked, though I was not the subject of his displeasure. "You have passed out of the draw time, when you might have avoided this which here begins. In crux, there comes an ending, from it new beginnings. That which will occur is, by my will, fixed. In a situation where outward influence is denied you, you will learn a thing: when one finds one's position untenable by reason of preconception and context, all that remains is to alter one's perspective, that comfort sufficient to secure survival may be maintained. That choice, survival, is open to you. Choose well." He indicated that M'tras might speak.

"The time"—M'tras stumbled—"is not up. You had promised another day. I would have returned her."

Khys shook his head. "You do not yet believe me, do you? I have complete access to your thoughts, for what they are worth. I am aware of your decision to use the return of Estri as sham behind which to conceal your true intention—that of destruction of the hides. I saw you reach it. I waited, set that time limit, that I might flush from hiding him who conceived this thing, him whose skills were sufficient to have kept him obscure. But all is now accomplished. I have what I needed from this farce. Thought you, really, I would spend life so extravagantly as to destroy a sphere of human habitation? Or was it perhaps a machine's conception, that would credit such dementia to a man?" The dharen's voice, so calm, so saddened, diminished M'tras as no harangue would have. "Speak, you who should have known better."

M'tras' face and hands were agleam with sweat. He seemed to have trouble finding words. "I am of some little value," he said, his voice trembling, "both to M'ksakka and my home world. Return me to them."

"It is not in the sort," said Khys.

V

Draw to Crux

I stood beside the Keening Rock of Fai-Teraer Moyhe. The wind, cold and wailing, blew inland off the gray Embrodming Sea. If flogged me with salt spray. I had confined my hair in a thick braid, safed the braid under the cloak Khys had lent me. Beneath it I wore only the rumpled silk. My feet were bare, upon the sea-slicked sand. At my left was the Keening Rock, ten times the height of a man; a pierced monolith. Seven holes are there in that spire, each singular. The northern winds long ago conceived it their instrument. And over that instrument have they gained mastery, I thought, standing there in the sullen midday, with the Embrodming pulsing bass to the wailing of the gale. Loud it was, and eerie, with high-octave tones that demanded and received sympathetic resonance from my very bones. Behind me, inland, amid the ragged coastal rocks, began the eastern wilderness of which none are empowered to speak. And yet, I stood here. Khys had bade me await him by the Keening Rock while he meted out judgment to those who incurred his wrath.

It had been, of course, Khys's barrier against which the Oniar-M had crashed. I squinted into the gray-green boiling sky, as if from here I could see it, where it encircled Silistra's solar system; a sphere of restraint through which no mechanical

craft could hope to pass, but by Khys's expressed
will. He had, when it pleased him, allowed the
M-class Aggressive entry into the space he had
taken out of common holding. There would be no
more such ships. I turned and looked at it, canted
slightly upon the beach, sunk a third of its length
in the sand. It was a sinuous craft, like a friysou's
wing. A damaged wing it was, all its golden plum-
age ripped away but pinfeathers, and they sticking
out from gray pimpled skin at unlikely angles. I
had seen such a ship with her great sails wrapped
tight about her like a Parsent forereader, the gold
glinting in the desert sun. At Frullo jer, I had seen
such a craft, when I had been tiaskchan of Nemar.
Long ago.

I sighed. There would be no more ships. Khys
had told me. Those now upon Silistra he would
give a set's grace, that they might take live cargo.
He wanted no more off-worlders upon the land.
The Oniar-M, before me, would not be leaving. It
could no longer perform its functions. All of its
machines were dead within it. The dharen had,
perhaps at the very moment my mind touched his
as he leaned upon M'tras' table, transported us
here. It was an awesome demonstration of his
power, that I had not even felt it occur. I should
have known, when he took the band from my throat,
but I had not. He had hested the ship, contents
included, to the eastern wilderness of which none
are empowered to speak.

I was glad to be again upon the land. I sank
down in the wet sand, overcome with emotion. It
was for me enough to sit there, a time. His bidding,
that I await him, seemed far away.

It had occurred to me that I might run. Down
the beach, amid the rocks. And I laughed aloud,
in the silence. There were none else upon the
beach. I had seen none of the Oniar-M's crew. The
dharen had told me, while he had knelt M'tras

before him, that they were all flesh-locked, and what he intended to do with them. And he had told me that even then was the M'ksakkan warship only a brainless hulk, upon the eastern shore of the Embrodming.

He would, he had said, turn them all loose deep in the interior. They might, he had conceded, survive both the wild beasts and the cahndor of Nemar, who would doubtless come to hunt them. All but Dellin and M'tras did Khys so judge.

They, I thought, blinking wind-whipped sand from my eyes, might lie within the ship, still flesh-locked. Or they might already be incarcerated at the Lake of Horns.

There would be no more ships: the lesson their cargo provided had been either learned or mislearned by the denizens of Silistra; the new teachings, helsars, had arrived. The old was now discarded. So Khys had informed me. The mechanical aid has place and purpose in the perfection of this human machine with which we are, by our choice, either blessed or cursed. And that purpose, brought to its apex in the teaching aid called helsar, is to facilitate the mastery of this threefold mechanism we inhabit while enfleshed; that machine which in potential may perform every task conceivable to its taskmaster, the ascending spirit. So the dharen had spoken, though I had not asked him to justify himself to me. I shivered, rubbed my arms with sandy palms.

I considered it again: I might run. But I did not know whether or not the dharen would give chase. Nor did I know if I could elude him, or even if that was what I desired. It would take a steadier stance than I presently possessed in the moment to outwit Khys.

I sat upon the rock, where a lichen climbed, staring out to sea. I reached for Khys's mind, across what seemed a great distance. There appeared to me a deep gorge, mist-enshrouded. Unscalable cliff face rose upon every side, except directly in my field of vision. In that cleft trail I saw black-suited figures, perhaps a yra. Many of those heads were blond. None that I could see wore flashing belts.

He had, then, done what he said. I awaited his return, and when it did not come, I reached another way. I sought Sereth, across the sea. Either I had not the strength, or his shield was all it had been rumored to be, and more.

I hested a waterspout. It caused me great effort. The first step, creating turbulence, was the hardest. I ripped at the inner scars that encysted my skills. I allowed myself no pain, for I had desperate need to prove myself, to myself, effective. The worst Khys had done to me was that; he had altered my self-conception. I habitually conceived weakness and failure, confusion and helplessness. He had taught me to do so. To function, I must first break those bonds. Tiny feats, I performed. But I did them. And I was strengthened, each success a girder of the bridge I built across the abyss. Khys, I realized, had allowed me this time for the purpose to which I had put it. So said the sort, and what I could see of owkahen. It was, I cautioned myself, too late to change occurrences so long abuilding. It had come to me: what I must do; but it was too soon, although the initial hest had been laid before Khys and I stood in each other's presence. I rubbed my naked throat, where the band had rested.

In the sand, my fingers traced a threx. Rubbing out two lines, I amended him with a threxman. My mounted threxman I gave the best of weapons, even a huija of Parset style. The drawing grew so complex I found myself needing the sharper lines my fingernails could provide. Four days, and more, had I lain drugged. It troubled me that I did not even recall ablutions made during that period. I thought I detected a sluggishness about me, drug residue in my system. I shrugged, and my thick braid flopped from under the cloak onto the threxman's rump. Cursing, I wiped my sand-wet braid. Then I erased the drawing with my palm, and turned about, to scan the rocks for him. Awkwardly I rose, brushed the sand from my knees.

He stood there.

"Khys," I greeted him, my eyes lowered upon my feet.

He chose to allow me that small defiance. "Think you," he queried, "that you can assay the journey to the lakeside alone?" I recollected the shriveling cold, the searing pain that had attended my previous efforts at such travel. And I had been, then, stronger.

"No," I admitted. "I would not even attempt it."

"Then I perhaps might be of help, for you have sufficient power to do so. It is rather a flaw in your method." I saw his eyes narrow, turn in the direction of the Oniar-M. I thought I detected the slight air flicker of the protective envelope he cast around the ship, before he split asunder each of its molecules one from the other, and shunted those now nonnative atoms into a universe where the physical laws to which he had reconditioned them obtained. I shielded my eyes with my forearm from that shadow-devouring light.

"You would teach me?" I disbelieved, blinking in the green afterglow.

"I have been teaching you, all along. It is my custom to do so. If you would scale even the most modest pinnacle of those to which you aspire, you had best apply yourself to my lessons." And he bent down in the sand, his long forefinger slashing illumination; the topography of the planes, did Khys set down for me; and beside them, a schematic for permeation. One does not push through; one but sets up consonance and demands synchronistic exchange. I sat back from it at last, my insteps aching, much disheartened.

"I am not mathematical." I despaired of the stringent parameters Khys set upon the obviation of space. I might never master them. Notwithstanding, I consoled myself silently, I had in the past performed creditably. Even with my sloppy and disordered methodology, I had met Raet, when Khys dared not. I had been first, also, to set foot upon Mi'ysten. Khys, with all his power, had not made that journey. Though he was more at home with shaping skills than I, he had not, to my knowledge, made a world.

"But I took a helsar," he said quietly, "when your great-grandmother was not even conceived. And what I have done, and come to be, I have brought into the time by my will alone. No help was there for me, in those early days, when the future of Silistra lay in my sole keeping. And I conceived the truth about the fathers while we huddled in the hides. Before that, we had been only reactive. Raet had toyed with us. We were unknowing. We had no chance; none at all." It seemed to me, then, that the centuries rolled away, and I saw through his eyes stop-frames of agony and desperation. They had sorted, those few, but there was no name for the skill. They had foreread, and none would harken unto them. And as the time grew close, the brothers and sisters gathered, like-mindedness being the sibling ship between them. Those who saw, and those alone, lived through Horoun-Vhass, the fall of man. Even did he show to me hide aniet, that day the gristasha tribesmen were ushered into the undertunnels, that their line might survive. "By you," he assured me, "and by our people, I would this time do better." He extended his hand to me. I took it, rising, and we obviated space, our fingers laced.

Upon the seal in the seven-cornered room, his

hand released mine. There had been no pain, no dragging of my substance through the void. Nor had it been any work of mine. I had merely ridden his wake to the audience chamber at the Lake of Horns.

Khys knew. He shook his head at me, reproving, that I had not even tried.

I opened my mouth to ask him why he sought me strengthened.

"No questions," he reminded me sternly. He turned, strode to the window.

I closed my mouth and blew out a breath devoid of words. I knew not even what day it was, though I guessed it Brinar third fourth. M'tras had accused Khys of being a day premature in his actions. My hands found the braid beneath Khys's cloak and loosed it. Would he, I wondered, restrain me again, now that he had no need to move my flesh through space?

"No," he said, his tone soft from where he held back the draperies, admitting the lakeside. "Not now. Our travel is not yet done." His voice seemed choked with sadness. "Leave me," he whispered. "Carth is in the baths. Ask what you will of him. At sun's set, seek me."

Trepidation attended me as I walked alone for the first time the halls of the dharen's tower. It is truly said that if one does not maintain the habit of triumph, its touch will pass unnoticed. It was nothing to me that I was unbanded and nominally freer. But it must be everything, for I sought stance in the time. Chayin, I must find, and Sereth also must I confront and make reparation for what Khys's Estri had said and done. And Santh. I took the taernite stairs two at a time, letting my momentum work for me. Down and around and down again, my bare feet took me surely over the well-dressed stone. Of Khys, I was hesitant to even think; what awaited was already fixed; in his sadness and solicitude he bespoke it. I put thought of him away, and from M'tras, Dellin, and politics did I free my mind. I needed more desperately other news.

What had the dharen seen, of what I still most dimly sensed?

Carth was indeed there, among the steam and the hissing rocks, as were a score of others. It was, I conjectured from that, late day. Late cloudy day, I amended my thought from the glimpse I had had of the lakeside. Silent, I threaded my way through the slabs toward his, nearest the steaming stones.

"Carth!" I shook his shoulder, moist and hot.

With a grunt he rolled to his side. His face was contused. Upon his right arm was a wound. It was no more than days old. "Do you not think you should have left that outside?" He grinned and sought my hand. I flushed. I still wore Khys's cloak and the silk short-length. "Presti m'it, tennit," he said quietly, sitting up. I took seat beside him.

"What happened to you?" I asked him.

"What happened to you?" he parried, eyeing me quizzically. There was a small thread in his black curls. I reached up and disentangled it.

"Khys said you would answer my queries." I unlatched the cloak chain at my bare throat.

"First let me congratulate you." His meaning was clear—the band.

"It is only a convenience, I fear. Tell me the date, Carth. And what occurred when Chayin discovered Liuma? And of where Sereth was, inform me. And what kept Khys so long at the lakeside?" One cannot get answers to questions unasked from such a man as Carth. "And how came you by those bruises? I would hear that tale."

Rueful was Carth's answering grin. It minded me of our first meeting, as crells in the pits of Nemar. The thought's trail touched him, and he rubbed his left wrist, scarred dark from chain sores. The man upon the next slab groaned and stretched.

"You seem to be yourself in entirety."

"And you somewhat bettered. Please, Carth."

"I am, actually, battered. I have come to sit upon the dharen's council." His tone was disbelieving. He touched his grin, as if to reassure himself.

"I think," I said with gravity, "that you owe me an apology." He had been so righteously angry with Khys's Estri when she had postulated that such a thing would have to come to be.

I regarded him, eyes half-closed, awaiting his response.

"In that," he said, much sobered, "and in all else I have done concerning you, I take no pride. But neither am I shamed." He went to rub his chin, encountered a bruise. "I will tell you what you need to know," he said, "but not here."

"Where?" I asked, sliding off the slab, my borrowed cloak over my arm.

"Upon the way to where you will want to go when I have finished my telling," said Carth wryly, easing his feet to the floor. Whatever had happened to him, I judged it more in the nature of a fall from height than man violence. There was much discoloration on his skin, a great stiffness to his movements.

We walked silently through the slabs. No word did we exchange as Carth sponged himself, nor as he pulled about him the unadorned robe of a council member. Nor as he led through a complexity of unfamiliar corridors. Not even when we passed between two arrars stiff and silent upon the threshold of a bar-gated passage did he utter a word. He guided me through it to some ill-used stairs behind a massive stra door. He knocked upon the stra, a pattern, and the door was opened from within. I heard chain hiss upon its ratchet, and thought it odd.

The stairs were torch-lit, the two guards respectively surly and taciturn. A growl apiece did they give Carth, who then ushered me down those moist-slick stairs. No ceiling stars had they wasted in this dank place. My skin crawled.

"Why did you bring me here?" I whispered as we made a better-lit landing off which three passages radiated.

"I wanted you to see the place. Have a seat," he advised. Against one wall were plank benches. I sat with care upon one, mindful of splinters, my cloak pulled well under me.

"Tell," I urged him.

He did not sit, but leaned an arm upon the wall. Looming over me, he began it:

"I was asked by Khys to keep him apprised of Sereth and the cahndor as best I could," he admitted hesitantly. "In doing so, I was upon the second floor when you were abducted. And thus it came to be that I was directly behind Sereth and Chayin as they hurried from couch with bare blades only to investigate. I could not catch them upon the stairs. I gained their side only because Gherein detained them at the stair's head."

And I recollected those footsteps I had thought I heard on the stairs while I faced M'ksakkans within Khys's keep. If they had reached me unobstructed, I would surely have been saved. Then I knew who of Silistra had aided M'ksakka.

"I am sorry, Carth. I lost the thread," I excused my wandered attention.

"I can see why," he remarked, but picked up where he left off.

"Gherein enjoined them to hasten outside, where they would find the body of Liuma. Estri, he assured us, was nowhere about. And when they would have passed by him he did not allow it, but derided them for their disbelief. He was, he reminded them, first of Khys's council. He demanded they prostrate themselves and show respect. That was not out of character for Gherein, and I thought little of it. I but soothed him, that he might step aside, allow Sereth to inspect the keep. It was a thing of iths!" He spread his hands, his eyes mere slits.

"Sereth," Carth continued, "was admirably restrained. Or so it seemed, he locked behind that shield. Not one word did he say, but brushed by Gherein as I engaged him. The cahndor, seeing this, turned and descended the stairs, running. I think he knew then, if not before.

"Gherein gave me tasa immediately following their departure. He took his leave in the direction of Khys's keep. It was iths, only, before Sereth reappeared. They must have passed in the hall. He was withdrawn, pale. His eyes sought his path before him. Then only did I think to seek you. And I did not find." His tone turned bitter. "I gathered my wits enough to follow him down the stairs." He stopped.

"Carth . . ." I touched his arm. "Carth, please."

He confirmed my guess of the date, in a low tone. Then he raised one leg up on the bench, rested his elbow upon his thigh. "Sereth did not hurry," he continued, and I began to see it—Sereth's back before him as they descended the stairs, his touch upon the other's arm. And Sereth's face, most terrible in Carth's sight, did I see, as he recalled it.

In silence Carth followed him down the vaulted hall with its archite floors and through the great inlaid doors. He did not deign to answer the attendant's demands for enlightenment, but half-ran though them and down the steps. Carth's mind sought the dharen, found him already upon his way. Out into the late day he followed Sereth's half-naked form, around the dharen's tower, to where Chayin crouched over the body. But for the fact that the back of her skull had broken open, she might have been asleep. The cahndor sat cross-legged beside her, his eyes closed. There was a small but prudent crowd, still as statues upon the white walk. No sound came from them.

Sereth stopped still a moment. He sheathed his gol-knife. Then he went and sat upon the right hand of the cahndor. His knee touched the cahndor's as he assumed a position identical to Chayin's. He, too, closed his eyes, his hands quiet in his lap. At Chayin's discretion, they would start the keening. But a time of silence, first, do Parsets give their dead, that the totality of the grief may be gathered before it is sung upon the wind. One loves, upon the moment of loss, as one can never love aforetime. The Parsets call it their greatest gift to the dead. It comes in silence and goes in song, the assumption of the chaldra of the soil.

Carth also sat, upon Sereth's right, for he had not well known the Nemarchan.

They still sat thusly when Khys appeared and stood staring down. Carth rose, thinking to calm the dharen, prevent him from breaking the silence. Khys's face dissuaded him.

"Sereth," Khys snapped, "I need you. It is over-long you have delayed. Implement my will. Bring me Gherein!" His knuckles were white upon his chald. His voice rang out over the Lake of Horns. An impious ebvrasea screeched, invisible in the clouds.

Sereth opened his eyes and regarded Khys coldly. "I am, at the moment," he said quietly, "otherwise engaged. Ask me another day."

"Now!" spat Khys. His eyes under arched brows caused Carth to step backward.

"When you again have what has been lost," said Sereth, and lowered his head, returned to the formal grieving aspect.

"By morning, or I will deal with you as I will

deal with Gherein," decreed Khys. And he whirled and strode back the way he had come.

"But Sereth did not seem to hear, nor Chayin either," Carth recalled. "They but sat there. That night, we heard their keening." And I feared, once again, listening to him. The hair rose up on my skin in that dank place. I pulled my mind from his, that I not see what else he had to tell. But I knew, then, that he had not fallen from any height. And why he had brought me here, I knew, also.

Carth, seeing my agitation, sank down beside me.

"At sun's rising, Khys bid me take ten men of my choosing. He also bade me try to keep the cahndor from becoming involved. That, I could not do." He shook his head, his countenance mere shadow play in the dimness. "We lost six men to them, all highly skilled, before we took them. I assumed you would see Sereth first. The cahndor is in the tower's holding keep."

I hardly heard him. I sought Sereth's mind. It should have been easy, so close. I found nothing.

"What . . . ?" It was inaudible. "What has been done to him?"

Carth shrugged, sank farther back against the stone. "We lost six men. We had to beat them both unconscious. Men do not heal fast while restrained."

I stared at him. I knew well what feats of healing might be accomplished at the Lake of Horns. I no longer cared about Gherein or Khys. "Will they live?" I asked, rising. I felt no inclination to sit by Carth.

"Neither will die from what wounds they sustained. Khys had set a date for Sereth's ending only."

"Of course. It is one thing to kill an arrar, another the cahndor of Nemar and co-cahndor of the Taken Lands." My voice shook.

"Do not be so sure," Carth said, low. "Khys has

judged them both, and his judgment was the same. Estri . . ."

I recoiled from his touch, my face pressed to the chill stone. I would not cry. I would see him. And I would give him aid, some way. "Take me to him," I said, pushing away from the wall, my eyes upon the taernite floor. I spoke no word to Carth as he led me down the middle passage. He was wise not to speak. Or to touch me. If he had touched me then, I would have leaped upon him and torn his eyes out. Fury trilled my nerves. My limbs trembled, but not with fear. Before a wisper-plank door like all the others, he stopped. I smoothed back my hair, handing him Khys's cloak.

Then I noted the difference in this door from its brothers. It had a number upon it: thirty-four. As Carth took from his robe a key and unlocked it, a mist came around me. I saw threxmen, mounted, and they were uncountable. Yes, I thought, Chayin at least would surely be avenged.

Then I stepped into darker dim of the cell; I heard a rustle, and something furry scaled my bare foot. Then it was gone. So there were yits beneath the dharen's tower. I found it somehow fitting that such would be the case. There was precious little light coming in through the hand-width slit near the cell's ceiling. My feet trod the lake rushes scattered upon the stone floor. He was slumped against the wall atop a pile of them. He had not enough chain slack to lie down. The manacles upon him would have restrained a hulion. He was not conscious. I knelt beside him, peering. In his hair was a mat of blood. Elsewhere upon him, also, was the work of Carth and his chosen. As I strenghtened him, I wondered at the fitness of my actions. It might, I thought, have been kinder to leave him free from his body, until the moment Khys called his mind back to attend his death. But I could not. And he was in great need. My hands did for him what they could. I spent much strength in that healing, before his spirit consented to return to his flesh. I saw its presage in his pulse and his breathing. His eyes roved beneath his lids.

I did not sit back, but knelt over him, my face close to his. His dark eyes saw me, a time, without recognition. Then he closed them.

"Sereth . . ." I choked upon it, dug my fingers into my palms. "Please, look at me. Forgive me for what has come to be. And for what I did."

And he opened his eyes. His hand, forgetful of his bonds, sought me. The chain links rattled. His lips quirked. "It is good to look upon you, little one," he said slowly. "I had concern for you."

"What can I do?" I whispered.

"Nothing. All is done," he said. "We seem to have exchanged positions."

He was, indeed, banded. "Sereth, submit to Khys. Beg his mercy."

His grin was a shadow of itself. "It is not in the sort," he whispered, straightening. I laid my head against his shoulder. He winced. "It is not," he consoled me, "as bad as you make it. I have been this close, before, to death." His tone was stern.

I sat back, pretending before him, that I not strip him of his own pretense.

"Why?" I asked him. "Why did this happen?" My tone betrayed me. I sniffled, put my finger between my teeth, and bit it.

"My sense of fitness got the better of me," he said. "Estri, let it be. Seek the sort for consolation. Or Chayin. I can give you none." And I saw then that he did remember those things I had said to him when I did not know him.

"Sereth," I pleaded, "I love you." I said it to him, as he had said it to me, when I recollected him not. We each had chosen strange moments for those words, so common and easy to speak with any but one truly loved.

He laughed a harsh sound dry of humor. His eyes rested for a moment upon Khys's sign, the only glimmer in this semidark. "That is reassuring," he said. "You had best keep such knowledge from the dharen," he added, and coughed. My heart constricted, remembering my plan to disenchant him with me for his life's sake. I had thought, in my arrogance, that I might do so. For his sake. And I would have lived a lie with Khys, to keep him safe. It never occurred to me that time might divest Sereth of what he felt for me. His shield was tight. As I rose from him, I wondered what kind of skills he possessed, that he could hold a shield while in a band of restraint.

"We will, yet," I promised him, "stand unscathed upon the plain of Astria."

Shifting of chain I heard, and his soft dry laughter. "Perchance. Owkahen has lately not favored me," he said as I turned away. "I would not count upon it."

Blinded with tears I would not show to him, I stumbled out the door into the lesser dim. Carth pushed himself away from the wall, secured the lock. **He** reached out to comfort me. I spat upon his hand. It has been said of me that my eyes, upon occasion, bear knives within them. I wished fervently that such was the truth, that I might pluck one out and use it upon Carth.

And he, hurt rather than angry, wiped his hand upon his robe. "Would you see the cahndor?" he offered, holding out my cloak.

"Yes," I hissed, "I will see the cahndor." I latched the throat chain.

I do not remember gaining the fourth-floor landing, nor walking that corridor that for so long had been all I was allowed to see of the Lake of Horns. Khys had not seen fit to incarcerate the cahndor of Nemar in his yit-infested prison. Once he had spoken to me of his dank dungeon, and I had thought it allegory, or some obscure humor.

Carth, telepath, partook of my thoughts upon those stairs, unspeaking.

"What is the date Khys set for Sereth's ending?" I asked as Carth stopped before the door to the holding keep. A shiver washed me, for the prison they had chosen for Chayin was the one I had first inhabited. Here I had languished while they stripped from me my past and my self. And here did the cahndor of Nemar await his death.

Carth, as he worked the combination lock upon the door, informed me that it was a set's time less one day until Sereth's execution. Six days. I nodded. Much could happen in six days. If I had not by that time freed him, it would be only because I, in trying, had ceased to inhabit flesh.

Carth held the door open. It closed with a muffled thump. Long had this place contained me. The cahndor lay upon the low bare couch, his face turned to the wall. Upon his belly he lay. His hands were braceleted behind. He was naked, and his rana skin shone with sweat in the light from the late-day sky. I went to that window, enclosed with a golden light that played ever across it and across the pale green walls, also. From this place, I knew, there was no escape. I tried the window. Even now, with no band of restraint at my throat, I could not force my hand through that pulsing barrier to touch the pane. I sighed and turned away from that too-familiar view.

"Chayin," I whispered as I knelt by his head, "Chayin," and I stopped. The cahndor did not need to be wakened. I sat back and waited, my eyes trapped by the glow of the band of restraint around his massive neck.

He rolled, when it pleased him, to his side. The membranes were full across his dark eyes. They did not snap or quiver. Greatly agitated was the cahndor, entrapped.

"Is this a visit," he growled, "or have you fallen from grace?"

"A visit." My hands sought my throat, met his eyes there. He bared his teeth, struggled to a sitting position. And he did not refuse my aid, achieving it. They had not been as hard upon him as upon Sereth, but they had not been easy. I sat back.

"I have seen Sereth."

I wondered what Chayin found to grin about as his kill smile once again gleamed briefly. It seemed the brighter for the darkening of the bruises on the left side of his face.

"Tell me," he demanded, "exactly what Sereth said."

I did so.

"Wear white that day. And even to attend Sereth's death, put no other color upon you."

I knew that tone. "Yes, Chayin," I said softly, and sought his mind for my answers.

"No," he snapped. I obeyed, though he could not have stopped me. "I told you once never to seek me that way." And I reached over and put my finger across his swollen lips to signify that I understood. He kissed it.

"The dharen remarked to me," I recalled, retrieving my hand, "just this midday, that you might in the future do some hunting upon the shores of which none are empowered to speak. To fulfill his prophecy, you must live that long."

"I have no doubt," said the cahndor, "that I will live that long." So did he reassure me, though it was he whose hands were braceleted behind him, he who languished, banded, in the dharen's most impregnable prison.

I put my lips to his ear, kissed a spot upon his neck that had been much between us. "Is there anything I can do?" I whispered. "None can hear us, except perhaps Khys himself." And at those

words, I formed it, a shield meant for Carth, who
doubtless listened beyond the gold-flickered walls.

"No," the cahndor said slowly, his nose in my
hair. "It is ours to do, and ours alone."

"I, too have grievances."

"Be easy," he advised severely. "Seek owkahen
and make yourself ready. Though I cannot see, I
have seen." His eyes gleamed, and the membranes
snapped sharply back and forth across them. As of
old, when none stood above him, spoke the chosen
son of Tar-Kesa. And I knew then that he yet
stalked.

"I might be of some little use," I pressed him. "A
timely visit, surely, would not prove unwelcome."
I had, already, a suitable plan. My hands went to
the chain that safed the borrowed cloak at my
throat, that I might implement it.

"That," warned Chayin, his lips nibbling my
ear, "most of all, you must not do."

I had thought to discard my cloak. Upon pretext
returning to claim it, I would have acquired the
rest of the lock's combination from Carth's mind. I
had half already.

"You must go with Khys, Estri. Accompany him
from the Lake of Horns. Trust us. Do as I say." His
lips hardly moved. His whisper was dialectic Parset.
And thought I had boasted that my shield could
protect us, I wondered.

"As you wish it, Cahndor." I agreed, rising. Khys
had informed me that our travels were not yet
done. Chayin directed me now to accompany the
dharen elsewhere. The sort, so clear to them, sat
easy with the hest shown to me on the sands by
the Keening Rock.

I stared down at Chayin, the bound dorkat. And
I was greatly saddened. Such a wild thing should
never know collar and cage. And yet, he knew
them not, in his conception. I shook my head in
answer to his carnivorous grin, trying to retain my

solemnity. But his called its mate onto my face. We had no need of sensing skills, Chayin and I. We had well known each other when neither would employ them. We had been, then, naive. But we had found, in those times, means of communication other than words. I had seen the cahndor, before, upon the kill.

"I must go, Chayin, before I become certain enough to be a danger," I said, turning from him. I felt his eyes upon me as I crossed to the padded, featureless door and pounded upon it.

"Tasa, Estri," growled Chayin. "Keep safe. We are short of crells in Nemar."

I flushed my back to him. My hand, of its own volition, sought Khys's device upon my breast. The door opened before me. As I stepped through, I spoke over my shoulder once more. "I will try to get you uris, lest you sweat to death," I promised, stepping into the hall.

When Carth's eyes rose from securing the lock, mine met them, accusing.

"You cannot withold uris from him. You might as well savage him as you did Sereth, and put him in yit-infested cell thirty-five, if you do that."

Carth looked away. "Speak to me," I jeered, "arrar, council member, vessel of justice and truth, explain to me this which you have shown me today. You and ten others you say, all highly skilled, did this?" I spat, "You must be deaf to your own teachings, to do such a thing." My fists wrapped in my chald. I waited. It took a time before Carth found words.

"You asked me also what kept Khys so long at the lakeside," he reminded me finally. "I will tell you that, if you will walk with me." His voice was very grave. "But ask me no questions of fitness. I have as yet come to no conclusions. I have my doubts, but I am undecided. When I have taken stance upon this matter, you will be the first to know." He met my gaze, unshrinking.

I let him take my arm, and we walked the hallway toward the stairs that led down to Khys's chambers.

"Khys," said Carth in the tone of a man who hopes to make sense of a thing for himself by attempting to explain it to another, "has long had problems with Gherein. And even longer has he been aware that someday it would come to this. But he was loath to do what needed done. He and others have suffered many indignities because of Gherein. Vedrast, whom Gherein swayed to his thinking, was not the only one. Such diversity to opinion within a group that links minds cannot long be sustained." He cast his eyes about the passage, his mouth a crooked line drawn dark across his face.

"Khys had come to this decision previous to your abduction. I believe, at this moment, that he even knew of it. But he waited, that he might have proof. In such affairs, it is well to obtain incontrovertible evidence."

"He did not need it, seemingly, with Vedrast," I interrupted.

"You do not understand. Gherein is the dharen's most vehement detractor. He leads some few others. He is volatile, unstable, contumacious, amoral, and exceptionally talented. He is sterile. He is Khys's son."

We were passing benched alcove. I sought it. "And what I wrote, what Khys's Estri wrote . . ." Nor was that all that had been revealed to me by Carth's words.

He smiled grimly. "We are dealing with it now. We have been coming aware. But until Khys replaced lake-born with a mixed-bred upon his council, none dared speak of it. Between father and son, that was the final insult. Gherein was

more than ready, with his M'ksakkan pawns. His
stance in the time is never faulty, only his use of it.
When Khys put a child upon you, and that child
matched his expectations, Gherein had to act. He
felt his ascendancy in danger. And well it might
be!'' With those words he confirmed what I had
seen. Over me, and the spawn of my womb, had
Khys and his favored son come to contest.

"Khys loves him?" I ventured.

"Doubtless. He has resisted any number of attacks personal and public, by Gherein. Rumor has
it that thrice he has allowed the son to engage him
in combat. And that thrice he has gifted him again
with life.''

"But not this time." I murmured. I recollected
Gherein's attempt to destroy me, while about my
assessment. And those things he had said to me
when I had been Khys's Estri, all uncomprehending.
At the feast had he spoken to me. And also there
came into my mind what Khys had said to Sereth
that evening. I had been there when Khys had
made the decision to set Sereth upon Gherein.
Even did I recall Gherein's words and manner to
his father from a new perspective. "Sereth once
id to me, when I criticized his treatment of his
son Tyith, that although someday the boy might
be able to knock the sword from his grasp upon
the second stroke, until then it was necessary for
both of them to know that he could not.''

"With lake-born, things are not so simple. Time
is the weapon; will, the sharpness of its edge.''

"And yet the weapon is no more than the wielder.'' I quoted again the Ebvrasea. "And owkahen
the circle into which we all daily step,'' I added, of
myself.

Carth picked a thread from his robe. "Khys has
not yet apprehended Gherein, though some feel it
was the first councilman he sought while he was
elsewhere, these last days. When he viewed Sereth

and Chayin, and spoke to them, he was more wrath-
ful than I have ever seen him. He reiterated that
he would treat them exactly as he would treat
Gherein. It was the sentence he had threatened
them with that afternoon they sat by the body of
Liuma. Witnesses had heard it. He could not do
otherwise. He will not," he cautioned me.

"Must you monitor me so conscientiously?"

"Yes, I must. I serve him still."

"And I serve him also. I go now to do so." I rose
from him in speedy leave-taking. "If ever you free
yourself of his yoke," I called back, "and take up
your life into your own hands, seek me. Until
the, keep an enth between us."

And I ran down the hall, away from him. Keep
an enth between us. It is an old, old saying, derived from an older proverb that states the value
of maintaining an enth's lead upon the now. If one
can but be appraised one enth into the furture, all
worth knowing will come to he possessed aforetime.
And one might then comport oneself with fitness,
in accordance to the exigencies of the sort. The
worthy man, fleeing his pursuers, seeketh only that.

I grinned upon the stairs. It had been the proper
insult at the most efficacious moment. We would
see what effect my work had had upon Carth's
shaken sense of fitness, what further erosion might
be wrought upon his surety. When a man feels the
meetness of his actions, none can sway him. When
he does not, he drifts from one master's hand to
another, seeking outside himself for what he cannot find within. The need for rightness in the self
cannot forever be denied, I thought, in a man like
Carth. It had been all I could do to so convincingly
deride him. But it had been necessary, lest he
catch the complicity within me. I had turned him
inward, which always serves. One cannot focus
one's attention in two places at once.

Upon the stair's landing I halted, smoothed back

my hair. Closing my eyes, I took a number of measured breaths. Before Khys, I must mobilize all that remained of my abilities. When I felt confident of my composure, when I had surveyed as best I could owkahen, I assayed the walk down that passage of ornithalum and archite squares. Past the hulion tapestry to the double thala doors I moved at measured pace, awaiting the moment.

The doors were ajar. Within, I heard sounds of converse. I smiled, a mere baring of teeth. Alone in the corridor, there were none to see it. Within, the voices grew low, sporadic.

It was not yet time. I separated my hair, brought half over my left shoulder. One must come down the passage first. Once more, I closed my eyes and awaited him.

The voices in the keep were silent when the blond arrar that had bound me and left me leashed to couch in the forereader's keep approached. It was as I had envisioned it. I motioned him closer. Three strides distant he was when I slipped between the doors into the dharen's keep.

It was shadowy in the keep. But for them. The entrapped stars were dead or spent for weapons. They opposed each other, glowing. Fire whirled in the air between them. Agonized was Gherein's countenance as he faced his father across that whirling conflagration. Khys's back was to us. Every muscle upon it stood high and ridged, and great shivers of flame coursed over his flesh.

Behind me, I heard the blind arrar shut the doors. Then he was beside me. I nodded, content. We were sufficient, for witnesses.

A cracking roar began, first like a blocked ear, then ocean's pound, then louder. They merely considered each other. Their forms were limned clear and bright by their motionless attacks and parries. Then clearer and brighter as the keep began to fade away about them. I felt their need, seeking

my substance to fuel their battle. I threw a shield
and held it, attentive. The need passed on seeking
easier prey. Doubtless it would come snuffling back,
if they both lasted so long. The arrar muttered. I
felt his hand upon my shoulder. And his fear was
very real. My eyes upon Gherein's black-haired
head, I widened my care to include the man beside
me. Why I did, I did not know, for he was Gherein's.

The dark around grew thicker. My feet found
themselves upon a different, more resilient surface
from which vegetation sprouted as the fighting
extended into another plane. I did not look down,
lest I come to reside there. My ears ached deep
in my head. The moving air from the whirl buffeted me with hot thirsty tongues.

Gherein's brows were in a line of pain over his
black eyes, from which the fire visibly dimmed.
They spoke to each other, somehow, in the cacoph-
ony that deafened me. Their mouths moved. Only
that. They were both still as death.

And then I began to feel it. The presaging was a
sly and vengeful smile upon Gherein's face. Doubtless he displayed it at great cost. Then as it faded,
the pain began. Consumed with it, entrapped, unable to break Khys's hold, Gherein fought back.
He took his agony and with all his considerable
talent broadcast it across the Lake of Horns. I found
myself on the mat, writhing, my own moans on
my ears. It took a time to know the dissolution his.
That time I spent reviewing my life. Then I realized the place in which I lay. Then that there was
another rolling upon the mat beside me. And who
he was, the arrar, and my name also I recollected
as I struggled to my knees, gagging upon the sudden unnamable stench.

I saw Gherein, weaving, stagger and fall. His face
hand form seemed blistered by the fire and emanated from him. While I watched, he crawled
forward, supporting himself upon hands and knees.

On his back, the skin and in some places muscle had been charred. It flaked away blackly. As he fell upon his face, I saw bone, gaping white through holes in his flesh. And then there was no pain. Only a settling. The fire-seeming spiral grew very bright. I shielded my face with my arm.

Lowering it, I saw only Khys. There was no stain or ash or sigh upon the rust-toned mat of Gherein. I regarded the bronze-scaled ceiling. There were no longer twelve stars entrapped there, but thirteen.

Khys stood very still. I did not venture to approach him until the fire faded from his flesh.

But I squinted at him though that glow like banked embers. And I judged him unscathed. The blond arrar caught my gaze. He was pale with shock and horror. I grinned and turned away. The dharen's body seeemed near normal, save for his lack of movement. In moments only, that stiffness was gone from his limbs. A strange place to do battle Gherein had chosen, neither here nor there, half in one world and half in another.

Khys ran a hand over his forehead. Behind him, the window showed dusk. "Gherein brought the accounting to me. Witnesses have seen it. Get out of here." He pointed to the arrar. Gherein's witness. "Do what needs to be done. Tell them not to seek me. None are to disturb my seclusion."

The arrar backed to the doors, his eyes upon the mat. He fumbled behind him for the bronze handle. When he had managed his exit, I locked the doors.

Khys sat upon the alcove ledge, looking out over the Lake of Horns. The sun had set while they were about their testing. I was glad I had been prompt.

I crossed the keep and filled two bowls of kifra, brought them to him. He received the bowl from me, absently. I stepped carefully through the morass of loose cushions, taking a seat upon the ledge's opposite end. He seemed a man once more. And in truth he was no god. I had seen gods fight, and such was not their custom. But it had been Gherein, surely, who had chosen the weapons and place of battle. Khys would have given him that choice, as Raet had given it to me. I sipped my kifra, taking rein upon my mind. His eyes ranged the lake's far shore. If he had heard my importunate thoughts, he gave no sign. I felt sorrow for him, that he had killed his own offspring.

"It was long coming. I tried three times to dissuade him. Upon the next occasion, I could avoid my duty no longer. I did what the time demanded. If not over you and our son, then over the number of clouds in the sky would we have come to contest." His voice was quieter than I liked. I did not know what to say. He had commanded my presence at his son's self-sought execution. I raised my bowl, not sipping. Over its rim I gazed at him. There was in him no grief, but a kind of weariness. That I caught taste of it bespoke its strength.

Letting the liquid lap against my closed lips, I searched some reply.

"Carth," said Khys as the knock came, without turning his head. He had the look of a man steeling for battle rather than meditating afterward. I went and admitted Carth.

"Dharen," he said, halfway to his master. "You know, surely." His whole bearing was distressed.

Khys closed his eyes. His lashes lay almost atop his cheeks, copper in the light from the thirteen entrapped stars. "Tell me, Carth, that it may go as I have envisioned it." He did not open his eyes. I saw the whiteness of his knuckles, tight fists clenched in his lap.

"The death of Gherein blanketed the Lake of Horns. It did not immediately identify itself as his. A number are injured. A greater number are profoundly disturbed, frightened. The council convenes."

"Witnesses have heard it," said Khys with a bare smile. "You are now first councilman. Appoint your own replacement. I will speak with you tommorow, mid-meal. At that time, you may, if you wish, seek corroboration from the off-worlder M'tras as to Gherein's complicity in these affairs."

"There is no need, dharen," Carth demurred.

Khys shrugged, his gaze still off over the lakeside. "Have a meal sent to us. This night I will give audience to my off-world guests. I want no interruptions. I will see no one, you included, before mid-meal next." And then he did turn, his majesty flaring from him like sun's spume. "When you know what you must come to know, attend me. You will soon have a thing to say worthy of my attention. Until then, I will not hear you. I bid you go and await the message you must transmit when next we meet. Leave me now," he commanded. "Carth! I bid you look well about you, for what you have not seen!"

Khys turned back to the Lake of Horns. The audience was over. I, too, turned from Carth, that I might keep at least an ith between us.

But I could not turn from the specter that hovered like a flame's afterglow before my eyes. Gherein had sent his respects to my father, Estrazi. What I had glimpsed of owkahen told me I might soon deliver them. Convey to your father my awe, Gherein had bade me, that he could put into the time such a force. Insightful was Gherein, I realized, as my stance in the time came clearer.

"That, in truth, he was," said Khys calmly. "Though enfleshed no more, his influence extends out into owkahen. We will feel his will, both you and I, some little while longer."

I thought of Chayin, in the holding keep, and

Sereth in his dank cell. I did not conceal my feelings.

"And you, who bring crux wherever you go, how dare you presume to judge my actions? I had thought to avoid much of what has come to be. And all of what owkahen yields up next. Yet, it rises. A man can only claim so much of the time. When one brings in a number of convergent hosts, in the heavy crux, where one mind has ceased, another may have started. There is, in truimph, a most vulnerable moment. How vulnerable one can come to be, I am ever learning. Beware, if you can, such prideful laxity. The time seeks the shape I have long denied it. The blacklash from my own inertia works another's will." A grimace, pretender of a smile, came and went. "I should read with greater care my own writtings." He studied me a moment, his countenance abstracted. "I wonder periodically whether you understand half of what I say. The time takes new shape with alacrity. You yourself have experienced such moments."

"I know it," I rejoined, but I felt no sympathy for his plight. I knew that he would not have it otherwise. That is the feeling that sustains upon the edge of the abyss. One walks the ledge, upon the substance of its simplicity. The life right rules. I nodded. I had been there. "Often in such times, one is offered a choice. It has been my experience that the option of stepping out of the circle is repeatedly given, though few seem ever to take it. Take it, Khys."

He crossed his arms. "Tonight we will sup here. Then you will accompany me to view the offworlders."

"You cannot deprive the cahndor so cruelly." I spoke of uris.

"I have done so," he observed. "It equals the weight upon the two of them."

"You cannot go through with this," I decried him. "The circumstances—"

"The circumstances demand this accounting," he interrupted. "You are thinking that they could have done no different, given their natures and customs. And I say to you that I can do naught else, given owkahen and life right. Do not plead for them to me. I will not hear you. I have spoken of their disposition before witnesses, and that disposition stands." It was in his most ringing voice that he intoned those words. Having done so, he rose up from the sill and took couch.

After a time, I went and joined him. He lay on his stomach, his head resting upon folded arms, and his reality was heavy, upon his spirit. So might mine have been, I thought, finally discarding the rumpled short-length I had worn since M'tras abducted me from the Lake of Horns. Much had happened in those five days. Tomorrow, I recollected as I rolled to Khys's side upon the couch silks, was the day he had given as deadline to M'ksakkans. But he had not waited. He had reclaimed me, aforehand.

His eyes were closed, his breathing regular. He had not pulled the silks around him, but lay atop them. It seemed to me he was asleep. I sought dimness from the entrapped stars, and they obeyed me, all thirteen. I wondered at the new one, at what it might know of its origin. But that wondering made me shiver, and I forsook it. I took pleasure in their obedience to my will. I thought I might seek some enlightenment from Khys in sleep. I found instead oblivion, and missed the moons's rise over the Lake of Horns.

Carth woke me. I had not known him possessed of a key. Upon the gol table was the service he had brought for the dharen. Khys did not stir. Carth, his hand upon my arm, asked a thing. Appraising Khys's chest, I doubted that he still slept. But I rose and accompanied Carth through the double doors into the hall. I stood there hugging myself, my feet on the cool stone squares.

"What?" I demanded in a whisper. The evening laid long shadows in the dharen's hall. The few ceiling stars seemed conspiratorially dim.

"I saw to the cahndor's comfort," he said upon breath. "I wanted you to know."

"What if Khys takes your generosity from my mind?" I suppressed a smile.

"He did not forbid it," said Carth, his brow furrowed.

"That is true," I allowed. "Now, if you could heal their wounds and remove their bands, you might have made some creditable start upon the reparations due them. And their freedom—perhaps you might consider giving that back to them."

"Estri—"

"Carth, I find it difficult to look upon you." And I pushed back through the doors and closed them upon his shadowed form. Leaning against their locked expanse, I sought calm. I dared not even consider how my work lay in the time.

"I mentioned to Carth Chayin's needs," I said softly to his prostrate form. "He found it in his heart to see to them." Then I pushed away from the doors and sought his wardrobe for wrap. By the time I reached it, he had risen.

I stood there in quandary before my belongings. The white Galeshir silk I had so favored had been lost to me. Liuma had worn it to her death. I was still undecided when he came and joined me.

"This is for you," he said, indicating a tas bundle next to my ors.

I opened it and found a tas breech, band, and tunic. "My thanks," I breathed.

"I also, as I had promised, found you a circle partner. But I doubt you will have time to try him," he said, taking up his dark robe.

"What mean you?" I asked, my pleasure swept away by his portent-heavy demeanor.

"It is my hope that you will be able to answer your own questions soon."

"May I get another white robe from the fitters? Mine is nowhere about."

"You may get what you wish from them," he said, eyeing me curiously.

To divert myself, I tried the breech and band. While I was about adjusting the lacings, Khys sought his meal.

He allowed, from the table, that since I had no robe, I might belt one of his about me.

I felt strange in the voluminous dark web-work. I could have pulled it twice around me. I bent the sleeves up thrice before my wrists came into view. Under it I had retained the breech and band. Tomorrow I would order a white robe.

When I exited into the keep proper, he was at the couch with a filled plate. Beside him lay another, bearing the food he had allotted to me.

He grinned when his eyes fell upon me. Khys smiled occasionally. Most times his face was composed, severe. Seldom did the dharen grin. "You look far too young to couch," he observed.

I pulled his robe around me and settled at the couch's foot. I did not move toward my plate, but waited to refill his. When he was done, I took it to table and replenished the harth and jellied gul. Also did I bring him brin, tasting it first for fitness. Such manners were lakeside custom. They rang loudly false to me, even as I employed them. He signified that I might attend my own plate. It was good to taste again Silistran bounty after the starfare M'tras had fed me. As I ate, I waxed hungry. I had not been, after so long abstaining. My stomach, although startled, was more than willing to take up once more its function.

He drained his goblet, handed it to me. "What

will you do with them?" I asked as I again got him drink.

"Who?" he said accepting from me the silver goblet upon which fog was forming.

"Dellin and M'tras," I said, taking the moment to reconsider. "What seek you with them?"

"It is what they will come to seek that is of importance."

"And what is that?"

"A way home." His words rose from the goblet's innards.

"Your explanation explains nothing," I objected softly.

He closed his eyes. I found myself upon my heels by the time he consented to open them. "Little savage," he said to me, "they are going to reside upon Silistra until they can provide themselves a means of exit other than in the belly of a machine. Between now and then they will come to be other than the men they presently are. And that which I am about, the widening of their conception, is an undertaking that should not confound you. Though the specifics may be tailored to the individual, the goals diverse, the practice remains the same."

And I shook my head, not understanding, shamed by my inability to grasp his meaning. I should not have been. Only such as Khys can set such far-reaching catalysts loose upon the time. Being one, I could not see siblings in the making. I was not concerned with the fate of Dellin and M'tras, but the speed of events, and the fact that Khys had at least temporarily ceded control of owkahen, greatly concerned me. They concerned my flesh and caused the hairs upon it to stand away, one from the other. I pulled Khys's robe tighter, but it did not warm my alerted flesh.

He bade me then accompany him to view them. I told myself, upon the way there, that their fate was no responsibility of mine.

Yet I think now that I must have known, after a fashion, for in all that followed, I felt no surprise, not even at first sight of them in keep number twelve. Although upon the same level, holding keep twelve differed markedly from Sereth's prison. I wondered if all were different. And I wondered also how many were filled.

The cell of rough-hewn brown taernite had no window, nor were lake rushes strewn upon the floor. They were not chained; they lay upon pelts spread over the stone. High above their heads, torches blazed in sconces reached from a circular gallery. One might have stood there above them, higher than one man could jump from the shoulders of another. From that gallery they might be observed, questioned, or slain. We made only cursory use of it upon our way to them.

The guards, so surly upon my first visit here, unbended themselves with fervor. One guided us to the gallery access, slid aside the ponderous plank door. A finger across his lips, Khys motioned me within the passage thus revealed. At its termination was a square of uncertain light. I found, when I stood there, that the platform was a man's length across. It followed the curving taernite wall. At intervals the torches that lit the prison floor below were sconced in the waist-high guardwall.

I sought the view, pressing myself against the brown stone. Below me they lay opposite each other on their pelts. They were reading. I read a thing into the opposition of their bodies, from my time in the Parset Lands. And I fancied I saw it, too, in the set of their frames. And in their silence did I feel the enmity between them.

"I thought," said Khys in a low voice, "that I would put them in a keep that would not discomfort their preconceptions."

The humor of it welled up in me. I stepped back from the edge, trying to swallow my amusement.

And it may have been hysteria, but it seemed truly fitting that M'tras should have for his first sight of Silistra this most ancient part of the dharen's tower.

"I am considering sending each a suitable fore-reader this night," he whispered, ducking by me into the passage. Such a move would feed their fantasies, I realized as I followed. And it bespoke once more Khys's humor. But I liked it not.

"M'tras much abused me," I said levelly. The guard slid the door across the access passage. "I think it unseemly of you to reward him."

Khys raised a brow. "I would not begrudge them women. They have, at any rate, each other." I had not thought of that. But I was angered, still, at the lightness of the hand of judgment upon them, in contrast to the weight of it upon Sereth and Chayin.

I walked with him, mute, not daring to press the matter. I had nearly forgotten it in the discomfiting realization that I stood but doors away from Sereth and could not aid him, when Khys spoke of it to me.

"M'tras mourns his ijiyr. I will give it to you. You may do with it as you wish. That, I assure you, is sufficient punishment upon his scales for any harm he might even have considered doing you. I shall inform him, also, of my decision." It was an official transaction, there in the undertunnel prisons at the Lake of Horns.

I bowed my head before his gaze, that my smile fall upon my feet.

"This is the first time," said Khys, "that I have truly marked the Shaper in you." His grim censure rang back from the stone.

"It is surely," I answered, "the first time I have marked such mercy in you." I let my mind seek Sereth boldly. I found only his shield. I had not expected to touch more. I had done it for Khys, that he might know me without doubt what he had called me.

Khys turned to the lock. "You feel that strongly," I heard him say as he cajoled the key.

"It is a blood debt. In his service, my life is forfeit. It is mine to spend, is it not? You have, already, that which you desired from me. The time calls me elsewhere. You must know it. I heard your name, too, upon the wind from the abyss. I have given you my word that I will aid you. Up to a point, I will do so. Where you go, I may be of some little use. You know it. Be assured that I know it also. Give me his life, and the larger thing might go another way. If I must be here for him, I cannot be there also." So did I speak to him of Sereth and destiny, and of our own parts in what was to follow. But he would not hear me. Nor would I have heard any other, had I been about the setting and holding of such hests and counter-hests as twisted the whole fabric of owkahen that evening, Brinar third fourth, 25,697.

"No," said Khys to all of it. Only that. Without looking at me, he pushed the great door inward and strode to the center of keep twelve.

I followed him, shutting the door behind me. I leaned against the rough ragony, searching.

M'tras raised himself to a sitting position. Still did he wear his form-fitting blacks, incongruous in this ancient holding keep. Around his waist was no blinking belt. He laid the ors aside, drawing his knees up against his chest. Those black-ringed eyes fastened upon me. He clicked. He seemed near thoughtless, waiting, poised like a forereader for the leap into owkahen. I sensed his physiochemical fear, his body's tentanus from shock and obviation of space and flesh lock. Worst—bad enough that I shrank from him and turned to Dellin—was his disorientation. His knowns were not simply threatened, they were shattered. Whole chunks of his conception had crumbled upon the flawed foundations of false assumptions. M'tras' reality had been

forcibly altered by his experiences at Khys's hands.
He floundered within himself, scrabbling for footing.
Perhaps for the first time without his machines to
aid him, M'tras sought stance in the time. He would
not, in my appraisal, gain it quickly.

Khys stood waiting. M'tras, as I, knew for what
the dharen waited. It was a foolhardy defiance. My
eyes met Dellin's as Khys began the widening of
M'tras' conception.

"I have little time," said the dharen to the
M'ksakkan mechanic, who could not yet answer.
"Let this be sufficient demonstration of the bal-
ance between us."

He stepped back, removing his hold. M'tras
waited out his tremors, unmoving.

Dellin of his own accord made obeisance to the
dharen. Khys raised him without comment. I saw
within Dellin a strength I had not seen before. He
was frightened, as befitted a sane man in his
position. But before the other, he was upheld, also.
And pride did he seem to take in Khys, in what the
dharen had done.

Khys called me to him. I went and stood there,
before Dellin and M'tras. That one's face was grayer
than I recalled, and the web of lines around his
eyes graven deeper. But he sat straight, his head
raised to meet the dharen's eyes.

"Further M'ksakkan perfidy has been made known
to me," said Khys sternly. "Before sun's rising, the
night will host two additional stars, if briefly."

"You would not!"

"It is past done. The light has only not reached
us."

"You spend life casually, despite your protesta-
tions," said M'tras.

"If you had not sent two unscheduled, unde-
clared vehicles to Silistra, you would not have had
to count them lost. The barrier is passive protection.
It only removes that which seeks to penetrate it."

"You have isolated Silistra from the rest of civilization," M'tras pointed out.

"Such was my intention," agreed Khys patiently.

"They will not rest until they have us back," M'tras said upon staccato clicks. His Silistran was fast becoming serviceable.

Khys, and Dellin also, found that to be amusing. Khys turned to the Liaison.

"You, then. Will you send a message to your people, informing them of what we both already know?"

"Allow me to serve you," said Dellin, squaring back his shoulders.

"And to your relations there, will you also send word?" Khys pressed.

"But tell me what intelligence you desire them to receive." Dellin, before M'tras, waxed ever more Silistran.

"Truth, nothing more," spoke the dharen, his eyes narrowed. "That you would remain here, to discharge chaldra and take an education. That you will remain here until you have taken the teachings of the helsar you claimed upon the plain of Astria. What say you?"

"That I am honored," said Dellin cautiously.

"At sun's rising, I will deliver you to your keep. We will together draft such a message. You will send it. I will then return you here."

Dellin's gray eyes grew shadowed. He weighed his loyalties. He looked at M'tras. Then again he raised his eyes to Khys. "I will do your will," he said.

"I would not try it," said Khys sharply to M'tras, his hands of a sudden upon his hips. "You will not be successful." Seeking within Dellin for the source of his newfound grace, I had sensed nothing from M'tras. But I recollected him and his ways as he clasped his hands to his head and rocked upon his knees before us, moaning. The remembrance steadied me. I only regarded him, the sweat and tears upon his face. Sereth, upon an occasion, criticized the vengefulness he saw in the cahndor and in me, and derided us both for our alleged lack of compassion.

Unmoved, I stared down at him. Aural symbolist, stochastic improviser though he was, upon the taernite of Khys's holding keep he begged and cried for mercy as sincerely as might any lesser man.

When M'tras was capable of speech, the dharen posed to him certain questions. From his mouth I heard of Gherein, and what twistings and turnings of justice and truth he had entertained in his conception. To rule Silistra, Gherein would have given much. He had given it, in truth, though it had not been his to give. As Khys had told it to Carth, so M'tras confirmed the dharen. Any, seeking to determine the truths involved, might now get them from M'tras.

I turned from him. Though it pleased me to see Khys instruct him, it never pleases to see strength brought low. I sought the torch play on the stone walls.

"Estri," said Khys to M'tras, "has your ijiyr. I have given it to her. And your life, also, I will give into her hands." I whirled upon Khys, staring.

M'tras fists were clenched upon his thighs. Seeing them, I remembered that which he had done to me, which had fitness only between men. I grinned at him.

He hardly saw me. He spoke a sentence in his musical meaningless language.

Khys laughed. "He objects most heatedly to being the crell of a crell. We have grievously demoralized him. Perhaps you might disabuse him of this particular preconception."

I looked at Khys. I knew what he wanted from me. Shivering, I bent my will for the first time to the diminishment of a man. But I could not complete the act. I could not. I spread my hands, helpless.

Khys nodded, as if I had pleased him. I ran my palms over my face. Both were damp. M'tras, tensed, looked between us.

"You must, it seems, take my word for our dhareness' proficiency. Or perhaps you might consult Dellin, whom I leave here to advise you. Listen well to him, Yhrillyan, lest in improvisation you lose cognizance of the root structure of the chord."

VI

An Ordering of Affairs

He showed me, later that evening, the lights in the sky. They seemed insignificant, viewed with the naked eye. And in truth their significance was great only to the world that had sent them. Silistra was never in danger. Other things he showed me, that night.

"What is this sudden ordering of your affairs?" I asked of him in a whisper when he had finished his extensive preparations.

"Exactly that. In the early day I will be absent with Dellin, at the Liaison First's. Carth will come to you before I return. Maintain your calm, regardless of the implications of his message. Be assured that you can render me no greater service than that."

I kissed him upon the shoulder. When one must hold calm within, against all rational instinct, it is of great service if there be calm without. It was a measure of his distress that he should plead my aid in what faced him. I promised him that service, not knowing how difficult its rendering would come to be.

When I awoke, he was gone from the keep. Knuckling the sleep from my eyes, I sought the window, that I might judge from the view the time and weather.

And I saw it then, but I did not mark it with

my sleep-dulled senses. I but turned away and
pulled on the breech and band. When that was
done, I went seeking rana and sun's meal.

I found them, upon the main floor. It was the
arrar's kitchen into which I wandered. None made
objection. The dhareness, I thought, getting in line
with them, might eat wherever she chose. I saw
there the blond arrar who had been Gherein's
witness. Upon that seeing, I turned away, that I
might avoid him, then back again when I realized
the futility of my actions. I was the only female in
that many-benched archite hall.

The men before and behind me were stiffly silent.

The server ladling out salsa-laced gruel screwed
up his face at me, and inquired after the weather
as he filled my plate.

"Will you have water in your rana?" he asked.

"It is for your rana I have come to this board,
rather than another's," I lied to him. "I would
chase the sleep from me, not stroll with it about
the lake." The blond arrar had a hand upon my
arm.

"Know you what has come to pass?" he asked
me.

"Of what, specifically, do you speak?"

"There are no hulions in residence at the Lake of
Horns."

"And when did they leave?"

"Upon my master's death," he said, pushing close.
I walked from the line. Others were waiting.

"Sit with me," he urged.

"No." I shook off his hand and sought an untenanted expanse of wall, squatting at its foot with
my food between my legs, Slayer fashion.

"Why do you tell me this?" I asked after a time,
when he hovered there still. I wished he had waited
until my head was clear. The rana, tongue-curling
and thick, steamed. I sipped it cautiously.

"It concerns you," he said.

"You give me more than I have, arrar."

"I doubt that." He grinned. He, I decided, must be longer awake than I.

"Direct me to the fitter's," I asked him.

He allowed that he would escort me there. I moaned silently. I had been a fool to come here. I had had other designs upon the time remaining before the dharen's return.

I gulped my rana, handed him the empty cup. "Get me, if you would, another serving," I asked of him. I waited until he had taken a place in line. The man ahead addressed him. His thought bristled, shielding. Of me, the other queried him. His guarded answer revealed nothing. But I felt ever more as I wakened the crux that crackled the very air about. I knew every nerve in my body. My pulse spoke loud. There were no longer hulions at the Lake of Horns. At Gherein's death they had left. I cautioned myself, lest I assume some false causal relationship between the two events. And what value might I attach to that piece of information, when I knew not the hulions' function, what service they had previously rendered at the Lake of Horns?

"Perhaps Khys called them elsewhere," I postulated to him when he returned with two cups.

He laughed. I liked not the sound of it. But I had not, upon first sight, liked anything about this blond-haired lake-born.

"What name have you?" I asked him, swirling the hot liquid.

"Ase," he replied. I had known another by that name once. It is not an uncommon name in the northeast.

"I had thought to do more of the dharen's work upon our new prisoners," I informed him. "I seek Carth, to get the keys. Know you where I might find him?"

"He is in seclusion, not to be disturbed until

Khys returns." He did not hide his satisfaction. I wondered what he found to gloat about in the hullions' absence.

"There is little time," I said determinedly. "I am afraid I will have to disturb him."

He squinted at me from above. I felt his mind's seeking, and showed him what served me. "I have the keys," he said, eyeing me speculatively. "I might take you down there, after you have seen the fitter. I would not want you to disturb Carth. He is, after all, a councilman." His voice dripped venom like a swamp slipsa's fangs.

He was as good as his word. And he was also the man Khys had chosen for my circle partner. A strong statement of power, was that: his placing my life routinely in the hand of his son's favored arrar. We descended many stairs.

"Get your gear," he urged me as we walked the halls. "I would try you."

I was more than pleased to agree. There fell between us then an assessive silence, ceasing only when our mental paths crossed.

"Why are you not grieving for Gherein?" I asked aloud.

"I still implement his will." His voice was hard-edged. "When I have finished my tasks. I will doubtless take time to consider him and his completed works." We crossed a nexus hosting six passages. I saw no windows.

"Are we below ground?"

He nodded, guiding me through the passage west of north. It was short, with no doors upon its length. It led to a door of stra plate. The door when opened to the arrar's fist revealed a huge chamber, compartmentalized. A woman from one answered the arrar's summons. From her I commissioned a robe identical to the one I had lost. Also I procured a white tas tunic; a cloak lined with shorn white brist; three silks long-lengths, all

white; a gol-knife; two straight-blades that I selected with care, and the leathers appropriate to
such weapons. One of the blades I chose was no-
ticeably heavier than the other. Even did I take it
from a different section.

"One should practice with the same blade weight
one intends to use upon the kill," he criticized.

"I have always done it thus." I had never done
so. "My master was Rin diet Tron, of Astia. Who
was yours?"

"Lake-born do not study Slayer's skills," His
voice said that it was favor he did me, that such
work was far beneath him. "The dharen assured
me you would not kill me."

"I would not be too certain," I said, adding an
additional gol-knife to my store. All but the heavier blade I had sent to the dharen's keep. That I
put in sheath, first knicking my arm with it. The
lake-born raised his eyebrows as I sucked the new
blood. Evidently one did not blood a new weapon
before sheathing at the Lake of Horns.

"Take me to your civilized and urbane holding
keeps, O effete one," I suggested, piqued.

He grinned and acquiesced, leading me a way
that twisted and turned and convoluted so that I
took fear of being lost forever wandering in the
soundless maze, with only the lake-horn and an
occasional ceiling star for companions. After an
agonizing time, we came finally to a passage hosting doors. They were high-numbered. We proceeded
down it.

"What keep do you want?" he asked me, fishing
out his keys from his robe.

"Thirty-four," I said, dry-mouthed.

"Here, then." He stopped, fit the key. Bent over
the lock, he regarded me. "How long here had you
in mind?"

"An enth, perhaps."

"That is long to wait."

"I will make the wait well worth it," I promised him.

"It is to be hoped," he said, shoving the door inward with his shoulder. Across the green-dark keep he strode, to disappear. I heard crackling lake rushes, then a sound as of flesh upon flesh. "Wake, arrar," I heard, and another muffled sound.

I felt the rushes under my feet. Straining for sight, I trod that dimness.

"Get out of here," I hissed at the looming bulk of the arrar Ase. He melded into the darkness. Wood grated upon stone; the dimness became more complete.

My hands found him first. He spoke a low greeting.

His form detached itself from the shadows as I whispered a return.

"Saw you Chayin?" he asked me. His manner kept me back, though I longed to lay my head upon him.

"Yes. He bade me wear white to your ending. I cannot see this. I am unbanded. I can deal with the arrar who brought me here. He has keys." I saw the ice in his gaze, and knew as I spoke that he would refuse. "Carth will seek me here, before mid-meal. If you held me, he would free you of the band. Upon my life, he would do it. You must not do this. Gherein tried him, Gherein is dead. The hulions are gone from the Lake of Horns. Khys admits he has lost stance in the time. Sereth, let me free you."

"You do not think I could prevail against him?" he questioned me very low.

And I sought his eyes. I could not meet them. They rested upon the dharen's mark, half-revealed by my open tunic.

"I see no need."

"Where could a man run from Khys? Estri, let me be. Keep your questions from the affairs of men. I will have a testing of him. It suits me. I would hear the manner of Gherein's death."

I told it to him. He slid down upon the rushes, his weight making them sigh and rustle. The chain upon him hissed. I wished it was over, decided. He asked me of the method and manner of the confrontation. He asked of M'ksakka. Not once did his gaze lighten upon me, not for one instant did I see in him what I had come here seeking.

When he was finished questioning, he bade me leave. Silent, I did his will.

The arrar, upon seeing my face and my early exit, did not press me to then fulfill my commitment.

"Sereth," I had pleaded, "let me serve you."

"One last time? No. When I want you, I will take you," he had answered. "Now, get from my sight. I have need of rest."

The time, I thought as Ase led me to the guarded exit, is obstinate in the extreme. I would have been elsewhere than Khys's keep awaiting Carth that morning. But that was where Ase delivered me.

He stood about, reluctant to leave.

"I will give you service," I said to him, at the lintel. "But not in the dharen's keep, with Carth's arrival imminent." He stood over me, very blond and lakeborn.

"We will see to it," he agreed, "at a more convenient time."

"You did not aid me for my use," I accused him.

"No, nor did you seek the Ebvrasea for his. But you are right. I sought something from the moment, something it failed to provide."

"I, also, got less than I had envisioned from that encounter."

"Doubtless," he said, leaning upon the door frame, "if the moment had been more fruitful, you would not have been here for Carth." He squinted, pointing down the hall. I then saw Carth.

"Truth," I said, my voice as wry as his. "Perchance we will do better in the circle, I, for one, am far beyond my depths in these matters."

As Carth approached, it seemed to me that he bore my destiny with him, a dark mantle that devoured light all around him. Carth walked in shadow, though the day came in the windows, and the ceiling stars attended their task. I heard Khys's voice, inward, asking from me composure, notwithstanding the message Carth would bear.

"You will excuse me?"

"Surely. I have a book to read," he said with a self-effacing grin.

"Upon hesting, no doubt." I picked it from his mind.

"Tasa," he said. Unwilling to meet Carth, was the blond arrar. He pushed himself away from the wall and was gone down a bifurcation in moments.

I shivered and awaited Carth, now first of Khys's council.

"Have you taken up with the opposition?" he snarled, pushing me roughly before him into the keep.

"Khys is not yet returned," I said, shaking free of him. Calm, I reminded myself, in the face of Carth's terrifying temper.

"The dharen has asked me," I managed through clenched teeth, "to try to maintain an atmosphere of normalcy in which he may function with minimal distraction. You are not helping." I sat upon the edge of the couch. Carth paced the mat before me as if Chayin's spirit had suddenly come to inhabit his flesh.

He snorted. "You would maintain that atmosphere from beneath the soil? I was apprised of Ase's intent while resting, so strong was it. And yours also. Do you think he did not know your scheme? He awaited it, that he might have cause to bring in another of his master's hests."

"Are you telling me Ase sought my life in the undertunnels?"

"As surely as you sought his," said Carth, stopping in mid-pace to glare.

I shrugged. "It did not work for either of us. Sereth awaits Khys's return. Chayin also seeks no help. Why? What possesses them?" I unbuckled the weapons belt, laid it by.

"Their maleness, I imagine."

"Maleness makes a man crave his own execution?"

Carth's fists found his hips. Derision twisted his features. "Why does a man reach his limit at one time and not another? I know not. With Sereth, I might guess it related to you and what you have become."

"Let us not discuss what I have become. I had more than enough of such instruction this evening past."

"But with Sereth, it is only a guess. In crux, little is revealed. He Places his hests. They are not ineffectual. His skills are not as ours. You have seen the attenuated effect of the band of restraint upon him. True Silistran, he may be, or a picture of what our children's children will become. Under these circumstances, with Khys bound by his own word to give him the chance he gave Gherein, his skills may aid him."

"You took him. How can he stand against such forces as Khys can command?" I whispered, seeing him, his wounds still heavy upon him, cold and defiant in his cell.

"Ten arrars and I went to the taking of those two. Sereth disdains helsar skills as weapons. And well he may, since none of mine could even slow him with mind. He demanded and received physical battle from us. His shielding protects him from all but steel or stra." Through Carth's memory I saw it: Sereth and Chayin, cornered upon the third floor. They bore that day no smiles upon them.

Between Sereth's legs was a corpse cleaved down the middle. The spilled organs made gory mud about their feet. Sereth had extended his shielding to Chayin, or the cahndor had learned its workings. Through it, periodically, did Chayin reach out with his mind. One stroke, that of contained turbulence, swept Carth off his feet and dashed him against the corridor wall. And I saw them taken in the rush of nine against them. Four more I saw die there, two by the cahndor in one desperate blade flash. From that stroke Chayin did not recover, but tumbled senseless atop the last man he had downed. And the five of them then took their leisure with Sereth. I broke the link. That I would not see.

"I am distressed," said Carth, "by your concern for them. Have you no feelings for Khys? You have long since ceased being a woman to Sereth. A symbol, you are, of his failure and diminishment and loss."

"Back to what I have become? Carth, I will not hear it. What I am, you and Khys have made me. What that is, I do not know. What offends the cahndor and Sereth, if offense it is, is beyond my understanding. But I have never understood fitness as it is propounded by men. I care not. I have feelings for Khys. They are mixed, in many areas. Of one thing I am sure. He has ruled overlong from the Lake of Horns."

Carth sought the window, his back to me. His voice came very soft. And it was filled with grief. "Shaper's spawn, we may see soon the end of that rule. And it would be a great loss, if such should come to be. It is a pity that none could give you perspective. But then"—he sighed—"we had perspective. It did us little good. You have served Estrazi's purpose. Khys dreamed you so weak and fragile that he might dally with you, forewarned, and come to no harm. He took a dream and made it real. But in those lands he became lost. And I

wonder if he will wake in time." He turned and
faced me, his hands clutching the still. "The child,"
he said, "is gone."

I looked at him, filled with thoughts of Chayin
and Khys and Sereth and crux, not understanding.
Then his words took meaning. I smiled at his dour
and careworn face. I stretched and rose. In my
seeing, I had been upheld. Crux notwithstanding, I
had received the match I sought—that of presage
with time-spawned moment. Our departure from
the Lake of Horns, I had seen. And where we were
bound—that also had been shown to me. But
though I had preguessed the reason, I had not
fitted it in its temporal position.

Calm, Khys had begged of me. Calm would I
give him. He, who had known even that my unau-
thorized seeking of Sereth would move Carth to
attend me before his return, would have my most
diligent assistance in these matters.

"Do you have no tears to shed for your son?"
demanded Carth incredulously.

"He was mine to bear, only. Upon this subject, I
gave Khys warning. Fear does not become you.
Khys doubtless has his reasons. If you love him as
deeply as your profess, give him the respect he is
due. He has not yet fallen. Let us all save our tears
for that event, lest we invite into the time that
which we least desire." And he did not choose to
hear my sarcasm, but only nodded and sank down
upon the alcove cushions to await the dharen's
return.

The sun sought the apex of its travel. I sought
the sort. Through great fogs and mires of crux I
plowed on. And came, eventully, to a recollection.
All that I had learned about blood debts and fitness I reviewed. Upon a certain scale, I weighed
what had passed between me and the arrar Ase,
while the both of us were intentioned on the other's
death. And the unclaimed blood debt he still owed

me, from that service I rendered him as we stood
witness for Khys and Gherein, came clear to my
mind; and even what that might mean, in consideration of a lesson Sereth had once provided.

Upon a time, I had held a man's life. His name
was Lalen gaesh Satemit. He had been a crell, late
of the city of Stra. He had come to be mine, among
other possessions, when I had taken up the chald of
the tiask Besha. I had freed him. He had later
proved himself more than willing to decapitate me
at Sereth's whim. And I considered Sereth and
Chayin, in their cells. And M'tras, whose life had
come into my hands. And I began to understand
what service I might render, and what I might not.
But I did not heed those lessons well enough, thinking them only what they seemed, insight into what
had occurred. That enlightenment, intended as instruction and preparation. I devalued and miscon-
strued. Only did I determine that I must beware
Ase, and keep a light hand upon M'tras. Not that
with Sereth and Chayin and what they hested, I
must not interfere.

Carth's eyes, boring holes into my scalp, ob-
truded into my concentration. "Your puerility never
ceases to amaze me," he said, still acrimonious
after our long silence.

"I suggest that you cease seeking within me,
since what you find puts you in ill humor."

What he muttered then was unclear.

"Tell me of hulions," I suggested. I rose and
circled the keep, all but the alcove where Carth
sat. Noticing the things I had ordered, there upon
the gol-slab table, I gathered them up.

Carth made no answer. I shrugged and took the
parcels unopened to Khys's wardrobe. I would not
have opened them before Carth. On my way, I
snatched up the blooded blade, explaining that
Khys had found me a circle partner. While within,
I exchanged the hide tunic for the white tas. It

covered completely the breech and band. "White, and no other color upon you," the cahndor had ordained. Also, did I get the cloak lined with white brist from my pile, and from its peg the true Shaper's cloak. Khys, I thought, would favor it for this journey. And I took up for him second-best leathers. He would not want, I was sure, to go overdressed. Those things I draped over my arm, then took to couch, arranging his on its left and mine upon its right.

Carth watched me, his face creating expressions that have gone ever nameless.

When I had finished, I sat at the couch's foot, upon my heels, as Khys preferred. I faced Carth, and that spot between us where the dharen would come to be.

Carth read thoughts. I gave him, then, some to read.

"Estri . . ."

"Carth, if I am as little in your sight as I am in theirs, then surely I can free the smallness within to work its will." I had considered, for his benefit, certainties I had about what would momentarily come to be. I took satisfaction in his ashen face even as it faded from view, replaced by Khys's form.

"Have you a message for me?" he demanded of Carth with asperity.

"Yes, dharen." Carth rose, suddenly awkward.

"You know it," he said. Then: "The child is gone, none knowing whither. It was at the moment of Gherein's death, when all were busy with its experience. It was not soon discovered, and longer was taken in its reporting. Those who might be considered negligent are in holding—"

"There is no negligence," Khys broke in. "None are to be held to account for this. Carth, after all I have done with you, do you still prejudge so blindly? Must there always be a ready culprit at hand, accessible? Who will hold the Weathers to account? What sentence will you impose upon the wind from the abyss? Can you contain crux in a band of restraint? Carth, I seek more from you than I can presently find. I pray you, make yourself ready for the weight you will come to bear. I have no more time to cede you. Get upon it!"

Carth half-ran from the room. I sat dazed, nearly drowned in the waves of his indignation.

"You found it necessary to test out my truths upon the Ebvrasea. Did he uphold me?" He sought the couch. At its side he stripped off his robe, garbing himself in those things I had selected.

"You know that he did," I said softly. "Nothing may be changed." He had told me: Sereth and Chayin awaited their moments. He knew them. He knew their sense of fitness. And he had spoken to me of it, when I could not chase thoughts of them from my mind. And of how they regarded me, he had spoken. I had been loath to believe him. All had gone as Khys must have known it would. My ambivalence rose within me, choking and sweet in my throat. He seemed loose, relaxed, his attention upon his fittings. But I felt him, searching.

"Does what you see please you?" I asked, my concern for him receding before his intrusion.

"You have your moments," he grunted. "It remains to be determined whether you can manage as long a string of them as the time demands. Do not fight so what rises within you. It may be all you have for sustenance soon enough."

"What mean you?"

"Only that. Make ready."

I set about it. "Do you want me as more than witness?" I ventured.

"I cannot say yet. If your sire holds you as lightly as you hold your son, you may be in some small danger. Keep your skills well about you. It could come to be that I am not available to aid you." He took seat upon the couch, then lay back. His molten eyes were distant, further than the bronze ceiling scales. "You should be prepared to make your way back alone."

"Do you crave release from your duties, to speak so?" I managed. My fingers upon the cloak fittings had gone numb and stupid.

"There is little danger of altering this time by an ill-spoken word or two. Would that it were so simple. Crux obscures, has obscured, will obscure, those specific truths with which we are about to become concerned. Most often, one may reach out beyond the point of blindness. I cannot make that connection. From that I can suppose a number of things, but I will not. Leave it at this: I might win what I seek. I will perhaps win other than what I seek. And I may trade for it what I have sought in the past. Or I may lose outright. It is crux."

"Have you a meeting place in mind?"

"An encounter point has been determined between us." He pushed up on his elbows, his chin tucked in. "If I should temporarily lose track of you, be assured that at my convenience I will again take you up." He lay back upon the couch once more. "You may go armed."

I declined. I could find no sense in bearing stra into such a battle. I sought the parcel that had been delivered to me. Even with pelted cloak and leather and wool upon me, I was cold. I leaned there in the wardrobe, my shoulder against the smooth northern thala. It was the most familiar of colds. I wondered if ever I would be without its portentous breath on my neck.

From behind, his arms encircled my waist. The strength of him, gathering for the moment, came clear. His readiness was staggering. I twisted in his grasp, pressing against him.

He chuckled, holding me.

If he went so greatly armed and was still unsure,

what small fraction of the necessary skills might I bring to bear?

In that time I came again to meet my ambivalence, and with no success. He only ran his hands over my back. He may have sought me, or the sort, or that which was about to commence. I know not. I knew then only that I could not raise my hand against him. Nor was it necessary. I had already done all that was needed, merely by being what I had been bred to be.

And Khys, who surely knew, only pulled me closer. If I had been he, I would have killed me. But therein perhaps lies the difference between the male and the female conception, that difference that was made once and for all understood to me in what was to follow. But not then did I know it, except in the way that all things, if only to themselves, admit their singularity to be dependent upon the effluence of their sex.

Then I only stood passive with him, aroused but in no way wanting his use, my thought bounding from him to Sereth to the cahndor and back like a bondrex in a Dritiran capture pit. The view from one place was no less forbidding than from any other. It occurred to me that they might all kill each other and leave me free. I doubted that I would survive, upon the next thought, if such came to be the case.

"Khys," I whispered, "reassure me. This calm you have demanded is as elusive as the sevenfold spirit."

"About whom or what?" he said. Because my cheek was pressed against his leather and my hair had fallen over my face, I could not see him. But his words gave message of the tiny quirking of his lips.

I stepped back from him as far as his arms allowed.

"That you will live long enough to give Sereth

the satisfaction of destroying you," I snapped, twisting free of him. There was a time when he would have dropped me screaming to my knees for less. That time was passed.

"I cannot," said Khys levelly.

I stared at him, blinking angrily. My tears brought that smile upon him.

I whirled and shouldered by him into the keep proper. Out the doors and into the hall I stumbled, seeking composure and a moment's respite. Before the hulion tapestry I halted and awaited him. It mattered not to me how the dharen ended. Or even if he did not. So I bespoke my heart. But my ears heard the falsehood and rejected it.

By the time he collected me, I had regained a semblance of calm. But only that. He regarded me, his eyes narrowed. He said nothing.

We walked the blue and green squares to the stairs and down them. I recall every one. Clear and sharp was the single path of crux. His grip light on my arm down the two flights, we wordlessly traversed the main hall.

In the audience room, upon the symbol that Khys shared with Estrazi and his Shaper kin and the Mi-ysten children, he extended his hand. I took it, his right in my left.

"Remember, mark you the route."

With real calm, that which attends me only upon such embarking, I promised to heed him. Upon the spiral, I felt only joy that the waiting was over. We were about it. That which had been long coming to be would stand revealed. It is never as torturous to do a thing as await it, I thought.

Then I cleared my mind. His fingers between mine became a grid of light over my closed lids, hot and great. Up the veins in my arm went the poisoning of power, a voracious drug in search of my present. There was a thinning of flesh as the network of our sensory systems meshed. I felt us,

rising like my nerves as they slid glowing out upon
my skin, dissolving it for leverage. And the bone
within glows golden at such times, when sensing
flashes red and seeks its macrokin spread all incon-
ceivable across the fabric of creation. Warp and
woof, we became. Fully distended, I heard us: whining wind we made over that place where an
instant's stop is overlong. Then came out to greet
us the beacon we had sought. Within that realm
are creatures from whose function Khys modeled
the concept "sort." And what do true sorters (all
widespread particles of self-conscious community
undulating multispectrum resonance) sort? Pregnant time from stillborn, entropy in its thousand
variations, natural laws and travelers thereupon
do they thrum and shunt from one alternity to
another. Upon another manifestation: silver drop-
lets heated molten, ever running; mercury asplatter
upon an eye's pupil. Third to the left, high in their
ranks, an eye the size of the Opirian Sea determined our destination. A hand better suited for
rerouting cataclysm and pruning stars came to
enfold us. We lay a time in what was chasm and
palm, creased. I looked up at it. It looked down at
me. The touch of Khys's being grew tenuous. I
fought to retain it. The circuited tide received us
from that dipping hand. Tumbling, he grasped me.
Eyes are never lost. Ours met. The father's fire of
his determination licked around me, and we ceased
falling.

We did not bounce or roll. We were underpinned
once more by world. Moist turf, beneath. Stones
strewn beneath my buttocks. His hand had solid
substance; fingers fleshed and of the shape and
form associated with such digits. I looked long at
them, enfolding mine. The sky was not Mi'ysten
sky.

It was not a land inhabited by such as Khys and
myself. I did not need to search the sky, comb the

grass. My sensing gave me sign. A young world it
was. Or a very old one. There was no worm bur-
rowing this earth, nor bird to eat it. There was the
rustling of leaves, the hiss and growl of wind. But
no insect clicked mandibles together. Then I sat
up. Far across the great rolling grassed plain was
a ring of trees, perfect and of a dark lush green. I
saw not one weed or flower or fruit. The laws
here, I surmised, must be greatly different. One
thinks of life systems interwoven. Here the chain
was either broken or the links not all yet forged.

Khys's hand was restless in mine. I thought to
withdraw. He did not allow it.

"This world is untenanted but for us." So did he
break a virgin silence.

I nodded, hesitant still to violate the peace. But
it was upon me. "And what we do here sets
precedents." I thus completed the first interchance
upon that world. Sequential time as man knows it
might now begin, I thought, looking at that unseen
sky, so vast and mighty. It had about it a blue
tinge, chilled still further by a cool sun's light.

"Do you think interchange is a precursor to evo-
lutionary life?" I asked him.

"It doubtless was the precursor, upon a more
protent scale. I do not know. You think they would
attempt to bind us with such responsibility?"

He actually asked me. The less-seeking light made
him young, uncertain.

"I hope not," I said, unwilling to deal with my
suspicions. Khys looked around him. He got to his
feet and scanned the great encircling stand of trees.

"That," he said, "is north."

"If it is your will," I said, dutifully fixing that
which I had conceived as north as True Declared
North. "You have directions," I postulated. Directions would have necessitated our declaring ourselves; we had determined north.

"Estrazi," I said to him, "is canny. Must we

traverse ground and make observational decisions to get there? Can you not mind-seek them?"

"Seek yourself. They are not yet present, nor do I expect them until we have gained the appointed ground."

"You know where this might lead," I warned.

A breeze came up and blew his hair, dull copper in the alien light, over his eyes. He raised a hand to brush it away. Here upon this world his skin had only the most modest glow upon it. Mine, I saw as I examined my outstretched arm, hosted none at all. I was further disquieted.

"We are natural to this particular conception," I said to him. He had been rubbing his eyes. He lowered his hand. His face was very grave.

"Whoever created this was familiar with us. Our arrival here was understood before the rock beneath us cooled." We agreed. The certainty within me grew. His eyes sparked. That, at least, was unchanged.

His left eyebrow rose. His nostrils flared. "I had not considered this," he admitted.

"I myself am only suspicioned. Let us wait, lest we bring it upon ourselves."

He reached down to me. I took his hand and by it gained my feet. I was light-headed, sluggish. The pull of the earth lay heavy upon me. Concerned, he noted it. His hands sought the sides of my throat, and I was much strengthened.

"You should not have," I objected, when I found myself with enough wit returned to realize what he had done.

"I brought you here. I should have foreseen this. Let us get done and away. Third rock, south of east. Can you walk?"

"Yes." The clouds were white with sienna tingeing. The sky was bluer than M'ksakkan eyes. I walked with him. It had been the journey that had weakened me, I told myself, that I might perhaps make it so. If what Khys thought it . . .

I found no further sucking away of my substance, upon the walk to third rock south of east. The sun seemed to parallel our course. Not once did it move from above our heads. He squinted at it, on several occasions. Once he glowered up at it a long time.

The quiet of such an untenanted world pressed in upon us. I looked around me at bounteous beauty and wondered why the catalysts of life had not finished their labors. I knew, of course, the answer.

"There is no respite from one's own creations," he reminded me.

"Of myself, I might say the same to you," I rejoined.

"There." He pointed.

"What?" I saw rolling ground only.

"The first rock south of east," he declared it.

"If it is your will," I said softly, trying to smile.

A rivulet of sweat ran down the trough of my backbone.

We walked. The ground was rich and resilient, the grass so perfect that my feet thought it the most elegant silken tapestry. Khys watched me as narrowly as the ground we covered.

Nightfall was a thing of iths. There was hardly a sun's set; a moment, a brief flame touch, and it weak and cool; then a blackness sliced assunder by a gleaming sword of stars. Steel in mid-strike with the light sparking off it was no denser than that swath of stars having the night.

There was no moon.

"Think you there might be a moon another night?" I asked him hopefully, after the first shock of dusk had passed.

"No," he said, calm, implacable. "There is no moon. Upon this night or any other. Would you have fire?" His hand sought the back of my neck. His fingers tightened there. I found I welcomed it.

"Yes, we have come too far for it to matter."

I heard his laugh as I knelt down in the grass. All was monochrome, noncommittal. Above me, he was denser shadow, limned in pearly fog. He knelt, half-turned, to his firing. The Shaper's seal upon the cloak's back flickered.

I closed my eyes and sent fervent plea to my father. I did not know what was right. I asked only rightness. I might better have chosen.

Khys had his fire, hovering above a shallow pit he had caused to be in the sward. It burned there upon invisible fuel. Hest and sort were unencumbered. None held limiting conception here. None but us. What we could conceive, in this place, could come to be without the bending and stretching of natural law required to do such upon Silistra. Khys, as he hested fire, further invested the time with stricture. Before he and I there had been only the possibilities unrestricted. Less than an enth (which also had never been before we came to walk the earth) we had been here. In us, we carried the world we knew. And upon a barely completed nature, we set a presupposed lawfulness. Wider, perhaps, than some others' might have been, but limiting.

The fire crackled merrily upon its invisible logs, all consuming, yet unconsummated. He sat cross-legged, palms up in the firelight.

"How far are we from the third rock south of east?" I asked.

"About a man's length," he informed me, gesturing to the left of the fire. I squinted, but saw only fire-deepened dark. I lay back upon the grass, watched the afterimage flames lick the sword of stars that cut the night.

"It is a world of great beauty."

"Thank you," I said.

"It is tempting in the extreme."

"Doubtless it was meant to be." Even my building of it had been part of Estrazi's conception. Thus far, I had been careful. I had not hested, nor had I shaped; it was my intention that this remain so. I had no desire to further entwine myself in the destiny of that world. I had promised once that I would return to it. I had not meant to keep that vow.

I saw two stars detach themselves from the sky, spewing long tails behind them as they sped downward.

"They approach," I said to him. He only nodded, his countenance adance with firelight.

Upon my left there was a breeze. It caressed my cheek, and I turned my head toward it. He sat there, in that most elegant male-form he wears, dark-cloaked.

Beside him was Kystrai, most beneficent of the fathers: Khys's own sire. Fathers sit not in darkness. I had forgotten them. Perhaps mortal mind cannot hold such images without scaling down. The fathers' fire made jest of the flame before us.

"Estrazi," I acknowledged him. His presence examined me. That compassionate mouth tightened. Those eyes touched my flesh, and I was strengthened.

"Son of my brother, I am not pleased," said Estrazi across me. Khys sat unmoving. He seemed not awed. "Have you become so indrawn and eclectic that you feel the need to alter even my conception of flesh as it clothes spirit?" He raised his hand, only. The fire died.

Khys made a sound. I strained to see him. I saw first a spiral, scintillant, part-obscured. It was the size of my palm. Around it from the dark coalesced Khys's bared chest, his hand upon the altered flesh. I dug my fingers into the turf. Harsh breathing filled my ears. I could not take my eyes from the dharen, so still with that wild fear in his eyes. As he had marked me, so had Estrazi emblazoned his flesh.

"One must be willing to bear judgment as one metes it out," said Estrazi. He lowered his hand into his lap. I watched the bronze glow wash his skin, the currents of life clear in their flow. Truly, I had not remembered him well enough.

Kystrai, beside him, looked wordlessly upon his own-spawned one. His concern was obvious. That magnificent head thrust forward, he gazed steadily upon his light-skinned offspring, as if by glare alone he could cleanse him free of flaw.

"You may speak," said father to son.

"You have something of mine. How may I regain it?" said Khys most softly. His palm still lay upon his breast. Through part-spread fingers, the Shaper's device glittered. Khys's eyes closed a moment. I saw him, striker, struck with his own blow. It showed like a saw-edged claw in the air, whirling around and spinning back. He threw himself flat, rolling.

And then he sat again cross-legged upon my right as if he had never moved. His chest heaved, and his pulse fought for exit at the base of his throat.

"Do not be absurd," said Estrazi, his amusement only touched with annoyance. "Shall I show you what might be decided here? You come before me with false assumptions. It is my pleasure to take my inheritor and school him. I may also extend that courtesy to his father."

"Calm yourself, Khys," advised Kystrai. It was he for whom I felt compassion, he whose spawn had come so far to stand upon the edge of the abyss. Their eyes met. "Why did you never seek me?" spoke Kystrai in a voice like embers fading.

"I might ask the same of you," said Khys bitterly.

"Is it not past time," broke in Estrazi, "that you

put away these repetitious exercises of children and address yourself to the affairs of adults?"

Khys looked from his father, to mine, to me. And to Estrazi again did his gaze return like some hypnotized yit.

"This," said Estrazi, "could be yours." The first among the Shapers raised his hand, and the world around showed midday, and that midday teemed with life. And we sat overlooking a sea. "And this . . ." I saw what swam in that sea. "And this," he said, dissolving from beneath us the world upon which our flesh had taken rest.

We depended, all four, from nothing, at the center of a sphere defined by pinpricked turbulence, all colored. Through it the stars processed, leaving great trails of wake. Out from a common center, streaming life, they rushed and bore us with them.

"Here," said Estrazi, "did we begin. Here will we never return, but by proxy." I could not make sense of my brain's imaging. I closed my eyes, blocked out that madness. It could be I saw chaos there. I saw what I could not see. "The child in question might, with the proper training, return word home."

We sat again before the hollow that Khys had made for his fire, and that was there also, its light yellow and puny with the fathers so near. "You could not have survived there longer." It was to me Estrazi spoke. I judged him saddened. He touched my arm. "Still seek you freedom from my work?" he inquired.

"Yes," I said, my eyes averted. "I need a time for reflection." My mind told him what else my heart craved, before I could silence it. He kissed me atop the head. "I can give you little respite," he said. "And you may find it to be heavier upon you than my service. If you find yourself insufficiently bound, apprise me. I will set you to work."

Kystrai stood now before Khys. He raised up his

son. Khys rose but shrugged the hand away. I watched, unbelieving, as Kystrai heard from Khys all manner of abrading without word or gesture. When the son had run dry of words, the father again touched his shoulder. Khys turned away. His face, full revealed, was awful to look upon.

"I will still contest with you, if you so wish it, for the flesh child," said Estrazi to him, stepping from my side. The bronze light flowed languorous after him as he moved. "I hate to waste you, after such lengthy preparation, but I will give you that choice once again. Let me point out, before you answer, that upon your own world you have imposed on others the like judgment. We are better qualified than you to attend the instruction of such a child."

With rage-contorted countenance did Khys regard Estrazi. For a moment I thought he would seek his dissolution. He did not. His face took its normal semblance. With only the flaring of nostrils and his narrowed eyes did he signal his wrath.

"I seek not your instruction. I seek it not for myself, nor for my son. If I had sought, I would have come here, long since. You set us into the time, disassociate us from the rest of creation, uncaring. Purpose notwithstanding, who has right to suspend heritage and withhold knowledge? Must we make the climb, to prove a point? Because it is postulated by you that once such occurred, must we mimic your trials?"

"You are not even close, abrasive adolescent, with those assumptions. We were not so lacking for company that we sought to create ourselves anew in space and time. What you interpret as whim is the learning process upon all levels." Estrazi looked at Khys inquiringly. That one made no answer.

"The creator," said Estrazi patiently, "can never experience his own creation from within. If he is potent, he may retain the experience of creation ongoing. But life, as flesh, may not be experienced from without. We sought, from the creatures of time and space, what they may yet become: a more potent creator species capable of multiplicities of awareness." Still Khys made no reply.

"It is beautiful in your sight, is it not?" Estrazi's hand drew the world within its circle. Khys only nodded. "I cannot know it. I am without. I may take flesh, but still I know far too much of the workings of reality to become immersed in it. My daughter, here, sent to me a plea for rightness." He turned upon me.

"At that moment, you declared yourself a creature of space and time. Committed you are, as never before, to its laws. I had thought perhaps to take you from such lands, for you seemed not well integrated. But you have become so."

I stared at the ground, tearful for the chance lost. But it was not chastisement he spoke to me then. Only in my conception was it interpreted as such.

"You make no such plea to me." He spoke to Khys. That one did not hesitate upon the chance nor fail to heed the warning.

"I make no such plea to you," said Khys clearly.

Between them a whorl of ominous proportions took form.

Kystrai stepped there. Within the counterstalking powers he came to stand, straight and severe, where nothing of flesh or sinew could ever have stood.

"Khys," said he from the obscuring roils of battle, "I would not see this. Long you have labored in the worlds of creation. Purpose did it serve, great and worthy if one might use your own scales to weigh it upon. But here there are no such divisions in fitness. All is fit, within one context or another. Only that which buildeth not change has censure here. The destroyer and the creator are one. The catalyst both disintegrates and recreates. By your efforts Silistra saw much change. You have brought to be all the change your conception holds. You have reached a most untenable position. One can do anything but perpetuate stasis. There is no holding that world to your conception. Upon what you gave them they have built. They are in need of a new creator, one who has as his foundations that which you in your lengthy lifetime built. Upon your works, that one will build that which you cannot yet conceive. Cede Silistra, if you love her. You stand obstacle in her path. All masters pass. The time is due for them to stand alone. And for you to seek a broadening of your conception. And for a father to share the fruits of his days with a son fit to be his inheritor." As he spoke those last words, the roil of contention dispersed.

Kystrai, legs spread wide, faced his son.

"Fifteen lifetimes I have lived upon that world. Of me, I gave her rebirth."

"None would take that from you," said Estrazi.

"Raet would have."

"Let us not speak of Raet," commanded Kystrai, who had spawned him. "What rivalry exists between the Mi'ysten children and the Silistran children is not our affair."

Khys laughed bitterly. His face was well known to me. He had found his stance. His decisions, though not revealed, were made. Looking at him, I knew he courted the life right. Kinship I felt to him, upon that realization, and a deep respect. His eyes flicked over me, noting. I sought longer consultation. He denied me.

"Send her back," he bargained.

"You will remain?" Estrazi queried him. "Without the distasteful alternatives?"

I recalled, horrifyingly real, my time in the holding cubes upon Mi'ysten. Above and below and upon all sides had been others, destined to inhabit those clear prisons until certain observations had been made of their behavior. Some of us, in those cubes, had learned a thing. I could have done without the knowledge, at that price. Khys partook of my thought. I was pleased I might give some small warning.

I had known. But I had not known how it would come to be. I bit my lips, recollecting the dream. "Take them, the father and the son both," I had said to Estrazi. Can one be responsible for one's dream? I had warned him.

"Send her back," Khys asked again of my father.

"This is not an unfit place for her," Estrazi answered.

"If you speak in good faith, do it." Khys's eyes adjured me to absent myself. I dared not try that returning alone.

"Khys," I pleaded, "do not make compromise upon my account."

Estrazi stepped between us. "Daughter, I would speak with you alone." And I saw Khys's mouth, opening to speak, over Estrazi's shoulder. Then I saw him not, nor Kystrai either.

We stood in the perfect green wood, or another wood swathed in darkness.

He stood very still, did my father. The bronze glow coming out from him lit the nearer trunks as if their bark had been dipped in molten metal.

Then he held out his arms to me. I took refuge in them. A time he stroked my hair. I pressed my cheek against his cool flesh and let my tears flow, unchecked.

"Shed no tears for that one," he said sternly. "He needs them not."

I did not answer.

"You found him unacceptable as a mate. Surely it cannot concern you, what I choose to do with him. He is badly in need of certain lessons, humility not the least of them."

"Do not chastise him upon my account," I begged.

"I will do what I have long intended," said Estrazi in a tone that allowed no answer. "What think you of the progress we have made upon this sphere?"

I thought of the sun, which had followed us overhead, then dived at dizzying speed into the sea of night. What rhythm had they imposed upon this world, that it lay cooled and green so soon after its inception? "Is it truly that world which I started?"

"It is. You did not have intention of completing it, I hope."

"No," I said, for I had not.

"As a sphere of holding for the dharen, it will do nicely. Here he may learn his skills and make his mistakes. There is a fitness, I think, in dealing with him thus."

"He knows better than that."

"I think not. He has made a start already upon the shaping of this world. He will, with little else to do, continue. And with each alteration he induces upon this nature will he be still further bound."

I shivered in Estrazi's arms. Here was retribution. Not the puny sort I had conceived, but a just and all-encompassing balance on the scales of power.

"And when he breaks those bonds?"

"Then he will be what he is destined to become. We will welcome him into the community for which he pretends disdain, but in truth has long coveted. Then he will be ready. Now he is but a precocious child with imagined grievances."

I recollected the Stothric prediction concerning the days of judgment: "He who goeth first to his fall will come again, and be last."

Estrazi brushed my hair from my shoulder. I felt his cool touch upon the dharen's device.

"Can you make me what I was? Will you remove

from me this mark and the damage done me by Khys and his minions?"

"I can. I will not. But I will return you to Silistra."

"Let me give tasa to Khys. His affairs are barely ordered."

"He has no Silistran affairs any longer. There is no need. You will see him again."

"And that other matter in which I sought your aid?" I ventured.

"As you comport yourselves, so will it go. I have, at this stage, no objection. But further use will I make of you both. There can be no permanent exemption; your own natures will preclude it." His face came close to mine. I drifted in his eyes, seeking understanding. I did not find it. But I found acquiescence in myself.

He held me back from him. "I thank you for the spawn of your womb," he said formally, in Mi'ysten. "Be assured of the service you have rendered."

"Do not send me back," I pleaded, suddenly spinning in the unconstrained time that devoured all else.

But it was late for such fears.

VII

Into the Abyss

I retain a moment of it: bearing witness to a light-rendered scene from Stothric tradition, wherein Ambrae, having found Dyin, her true male complement, and made that hermaphroditic match which opens the pair to universal points of power, is taken by him to a sheer pinnacle overlooking the very chasm in which I floated.

"Fly with me," he proposed, his feet straddling that great peak that obtrudes into eternity.

She peered about her into a place of cold and darkness. "I cannot. My sight is obscured," she demurred silently, for her head was all covered over with woolens to keep her eyes from the blinding wind that sought to freeze them dead, and she could not open her mouth to speak.

"You must find another way to see," he instructed her, and cut away a tiny hole in the glove she wore so that the tip of her little finger lay exposed.

That being done, he then launched himself, and by his grip precipitated her also into the abyss.

As Ambrae, in desperation, I conceived a way to sensitize that part of me which did not normally see, but retain within its structure the capacity for seeing. As she changed a finger's nail to an organ of sight, thus surviving her mate's required test and teaching, so did I, amid harmonics ever forming, recreate the progression home.

But in two respects my sojourn contradicted the mythological model:

I was alone.

And I was there overlong.

VIII

The Passing of Khys

Upon the white walkways of the Lake of Horns I found myself, and they were red with blood. All about me was the snort and squeal of threx and the screams of men and women. The sky was thunderous and dark.

A threx sped past me, throwing up clods of turf. To my right it passed. Then stopped, whirled savagely around by its rider. I scrambled to my knees and ran. I ran past corpses and struggling knots of men and women. I leaped a forereader, trussed Parset style, wrists to ankles. Her eyes were wide. Her mouth was gagged. More threx did I see, and more. Louder and louder grew the hooves behind me.

I was in sight of the steps of the dharen's tower when the huija bit through my tunic and cloak. Thrice it curled around me, imprisoning my arms at my side with its fanged leather. I screamed, jerked off my feet. For a moment I dangled in midair, the metal teeth of the huija biting deep in my flesh. Then the rider had me.

His strong arms thrust me facedown across the threx's saddle. He jerked my wrists behind, bound them, and disentangled the huija in a practiced motion. I moaned as its teeth, pulling away, lifted tiny chunks of my flesh.

I struggled to raise my head to him, to explain

my identity. But the threx was running, bounding, jumping. A hand at the small of my back steadied me as he jerked his beast right. Before my eyes, all lay revealed. Gasping breaths between the threx's bounds, I tried to estimate their number. I made it well over a thousand Parsets. My estimate was later to prove low. Then it seemed very high.

My captor leaned low in the saddle and skewered a lake-born man. I saw surprised golden eyes. Before knowledge came to him of his death, we were gone, seeking others. I saw a tiask, bent over a trussed lake-born. What she paused to do with him there upon the field of battle that had been the placid lakeside made me retch. The saddle grip dug into my stomach, refused me breath.

The pedestrian lake-born defenders had no choice against mounted Parsets. They seemed not to know. My tears washed the vomit from my chin, and the dust and dirt from my eyes.

Up the great steps of the dharen's tower and through the open doors did the threxman urge his mount. Those steel-shod hooves threw sparks upon the archite and ornithalum. Its hooves reverberated like kapuras in the vaulted hall. Bodies adorned its length. I was sobbing, and I could not stop. Through the halls the threxman raced his beast, killing whatever moved within his sight. Nor was he the only one.

In the seven-cornered audience room were six threxmen.

He who had me drew his mount up with theirs. It blew and heaved and shook spittle upon me. I raised my head. The rider slapped me upon the buttocks. Further I squirmed, that I might get my rider's attention. He cuffed my head with his booted foot.

"Did you find them?" I heard dimly.

"Not yet. Where shall I put this one?" said the voice of my rider.

"Is she marked?" Again I tried to rise.

"I know not."

"Let me see her."

The rider raised me up roughly, setting me before him in the saddle.

"Please," I said, before his hand covered my mouth. I bit it. He grunted and set about gagging me with my hair. I wriggled from him. My eyes pleaded with the jiask who sat opposite us upon a brown threx. The screams and sword sound and threx noise rang through the audience chamber. Behind the threxman, the hangings had been torn from the window. Through it, I witnessed the efficiency with which the Parset forces invested the Lake of Horns.

"Let me see her," said the jiask upon the brown threx again, sliding off his mount. Wadded hair was forced into my mouth, bound with other locks behind my neck.

"She is mine," growled the rider who held me. I heard the hiss of his blade as he drew it.

"If I am not mistaken," said Lalen gaesh Satemit, "she belongs to those we seek."

"That one," growled my captor, "would have worn only white. This one"—he demonstrated, ripping from me cloak and tunic—"wears leathers."

"Nevertheless," said Lalen, his eyes crinkled with amusement, "she belongs to the cahndor and the Ebvrasea." He noted upon me Khys's device. Nor did his eyes miss my chald, set with gol.

"If they live," growled the voice, even deeper. "And if you are not mistaken. All I want to know is where I can leave her. I would pick some more of this lakeside fruit."

Lalen looked at me. He shrugged. I tried to speak.

He turned from me and walked to his threx. "She might know where they are." He grunted. "She might be of some help. But put her in the undertunnel keep with the others. Number four keep. Down three flights, left at the turning." He mounted his threx. "I think I might pick a few myself," he said, and urged his mount by that of my captor.

At the stra-doored stairway he was forced to dismount. We had seen no living thing in the halls, but we had seen many that had once lived. He left the threx, pulling me down into his arms. I could only implore him with my eyes. The soaking hair in my mouth threatened to choke me senseless.

"Be still," he advised, as I writhed in his grasp. I was still. At the stairs' foot lay the guards of the undertunnels in their own blood.

A Dordassar jiask lounged against the door of keep four.

"Did you mark her?" he grumbled, surly at his ill-drawn duty. "I cannot keep track of them." His dark face bore a disgruntled frown. His membranes wavered, receded.

"I will know her," said the jiask. "Lalen says she might be the cahndor's. I would not mark her until I am sure she is not. Here." He handed me unceremoniously into the guard's arms. That one kicked open the plank door with his foot. My captor's face split in a grin, teeth showing bright in his dark-skinned face.

Then he turned and ran up the steps two at a time. I raged and yelled around my gag of hair, but to no avail.

"Quiet, little crell," the guard said, laying me among perhaps two yras of women. Some of those I saw had marks such as I bore upon my own breast. I considered the refuge of madness. Crell, and crell, and crell again. He dropped me between two others and took up his stance outside the door.

It was long I lay there while the battle raged above. Thrice men came with lake-born women they had claimed.

I struggled to free my wrists of the braided leather

that bound them. The Parset had known what he was about. I could not even loosen the bite of that thong.

Lalen, I thought, would surely come. No matter how he counted me, he did not hold Sereth, nor Chayin, that low. And if they were those that remained unfound, my aid was needed. I screamed in frustration, and the sound was only muffled gurgle. How long a time I lay there, I know not. My wrists had ceased to feel, my fingers were no longer even cold when Lalen brought a forereader to the holding keep.

Without comment to the guard he stepped within. Then did he take his gol-knife and upon the trussed forereader's bottom trace his sign. Hair-gagged and bound, she only shivered.

He sheathed his knife and looked around him, his prize at his feet.

I struggled to my knees.

He ran a tanned hand through his blond hair and chuckled. Insolent, he came and stood before me. He did not move to free me of my bonds.

"Know you the whereabouts of Sereth and the cahndor?" he asked.

I made noises and nodded my head vigorously. Behind him, two jiasks, similarly laden with quivering battle spoil, entered. Both were familiar to me, though not well-known.

Lalen turned away. The men compared their new crells. I rose unsteadily to my feet.

"A Menetpher took that one," he said to them, pointing in my direction. I closed my eyes. Tears of relief squeezed through my tight-shut lids. "She says she knows where the cahndor is."

"Do you believe crells, Lalen?" spoke one who had been with us at the investment of Well Astria.

"It might be a likely chance," said Lalen. "But I seek no confrontation with that Menetpher."

"Let us free her tongue and see what waggles

forth." At my feet, a girl bound hand to ankle moaned and turned, pulling her hair from under my foot.

That one came toward me, gol-knife drawn. Shaking my head, I backed from him, stumbling over the limbs of a woman slumped dumbly against the wall. He kicked her, on his way to me. She did not even notice.

With the gol-knife he cut the hair that bound my mouth. I closed my eyes, feeling the short lock swing free against my cheek. His fingers sought the wadded mass between my teeth. At my throat lay the gol-knife, in his other hand. "Do not bite," he advised.

I spat, trying to rid my tongue of a strand that wound around it, dangled down my throat.

Lalen gaesh Sratemit came to stand beside that other, his face expressionless.

"Know you where they have imprisoned the cahndor, crell?" he asked me when I only stared back at him.

"Have you not had enough amusement with me, Aje?" I hissed, using his crell name.

"Miheja," he retorted using mine, "I have barely started. Where are they?"

"Sereth, when last I knew, was in number thirty-four, this level. The cahndor is in the tower holding keep, on the highest level." All three wheeled and ran from the chamber.

I sank back upon the floor, my wrists jerking their bonds. The guard peered within. He grumbled a curse, that they had not gagged me.

I closed my eyes, that I might shut it all out, the Parsets, the lake-born, the terrible culling in progress around me. I had not used my skills upon the walkways. It had been too fast. And against whom would I have raised my hand? Against Khys's people, or Chayin's? But I had not thought of it then. More proof of the conditioning to which Khys had subjected me. I fled in fear. From fear one can find no stable place to make a stand. I had run from them in fear, as would have Khys's Estri, who yet looked out through my eyes.

I got to my feet, a decision upon me. I had cried and groveled and feared and been crell since I had become Khys's. No more would it be so. Before such as Lalen I would not restrain my skills, in pursuit of some unattainable fitness. With what little courage I could summon, I sought Sereth. I found him not in keep thirty-four, but another place. I turned my mind upon the leather that bound my wrists. Such are not my strongest skills. I burned my wrists, while at the weakening of that leather. Mind sought to part it. Precious iths were lost while I attained certainty. Fast attendant upon it came the parting of the thongs, with the smell of singed hair.

I leaned against the wall, my wrists still behind my back. With one I rubbed the other, until they once more knew me. I remembered thinking that I should not mourn for the Lake of Horns. And I called also my own attention to the moment. Upon action's verge, I floated detached. This is now. It is real, I reminded myself. Lose or gain, the moment rises.

Then I struck the guard from behind with a neatly turned turbulence the width of my arm. I pushed away from the wall and stepped over the lake-born women. Some had doubtless been Khys's. They lay, and they did not beg to join me. Not one so much as raised a glowing head. I wished I could do the same, for a moment, then struck the ambivalence savagely aside. My stroke, I determined, turning the guard, had not been hard enough. He would, left to his own, regain consciousness momentarily. I sedated him further.

Down the torch-lit corridor, I heard voices, echo-loud bootfalls.

I set off up the stairs, running. It would be Lalen.
If he gave me cause, I would kill him.

All of it, I reminded myself, upon the first landing.
And I did use all I had that day, and I used it as I
saw fit.

None challenged me at the stra door. The threxmen seemed nowhere about. I took narrow turnings,
gained the back stairs of taernite. My sensing was
out, always. I saw what occurred in the seven-
cornered hall. I saw Lalen, with the unconscious
guard in the under-tunnels.

I smiled to myself upon the second-floor landing.
I heard Jaheil before my mind knew him. I did not
approach him, where he raged at his jiaskcahns.
We would meet, soon enough.

I was challenged, as I had expected, at the third-
floor landing. Three lake-born held the entryway.
Their minds touched me, drew back.

Show cause, they demanded. By that time they
could see me. They asked no more, but parted. I
hardly marked them.

I half-ran that hall to the dharen's chambers,
through the resting and the wounded that were
strewn like yris-tera pieces along its length. All
lake-born here. I saw few forereaders. There were, I
noticed as I called Carth's name in the enquieted
corridor, no light-chalded men. What resided here
was the resistance I had not seen upon the walkways. No whorls of fire, no hovering swords of
light had barred Chayin's tiasks and jiasks from
the Lake of Horns. Some of them, it seemed, had
fought, after all.

Some, I saw as Carth opened the double doors to
admit me, had not. And then he pulled me roughly
within. I made no objection. I, as he, had heard
the rumble of Parsets like a rockfall upon the back
stairs. I, as he, had seen those scattered in the hall
rise and prepare.

Carth turned from the doors, pressing back

against them, his hands still clutching the bronze handles. His dark face was care-clouded, his black curls light with dirt. His robe was ripped and stiff with blood at the left shoulder.

"Have you word from him? What am I supposed to do?"

"Cede the Lake of Horns. Khys attends the teachings of the fathers. A new time, and a new dharen to attend it, will preside over the next sun's rising." Looking around the dharen's quarters, I made them thirty-three, not counting. Sereth and the cahndor. These had not met steel, or had met it so well as to be unscathed. I recognized Khys's council members. I saw the blond arrar Ase, among what must have been near all of his brothers. They were silently, separately engaged. Unmoving, they were desperately busy. They sat or leaned or stood like statues, each upon his hesting, removed from flesh. Intently absent they were. The air pulsed and stung like hail-lightning.

I liked it not, this fighting in which they engaged. A man cannot forsake body for mind. In my sight, those men had a responsibility they were not discharging.

"Are the arrars too precious to fight Parsets? What do you here, when the lakeside falls about us?" I demanded, forgetting Sereth and Chayin, manacled together upon Khys's couch.

Most failed to even acknowledge me. Ase laughed. Carth forsook the doors and grabbed me by the arm.

"What say you, Carth?" pressed the blond arrar, approaching. "Shall we cede them the Lake of Horns? Or those two?" He thrust his sneering face toward Sereth and Chayin, helpless upon their bellies. I then knew what they did here, the elite of the Lake of Horns. In Ase's glare and Carth's taciturnity I read an argument ongoing.

Carth's answer was drowned out by the first

shudder of the thala doors. From without, louder and louder, came the pounding. The great doors shuddered. A slit appeared momentarily, and the flash of stra. Splinters flew. In iths the thala would be kindling as the jiasks hacked their way to their imprisoned cahndor.

I looked about me, at the lake-born.

The councilmen rose and came to Carth. Their faces glowed with their blood and their sweat. And yet the heat of a man embattled I saw not, only a coldress. "No, Carth," I disbelieved, when his mind gave me trace of the council's intent. "Bargain with Jaheil! You cannot—"

"Ase," Carth said sharply. I backed from Ase toward the couch. The council joined hands. No word was spoken. All about the room the arrars rose, ringing the council, swords drawn but loosely held. The sword-battered doors rattled and shook.

Ase reached out. "Do not," I advised. He grinned. I felt the couch at the back of my knees. I met Carth's eyes just before he closed them, where he stood in the council circle.

As Ase grabbed for my wrists, the screaming began, and a high crackling whine. I smelled the pungency of burning flesh. And it was time. I let it come; the hallway, and Jaheil's men screaming their retreat before the great fire the council set there. From all sides the council's whorls stalked the entrapped Parsets.

At Ase's touch, I was ready.

I sprawled back upon the couch, letting myself fall. Off balance he was. I heard him grunt as I hit the couch and the captives, while with all my need and desperation I threw him into the midst of the council-spawned flames in the hallway. I saw him flicker. Then I smelled the hair and leather and flesh, acrid, cloyingly strong, and shielded my own eyes from the light. But I was not there; it was the arrar Ase who screamed his death denial amid the council's work. With all his skill he fought them, and they, before their own, were of a sudden unsure. The flame thinned, and I took my chance. With Ase, I reached for life. He sought return to the council ring. I aided him, that he might bring his dying rage back upon them all. Their flames accompanied him into the dharen's keep, while they wavered, undecided. Only that I did: guide their force back upon them. Ase's departing spirit and their own agony did the rest.

In that instant, as the whorls homed in upon their makers, I let go of them. And dived for Carth, stock-still in the first licking flames.

Carth I attacked with mind and body both, horrified in realization. I ran to him, uncaring of the holocaust raging, throwing myself at his tranced form. And dragged him back as the conflagration, fueled by the will of those who birthed it, grew; smoking, crackling, bright. Then dimmer, as the dying sought relief. Slowly the great whorl died. Around it lay arrars: singed, burned, two missing limbs. The doors shook, dissolving. It rained black splinters and sawdust and a torrent of jiasks.

I hardly noticed. Through pain-dulled eyes I peered at him. Faintly, faintly resided spirit in the arrar Carth. Jerking and dragging him across the mat, I recall, and the steady stream of sobbing curses that were mine; and the terrible afterimage of the cleansing fire in my eyes. Closed or open, I saw it the same. And little else. Fighting a glittered mist, I bent close over him, deadweight in my grasp. I thrust my face close to his, and I knew I had not done well enough.

I looked up dully and saw the arrars still able setting their swords against the multitude. Stra clashed steel. I bent over Carth, begging life forth. I had little to give, little to spare. I sought him. In repayment I received a phantasmic breath, a sporadic wander of eyes under closed lids.

I lay a moment, gaining strength, despondent, my face against his and my hands upon his throat. "Carth," I demanded, sobbing, of his flaccid features, "do not die. I beseech you. Not yet." I heard it, and the succedent mutterings, but did not recognize the words as mine. I knew only that I dragged Carth barely before the tide of combatants.

I sought the couch. I sought Sereth and Chayin, who yet wore bands of restraint. "Carth," I pleaded as I crawled with him, holding him by the arms across my back, "Carth, live for me just this little while longer."

Ith-years it took to reach the couchside. He slid thrice from my debilitated grasp as I pulled him up. The arrars fought jiasks to my rear, their curses dream-growls in distended time. Sereth's eyes met mine above his gag. I prayed and tried once more to raise Carth. His hands seemed too cool as I dragged his torso up on the couch.

I scrambled atop Sereth's back, that I might have more leverage, tears streaming down my face. Some senseless stream of demands flowed forth from me while I formed Carth's fingers into the proper pattern. As I almost achieved it, he slipped out of reach. I put my arms around his hips and pulled his inert form half over Sereth. I had, with that second try, success. Carth's fingers, by my manipulation, freed Sereth's throat of restraint. The band, loosened, parted. I took a gulping breath. My knees around the cahndor's hips, I pulled Carth toward Chayin, across Sereth's helpless back. Dread opposed me as I fumbled with Carth's hands. The thumbs must be together at a certain angle. I heard man sound. A shadow fell over us.

At that moment, Chayin's band relaxed. I tried to shake off the hand that came down hard upon my shoulder.

"Estri," said Jaheil, seeking to lift me from them, "it is over."

"The bands!" I protested, sobbing, as he tried to drag me away. "You must let me finish!"

Jaheil released me. "I know nothing of bands," he rasped, uncertain.

I threw myself upon Chayin, grabbing the loosened band from his throat. With trembling fingers I closed it back on itself and threw it down. Then Sereth's was in my hand, and it too I closed, harmless, that it might encircle only air.

They took Carth. I knew it only as his limp thigh was dragged from under me. I raged at Jaheil, but he would not hear me. I crouched there, half-crazed, threatening curses upon them if Carth did not survive.

Jaheil, huger even than I had recalled him, loomed above. It was only as he helped me down from where I huddled by Sereth and Chayin that I realized the enormity of what I had done. He tried valiantly, as befitted the cahndor of Dordassa and co-cahndor of the Taken Lands, to keep his eyes from Khys's device upon my breast. He could not do so.

"Keys," he snapped to the jiasks not occupied with corpse or prisoner. I took thought for Khys's rusty mat, and its ruin. Then I laughed, and got Khys's own master keys from his library, where they were hidden with his charts and precious writings.

"Get water," I heard Jaheil bark, as I turned from the library, sliding the panel across until it locked.

"Where is Carth?" I demanded, handing the keys to him. "Do not lose them. They and they alone are the full set. There is only the set the dharen has, and these, which are complete." I saw Lalen, who had paused to extract information from a wounded arrar, rise up.

Jaheil bent over the cahndor, fitting the keys until he found one which worked upon the lock's fetters. Lalen gave his prisoner over to two jiasks and strode to the couch.

I took up a gol-knife that lay upon the mat. With it I freed them each in turn of the gags, slitting the thongs and then pulling the soured packing out of their mouths.

A jiask handed me a southern water bladder. Under his watchful eye, I gave first drink to Chayin.

The cahndor growled and spat. "Get away from me!" he ordered Jaheil. "Attend Sereth!" The manacles that had bound him clattered to the mat. I saw his stiffness. His hands had been long bound behind. He raised himself slowly, every muscle of his dark frame straining. He reached toward me, wordless, for the bladder. His hands, taking it, shook. His face was forbidding as he strove for command of his flesh. His dark eyes would not relinquish their membranes' protection. Unblinking, he stared at me. I dared not look away. He drank, and the water spilled out, sloshed by his muscles' tetanus, and ran down his arms.

The silence of the keep, as thick as befitted such a day when so many took up the chaldra of the soil, pressed in on my ears. Even Sereth's low whispers, and Jaheil's demands that he stay still, seemed importunate.

I huddled there, only watching, tremors as heavy along my limbs as if I had been flesh-locked. Chayin's eyes fastened upon me and held.

Sereth, grunting, ordered Jaheil and Lalen away from him. He would not lie there and let them knead life back into his limbs. He hissed them away, rising to his hands and knees, his head hanging low. Men do not heal quickly in bands of restraint.

At Chayin's behest, I edged toward him, offering the bladder. Without looking up, he shook his head.

I dared not force him. I implored the cahndor silently.

Chayin turned upon the couch, wincing. "Drink, man," Chayin urged, his long-fingered hands clenching up the silk.

"In a moment. Give me grace." Sereth's voice was loud as a wind-borne leaf dashed upon the grass. He raised his head cautiously, then sat back, steadying himself with straight arms.

Once more I sought to aid him, silent, the bladder in hand. His eyes would allow no approach. With a gesture he indicated the couch's head. I went and sat there, upon my heels, the bladder resting on my thighs.

"Jaheil . . ." I heard Chayin's voice, stronger. "Get you out of here. Surely there must be more to securing the Lake of Horns. Attend it. When I can walk upright as befits a man, I will join you."

"As you wish it, Chayin," grumbled Jaheil. He and Lalen exchanged glances. "I will leave you Lalen." He waved his men toward the doors, which were no longer. Those few jiasks still in the keep hoisted up their wounded and left.

"No," said Chayin wearily to Jaheil. "There will be none here but us."

Jaheil pulled upon his beard. His eyepatch wriggled with his brows. Then he shrugged, and took from his belt a small pouch. He threw it to the silk near Chayin's knee. "You heard him," he said to Lalen, who yet hovered there. Lalen took his leave.

"And you, too, brother," said Chayin, implacable.

The cahndor of Dordassa walked slowly to the gaping hole that had been the doors.

"I am pleased to see that you live," rumbled Jaheil. "Godhead is a burden in which few share fraternity."

And he lumbered away. I heard him setting guards in the corridor.

Sereth tossed his head and crossed his legs under him cautiously.

Chayin tipped the uris pouch back, his eyes

closed. By it he was greatly improved. His membranes began to flicker, where before they had been full extended. They snapped a time across his eyes. He grinned and handed the uris pouch to me. His fingers sought his throat. I recalled all too well what it had been like.

"I told you to wear white upon you," he disapproved, as I partook of the pouch.

"Upon the day of Sereth's execution," I said, my tongue at the pouch's rim. I wondered how I had lived without it. Then I handed it back.

"This is that day," said Chayin. "It is Brinar third fourth. Where were you, that you know not the date?" His hand reached out, took hold of the short lock that hung upon my cheek.

"Where I was, I cannot tell you. A place where five enths equal five Silistran days. But I wore white, and one of Menetph ripped it from me. And that lock of hair I am missing was shorn by a Nemarsi. Lalen of Stra, who did not aid me, I would see disciplined."

Chayin laughed. "You would discipline a man for that? Little crell, I wanted you in white so that none would claim you. It seemed safe enough to me in the undertunnels. You should have stayed there. We would have triumphed without your aid."

I pulled my hair from his grasp, flushed, furious. I said nothing. I had adjudged the signs upon them. They prepared for battle. Chayin was acerbic, distant. Sereth had upon him the look of a man who will not be touched. I shook my head, uncomprehending. It was Brinar third fourth. Estrazi's humor, perhaps? The uris sang within me.

Sereth drew up one leg, rubbed his calf. He looked at me from under the mass of his blooded, filthy hair. Long did he assess me. I did not mistake him. He considered my worth. I longed to touch him, give of my strength, tend his wounds.

"Get what weapons there are here," he said. "Bring them to me."

"Chayin, give me that." And he held his hand out to the cahndor.

That hand, as he held it there, trembled. Yet I knew him stronger. No longer was he banded. It seemed to me I saw the bruises on his skin fading as he worked within. But his hand shook, as he received the uris from Chayin. And in touching that pouch to his lips, Sereth amended his long-standing custom. Never had he used it, in all the time I had known him.

I got them the weapons; all that I had procured from the fitter, and two blades of Khys's. While I fetched them, I worried the implications of their manner. Chayin would not miss it if I sought within him. Sereth was inaccessible behind his shield.

When I brought the arms before them, Chayin had his hands upon Sereth's back. With each other, they shared strength.

I spread the tas, exposing what blades I had chosen, and added to them what I had taken of Khys's.

Sereth, after a momentary hesitation, took that blade I had blooded, that one I had worn into his cell.

"That is the one I had meant for you," I said softly.

A tiny humor came over him as he reappraised it. "It is near the weight I favor. Let us hope it is near enough." Still did he have that isolate bearing. I had seen it before on him—upon the kill. From it I sat back.

"Chayin, what rises?" I demanded in a whisper as Sereth got up from couch to try the blade and his limbs.

But Chayin did not answer. Then he, too, was standing. I found myself, in my turn, shocked to my feet.

Khys weaved, legs spread wide, upon the rust-toned mat. The spiral Estrazi had put upon his chest glittered malevolently. He had lost all but chald. Upon the left side of his face, and in a strip down his chest, great chunks of the flame glow that once lurked ever about him had been torn away. The dull and darkened skin, exposed, seemed to shrink from the air. His eyes were gleaming slits. From out of that countenance blazed such anguish and fury that I moaned and shrank back. Chayin took me in his arms and from behind. He put his hand over my mouth, even as the dharen's name escaped my lips.

"Sereth."

"Khys."

"Thought you I would quit the Lake of Horns?"

"Never for a moment."

"Do you hold stra by reason of choice?"

"It is the weapon with which I would meet you."

I opened my eyes.

"That choice I have ceded you," agreed Khys, his stance firm. But I knew him, and what was meant by the ridges upon his jaw and neck, by his knotted belly. And tears rolled out of my eyes onto Chayin's hand as he crossed the mat. Slowly and with great dignity Khys approached, to take up the chosen weapon.

Sereth threw his head, his eyes narrowed. He stared at Khys's back, his wrist and forearm of their own accord making ready.

Khys, as I had known he would, chose the chased blade, its hilt a single fire gem, which bore the seal of his own skin mimicked. When he raised up, his glance slid by me. Sickened by what the fathers had wrought, I was. And he knew. He touched gaze and mind to Chayin's. They communed a time, and while it occurred, the cahndor's every sinew pulled tight against my back.

"I will give you quarter," said Khys, turning around to Sereth.

"I will give you quarter," Sereth rejoined, his crouch belying his words.

"For the Lake of Horns, if you wish. For all of Silistra."

"I can put nothing against that but my life."

"It is enough. Witnesses have heard it."

I moaned under Chayin's hand and wriggled. He slid his other arm around my waist.

They stalked.

They circled, and as they did so found that infirmity had even the odds between them. I saw it clear, in Khys's uncertain advantage, and in Sereth, who slipped ever out of contest. I threw myself hard against the cahndor's imprisoning grasp.

"Hush, crell," he whispered. "We will know your new master soon enough."

At first it seemed no battle of mind between them. Even the clash of stra was sporadic. They still tested, limbering, each awaiting his body's own signs.

Through blurred eyes I saw Khys's first strong pass—a slash across Sereth's chest. And sobs racked me, that these two had come to contest. The wound seemed to wake Sereth, to free him, as if he had been elsewhere. He shook his head. He reached, and connected with a side cut to Khys's neck; unexpected upstroke, a hair's breadth from death cut.

Khys stepped back. The blood raced in a dozen streams, eager, down his chest. The shock of the cut, the burning, coupled with surprise at his own fragile, fickle flesh, came first. Life right warred with honor within him. It consumed his shield, pouring over me, freezing my tears. He noted. He could no longer afford attention to shielding, not even for privacy. Victory, cold, bitter triumph that his body would not understand, flooded him while his physical form poised shocked and shivering upon the edge of the abyss. He sorrowed, momentarily, that he had no time to explain to it, that collection of muscle and nerve that demanded to survive, that he had sold the years it held yet banked within for this moment, for freedom from all detested manipulation, for an act and consequence solely of himself. Poised there, by his will, he laughed through the waves of anguish and loss and his body's terror that he would no longer heed its needs. He laughed again, realizing that at this moment, which he had chosen, even such an eloquent statement of fully actualized will became as nothing, for where he went no fathers reigned, nor self recalled. Freed of them, and even his mind's craven judgment of the precipitousness of his folly, all that remained was the act itself. He strove desperately to retake control of his fear, grinding his teeth together to still their chatter. For out of presage came an awful foreboding, a terrible yawning chasm of possibility: that even this would be denied him, that this death toward which his life had labored would be aborted.

With an effort of will that had me lunging mindless against Chayin's restraining arms, he closed with Sereth. Out of the sharper weapon of turmoil, wielded by ineluctable decision, he thrust.

Sereth met him. Sparks rained as the dharen's edge rode grating to Sereth's hilt. They hugged close, blades between them. I could not adjudge it.

They disengaged, closed again as if a wave thrust them asunder, swells dashing them together in its wake.

Ah, Khys was eager. He welcomed Sereth against him like some long-lost lover. *Now, upon this moment!* He begged it of the time, demanding, afraid he could nor longer hold firm before his body's lust for life. I felt the cold burn of the blades against my own breast; and a heat, blinding, borne on a rushing sigh that lasted forever in that convulsive moment when point impaled heart. The muscular contraction caused the blade to scrape between two ribs. Relief flooded him. It was done.

Then they backed from each other, facing off. Khys's fingers, about the blade which pierced the spiral on his breast, did not feel the blood beneath them. He coughed, and choked, swallowing hard. He tasted metal, and salt, and success.

Sereth's chest heaved, and sweat poured down his spine, rode the ridges of straining muscles, gleaming. That, only, I saw. But it was not sight that mattered then. I felt the sharp, clear heat, then vertigo, then rejoicing that it was all so easily accomplished. The pain receded, and sight and sound took on a different hue. Khys felt his legs, trembling, fail him, and a far-off thud as his distant, numbed flesh struck the mat.

Upon gasps of anguish, I merged with him, freed of tears: a cessation of pulsing, of final, sweet regard for those things left undone. Then even the victory evanesced, leaving only a last wonder as to what it had meant. He could barely feel his body fluids, draining, though a detached part of his mind bespoke the progress of his death, chronicling, one at a time, the failure of those systems that had long been the sum total of his world.

The grains that prickled his vision spread, multiplied, became all colors. A wind whirled him up and away.

He saw us, and Sereth, arm with upraised blade wavering, from a place above and behind the flesh he had known. Tenderly he bade farewell to it, the form that had so long and well served him. He knew a faint, sinking tingle, one last shiver of spasm along nerves he would never again command. Its counterpart trilled through his mind, a tardy quailing before the immutability he faced. This decision, made, could not be recalled, nor

rethought, nor even recollected. He reached out
tentatively for his body sprawled upon the mat.
His attempt to move it from where it lay impaled
upon his own blade, to see once more through the
eyes of flesh, failed totally. He could not remember those skills, once employed without even need
for thought.

And then that thickened dark birthed a new cataclysm of light, and from that beckoning change
came a melody he must needs follow.

As he strained to find a way through all the
coalescing beauty around him, a form which he
first knew to be friend, then to be a woman, long
passed and longer mourned, extended her hand to
him. As he took it, a sound like shining attracted
his attention to a door he had not before seen.
Their hands met.

Sereth stepped from my view.

Khys lay crumpled small upon the mat, deflated,
his body fluids a red pool all about. From out of
the Shaper's seal, Sereth drew the dharen's sword,
around which his life still bubbled forth in lesser
and lesser spurts.

His eyes were closed.

I bit Chayin's hand, grieving.

Sereth paused a moment, then retreated. And
again advanced. To stop as if frozen in flesh lock,
though his next stroke would have been fit and
merciful.

Estrazi manifested there, standing bronze and
incontestable, his great arms folded over his chest.
Not since my conception had the Shaper come
among Silistrans, and before that not for two thousand years.

Sereth retreated another pace. There he halted,
and dropped his blade, and the dharen's, before
my father's feet. His hands found his hips, curled
into fists.

Estrazi surveyed us, and Khys upon the mat. "I will take him," said my father, his cauldron eyes compassionate. He gathered Khys up in his arms. The dharen's blood rolled down Shaper flesh. Like some child, Estrazi held him, his hand covering the seal he had put upon Khys's chest, and the wound it hosted. Khys's limbs dangled, swaying gently, his form limp and unknowing.

"He has left you no easy legacy, flesh son," spoke Estrazi to Sereth. The flame tongues over his dark form seemed to thicken, to envelop Khys. "You have in the past well served me." So did Estrazi acknowledge Sereth, who had not moved.

"If again you use me," said Sereth in his most quiet voice, "I would appreciate being informed beforehand."

"Then," allowed Estrazi, his form engulfed in the crucible of creation, "I will inform you." The wave of his words hung in the air. He was gone. He had left without word to me, his daughter.

IX.

The Law Within

"For the Lake of Horns," whispered Sereth, half to himself. Upon the mat where Khys had been lay lay dark stains. Among them, gleaming wetly, lay the dharen's chald.

He walked there, his stride slow and deliberate. Before it, he squatted down, a hand out to steady his weight. He took up the chald and ran it through his fists. He said a thing, too low for us to hear, and tossed his head.

He brought it with him, to where we still knelt, and sat himself down.

"Find work to do, or I will assign you some," called Chayin, his head twisted around. Only then did I turn and see the silent jiasks crowding the hole where the doors had been.

The cahndor rubbed his neck. He regarded Sereth and the chald a time.

"Witnesses have heard it." He bespoke it as last.

"Think you it was still his to give?"

"In deed and truth, it was his. And a gift he made of it to you."

Sereth, for the first time, raised his head to us. I saw two things unexpected: tears and anger. "I want no rule over men. All my life, men have sought to rule me. The law within is enough bondage for any man."

"It is your chaldra," said Chayin pointedly.

He looked down at the great chald of Silistra and back at Chayin. The wound on his chest rolled one last tear of blood.

"You know what I wanted. You stalked it for me. What there is left of that dream, I will take. And I would get out with her, out of the lands of men."

"What will you do?" asked Chayin gruffly.

"Hunt, perhaps. I know not." The grief that shrouded Sereth then made me rock back and forth upon my knees. Barely could I withstand the impulse to keen. His eyes went over me, in great detail, as if finally he could fill his hunger replete. When his gaze met mine, I could not name the emotion there, for it was spawned of owkahen, and what it had done to us.

"It is my father's sign," I offered, very low, not wavering.

"It is not the marking of the flesh but the marking of the spirit that concerns me." He rose up. Glowering, he snapped his fingers. I did for him what he required, as I had for Khys so many times.

"She is truly crell," said Chayin. I saw nothing but the hair fallen around my face.

"It is not that. It is that she learned it at another's hand, and to a different taste. Rise up."

I did so, woodenly. He was grinning. He pulled me close. It seemed he touched every part of me, reacquainting himself. I protested.

Abruptly he spun me toward the cahndor.

"See for yourself," said Sereth to Chayin.

I endured the cahndor's probing, until I could not. Then I struck out with mind violence, all I could command. Without even a hesitation in what else he did, he parried the blow. "Do not ... No longer can you hold that above us. At my convenience, I will take reparation from you upon this account." His dark eyes had no hint of film.

He pushed me from him. I stumbled, caught

myself, straightened, halfway between them. I saw Sereth's eyes, hard and resentful. But I had seen what else lurked there. I tore my hair from my face, squared my shoulders under his scrutiny.

"She called Khys's name when he and I faced each other," Sereth said to Chayin.

"Crells and owners—thus it often is with them. If she had been less to him, she would be less to you," opined the cahndor. I heard jiasks, sharp laughter in the hallway. "But she was not obedient when I bade her stay her hand from these affairs."

"Shall we take that chald off her?" Sereth suggested.

"Immediately," the cahndor agreed.

They cut it from me. I did not object. It was of no value to me. My mind was full of them, and what they were, and the rightness of Khys's predictions as regards them. Though I looked at Sereth, all my love offered up with my eyes, I said nothing. I was his—a spoil of the circle, crell, whatever he chose. That which had driven him to contest with Khys still raged in him. He would vent his anger on me, doubtless. I stood very still, pliant, that I might not worsen his temper.

I recalled a time I had seen Sereth and the cahndor match blades. They had been only working their skills. With weapons, I had never seen better. They were, perhaps, the best on Silistra. And I considered Khys, who had gone against Sereth with sword. Knowing his skill, Khys had fought him. And it had not been as other times I had seen Sereth wield stra. There had been no skittering of Khys's blade from his grasp upon the first or second stroke. Khys had chosen his successor. Estrazi had ratified the choice. And Sereth stood regarding me from under his blood-matted hair, thinking.

"Tell me of your abduction," he ordered.

"Do so," added Chayin from the alcove window.

I thought of what concerned me, and I thought of something else. "Sereth, what choice will you make? I care not about the rest. My father and Khys both meant Silistra for your hands. Who will take it up? Chayin cannot, else he be ever engaged in riding around the perimeters of his holdings." Parsets believe that to own a thing, one must make use of it.

"Tell me of your abduction," repeated Sereth very quietly, approaching.

"Ask Dellin, who was there with me. Or M'tras, whose work it was."

I retreated a step, halted, hopeless. He took hold of my shoulders. "Estri, at moon's rising you are going to wish Khys yet ruled at the Lake of Horns."

His fingers dug in my flesh. "Sereth," I whispered. "Go into the prisons. See Dellin and M'tras, in keep twelve. Hear what they have to say. See the others, the killing, the carnage. Then tell me again that we will hunt, away from the lands of men."

"I will tell you again. We will hunt." But he stuffed Khys's chald in his breech.

Chayin forsook the alcove in a flurry of cushions. His countenance was grim. "Let us go and see Dellin and this other. She is, after all, her father's daughter. Though crell, of course." His eyes, touching mine, softened.

"That is precisely the problem. But we will go." He took up the fallen swords from the mat. Khys's blade he tossed to Chayin, who found its sheath among the weapons upon the couch.

I followed the cahndor, thinking of the light blade. He put his arm around my shoulders. "You are superb," he whispered, then released me. I backed from him, into Sereth. I shook my head, turning away. But I should have known that Chayin saw. He, too, had been with Sereth at the sack of Astria. He, as well as I, knew Sereth. Those three words sustained me, upon our foray through the halls to the undertunnels, past the groaning and the maimed and those who could groan no longer, those to whom bodily ills were not pertinent any longer.

We went the route of Sereth's choosing, down the front stairs and through the main halls. As we proceeded through that Parset slaughter, his brow grew furrowed and his hand sought frequent communion with his hilt. Thrice he stopped and examined men left in the halls, those Jaheil's Parsets had adjudged no further threat. One man he slew. The second was dead. The third he hoisted upon his shoulders and carried into the seven-cornered chamber, in which the Parset wounded and some few prisoners lay. With a forereader who had been freed to serve, he left instructions.

As he turned back to us, a banded woman was carried in. A blade had pierced her through.

Chayin stopped the man who bore her. Sereth strode close, his carriage ominous. The man explained that the woman had thrown herself upon his blade. His tone was one of amazement. Sereth bade him put her down. He knelt close to her, spoke very low. Her lids flickered and opened. She managed some soft words upon her death breath.

Sereth straightened. He took my arm and led me to the door. The cahndor stayed a moment, then followed.

"The man who put her in restraint was dead, slain before her eyes. She had no wish to live that way." It was Chayin who informed me, when he gained my side. Sereth was far from the lands of speech.

"Speak to me of those we seek," proposed Chayin, as we passed the barred gate. Sereth would take us through the maze that ended with the high-numbered cells. Upon that way, there would be sufficient time for him to think whatever thoughts he might choose.

"Only will I say to you that they must not be harmed. Khys put M'tras' life into my hands for safe-keeping. Since I can no longer keep him, it falls to you both. He is to be taken to the plain of Astria. There he will find his helsar. Dellin also is to take a helsar."

"Do not speak to me of Khys's will, Estri. Not just yet." And Sereth's tone kept me mute the whole way through those extensive passages. We saw, as we had above, jiasks and tiasks. I wondered at this, when the first group of five challenged us, but then I recalled Chayin's knowledge of the Lake of Horns. Maps can be made. Directions are easily passed from one hand to another. I had drawn a threxman upon the shores of which none are empowered to speak. Chayin had assured me of his safety, while in the tower holding keep. Khys had spoken of rebellious tiasks in the south.

We were approaching the cell corridors when it came clear to me, and I risked an inquiry.

"I had heard that there was great unrest in the south, that the tiasks roamed the lands in gangs. And yet I see tiasks wherever I look. Have you come to terms with the rebels' leader, cahndor?"

His laugh rang out and back from the taernite. His white teeth gleamed in the torch flame. "The leader of the rebellion. Yes, you might say I came to terms with him. You see, he had access to my most secret thoughts. My most devious plans were always shown to him. Whatever steps I took to quell the tiasks, he was always an enth before me. More and more yras of jiasks did I send after the renegade tiasks. I but drove them farther north."

"And when they were in the northwest," interjected Sereth, "Chayin had no longer need to make war upon himself."

We turned down that taernite undertunnel, torchlit, rank with mold and seepage, in which the dharen bred yits and incarcerated evildoers.

"How did you get the falsehood past Khys?" I wondered.

"It was no falsehood. The rebellion was real enough, only was it mine. I but stayed at my hest. Crux did the rest."

"You used me against him," I accused. Chayin had told me twisted truths, that Khys might take them from my mind.

"He used you against us," Sereth said, his eyes upon the cells, each as we passed it.

Man sound came to us from somewhere down the shadowy hall.

Keep number thirty-four lay open. As we passed it, Chayin spoke of what concerned him.

"I have paid highly for this domain you spurn," he said, toneless, to Sereth. "When I conceived this investment, after returning to the south from my helsar training, it seemed meet. I thought then that I had not given you couch-gift. It seemed fitting at the time. I would have avenged myself upon him then if neither of you lived. I am not one to judge men, other than myself."

Sereth stopped in the hall. "I do not take your meaning."

"We are all very different from what we were. I see in that difference a sameness. If you will not have the Lake of Horns, that is your affair." They stood opposite each other in the hall. Then Chayin purposefully moved to Sereth's side. "Come back with me into the south. Roam the Taken Lands. Regent for me—all that is mine is yours. Or raise threx upon Mount Opir. The grass is good there."

"Yes, the grass is good there," said Sereth quietly. They embraced, and I turned away. From the low-numbered cells, jiasks advanced in a group. Before each cell they paused, opened, inspected.

And I knew that he considered it, as did I, and that such a move would sate the heart and salve the spirit in each of us. A part of me screamed

silent assent, but I could not force the words out.
His decision, and his alone, it was. And from that
decision would spring all that might be seen when
the crux time cleared away. I had done my part—I
had brought him here.

We met the knot of jiasks before keep twelve.

Among them was the Menetpher who had taken
me. I grinned at him, safe between the cahndor
and Sereth. He grinned back. My fingers found the
tiny holes the huija had chewed from my upper
arms. They were quiet, awaiting Chayin's words.

He gave it. He bade them find all those who
bore bands of restraint and put them together. The
cell checks, he assured them, could wait. From
their leader he got the keys. And Jaheil, he ordered
them seek, and invite to the dharen's keep at sun's
set. Also he inquired of them about hulions. None
had seen even a single one of the great winged
carnivores. Hulions' favorite food is threx. He sin-
gled out that man who had first taken me, and
another, and bade them organize a watch for the
beasts. The men, dismissed to their tasks, scattered.

As Chayin chose a key and tried it, Sereth bade
him not fret over hulions.

Chayin grunted, his shoulder to the warped door.
The swollen wood protested its way across the
stone.

Dellin and M'tras sat as far from the door as
they could, huddled together under the gallery's
shadow, against the wall. Their frames showed
some signs of cursory interrogation, Parset style.

I looked up at the gallery. None stood there. But
there was a razor-moon upon the stone, one edge
dulled reddish brown. I got it from Dellin's mind,
even as Sereth took up the weapons; as he scrutinized them, where they sat watching. Jiasks, three,
had taken time for oejri-anra, a target game played
with razor-moons by men with the skill to make
them return to hand after they are cast. In these

close quarters, the game had been a true test of skill, with Dellin and M'tras the live targets. The flesh wound M'tras had sustained lay upon his right thigh. That had been after they had been questioned.

Neither man moved. Their eyes lay upon us. They did not cower or plead or accuse or resist. They awaited.

By M'tras' side, upon the stone, lay two ors. One was open.

Sereth squatted down before them, spinning the razor-moon absently. Dellin stared from the cahndor to Sereth, to me. He thought of what we had done to him, when last the three of us had held his person. His eyes locked upon the cahndor with such abject terror that Chayin smiled. M'tras just observed. He did not know enough to be frightened.

The cahndor leaned against the curving wall. Sereth called me, and I went to his side.

"Estri tells me," he said to Dellin, "that you were with her when she was removed from the Lake of Horns. Chayin seeks vengeance for the murder of his couch-mate. I seek some reason to keep you from his hands. If you have any suggestions upon this matter, I will hear them."

Chayin growled something unintelligible and shifted his stance against the wall. I smiled at M'tras encouragingly. Dellin closed his eyes and said nothing.

Chayin leaned over and spoke in his ear. He shivered. Then he told all he knew of what had taken place; of Khys's appearance before him, his flight from the dharen's wrath. M'tras' plan to destroy the hides, the crippling of the ship upon the sphere of restraint that now encircled Silistra. That point, and what Khys had done with the crew of the Oniar-M, and with the ship itself, took Sereth's interest.

"Chayin," he interrupted Dellin's telling, "it

seems that we will indeed hunt, and together. I have long desired to see what rises across the Embrodming."

"I would welcome your sword. Though it lies heavy upon me, I must discharge my obligation to Liuma's shade." That kill smile flashed over him, a moment out of hiding. I thought of Khys's words to the M'ksakkans when he released them into the wilderness, that Chayin would doubtless come to hunt them.

Sereth turned back to Dellin. "Are you telling me we are rid of M'ksakka and her confederates?"

"All I know is what he told me. Our people had a set to get off-planet. At the end of that time, the barrier became impenetrable from within, as well as without. If it is true, you are by now looking at the last two off-worlders upon Silistra."

"And why did he make you the exception?" snarled Chayin.

"I have no idea," said Dellin.

"He wanted them to take helsars," I supplied. "Dellin's uncle became M'ksakka's adjuster when you killed Mossennen." It was to Sereth I spoke as the pieces fit together in my mind. "He wanted them to remain here until they had mastered sufficient skills of mind to return to their own planets. They are both high on their worlds, Dellin by blood, M'tras by skills. They are his envoys, the ongoing perpetrators of his hests upon the time. Look at the hesting text. It is for such as M'tras it was written. In time they will bear Khys's works home with them."

M'tras, hearing this, sat forward, his hand upon the ors by his side. He shook his head violently, as if his ears had taken water.

"Estri," warned Sereth, "I have told you once: Khys's wishes do not concern me." Thereupon, Sereth found M'tras of interest. "You seem no M'ksakkan," he remarked. "What is your world?"

"Yhrillya."

"And how do you find Silistra?" Chayin also spoke to him.

"Inhospitable," M'tras said, his black-ringed eyes, circled with bruise, steady.

"You are chaldless," Chayin observed. "When speaking to chalded, it is customary to include some form of title or name." He drummed his fingers upon the fire-gem hilt of the blade that had been the dharen's.

"But tell me the proper form of address, and I will use it," said M'tras carefully in his stilted Silistran. I knew then that Chayin, for whatever reason, would not kill him.

Chayin, most pleasantly considering the circumstances, gave his titles.

I shifted beside Sereth, recalling what M'tras had done to me.

At their bidding, M'tras told them what he had done. He told it well, with the directness of a man who takes pride in his craft. How he had come to be upon the commission, he did not explain. But all else he told them, even that I had seemed to him small in the hips.

Sereth, at the last comment, laughed. I stared at him, that off-worlder in whom Sereth had taken interest.

"I have your ijiyr," I said softly to M'tras. "If you would ever regain it, watch your tongue."

Perhaps Sereth and Chayin sensed some obscure siblingship with M'tras. I found in myself no echo of it.

The cahndor came and took hold of my arm. I shook off his hand.

"Take her out in the hall," said Sereth sharply to Chayin, who obeyed him.

"I cannot stand it," I hissed at him, leaning against the passage wall.

"You will doubtless find the strength," Chayin predicted.

"What care you?" My limbs shook, and my head throbbed.

He grinned. "It has been long since I have seen him so well."

"You did not take revenge upon M'tras for Liuma."

"M'tras looks of more worth than Liuma. And there are the others."

"What should I do?"

"Be silent. He will do what he will do. Just wait."

"What brought it to this?" I found my vision blurred.

"We did," said Chayin, taking me against him.

We stood thus a time. Down the hall came tiasks, singing, their bladders full and plump. Chayin commandeered one and bade me drink. I did so, also taking the uris he offered up. With it came to me the remembrance that Sereth had this day used uris, and that such was not his custom.

I had just handed it back when Sereth took his leave of Dellin and M'tras.

"I bade him seek us in the south if he wishes," said Sereth. His eyes seemed a stranger's.

"M'tras? Good. He is worth having." Chayin released his hold, stepped from my side.

"You have something of his," Sereth said to me.

"You have it. I had it. It is with the dharen's papers." I snarled it, without volition.

Sereth and Chayin exchanged glances.

"Would you do me service?" asked the Ebvrasea very softly, of Chayin.

"As ever," Chayin replied.

"You meet with Jaheil at sun's set. Consider this: there is no need for a dharen upon Silistra. The council is dead. The slitsa's fangs have been pulled. The outside world will not crumble if there is no rule from the Lake of Horns. The value of such manipulation by a group of elite inbreds is questionable. The blood has value, I have been told. Good. Take those women and men that please you, and use them in the south. The gene pool will be widened."

"Just leave it?"

"Wreak some dissolution. Take the finest women, breed them. Reap what spoils you choose. But leave not enough of the Lake of Horns that they may rebuild empire. You need not kill them, those you find unworthy of the crell pits. Perhaps they will become a city. Let them, with your leavings, instigate a Well. Let them, like the rest of Silistra, do work. Let them flee, or stay, I care not. I would see the place torn stone from stone, and its inhabitants scattered to the edges of the world." He grinned bleakly. "But it would take too long."

"That is your will?"

"It is. We must break the pattern, lest Khys with his hests continue to control us. I am no caretaker of his designs. I do not intend to implement them."

"But you will go with me across the Embrodming?" Chayin pressed.

"Yes, I will do that." I studied him in the light of what he had revealed. When speaking of the lake-born, his bitterness had rattled like death in his throat. I well recalled what Khys had said to him: that his sperm was inferior, that he was not fit to breed one such as I. I shivered. My hips found the stone wall of the corridor. It was as damp and slick as my skin.

"You will not go with me to Jaheil?"

"No, not yet. Do me another service."

"Name it."

Seek Miccah, the high chalder. See that he, or some other if he is dead, leads you to the bands of restraint. Key and close them all. There are none left capable of producing them, thanks to Estri."

Chayin looked at me. Then he nodded. "It has a certain fitness," he remarked. "Think upon which of the Taken Lands would suit you."

Sereth smiled. They exchanged a grip, one of five turns. It was the jiasks' grip of triumph. The cahndor strode away. The torchlight fired his rana skin bronze as Estrazi's. "At moon's rising, where will you be?" Chayin called back over his shoulder.

"Attending to the discipline of a certain crell I have come to possess. You are welcome to assist me." Sereth took up a lock of my hair.

"I will have a meal set. Such undertakings are often lengthy," the cahndor laughed.

"You would not," I said, incredulous.

He wound the length of my hair around his fist, by it pulling me toward him. I had thought, when I suggested we view Dellin and M'tras, that he would be apprised of the injustices around him and make reparations. He had not been. Rather he had determined that Silistra had no need of a dharen.

His hand, at the nape of my neck, tightened painfully. "Estri, cease this," he said, his eyes intent. There had been, when he spoke with Chayin, laughter there. Now I saw none.

I stared up at him. "I thought you did not read women's thoughts," I accused.

His other arm went around me. My head was pressed to that wound he had so recently taken. My body knew his. I ignored it, making myself stiff.

He picked me up and carried me down the cells. "Not when I can help it," he said. "Woman, what is wrong with you?"

And then when I did not answer: "What is this sudden thirst of yours for fitness? Are you some lake-born?" He found the cell he had sought. His old one. He laid me upon the rushes and closed the door.

I knew, though shadows masked him, that he was slouched against it, his arms crossed over his chest.

I sat up on the lake rushes. They were damp and fraught with jabbing ends.

After a time he came and stood over me. My eyes, adjusted to the scant light from the tiny oblong window, saw his hesitation as he disrobed.

I found I sat upon my heels. I realized it when he knelt before me and took my palms from where they rested on my thighs. His anger was for Khys, and his teachings, but I felt it in his driving use. He held my hands from me in that first wordless couching. It was a thing of claim and conquest, of need pent too long, and under him I wept, praying to I knew not what that he would find in me that thing he sought.

And it came to pass that I spoke much truth for him there, in his cell. I had come here once and tried to free him. I had proffered my aid. Failing that, I had offered my use. Did I not think him Khys's match, he had asked me. He recalled it, reminding me of what he had told me then; when he chose, he would take me.

I spoke to him of how it had been for me: that I had dreamed of him, so often; that even unknowing myself, I had known his touch more than Khys's; that my body had never failed to recollect him, even when my mind did not. And I marked his light, deft touch in my mind.

There came a moment in that couching when he also spoke of what concerned him. It was not until he had, to his satisfaction, reclaimed my flesh. I lay with my head in his lap, my lips tracing an old scar. In my heart, at that time, there was no ease.

"I have a problem with you," he said, very low. "You question me. If I am fit. If I am right. You risked yourself and all our lives when you tried your skills on Khys's council. If Carth had died,

Chayin and I would be yet in bands. I told you long ago, when first you revealed yourself, that you must not initiate precipitous actions."

I said nothing. "At that time, I was seriously concerned with the problems such skills might engender. Now I have similar skills, and I am still not unconcerned.

"Estri, if it had not been for you, I would have dealt long ago with Khys. It was his possession of you that held me back. You have come, like the lake-born, to regard men with too much concern to the color of their skin and the nature of their ancestors."

Then I did speak. "I wrote a critical essay for the dharen upon that subject. Carth tore it up." Sereth spat a single word of condemnation, sufficient in his sight for Khys, Carth, and the written word.

"Let me make this clear. I fared reasonably well against Khys. My sense of fitness is not impaired. I know what I am doing. I expect no less from you now than I expected upon Mount Opir."

I recalled it, that time. In all things had I deferred to him.

"You struck out at Chayin with mind. If you try such a thing with me, I will not be so easy upon you as he might."

"I love you," I whispered, my lips against his thigh.

"And I have lost many enths of sleep over you. I intend to lose no more. I know you are confused. Things will become clear to you. Seek the sort."

I kept silent, in fear of his displeasure.

Exasperated, he pushed me from him. "Estri, speak your mind. How dare you be so affrighted of me?" he growled, shaking me by the hair.

"I have lost the habit," I said when I could. And: "Please, this is not what I seek with you." I wanted nothing else but him. And yet the current of the time clashed us together like unmanned derelicts upon a full-roused sea.

"If you can, relearn it. I do not fear your thoughts or your skill." He pulled me onto his lap. "To own a thing, one must make use of it."

His hands upon me are not a thing that can be described. Beside his touch, all others' pale spectral. "I will settle for no less than I have ever demanded from you," he informed me twice more.

"Take your reparations," I begged him. "I am yours, crell without doubt."

Later we walked the dharen's tower, enquieted, arms around each other's waists. He sensed my fretfulness, and allowed that he would teach me the shield that served both him and Chayin so well. I rested my head against his shoulder as we came upon the third-floor landing.

The night's stars were framed in the darkened keep's window. He led me there, not allowing the ceiling stars to glow.

"I would speak to you. Will you hear me?" he said quietly, throwing his leg over the ledge.

"You know me," I said.

"I know what I feel. There was a time when you would have spoken of your own accord. You must understand me. I know the hest, and the sort; and I know where hesting blends with shaping and becomes unnatural constraint. You yourself know the rules. Even Khys could not escape them. And many take helsars. The time is sorely beset."

"I do not understand you," I said.

"There are stars in the sky," Sereth observed. "Once, I might have gone out among them. Khys felt it better that we be isolated. I cannot now hunt among the stars. Hear me, ci'ves," he said, the shadow face turning to regard me, and then back to the stars over the Lake of Horns. "I might not wish to go. But I would like to regain the choice. I may set my will to that barrier. I cannot say. There is the Embrodming Sea, and what lies beyond. I have reclaimed you. I am reasonably content. In time, you will better recollect yourself. I will see to it. You are not as stripped of skills as you pretend. I invite you to take them up. I advise you to do so. We will all need what weapons we can muster. The helsar children roam the land. The law within will be greatly tested."

He paused. I waited, lest my word cause him to retreat once more into his taciturnity. My hand found his thigh, lay there quietly. His finger traced a pattern along its back.

"Perhaps he is right to contain us," he mused. "And perhaps your father is right. But I do not think so. The helsars have come to be, premature. We will have to deal with them, and the resultant strains upon owkahen. What Khys has done, right or wrong, is upon us. We are reaping his fruits. Storms rage upon owkahen, turbulence abounds. The wind from the abyss howls hungry. If we are not mature enough to limit shaping skills, they will destroy us. As they destroyed him. It was not I; I was chosen executioner, and pawn ongoing. It was not I, but owkahen. His own works destroyed him. He used the time coming to be like a bow. By will he notched the shafts of his conception, and at length, the tension being untoward, the bowstring frayed, snapped. The bow snapped back. And we are left to seek what we may.

"I have found it necessary to put restraints upon my own skills," said Sereth, almost inaudibly. "I choose not to obviate space, when I might walk or ride or sail. I choose not to shape, nor to intrude upon the minds of others. I do this not because I am weak but because I am cautious. I enjoy my body. I would continue to inhabit it. We live in a world subsumed with natural stricture. I would have it no other way. I find it comforting that the sun rises and sets dependably. I like to know that the ground will not dissolve from beneath my feet between steps."

His shadow face regarded me. "You have felt the backlash from imprudent twisting of those laws. It was you who first spoke to me of such dangers. Khys might speak even more eloquently, had he survived them. But he was mad, too long enfleshed. Though brilliant, he was mad. And no book of cautions is going to tame the helsar winds when they blow."

And I saw him in my mind's eye: Khys, who locked doors though none who might threaten him could be by such means obstructed; who wore stra, though none of Silistra could stand against that armory of mind the dharen possessed. And I saw the helsars, in their thousands, aglitter on the plain of Astria.

Shaking the phantoms from me, I tried to pierce the darkness that hovered around Sereth. Never had he spoken to me thus. My hand lay limp upon his thigh, cool upon his heat. I stared into the darker shadows where his eyes must be.

"Perhaps we will learn to contain our skills and use them lawfully," I ventured. "Those who do not will be, by their own works, destroyed. Owkahen takes reparation from those who would rule it."

He took a sibilant breath, spewed it out. "It might come to be," he said with a voice like driven sleet, "that we destroy all the order on Silistra, and, like Khys, find ourselves bereft of choice, surrounded by chaos born out of our inviolability. It might be that with so many engaged in ordering the universe to please them, Silistra will become divested of sequentiality—a sphere where there is no certainty, no surety upon which a man can count. One must have a place to stand. It comes down to this: we either order our skills or be destroyed by the crux we engender.

"I would not have it so," he whispered. "Nor

would I attempt to legislate morality. Each must choose for himself. As long as I can recall, I have hested and sorted. I did not need Khys or a helsar to teach me. Man comes, of nature, to the sort and the hest. No more.

"Now," he said, touching my cheek, the shorn lock that flopped there, "do you understand why I would not hear of Khys's will, or Estrazi's? If I must be responsible for my actions, they will be in my sight right. Always have I done it thus. I know no other way." I kissed his fingers as they played upon my lips.

X.

In Deference to Owkahen

In the predawn I left them, soundless. I stood over them a time, where they were melded by the shadows into some many-legged creature not of my acquaintance. I thought sure my breath would wake them, roaring down through my nose. And what I would say, when they caught me, I conjectured. Almost, I lay back down beside them.

As one embarked upon a nightmare, I got gear from the wardrobe. At any moment I expected a hard grip upon my shoulder. And then their anger. The breeze of my painfully slow movements raised every fine hair upon my body. But I had gained the hall. And then I ran, fittings in hand, down the rear stairs, my breaths barbed and my mouth full of tongue.

One comes, inevitably, to the great doors with their inlaid golden beasts. I took an alcove, therein garbed myself in the tunic and cloak, and belted the light blade about my hips. And I congratulated myself. Sereth is the lightest of sleepers. Chayin has desert ears.

The guards at the open doors dozed—all but two, who had found amusement with each other. They did not look up.

Out I walked between those bronze doors twice the height of a man. My bare feet trod the cold stone steps. The evening bristled with Brinar chill.

Wirur, constellation of the winged hulion, glittered faintly in the coming dim.

Upon the ways were a great number of threx, strung on ropes, their gear piled before them, as is Parset custom. There were, of course, no saddle-packs or saddles. That, also, is Parset custom.

I chose a young-seeming male who slept upon his feet. He slept no more when I started toward him. He gave me scrutiny, his pointed ears flattened. Then he snorted softly and tipped them to my croon. He did not know me. He snapped his huge teeth together. But he was interested. I have, with animals, some small skill.

Out from the Lake of Horns in the first outpouring of dawn I rode him, bareback. His stride was clean and fast, his manners and mouth soft and sweet. We could not, I adjudged, shifting my knees lower on his barrel, gain the trees before true day. Where my thighs had clutched him, the hair was dark and sweating and the sweat frothed white. Not by true day, I thought, leaning forward, low upon his neck. I hoped, as I urged him for speed, that those who watched for hulions atop the tower would not see, or in seeing, mark only the threx, running breakneck toward the encircling trees.

We did not make the trees by true day. But we were not much later within the dappled dark-light they filtered.

I drew him up. We rested, blowing stentorian breaths. I sluiced froth and sweat from under my legs. In that air a fog streamed from us, not dispersing. The tree trunks were immense. The first branches started far above my mounted head. The day seemed hardly noticeable; the cool Brinar light, weakly piercing the tree cover, had not even the strength to dry the leaves.

I kicked him moving, lest he be done ill by standing and steaming in the damp. He snorted. The

night water showered us from above. I did not
mind.

I gave the nameless threx his head. I did not
know where I was bound. I had run from Sereth. I
had not run from Khys when the opportunity presented itself, nor from Chayin, though I had had
many chances, nor even from Dellin so long ago on
the road to Well Arlet.

I wished I could cry. I wished also that the
young threx was possessed of a less protruding
backbone.

I had not thought I would get this far.

The green-dark deepened. The threx lowered his
muzzle to the ground and sniffed rumblingly as he
picked his way.

I had run from none of them, but I had run from
Sereth.

The evening past had yielded much. They had
meted out justice, in their fashion.

They had returned to M'tras his ijiyr. He had
thanked them, and played for them a dark and
explorative piece that ended unresolved. He had
said that the power source, self-contained, would
last a thousand years.

"And then what?" had said Sereth soberly.

Chayin and Dellin had laughed. M'tras had not,
but only placed the ijiyr again in its case.

Then did Sereth and Chayin give to them the
threx they had appropriated. Sereth had spent some
time searching a gentle beast for M'tras. Such are
not too common among tiasks and jiasks.

M'tras looked upon the beast warily. He clicked
and muttered something in his own language. The
stars were only rising above the lake. The fattened
moon, just clearing the trees, was smeared with
blood.

M'tras' uncertainty had been a palpable taste to
us all. How strange and terrible and crude we

seemed to him, great bloodthirsty animals riding upon their like.

"Just assert yourself," Dellin advised, mounting his own beast. When he had it settled, he took M'tras' threx by the head stall.

Sereth helped M'tras mount. We watched them as they departed. Dellin, anxious to be off, still held M'tras' beast when the dark consumed them. They went gladly to the Liaison First's upon the plain of Astria. The last we sensed of them was their relief, floating back like scent upon the breeze.

Though Sereth knew of Khys's hest and their intention, he did not speak to them of helsars.

He had spoken to them of the Silistrans trapped upon the space worlds, orphaned by Khys's barrier. I had given little thought to them—the wellwomen, the telepaths, the teachers, and the dharen's agents. Dellin and M'tras and Sereth and Chayin had long discussed them.

It was then that it came to me, while I strove to separate Sereth's silhouette from the lakeside night as he stared longingly after Dellin and M'tras. I caught taste of him then; that shield for a splintered heartbeat of time crumbled by his need. How greatly he envied them, unbound and free, off upon whatever errands they chose. And I saw his life as he perceived it—and I saw that although in a sense he had won his freedom, he considered it putative. Sereth, child of owkahen, had served his master well, that he might win surcease, and had become even further bound. I shared my thought in a moment of privacy with Chayin, and he upheld me:

"It has been before us all along," he agreed, lying amid the cushions, his membranes attesting to the strength of his conviction. "We saw, but we did not realize. Both of us, who love him, failed to see." And what we had overlooked—that he was in a sense Estrazi's hest that all the fathers had long sought, all that Khys so long obstructed—most discomfited us.

He is hase-enor: of all flesh. In my research, during my early pregnancy, I had not neglected him. Sereth, who bears every bloodline upon Silistra, had been of use to me in my criticism of Khys's genetic policies. It is Sereth who is first-come to time and space, presage of what the future might hold, should all be free on Silistra to mix their blood.

Chayin and I are both catalysts forced upon the time. Sereth is natural to it. He is owkahen's son. To sons, fathers have been known to set tasks, and ultimately to show favor. Should the son prove worthy, it is often so, between fathers and sons.

Upon that determination, I knew what I must do. I showed him Khys's most secret charts and papers. He was unconcerned with them. He had, he said, just come from seeing Carth. Carth, he assured me, would live. His eyes were far indrawn. He had been long among the wounded and maligned.

It was then that he adjudged us both lacking in compassion, and I sensed in him the distance the time had put between us. Before, he had not met my father. It seemed to me, hearing his words, that we might never span the gulf of our divergent heritages. All of Khys's knowing words came back to me. I rubbed the seal upon my left breast and let my eyes drink of him, for that drink would have to last me long.

He watched me, sidelong, but made no attempt to aid me up from out of that particularly female pit of self-abasement into which I had fallen. And Chayin, angered, rose up and left, growling that he must see to his child. I had seen the child, in the arms of that well-woman who bore Sereth's seed. Sereth seemed to barely recollect her. I had asked of her disposition and been told that she was destined for Nemar, crell to the cahndor.

The threx stumbled, his forefoot caught momentarily in an exposed root. I patted him reassuringly, and urged him forward. His shoulder, under my hand, twitched and quivered, but he quickened his pace.

The hulion's roar stopped the threx so suddenly I grabbed his neck for support. I cautioned him to silence, slipping off his back.

The hulion, roaring repeatedly, appeared between the trees. The threx, affrighted beyond sanity, waited no longer. Even as those gold-gleaming eyes fixed upon it, it reared screaming upon its hind feet. The reins, jerked from my hand, flapped wildly. I made one abortive jump for them. A steel-shod hoof creased my skull. My vision became particles of light. I felt no pain.

When I felt again, it was a great rough tongue scraping my arm.

When I saw at last, I saw a face. That face loomed against darkness. I put my fingers to my right temple, encountered another's there.

I tried to raise my head. The hand would not allow it. The scraping of that dry abrasive tongue upon my flesh ceased. I peered at the circle of light that seemed to belong to the hands. After a time, it coalesced into a familiar pattern of tone and feature, behind which the blackness undulated queerly. I continued to peer. Then I knew what I saw, and closed my eyes to the blur.

I heard an entwining of sound.

"Little one, look at me." It was a number of times he said it, before I could disentangle his words from Santh's plaintive mutterings.

I opened my eyes. The new day's light, bounding and rebounding off the thinning foliage, played upon them like running water. Santh sat with his forelegs tucked between his hind, his wedge-shaped head lowered, his ears cocked askew. And before me also was Sereth, squatting down with his hand upon my brow.

"Do you not think," I said slowly, "that we would all fare better apart?"

"If I thought that," he said, "I would not be here."

"And how did you find me?"

"Santh."

"He serves you," I said, raising my head and letting it fall. The world wheeled in stately procession, with my eyes as axis of its languid rotation.

He laughed. "Ask him."

From Santh I received a greeting. And a question formed of allegory. Hulion thought is not as man thought. They are not symbolizers such as we. I saw a light she-hulion, and marked her as Santh's mate. I saw her, and him also, engaged in their mating ritual. And then, superimposed, the tawny one, fleeing his dominion. And the thought was full with heat, and the courting customs of his kind. If he had bespoken me as a man, the question might have been: "Why do you flee him? Is it thus?" But it was a hulion's question, subsumed with acceptance and harmony, and the love of the chase.

I could not gainsay his truth. I turned my face into Sereth's hand and wept, at last.

"There is much left undone," he said, his callused fingers tracing my brow. "Sit up."

I once more lifted my head. The forest spun liquidly. I lay back upon the mulch of moldering autumn, content to rest, with his hand upon me and Santh's mutters like settling rocks in my ears. It was beyond my power to do more.

"Sereth," I said, "I cannot." I had spoken clearly. My own ears heard the words loud and strong. But Sereth did not hear them. He leaned close. I could count his lids' lashes, judge the widened pupils of his dark eyes.

"Speak again, ci'ves," he whispered, as the scar upon his cheek took life and crawled off his face to encircle his neck like some hideous band of restraint.

He put one palm over my eyes, his other cupping the back of my neck. It was only then, as sensation, identifiable pain, coursed over me, that I realized I had been without it. Now, as my back and ribs throbbed and my left leg demanded attention, I was terrified, for I had not heretofore felt them. My whole self shrunken inward with fear, I assayed the drawing up of my damaged leg. I heard him grunt. He removed his hand from my eyes. Santh, paw before paw, stretched himself full length, yawning.

"Where were you bound?" he asked. Now, only, was there trace of anger upon him. It rode his voice, cowled in relief. With his aid I sat, my left leg stretched out straight.

"I do not know," I said, regarding the swollen knee. Below it was a bandaged gash, but that was of little moment. I put my own hands upon it, closing my eyes. What I sought, I received. Under my palms the flesh cooled and subsided. "I do not know," I repeated, folding the leg experimentally.

"We will meet Chayin," he said quietly. His gol-knife excavated the mulch between his legs as he squatted there. "I will not be pleased if you make such wanderings your practice. I know you have been long sequestered. You will get enough destinationless wandering, across the Embrodming."

"If you would avoid my father's service," I said to him, "do not again take me up."

"We will go first with Santh. I have something to share with you. Then to Astria. You may bring in your hest there. In Port Astrin we will take

ship—Chayin's best, and a picked Menetpher crew.
The men of Meneth are excellent sailors."

"If it is your will," I said, putting weight gingerly upon my left leg. Sereth and Santh rose as
one. I looked between them, taking a testing step.
My work held.

"You can ride?" He disbelieved, critically.

And it was upon hulions, Santh and Leir, who
was waiting amid the trees, that we rode to that
mountain holy place priested by hulions. It is of
their deity and deification, and not man's; therefore the mountain has no name. It is but one of
many in that cragged fastness where no man
dwelleth: hulions rule the impenetrable west.

Upon the way there I learned that Sereth, through
Leir, had come to be held high among them. And
that hulions, also, had taken a knowing part in
Khys's destruction. They had willingly absented
themselves from the Lake of Horns. It had been
between them, and Sereth decided: if thus-and-
thus occurs, such will be done.

From Santh I could coax nothing of reason or
motive during those two days. Nor would Sereth
enlighten me, except to say that only selected
hulions ever frequented the Lake of Horns. His
implication was that the hulions gathered such
intelligence as concerned them, while seeming to
serve the dharen. There is no way any of us will
ever be sure.

"I care little for their reasons. I took the chance.
It proved lucky. They aided me, or I aided them.
Or it was a coincident serving," Sereth had said,
as I pressed him in the firelight that evening. But
he had not been angry. Little would have angered
him then. Before his fire, he lounged upon the chill
ground as loose as the hulions stretched with their
bellies to the fire's warmth. Above us the full moon
danced, impaled upon an audacious peak. The fire
showed me the easy inward smile upon him. The

laughter rekindled in his dark eyes that night, as if the flame cleansed his spirit. I recollected that look, from when I had first known him in Well Arlet. And I began then to fan within me the banked coals of my own faith. If he might find contentment upon such a night, how much less could I show myself to be?

He had sought owkahen, and found it pregnant and new. What he chose, he might now do, with the crux time clearing away. And he found no shadowing upon it that troubled him, although I had found my ardor much damped by what I myself had seen.

The storms grow upon owkahen. We saw them then. We feel them now. But still, there is time. The ship rocks under me. The waves make a wine-sot of my not-ever-precise handwriting. The sea's pitching has this past set taken a different rhythm. Chayin says we will soon sight land.

There are various observations that I would like to make upon what has come to be. But there remain certain outcomes, if such they may be called. The cahndor maintains that little of life may be neatly tied up, and even less of those particular events with which I have here concerned myself.

None will know, Chayin is sure, what disposition the fathers made of Khys. And yet I saw him, when we sat with the hulions in their cavernous temple. Luminous veins riddled the rock with greenish trails that seemed to pulse. The only other light was that of their eyes—pair upon pair of glowing pools, all shades from palest yellow to brooding red. Their rumbling, magnified and returned to us by the subterranean vault, might have been that sound a sphere makes, turning. I was visited, while kneeling among them therein, by a number of truths. Among them was a sense of Khys's presence. Since that time, I have doubted his demise. Though for his sake I hope that he achieved it, that passing he so concertedly sought, that inalienable freedom to which we are all entitled. Those teachings he so venerated, those masters whose works he emulated, bespoke it far better than I ever might: all come to the abyss, there to partake of the definition of life, the catalyst death, that beginning toward which all life labors.

Still, in my mind, he lives. Upon all of Silistra he thrives, through the metamorphosis he has brought about. Where men erect yris-tera boards and throw, is Khys. Where the children are conceived, does his spirit rejoice. Upon the chalder's anvil are his blessings ever forged. In the Day-Keepers' schools and the Slayers' hostels and about the waists of wellwomen and parrbreeders and weaponsmiths and pelters one may see him. Sereth weighed him, and found him mad. It may be so. A relic from a long-dead age he was, in truth. Those teachings that he gave unto us were not those that he had learned. In a way, he was never of us, but only with us, he who was a Stoth priest even before the holocaust. Perhaps, as said Sereth, he never truly partook of that morality he taught. I have presented him, to the best of my ability, as he presented himself to me. I make no judgment upon him. In accordance with that Stothric tradition into which he was born, he lived. And in a Stoth manner, he sought his death, not in flight, but as a fitting resolution to his life.

They judge me recovered from what he did to me. I wonder if any of us might ever recover. That which one experiences is not other than oneself from that moment ongoing. I no longer cringe when a hand is raised unexpectedly within striking distance. I have made some progress in excising from my behavior the fear and timidity he taught. But I yet bear his sign upon my flesh, and in my heart also. If it were within my power, I would change his ending, if it be death or confinement or the anguish I sensed when I knelt amid the convened hulions of Silistra. Why they deserted his service and turned their absence to Sereth's aid, I know not. Nor why they held service in his honor and sat vigil for his spirit, do I know. Suffice it to be that such was the case—that it was done, and I was present, and Sereth and Chayin were also there. And we each gave up, in that cavern with the deep-throated hulion hymns vibrating the stone upon which we knelt and the bones of our bodies, what recollection we had of him, into a pool of communal reliving. And when that pool had no bottom and no surface, when all ever known of him had been entered therein, the hulions walked one at a time, with measured stride and solemn demeanor, through the harvest of his years. When my turn came to enter that darkened depression in the circled mid-cave, it seemed to me that I stepped into cold, fast running water. Down the unsteep incline I proceeded, at each step the tingling chill of immersion rising higher up my body. As I had seen the hulions do, I stepped onto the down-spiraling ledge and followed its ever-tightening course until I stood at the pit's center. But I saw it not. Rather did I see Silistra, her copses and groves, her precipices and seas. I saw her burned and steaming, oozing foul putrefaction upon the land. And I saw all those years of her tending, that she might once more raise bountiful eyes to the sun.

And he came to me there. First it seemed he bestrode a lake sheeted with ice. Across it, toward me, he came. The sun lit the ice tawny. Where he lifted foot, deep tracks appeared, as if the fire of him melted the surface beneath his flesh. And he held out his hands to me, his face becalmed and peaceful, as the ice began to rumble and creak. With sounds like bones snapping, in an air turned dark and awful with crackling chuckles, the surface of the lake broke asunder. As if some great sea beast desired exit and beat against the ice sheet from below, the cracks spread and heaved, whole chunks the length of a man rearing up into the air and crashing down to smash what ice remained. He danced, scrambling for purchase. With more than man's effort, he leaped and scrambled. I saw him fall once, feetfirst, into the ice. Hands, clawing, seized the chunks afloat. He struggled upon one and lay there, his face turned away. Beneath him, it crumbled. And I saw him swimming, first desperately, then sluggishly, then a mere flailing of hands. And he met my eyes once with his. And then he was no more. There was only the lake and the tiny crystals of slush that floated gray upon the surface. That, and only that, was revealed to me, as I sat with the hulions, of the fate of Khys, once dharen of Silistra.

Of my son, all that remains is a name: Jehsrae.

We went, upon the first first of Decra, by hulion out from that place. It was a set later we stood upon the plain of Astria, Sereth and I, unscathed, as I had so long ago hested. And indeed, I could not excise the crawling, mewling wounded from my sight of that place, nor the corpses over which they crawled. All around us I met the shades of our dead. We did not stay long there among the helsars. The hulions had refused even to enter that place, but waited past the stand of trees in which Sereth had secreted his archers to await the closing of battle in Amarsa, '695.

Chayin was first to speak it, but we were all, by then, apprised of the need to be gone from the plain. As we had been of the need to come, to offer our silence to those who had perished in our service, a thing we had not been able to do that day.

We avoided, by my will, Well Astria. Let Vedrast's daughter reign there. It matters not to me. "Guard Astria, or you will lose it," had written the Well-

Foundress Astria in her warning. One should not go about groping for the joys of youth to which maturity has made one unsuited.

Sereth, surely sensing my melancholy, led me gently from the field. My eyes, upon my feet and his, saw here and there, among the browned grass, helsars, awaiting those who would sometime claim them. It was said to me once by the dharen that helsars have been provided for all ever meant to take them; that a helsar knows no sequentiality, no waiting. To them, every man who will come to claim them, every woman who will pilgrimage here, stand all together upon the plain in one moment encompassing all of time. There must be many still to come. Upon the plain of Astria are enough helsars to bestar lavishly a virgin sky. Enough, perhaps, to make a necklace for a universe mother, should such a *she* ever care to appear bedecked before the creator spirit to whom she is in service.

I wondered briefly if Dellin and M'tras had come and gone, or if it still remained for them to lessen the field of helsars by two. And of what they would become, attendant to the helsar's teachings, did I take thought.

The hulions left us upon the outskirts of Port Astrin. I made a blurry-eyed farewell to Santh, and wished his mate Tjeila a fruitful birthing.

Sereth arranged with Leir a meeting for mid-Macara of the new year after next.

Chayin sent his regards to Frinhar, watcher of the clouds, whose eldest son had borne him hither.

We watched them in silence until they were only specks in the greening sky. When a hulion departs, the world seems shrunken and muted. Their perceptions, withdrawn, leave a flat and longing emptiness. They have the oneness, the wisdom of creation, within them. They see it in the leaves, they rejoice at its outcry in the thunderbolt as it carves its smoking likeness upon the rock. They are not as we, and there is much we might learn, should owkahen allow it, from Santh and Leir and their brethren.

I looked at Chayin, just turning away toward the twisting anarchy of Port Astrin's jumbled streets. He stared with narrowed eyes at the city, then at his booted feet. Stooping down, he plucked a blade of withered grass and sucked upon it. His marks of godhood were covered by the loose sleeves of winter leathers. All in brown was dressed the cahndor, unassuming, with just southern short sword and gol-knife at his waist. But I knew what weapons nestled in the lining of his brown cloak, and even in the tops of his high boots, for I bore the like about my own person.

"Here," said Sereth, holding out something in his hand. It was a chald. Upon it were strands to which I was entitled. I took it, circling it around my waist. When I had fitted the key in its housing, I saw Chayin's snap-membraned stare.

Sereth bore at his waist an arrar's chald. But it was not truly his, any more than that about my own waist was mine. And he might have borne another chald, that of Silistra's dharen.

Chayin spat upon the ground and rose up. "I will never understand you," he spoke to Sereth. "You take up and put down chaldra the way other men take up and put down women." The cahndor's first act upon addressing his triumphant troops had been to rip from his waist the northern chald Khys had forced upon him, and replace it with his own, feathered and trophied. As he donned his southern chald, he bade each of his men do likewise. And he bade them also rip as quickly from their hearts all amendments of their custom that had been forced upon them. I had not been there, but I had heard tell of the cahndor's impassioned speech to the jiasks and tiasks of his realm.

"Chaldra," said Sereth, grinning, "is carried about the spirit, not about the waist. And besides, would you have me cut down for chaldless by the first Slayer we meet in the city?"

Chayin snorted. "Just the same, I like it not."

And I liked it no better.

"While Carth remains alive," said Sereth soberly, "I have a right to this." He ran his hand along the supple chald nestled gleaming above his weapons belt. "And Estri has surely earned the chald of messenger. You would see us in southern chalds, I suppose."

"It would please me," the cahndor admitted.

"If your ship and your sailors are half as skilled as you claim, we may live to collect some." He shaded his eyes with his hand, looking out past the city, where the gray-green sky met the gray-green sea. The harbor, from this vantage, was abristle with sharp-masted craft. "Let us get upon the trail. I would be there and at a meal by dark."

Down the yellow-brown hills that sloped to the city and the shore we went, cross-cutting to take the wide and well-kept thoroughfare that led to the Well-Keepress' gate, so called because it offers northerly exit toward Well Astria. The road, though there were some carts and one caravan (from Galesh, surely; gaen-hauled wagons, tasseled and belled and enclosed in colored silks, humped archeon packed to twice a man's height with woven baskets, their bottoms sagging with produce; the fruit smell wafting back to us, sweet and sharp), was sparsely traveled, for such an enth.

And within the gate, at which we were not checked, but only noted upon a wax tally by a portly guard who judged us unworthy of even a two-eyed scrutiny, I saw more clearly what the loss of the star trade might come to mean. Shops were boarded up. Men hawked off-world goods at ruinous prices in the sandblown streets. Where

M'ksakkan or Itabic or Torth legends showed upon
hostels and inns, those signs had been defaced.
Perhaps a third of the businesses were closed
altogether. Port Astrin, more than any other place
upon Silistra, had made off-worlders at home. She,
of all Silistra, would most lament their departure.

"There seem an inordinate number of beggars,"
Sereth remarked, silencing one mendicant in whining approach with a scowl that sent him stumbling over his own rags into a doorway.

"Things will right themselves here," I said. Chayin
put an arm protectively about me as three raw-
faced seafarers came by us.

We found an inn of Sereth's acquaintance that
was not closed. In the old section of the city, high
over the harbor it rose, hulking blocks of taernite
so thick that not even the shifting coastline had
been able to dislodge them.

Over a meal that displayed the sea's bounty upon
our table, they spoke of ships and courses, of tides
and straits and what might lie in the uncharted
waters between the Astrian coast and that shore of
which none were empowered to speak.

"We cannot keep calling it that," Sereth decided,
slid down low upon the padded bench, a pipe of
good danne, courtesy of the innman's girl, glowing
red in his hand. "We are speaking about it all the
time."

"Let us name it when we set foot there," proposed Chayin, flashing his white teeth expectantly.
"That is the way such things are done."

"The Keening Rock has a name. The shore upon
which it sits has a name. Might we not be presumptuous, planning to name a continent?" I said
it softly, my finger drawing the Keening Rock's
likeness in the wet rings the kifra goblets had left
upon the striped ragony of the round table.

The innman's girl took bellows to the fire against
the encroaching salt chill. By my shoulder, the

cold panes sweated. The calk-and-beam ceiling had depending from it brass oil lamps upon chains. She turned to their trimming, from the fire burning renewed upon the hearth. Its dance caught me. Within dance is ever story; within flame, glyphs of life. I saw Khys there, his glowing eyes heavy-lidded, as he had been above that blaze he had made upon the planet of his entrapment. And Sereth I saw, and the trail to Santha. And all that had occurred since then: upon Mi'ysten; in the Parset Lands; Hael dark beneath Raet's likeness, underlit by chalder's fire; the flames of the helsar gate; the fiery agony of childbirth; and my trial at the dharen's hands. Then I saw hulion and uritheria. Father, give us respite. And Gherein roasting in his sire's flame. Free us from this blind striving in thy name. And Kystrai, standing in a greater conflagration as if he stood beneath a beneficent waterfall. Khys, my grief is never-ending. Accomplice inconsolable, I stand bereft of even tears. Long had they lain in wait for you. I was born to destroy you. Golden lashes, so long his eyes seemed oblong. You would have fallen, then, without my betrayal. But I am the vessel of their chastisement. The herb that will be ground and sold for poison of an old weak man for his holdings—can the plant be adjudged guilty of the crime? If only you had gone to them . . .

"Estri?"

"No, Sereth. No more kifra." His arm goes around me, silent comfort. He knows, but he will not speak of it. He is free from fear. I draw peace from my head leaned upon him.

"And yet, I might speak of it," he said. "Or repeat it, at least. Before the battle of Astria, you spoke it: we are it. Se'keroth, I thought for the thousandth time, and put the thought away."

Chayin pushed the kifra aside, leaning his elbows

upon the table. " 'Thrice denied and thrice delivered/ Lost and bound and found and tempered. . .' "

" 'Sword of severance,' " I repeated, as Chayin broke it off, that oldest of prophecies whose refrain was all too familiar. I pressed my nose against Sereth's leathers. My eyes searched the fire. Khys and the anguish of my life no longer burned therein.

"Did you know I was born in Nin Sihaen?" offered Sereth gravely. Nin Sihaen, across the Karir-Thoss, is the most western city of known Silistra. " 'One from the east, born of ease and destined/ One from north of Lost and bound and found and tempered . . .' "

" 'The third from out the west, astride a tide of death,' " quoted Chayin. He was not smiling. It is a long epic. All has been foreseen. We all know that tale's end.

"A man thinks," said Sereth softly, "that it cannot be him, as his life first bends to fit itself to some metaphysician's metaphor. It cannot be me, I thought, at first with amusement and later with great fear. I admit it. Those old forereadings—they are detailed. The legend's blade, it was said, would be forged of substance from the Sihaen-Istet hills. It is told to children in those lands. It was told to me, for I was raised there. And when I set off to test for a Slayer's chain, the town boys laughed and called me 'seeker after severence.' " I craned my neck to see him. His gaze rested in Chayin's. I had known his birthplace. I had never heard him speak of his youth.

I remembered a time in Nemar North, with Chayin, when I had revealed to him that I was at war with his father, god of that land. And he had named himself spawn of chaos. " 'Out of fear's belly did I come,' " he had said then. I shivered.

" 'Son of dark gods, son of life/ She between then blessed with light,' " I said. The words came from me slowly, involuntarily, as if dragged up from some primal foreknowing spirit pit, like the child that knows, in paralyzing realization, that *this* time that which lurks in the dark is no phantasm, but the reality of which phantasmic monsters are but racial memory.

In the Sword of Severence, there are four ors. They are concerned with a time of cleansing and rebirth come upon Silistra, indeed upon all the universe. And it is concerned with the instruments of that cleansing. And there is a sword, and a scabbard, and a hand to bear it. There are two men and a woman. And there are labors the extent of which have these thousands of years relegated the prophecy to the pertinence of epic drama.

"Some thought it fulfilled by the destruction of the surface cities," Chayin said at last, uneasily shifting in his seat, as a brist might ramp back and forth at the smell of men.

"Would that I could believe that," said Sereth. "If we make this journey, we will know for certain."

"If?" I said, pushing away. I found my dry mouth in need of kifra. I raised hand to the girl. Sereth slid down lower upon his spine. He took his knife and with the blade cleaned his nails. The knife was all stra, hilt and blade both. Its butt caught the firelight.

"If we do not return from that land, we cannot be they." A log burst, snarling sparks.

Chayin rubbed his left bicep, upon which, under the supple tas, was inscribed the slitsa wound about a recurved blade. His hand trailed to his shoulder, stayed long at his neck.

A very small part of that prophecy I knew we had fulfilled. Great harm had come upon Silistra from out of the south. *We* had come. We had been, the three of us, responsible for more deaths by violence than are normally written upon the Day-Keepers' Roll in twenty Silistran years. And we had done it in little more than five. And the dying was not over. Those who tried the helsars—a good number of them would die.

Perhaps as many as had died at the Lake of Horns. I hoped not. Over two thousand Parsets invested the Lake of Horns. They killed close to their own number. More than a hundred of those corpses were children. I had not been at the burning. There had been too many to bury. The corpses, piled high, had been fired. A number of the restrained had thrown themselves, alive, onto those pyres. None moved to stop them. It had been Chayin's order that those who were in lifelong restraint not be interfered with in any way. For those still living, there can be but little comfort.

"Carth," said Chayin, "led the ceremony himself. Supported by two of his arrars, for he could not stand alone, he led the lake-born in prayer." He had turned to Sereth, smiling. "I think you were right about him." Another log burst. Chayin's recollection of the pyres blazed bright before me.

"I hope so," said Sereth, who had laid the dharen's chald into Carth's hands, along with his life and the Lake of Horns. Certain terms had Sereth and Chayin dictated to Carth, highest living of the dharen's council. Those terms, Carth almost gratefully accepted. He ruled in regency for Sereth. The focus of his efforts was to be not the reconstruction of empire, but the fortification of the law within. As Khys, in his youth and brilliance, had envisioned it—before ego and power and hardship stripped him of his objectivity—Sereth would have it become. Sereth asked no alteration from Carth in the teachings of his master—only that those teachings be put truly into practice. Before Miccah, the high chalder, oaths had been sworn. And Sereth had taken up an arrar's chald for himself, and one for me, and instructed Miccah as to their alteration.

And Carth had shaken his dark head, from which great clumps of hair had been singed away, and his demeanor had turned darker, but he had not spoken. He lived, spared by their mercy. That had been made clear to him. And yet he seemed to me not servile. Sereth, toying with arrar's chald, had regarded him questioningly.

"Have you something to say?"

Carth, lying propped up against the austere wall of his own small keep, said, "Am I to exercise your authority as I see fit, or as I might conjecture that you would see fit?"

Sereth looked at him in that very chill countenance of his. Chayin shook his head as if his ears deluded him, that such impertinence and impropriety could come from a man who by all rights should have burned with his brothers. "What I want," said Sereth very quietly and at length, "is no more than minimally difficult to understand. Since it is unacceptable to everyone but me that there be no dharen upon Silistra, and since I have no intention of staying here and being dharen, it falls to you. I can kill you, and it will fall to someone else. I would rather not. Be dharen—not as I might see fit or you might see fit, but as best serves Silistra. Keep a light hand upon her. Aid as best you can the helsar children; school them, counsel them, but above all keep cognizant of them. Teach restraint. Let the time go its own way awhile, that owkahen will settle . . ." He broke off, unwound one hand from his chald, brushed hair from his eyes with it. The wound upon his skull was nearly healed. He frowned briefly at Carth. "If I thought you really did not know what was needed," he said softly, as if disappointed, "I would use another. How we regard each other matters little at this time. You may think what you will of me, as long as it does not impair your judgment in my behalf. If you need me, send word. I will receive it."

He rose up. "And recollect this well: it is to the

south you must send in your need. Then, only, will you suffer any northerner to set foot there. Should there be any reprisals, we will in truth tear these buildings down, stone from off of stone, and Silistra will live beneath the beneficent hand of the chosen son of Tar-Kesa."

Carth had turned away, though movement was costly to his bandage-swathed body, humped but hardly hidden beneath the couch clothes.

It was to Miccah he twisted. The white-haired high chalder, his seamed face distraught, hurried to his side. They whispered together. A cloud begrudged us even the slatted light streaming weakly through the six narrow windows.

Chayin motioned Sereth to him. They also conferred. It was this that had brought us to the lakeside so soon after Khys's reliving. I had little attention for the moment that day. My flesh was racked with chills, and I could not more than huddle in this corner or that. So did I attend it, Carth's assumption of the dharen's chald, a set's time after I had run from Sereth and my guilt. For better or worse, Carth, who had been once crell in the pits of Nemar, would rule from the Lake of Horns. On Brinar fourth fifth, 25,697, did a hase-enor, and a telepath, take up Silistra's care.

The silence was long. Neither Sereth and Chayin, nor Carth and Miccah, seemed anxious to break it.

"Excuse him, lords." Miccah straightened at last. His chins puffed as he worked his mouth. Confronting their austere authority, his message would not come forth.

"Excuse him," he sprayed. Tiny bubbles formed where his lips met. His eyes darted here and there in their bloodshot milky pools. "I beg you. Carth has no more strength for words. In his last breath, he bade me tell you he will humbly and to the best of his ability carry out your will." The words, springing forth all together in a jumble, were nearly unintelligible. Mouth agape, Miccah waited, hands thrust deep into his hide apron, feet wide and figure swaying. Still half in shock seemed Miccah, and yet grieving for the dharen.

Chayin, arms folded over his chest, looked at Sereth meaningfully. Then both turned to Carth, who lay in his body like a yra of binnirin grains in a two-stone sack. "Is that what he said?" queried Chayin innocently.

"Yes," affirmed the high chalder.

We can only hope that Carth will keep his proxy's promise. What he does is done in Sereth's name.

"Se'keroth, Se'keroth, direel b'estet Se'keroth," growled the cahndor, as the girl served me kifra. His eyes measured her as she leaned over to pour. She had evidently spoken to me. I had not heard. I had been with flame, once again.

"She is not yet well," said Sereth, half to the innman's girl and half to Chayin.

"Would you want three chambers, Se . . . arrar?" I heard her through the sea pulse, breaking upon the jetties and my eardrums.

"Two," Chayin said, "with access between."

Sereth's shifting, as he dug dippars from his pouch, was more immediate. I resettled myself against him.

"Re Dellin has been here, and left instructions that he be the first to know should you happen this way." Under his gaze, she preened herself, patting her hair with a sturdy wrist.

"When?" Sereth was tense-stiff, his quietest.

"Just this rising," she murmured, deferential, "if it should please you, arrar."

"And if it should not?" he snapped.

Sereth tossed three coins. The third was titrium half-well. The girl smiled, eyes lowered demurely, Chayin twisted around in his seat as she bent to take them. She brushed against him. She hesitated, her breast against his shoulder, her fingers upon the coins. "Should I send him word, then?" she asked.

"No," said Sereth.

"Se'keroth, indeed," I whispered as the girl withdrew and gave me back view of the hearth. Others entered then, to dine and chase the salt chill from their bones.

My fingers found the arrar's chald at my waist, and a certain knife that was sheathed upon the parrhide belt. In its hilt was a single gol drop. It had been given to me by Sereth, upon Mount Opir. Or its mate had. He had commissioned them, both alike, when I had been accounted dead. The gold drops in their hilts had been gift to us from a golachit we had aided, high in the gollands of the Sabembe range. Khys had taken them from us. We had, upon rediscovering them, learned the faithfulness with which the weaponsmith had followed the Ebvrasea's intention: "Tempered and remade the same, so that one may not be told from the other, Se'keroth."

At length, we each took one. There was no telling them apart.

The fired blade must be quenched in ice. We would not reach the eastern shore much before winter solstice, first first of Orsai.

I sat up, away from Sereth. Chayin looked at me, pensive, expectant.

"There is no proof. Beware use by prophecy in search of fulfillment," I warned him, knowing that if any could have warded off such forces, that one was no longer among us. He caught my thought, for he glared at me severly. I shrank back, upon reflex, from his displeasure. Then straightened. I had made no secret of my hesitancy to undertake this, or any, journey. They had both separately informed me that a time of peace and reflection was not in the sort. I think, rather, it is not in their natures.

The cahndor massaged that old wound, often his prelude to speech. It has long since ceased to pain him, but the habit remains. He seemed on the verge of comment when the innman's girl again approached. With her she bore a rolled document—documents, actually two, the larger serving as post around which the smaller had been wound. Then the whole, the larger, orangish fax, diapered with bone-white parchment, had been bound up in a strip of tas, upon which the Liaison's device was stamped in gold. One newly seated guffawed over his mug, across the room. His fellows joined in.

It lay upon the striped ragony, amid the wet rings and crumbs of our meal.

Sereth only regarded the girl, who without breaking her silence laid two brass keys beside the tas-bound tube.

She seemed to quiver all over, like a startled crier poised upon invisible wings above some scum-choked pond. "He said," she gave forth at last, "that if you would answer 'no,' I was to give you this." Her eyes had swelled to the size of copper dippars. She seemed flesh-locked, under his scrutiny.

"And you have done so," he said, tossing his head. The movement seemed to free her. She staggered slightly, like one who, long pushing upon some aged, recalcitrant door, stumbles forward in surprise when at last rusted hinges recollect their task. And like that door her retreating steps were jerky, as if she had long forgotten her body's command. She drifted between the tables, toward the men seated by the far wall.

None of us spoke for a long while. I looked after the innman's girl, now wiping her brow like one come out of a fever. She had seen—what? She did not know: a glowing, as of eyes more than mortal; two great beasts, abattle beneath a sky transformed; a room of seven corners, in whose center a spiral bound a woman in flame. She trembled. It ran from her head downward like a dorkat shedding water. It was a mark, only, she had seen, some odd bejeweling upon the foreign woman. I pulled my mind away, my fingers finding that device I still bore—the Shaper's seal, and Khys's most audacious statement of disrespect. He had appropriated it, as he had mimicked their councils and assessments. If I chose, I knew, I could divest myself of it. As yet, I have not done so. Upon a certain scale, it has value, as does even the most painful of remembrances, and on another, I have a right to bear it. And no move so simple as removing the dharen's device from my flesh will erase from Chayin's mind, or Sereth's, or mine, what Khys, in his battle against the father's will, chose to do with us. What will they say of him, those like the woman who still regarded me across the inn's common room? And of us? Will we be turned by the ineluctable chroniclers of events into liberators or villains? Those for whom such wars are waged have not yet breathed their first breaths, had said Chayin to me. And yet, the validity of Khys's sphere of restraint, the helsars' final testing, the loosing of the lake-born onto Silistra all loom imminent; as in Se'keroth, they approach, bringing with them that judgment of which all words will speak. Such as she would see a legion more of us, all bearing in our genes the legacy of Khys's bestowal.

"What think you of this," rumbled Chayin, poking once at the missive, then again, each touch pushing the tube closer to Sereth.

" 'And all the worlds of creation hearkened, and some even lent their hand unto the task. Let them be blessed,' " I recited dully, as Sereth's stra blade severed the tas, halving the M'ksakkan seal. The parchment, with a will of its own, uncurled from about the longer tube of fax and lay like some cornice upon the ragony.

He pulled it out, spread it flat. His elbows on the

table, he scanned it. Then he put his head in his hands. After a time I took it from him.

When I had read it, I passed the parchment to Chayin. It had taken up water from the table, and some of the words blurred indistinct as if they would disappear from the page. A wayward gust howled down the flue. The lamps' flames cowered.

Dellin played his part well. After greeting, his message was sparse of words:

> My appreciation for my life, and that of my world, also. Notwithstanding, I must, while I do live, perform my function. Enclosed find maps and intelligence pertinent to that journey which I have been informed you will undertake. It is my hope that you will accept them in the spirit of the giving, and take heed to my requests.

> Be those men and women you seek alive, I ask you to return them unharmed to us. It is upon me to discipline my own people. M'tras, or I, or both, would most willingly accompany you, that they be bloodlessly apprehended.

> I have long been charged with the care of Tyith's son. I could find no way to broach the subject under those circumstances you must well remember. I am bound unto that duty. I do not seek relief of it, but inform you lest you learn it from another and mistake my silence for ill intention.

> Presti, m'it tennit. I will be at the Harth's Nest upon the Street of Greaves until Decra third first."

And at the bottom, above his seal, he gave Sereth tasa.

Chayin threw it. It sailed upon a current, to drift to the floor by my foot. Sereth raised his head and reached for the fax.

What had the serving girl seen upon us? She who now leaned against the hearthside, what could she have known of us? Were we so set apart now, that any could see it?

And Dellin, who knew little enough of Silistra that the whole extent of his knowledge might rattle around in some child's thimble, how came he to serve owkahen's will?

"Will you see him?" asked Chayin, his eyes devouring the map of that land which no Silistran cartographer had ever charted.

"No, I have what I need."

His voice echoed, forlorn, up from the abyss. I touched his arm. He took me in under it. We gave each other warmth there, as one can in certain moments when the barriers between spirit and spirit turn thin with remembered grief.

It has passed now, that aching time for us. The sea has salved our wounds. We have found new ways to look upon each other, freed from the shades of loss.

He has said to me, so soft, holding me in the night with the world's womb rocking us gently, that he would not have it otherwise, that he is content.

Chayin bespoke it: If owkahen, or prophecy, or the fathers use us, what of it? If we come to be such instruments, we shall do so of our own will. So is it, always. It is the self that predestines, the mind that compels.

Khys fell to Estrazi, knowing that he would. As long as he fought them, that long did he create his own ending. A man, disoriented, running at dusk in the forest, circles and comes at last to that same brist-shaped rock from which he first took flight. Had he gotten me with child and presented me pregnant to my father when first I set out to discharge the chaldra of the mother, it would have fallen out the same. Did he know, then, all or only part? And how goes such choosing, upon what scales might such decisions be weighed?

Might we come to learn, upon this shore, of such burdens? Perhaps. It was Khys's will that we come here. He took time to put his affairs in order. He designated his successor. In deference to some rhythm heard by his ears only, he passed from us. We must seek what we may.

Sereth and Chayin have sought, assiduously, in endless evenings of debate, some way to unify those lands which between them they hold. And they have forged, I think some basis upon which such a dream might be built. Upon the crell system, and the fate of chaldless in the north, they have shared much thought. No, they have not wasted this peaceful interlude, and in time all of Silistra will taste of its fruit.

In no respect has it been an uneventful journey, but those whim-spawned attacks of nature have tithed from us no life. We have seen no other ship, nor sign of man.

Where the currents run warm, not here, surely, the sea abounds with life. There is a beast, slitsalike, that we have named sinetra-e'stet (night shiner). They travel in groups hundreds strong. One full-moon night, Sereth called me up to see them. Their rubbings against the boat had not prepared me. They were as glowing waves upon the sea. One could have walked upon them, so thick were they, their coils shimmering unnamed hues over the waves. They average thrice the length of a man. Their fanged heads seem all jaws and streamers. We caught a small one. The streamers, a fringe around the head and upon the dorsal side, look silken soft. They are barbed and poisonous. I was well relieved when we passed from their domain, and glad all that time for the stra plating of the Aknet's hull and her warship's protection. Less glad I am for the likeness of uritheria at her prow.

Here it is cold, and the snow lies thick and deep. We will sail the coast south, seeking a more clement port. But they had to behold the rock, to stand there, that they might hear its soundings. Winter solstice is two days gone. We will not hunt M'ksak-kans until spring.

At night the sky is alive with light, behind the Keening Rock of Fai-Teraer Moyhe. This far north, Sereth has assured me, such displays are not unusual. He and Chayin are as children, eager to tramp the woods and find what lives within. And beyond.

Last night, tiring of the night sky's festival, he came to me, earlier than has become his custom.

"Cold chase you in?" I said, putting down the work I had in hand. I had known by the step upon the stairs. I pulled the brist pelt around me.

"No," he said, ducking his head in the narrow stairwell. Even bundled in heavy cloak and fur-lined boots, his movements flowed like fast brook water. Stooping lest he bang his head upon the crossbeams, he threw off the cloak and cautiously, with a glance upward, straightened up, his hand at the small of his back. "I came to get you out from here, and away from your accursed reminiscences. When the world freezes as cold as Fai-Teraer Mohye, you will be still at it. And forever left at it, hunched over your scribbling. Had I known, when I took you from Khys, of this more insidious rival, I might not have bothered." This last he grunted as he lifted me bodily from where I sat. His fingers upon my arms were icy shards.

Still holding me against him, he plucked a page at random from my pile. I wriggled, away from him and his chill leathers. "Is this, truly, what you think of me?" he demanded.

"Let me see it," I said, feeling the flush crawl up my cheeks. "Yes," I admitted. Not before had he taken interest, muttering that as long as I did what he required of me, my free time was my own. And little enough he allows me. Daily I must face him, and often Chayin, with what weapons they choose. Under their tutelage, I have become much improved. And dhara-san, also does he require of me, that toning of the body which I have long neglected. "Yes," I repeated.

Not releasing me, he put down the page and took up another. Humor tugged at the corners of his mouth.

The ship rode a deep swell, setting the oil lamps depending from the beams aswing.

He pulled me with him down upon the slab that serves us for couch in our cramped cabin.

"You said all of this," he accused, while the scattering shadows steadied, "yet you have not said what is important. Child of owkahen, am I? Of my mother and father, so they swore while they lived." He relinquished the page and lay back, his hands under his head.

"And what is important that I have not said?" I asked, twisting upon the narrow pallet. "I have spoken of Se'keroth. I have not left it out."

He groaned as if in agony, and put one hand over his eyes. After a time he spread his fingers and stared through them.

"Se'keroth, yet. That, little one, was a tale spun of danne and kifra, the maunderings of two men between battles. That is all. Come here."

Fitting to him, my cheek upon his shoulder, I felt it, beneath the thin cushion that makes pallet of two unyielding boards. "Yet you keep it," I said of the blade secreted there. I well recalled it, that stra straight-blade; its hilt, inlaid with titrium wire, carved from a single fire gem; its length and scabbard chased with the Shaper's seal. And it bears, also, engraved into the blade, a legend in Mi'ysten. And I recollected that moment I had first looked upon it; and that refrain I had been humming when

I closed my fingers upon its hilt, come to me, unbidden: Se'keroth.

He shrugged. "I kept your couchbond chald. Those two things are little enough to take, from such wealth as rests at the Lake of Horns." He rose up on one elbow. His lips touched my closed lids, then my temples.

"And what, then, have I not said? What is important?" I whispered, locking my arms around his neck. His eyes saw deep within me, took pleasure there.

"That such moments as these are made precious," said he, solemn, his breath hardly a breeze upon my cheek, "by what we spend to acquire them. Without suffering and adversity, how would it go? Where would be the sweetness? And whence would come triumph, but out of loss? We create them, ci'ves. The only injustice is that, too often, we forget what we have done."

"I think I have said that," I whispered, pulling myself up to meet his lips. "But I would gladly add any words of yours."

"Say, then, that we are all bound, the highest no less than the meanest."

So I say it to you, as he said it to me, from the shores of which none are empowered to speak.

—first third Orsai, 25,698

Appendix 1

The quotations made by Estri, and by the cahndor and dharen, come from the third ors of Se'keroth, or what is called the arcane cycle. It is in the final section of this work that the line "Thrice denied and thrice delivered" signals Laore's passage from the factual to the allegorical, a journey which was to subsequently cost him his life. The application of current events to such a critically obscure and castigating document was as inevitable a development then as it still remains; in such a work, where a mirror bright and clear is created by the author, that the self of the reader may shine forth, interpretation remains in the mind, potential of the reader, ever transmutable, evanescent, a primary example of Laore's postulated "Differentiating Unfixed."

It is not the author's purpose here to attempt to determine the validity of the Se'keroth legend, nor to put forth any new theories as to what allegorical meanings are contained therein. Too many similar projects have been undertaken, and the resultant confusion from such a large number of theses (each redolent with biases and politicized to serve its creator's particular postulates) no more needs another fragmentizing interpretation than the fathers' fire needs oxygen to burn. The intent here is only to outline the legend as Laore propounded it; and thusly as Khys believed it, that we may consider the extent to which the dharen's actions were affected, indeed at times dictated by and predicated on this belief.

The kernel of the Se'keroth legend is thus: the sword was created from the substance of Silistra by a Superior Entity, presumably an agent of the fathers, in the dawning age of toolmaker-man. (The primary Se'keroth legend was rendered in the tongue ascribed to the seed-sowers, Silistra's first written language.)

Se'keroth's magical nature ensures its possession by those chosen catalytic personalities that shape each ensuing age, all of whom undergo rigorous purification before the sword falls into their hands, at which time the blade is "retempered and quenched in ice." He who wields Se'keroth is himself that weapon, is himself wielded by the same power which transmutes the gross into fine. Se'keroth, or the artifact believed to be this fabled blade, has been clutched in the grasp of every man who has catalyzed a "change of ages." It has drunk the life of those visionaries responsible for Silistra's three principal spiritual schools: "by their death gifting them with life." The blade has been borne into every Silistran civilization's history by one hero or another, even managing to insinuate itself into the mechanist wars under the aegis of the dharen Khys.

It was precisely this cyclical manifestation that so concerned Laore, and motivated him to chronicle in his four-volume epic the momentous changes, spanning nearly the whole of Silistran prehistory, that the various agents of Se'keroth had wrought; and to predict the exactitudes of a projected cycle extending ten times as far into the ages to come, even including those long periods of dormancy upon which Khys based his macrocosmic approach in his own work on Se'keroth.

Knowing so intimately the work of Laore (it was Khys who initially created a schism in the Laonan church by his reinterpretation of the great adept's teachings, and who subsequently shaped the Stothric priesthood into the force it was destined to become), it is no wonder that Khys structured the impending change of ages in such a way as to make Se'keroth both the instrument of his own death and projected martyrdom and to ensure its reception by Sereth crill Tyris, his chosen successor not only to know Silistra but also to those shores of which none were heretofore empowered to speak.

The similarity between Khys's death and Laore's cannot be denied, but it is Khys's conscious effort to evoke congruency which bears the greatest import. Laore predicted his own death by Se'keroth, "at the hand of one who will by this act seek to discredit me," and true to his word, the manner of his execution was decreed primarily to cast upon him and his teachings a taint of evil. Se'keroth in its best understood function being designated as the inculpator of iniquity, it was thought by the tribunal that its use as the weapon of Laore's execution would disprove his claim of sonship; instead, it raised him to a pinnacle of veneration never equaled by any other Silistran individual. Khys explored at great length in his papers the influence Se'keroth held in his decision-making. He was not unaware. In his own annotated *Ors Yristera* are various assignments of the prophecies contained therein to specific individuals, dates, and occurrences. Among these are interleaved much more detailed prophecies, often with mathematics appended, and one concerning the mode of his passing and what significance might be derived therefrom. Beside that page there are three dates, one being Brinar third fourth, 25,697, the actual date of his demise.

Appendix 2

A biographical sketch of the dharen Khys, born Khys Enmies, pre-hide year 2831, presents certain problems, not the least of these being the sheer volume of noteworthy accomplishments with which he is credited, coupled with the fact that most of the fertile periods of the dharen's life have been elsewhere chronicled to a depth not even to be attempted in this brief sketch.

His birth, 760 years after the demise of Laore at Fai Teraer-Moyhe and 738 years from the publication of that one's *Forewarnings*, was the source of great tribulation and scandal to the prestigious Enmies family. Khys's mother, Ismarah, after enduring ten years of psychiatric treatment (demanded by her spouse, Braese, and ceded him by the courts after an interview with the lady in question, during which she refused to recant her insupportable position that the son she bore was not Braese's, but rather of supernatural siring), was remanded into the care of the Stoth priesthood, whose dogma she embraced with ever-increasing fervor until her suicide in 2149, on the day following Khys's eighteenth birthday. Khys's father, twice respoused since the judgment of incurable insanity against his first mate, at that time applied considerable political pressure to regain custody of his son from the Stothric church, but to no avail. Ismarah, though adjudged unsound of mind, had delayed her life's termination until the boy had reached the age of consent, until, in fact, she had witnessed Khys's assumption of his Laonan vows and his consecration as a Stoth neophyte.

It was possibly this attempt upon Braese's part to "secularize" his firstborn and force the boy into assuming the responsibilities of the Enmies fortune that resulted in Khys's dramatic assignment of his considerable inheritance to the Stothric priesthood upon his lay-father's death, which occurred in a sudden and catastrophic yachting accident that killed not only Braese but all other claimants to the Enmies wealth exactly five years after Khys's mother's passing.

It was at this point in time, Cetet, 2154, that the youthful Stoth initiate made the acquaintance of the Darsti-trained Gyneth Frein and her brother Wialer, the former to become, six passes later, his life mate, and the latter his coexperimenter and confidant during those years of Khys's absorption with the life sciences that laid the foundations for their joint discovery of the Silistran serums just prior to Haroun-Vhass.

Upon that discovery, the Stoth priest, now fully confirmed and entered into his adeptship, went before the Mechanist Union with a proposal to distribute the drug, which retards deterioration of cell generations and extends the number of such replications per organism as well as conferring extensive immunities, throughout the thirty-seven nations. The Union, caught up in its wars and facing seemingly endless famines and profligate overpopulation, not only refused to embrace the project but pressed through an injunction against private distribution of the serums outside of the Stoth hierarchy itself, allowing this exemption for two reasons: firstly, the serums had already been distributed within the Stoth priesthood, which was to a great extent a static, nonreproducing population (the schism of the Laonan faith, though already pronounced, had been contained by those concerned; the replicating priests had been neither excommunicated nor denounced, and by such time as this move was contemplated, Haroun-Vhass aborted its completion); and secondly, the Union feared the power of the Stoths, who had not declined to infiltrate the power structures of the Mechanist Nations.

In all things, the Laonan faith had retained sovereignty over itself and its doings; if she had not done so, I would not write this today. Exempt from secular law and court proceedings, freed of all tithing obligations to state, bolstered by such economic bestowals as Khys's own gift of the Enmies' transnational cartels, it was the Stoth brotherhood which conceived and constructed the hide system. None else could have accomplished it, gained the waivers of right-of-way, claimed the exemptions to tax that made the project economically feasible, and coordinated such a gargantuan undertaking. Left to any secular force, the underground life-support complexes would have aborted, lain fallow under miles of factionalism and profit-loss, perhaps languishing half-completed, a final mute memorial to the race of man, untenanted, while Haroun-Vhass destroyed us all.

During that period of intense and single-minded concentration, Khys and his mate grew distant. Gyneth, childless by choice, had not chosen to embrace Khys's reinterpretation of Laore's teachings; she clung to the old ways, the celibacy, the fatalism, of the conservative Laonans; though Stoth and eligible, she refused the serums, and by so doing refuted the work of both her brother and her life mate. Thus it came to be that she stood on the one side of the schism and they on the

other. Because it would have been a repudiation
of her own faith to break the life-mate bond,
she did not dissassociate herself from Khys, nor
seek quarters elsewhere, but their relationship
grew greatly strained, disintegrating entirely when
Khys and Wialer together contrived to surrepti-
tiously administer the longevity serums to her.
From that time onward, though she lived in close
contact with her brother and cohabited Khys's
bed, she spoke no word to them other than those
simple exchanges necessary to maintain civility—
indeed, up until the onslaught of the Final Passes,
when Khys set off with Wialer and some few others
to regain Se'keroth from across the sea, she kept
her silence.

Upon their return, triumphant, they found a
note ceding her hide place, to which was appended a short and heartfelt prayer for their
erring spirits. She took nothing, she left no trace,
she merely disappeared among the multitudinous
doomed.

Khys from that time ongoing took no woman in
couchbond until the advent of Estri, choosing instead to instigate the common-holding practice,
by which means he produced close to a hundred
children.

His treatment of Estri, though harsh by Silistran
secular standards, was neither unusual nor uncon-
scionable by the pre-hide Laonan doctrines into
which he was born, but rather an attempt on his
part (despite her unknowning state) to enter her
into the Eleventh Embrasure of dhara-san, that
transcendent sexual ritualization that Estri refers
to as the "hermaphroditic match," and to which,
perhaps understandably, she failed to respond. His
notes upon this subject are extensive. He felt that
by this means alone could he elude the fathers
who so assiduously stalked him. His predictions as

to the results should he fail to achieve such a match were borne out to the letter. Among these was *Meditation on the Nature of Death*, from which comes the following quote:

. . . the violence of expulsion from the womb, the first blow that attends the drawing of breath—how may we know these things? What is thought, while wombbound, of the terrors soon to be faced: the beginnings of life? Perhaps there is a correlate here; the violent entry into flesh, and the precipitous evacuation of it, might these seemings truly be only a diversity of expression of the same principle? For myself, I must conceive it not as the final mystery, but the penultimate. Come early, come late; come with expectation and preparation; come empty-handed and guileless like a child; all come to the abyss, therein to partake of the definition of life, the catalyst death (.) which ends one sentence even as it signifies the beginnings of the next. And if, perchance, some will adjudge me overanxious, then let it be so. Those answers I seek can no longer be found in this flesh that trundles me about like some faithful beast of burden; and like that fleshbeast, though it might at first resent idleness enforced and run the length of its pasture peering over the fence at the young beasts come laboring down the road, thinking all the while of its years of service rendered, craving the feel of harness once more chafing its hide, it knows, in its heart of hearts, that strength spent is irretrievable but as interest accrued in memory. And might he not then turn his head from that road, and sniff with white-haired muzzle along his own joints, worn past renewal, and wonder at it all: that which has gone and that still to come, and therein find a road whose twists are never-ending and whose boundaries elude the vision free of fence and gate? I shall see.

—at Estri's request: Carth

Glossary

S = Silistran
St = Stothric
Y = Yhrillya
P = Parset

archeon: (S) A splay-footed, cursive-horned her-
bivore, the archeon prefers swamp and marsh
and is the indigenous Galeshir herd beast. Larger
than denter but smaller than gaen, the archeon
thrives both in a domesticated state and wild in
prodigious numbers among the wallows and
sedges so prevalent along the southern Karir-
Thoss. The Galeshir highly prize the archeon,
and lavish upon their beasts all manner of
consideration. A man of Galesh, when assessing
the substantiality of a stranger newly met,
looks first to his archeon and the opulence of its
fittings.

archite: (P) Beryl-toned igneous rock, often veined
with gold or blue, which takes and retains a
high-gloss finish and is prevalent in decorative
stonework and in statuary. Archite ranks with
ornithalum as the most prestigious of architec-
tural stone, and is widely employed in Silistran
administrative structures, as well as in the homes
of those of means.

Cete: (S) The nineth pass of the Silistran calendar.

chald: (S) (Stothric: spirit-bond.) A belt of chains commonly soldered around the waist.

ci'ves: (S) A small furred predator common in the Sihaen-Istet hills and in Nin Sihaen itself, where it is not unusual to find three or four ci'vesi in a household. There they earn their reputation as talismans, keeping their masters' holdings free of slitsas. Although the ci'ves makes an elegant and devoted pet, and also by its very odor discourages the establishment of yit colonies in keeps that it prowls as its own, it is this natural antipathy to slitsas that has earned the ci'ves its place in the hearts of the Sihaenese, for whom the slitsa is a ubiquitous and often deadly peril.

Coryf-denne: (C) The Coryf-denne entered provisionally into and at length withdrew from the Bipidal Federate Trade Union upon the grounds that insufficient similarities in physiology and culture context outweighed whatever potential value existed in the "satiation of curiosity and mentality between two such diversely evolved intelligences," thereby grouping all the Bipedal Federate members into one phylum, at which point further attempts to dissuade them were discontinued by unanimous vote.

Decra: (S) Twelfth pass of the Silistran calendar.

Dydian chromatic: (S) The Dydian chromatic derives from the Silistran Parent Scale, that tonal organization from which the diverse scales and tonalities used in Silistran music are sprung:

Parent Scale

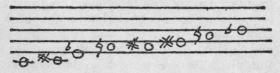

However, as may be obvious, the Parent Scale is not a key center from which diatonic relationships can evolve. Native Silistran songs are based on "randomly" selected, mathematically arranged notes (Scion Scales). One of the most common of these Scion Scales is the Dydian chromatic:

Dydian chromatic (derivative)

Dyri-yiil: (S) A Central Clusters resort world, possessed of four small atmosphere-bearing satellites who circumnavigate her while she in turn negotiates a stately figure eight about the two stars that share her attentions.

Fai-Teraer Moyhe: (Stothric: Cove of Resurrection; literally, fai, to begin again; teraer, birth; moyhe, inlet.) The physical characteristics of Fai-Teraer Moyhe as delineated in the text fit with exactitude those of the fabled spot upon which the adept Laore was disemboweled after being convicted of necromancy, heresy, and sedition; and from which he rose whole of form seven days later to begin the dialogues with his waiting adherents, which were to form the bases of Stothric thought in the ages to come. It is legend that upon his reemergence from the sea, he looked about him and the proponents of his faith numbered only forty-two. Of these, only half remained through that first night, the fainthearted being frightened away by a terrible keening that came out of that moonless darkness, and of which Laore said: "What you hear is the last sound and the first. Go if you will, but know that from this place there is no escape, but only return, and from this song no respite, but for the deaf and the dead." And upon the sun's rising, those who had accepted on faith Laore's explanation woke to find that he had spoken the truth, for they saw before them the pierced spire of the Keening Rock, about whose base were strewn forty-two severed ears, struck off each pair by its owner's own hand as prelude to their crazed and craven flight.

hase-enor: (S) "Of all flesh," the purported goal of Silistra's long-standing genetic-mixing policy—a homogeneous single race, one whose genealogy includes every bloodline still manifest upon the planet; a thoroughly admixed individual.

hest: (S) To bend or twist natural law to serve the will; to command by mind; to cause a probability not inherent in the time to manifest. (The line between hesting and shaping is somewhat difficult to define when highly skilled individuals are concerned. The rule of thumb is held to be thus: if natural law must be remade or totally superseded, as in creating a permanent object such as a fruit or a star, one is shaping. If one is simply controlling an already existing object or event, as would be the case if one caused a fruit or star already in existence to alter its behavior but not its structure, one is hesting. The fruit or star one moves to the right or the left or higher in the sky by will would not have behaved in that fashion, but is still the same star or fruit as was a natural inhabitant of the time before the hest was applied. If one, on the other hand, creates fruit or star, one has brought into the time, by a suspension of natural law, that which heretofore did not exist. One shapes matter. One hests time.) In usage, bringing in a hest, affecting probability.

Haroun-Vhass: (Stothric: fall of man.) The cataclysm precipitated by Silistra's thirty-seven mechanist nations; according to Laore, the final cleansing of the "prehuman" protomen. ("From the bowels of the earth will the race spring forth anew, freed of all self-aggrandizement that has gone before. He who harnessed the wind and despoiled the seas and neutered the earth will perish by his own hand—in truth, he will fall from the skies over which in delusion he has prematurely claimed sovereignty." —*Forewarnings*, pre-hide year 2093.)

ijiyr: (Y) Yhrillyan tonal synthesizer, possessed of both strings and keyboard, allowing multiple attack and wave variation, even to a self-contained phasing and digital delay capability. Formerly displayed electronic synthesizers (the M'ksakkan and Torth devices) have held little fascination for Silistran musicians, their bulk and complexity emphasizing their distant and, for some, putative propinquity with musical instruments as Silistrans are willing to conceive them. The ijiyr, however, self-contained, compact, and versatile, has evoked interest in many circles. The Musicians' Seven have, at the time of this writing, entered into negotiations with Trasyi of Yhrillya to acquire, on loan, this instrument for further study.

krit: (S) A tree-dwelling, furred Silistran mammal. Krits "fly" from branch to branch by launching themselves into a spread-legged glide, facilitated by the webbing or flaps of skin that connect its four six-toed appendages. A fruit-and-nut eater, the krit, whether bush-, yit-, or stub-tailed, hibernates in winter. Weather diviners and woodsmen alike profess to be able to adjudge the length and severity of approaching winter by the krits' autumnal preparations.

lake-born: (S) An individual procreated according to the guidelines set down by the dharen Khys in an attempt to stabilize "desirable traits"; in effect, those double-bred and inbred scions of the Shapers' spawn. It is not unusual for a lake-born to be able to count among his progenitors two or three of Khys's own children, or even two parent connections to a single dharener or council member.

litir: (S) The ubiquitous Silistran stringed instrument; usually possessed of thirty-two frets (but sometimes fretless). The scale length, body configuration, and octave range of litirs vary greatly, the inclusion into this class of instrument being determined by the presence of a soft-wood sounding board joined to an extended neck from whose tip strings of metal, web, or gut are stretched. The one differentiating factor between the class litir and its cousin, rissir, is that a rissir must be bowed, while a litir may be plucked or struck, but never sounded by use of another device that is stringed; hence, a "standing rissir" and a "standing litir," though to eye and ear not dissimilar, are considered by musicians only distantly related.

luricrium: (S) A highly malleable, ductile metal, grayish black in color, used as a catalyst in metallurgy (luricrium salts) and in jewelry, luricrium is highly conductive and considered "rare," although it occurs naturally in deposits of up to 10 percent purity in those areas previously exposed to high-intensity fission reactions.

Nin Sihaen: (S) Silistra's most westerly city, Nin Sihaen lies above hide crill, amid the Sihaen-Istet hills, beyond the Karir-Thoss river. From the Sihaen-Istet, she receives stra ore and some gemstones for trading, but remains (as she has been since her founding), a self-contained economy, as much because of her inconvenient and isolated location as from any conscious or predicated attempt on the part of her Well-Keepress to maintain her dependent city in its reclusive, hermitical posture.

oejri-anra: (Parset: "returning of moons.") A method of casting razor-moons which obliges the weapon to describe a circle and return to the hand that cast it. The object in oejri-anra is not to embed the razor-moon in the target, but to touch-strike with sufficient force to mark, but lightly enough not to alter the moon-caster's trajectory. The greatest difficulty of the game is not, as might be expected, encountered in causing the razor-moon to perform in the desired manner, but in reclaiming it without harm to one's own hand. To this end, thick parr gauntlets with stra-armored palms are often used while honing one's skill. In moon-casters' circles, however, use of these protections in actual competition is considered an admission of cowardice, a negative assessment by the moon-caster of his own prowess. (The type of razor-moon used in oejri-anra is without exception the crescent; only a fool would put a returning cast on a full disk.)

ornithalum: (P) An igneous rock, cerulean to azure in tone, quarried almost exclusively in the southern regions. Prized both for its permanence and its beauty, ornithalum remains the most prestigious material (exempting gol) for structural art.

Orsai: (S) The first pass of the Silistran calendar; the pass of winter solstice, which occurs either on first first or on first second Orsai.

razor-moon: (S) Although the variations of razor-moons are extensive, we will discuss here the two major types: the full disk, or one-way razor-moon; and the crescent, or returning.

The full-disk razor-moon, like its cousin the crescent, may be made of either steel or stra. It is in general smaller, never exceeding a hand's width in diameter. The central thickness of the full disk may be up to fifty times that of the honed outer edge, which has no "grip" or blunt area by which the moon may be caught or grasped, making it, unlike the crescent, a weapon against which there is little or no defense. The full disk is an exceptionally lethal weapon, and in competition is never cast against an opponent, but only at an inanimate target.

The crescent moon, sharpened along every edge but the outermost central mid-curve, varies in size but is seldom smaller than the full disk or larger than twice that in diameter. Because of its "returning" qualities, it is favored for competitive sport but seldom used in combat situtations, where one runs the risk of finding one's own projectile caught by the enemy and launched back upon the caster.

Razor-moons remain basically a boot-sheathed weapon, although some moon-casters have lately begun bearing them in arm-scabbards that hold five or six of the smaller variety strapped to the forearm.

Se'keroth: (St) The legendary blade of which Laore wrote, and with which, by all accounts, he was slain. The premechanist legend of the sword of severance differs quite markedly from the four-volume epic the Stoth adept produced in his youth, and which was later used as evidence against him in his trial and subsequent condemnations, but it is Laore's version, subsumed with revolution and revelation, that is quoted in the text. (See Appendix 1.) The blade itself—Se'keroth of the fire-gemmed hilt—was reclaimed by Khys at great personal peril in the last pass before the onset of Haroun-Vhass. With six lesser priests, he crossed the Embrodming and liberated the sword from the Brinjiiri Laonan Museum, in the midst of that enemy's capital. The escapade has never been subject to procedural documentation, but Khys, who in many respects emulated Laore both in his life and his death, risked his hide-place to acquire the blade, which he believed was the genuine artifact. His own research and attempt at documentation of the sword's authenticity is extensive and available under the title *Se'keroth: The Motif of Catalysis.*

"Se'keroth, direel b'estet Se'keroth": (St) "Se'keroth, light from out of darkness by the sword of severance"; the legend said to be inscribed upon the blade of that fabled weapon; an ostensible simplification of the aphorism "reduction/resolution" that pervaded early Stothric attempts to deduce the relationship of substance to matter.

Sihaen-Istet: (S) Those hills said to be the birthplace of mankind, once in mid-continent, but since Haroun-Vhass the continental perimeter; the western shores.

sinetra-e'stet: (S) The sea denizen discovered by the Menetpher vessel *Aknet* on her journey to the eastern wilderness; a prognathic sea slitsa, venomous and luminous, that abounds in the northeastern Embrodming.

sort: (S) (n.) The probabilities inherent in a specific moment of time; those alternate futures available to one trained to seek them.

sort: (S) (v.) To "sort" probability; to determine in advance the resultant probabilities from postulated actions.

taernite: (S) A variety of the mineral SiO_2, brown to red-brown in color; an attractive and proliferate building stone, of little worth upon Silistra, but highly prized by some B.F. planets where silicon strata is not common.

Yhrillya: (Y) A provisionally entered planet presenting auditing of the B.F. worlds, possessed of a highly advanced mechanist culture about which little is known.

zesser: (S) A leafy green vegetable with a high sodium content, zesser grows close to the ground in round heads and prefers stony soil in a temperate climate.

Silistran Calendar

pass of winter solstice   Orsai
    Tisera
    Cai
    Macara
    Detarsa
    Jicar
    Finara

pass of summer solstice   Amarsa
    Cetet
    Enar
    Brinar
    Decra
    Sisaen
    Laoral

RETURNING CREATION

JANET MORRIS